HEXED DETECTIVE: A THREE-BOOK COLLECTION

HEXED DETECTIVE | FATAL MOON | NIGHT TERRORS

M.V. STOTT

BECOME AN INSIDER

HEXED DETECTIVE

1

Neil Stevenson was about to die.

It would not be a natural death but would be treated as such. Only Neil would know the strange truth of it; only Neil would know about the voice and what it made him do.

Many people thought Neil to be odd, his own wife among them. He would iron his socks, and sing lesser-known Billy Joel songs to break an awkward silence. Then there was his morning routine. He'd get up at the crack of dawn, whether it was baking with summer sun outside or freezing with winter cold, and out he'd go with a whistle on his lips and a towel in hand.

He'd walk the short distance from his house to the beach, putting on his swimming goggles as he did so, ready to wade into the sea.

'A dip in the big blue,' he'd say to anyone who'd listen, 'twenty minutes splashing around in the sea and you'll be astonished how it jump starts your mental faculties.'

It was one of the main reasons Neil had lived in Blackpool his whole life; that faded tourist trap on the North West coast of England that had, most agreed, seen far better days. Now the tourists were smaller in number and the crime rates were reaching record highs. Cars rusted as the salt air nibbled at them day after day, and people walked with their heads down as whip-crack winds struck out from across the water.

But the sea.

Being so close to that seemingly endless expanse of water.

It made Neil Stevenson's heart sing.

Unfortunately, on this particular morning, it would also make his heart stop.

Neil took off his shoes and placed them on the sand, tucking his house keys into the toe of one of the loafers, then placing his towel on top. He breathed in forcefully through his nose, then did some vigorous squat thrusts, the half-wetsuit he was wearing squeaking each time he rose.

'Right then,' he said to himself, running his hands through his thick, black hair and striding towards the water.

The sea that met him was cold; it was always cold. Neil didn't mind. The cold was the point of it all.

He was halfway to the buoy, which bobbed 100 metres from shore, when he first heard the voice.

'Neil.'

At first he only half heard it. A whisper on the breeze; a sound he dismissed as the water sloshed past his ears and he felt his brain crackling to life.

'Neil.'

I mean, it was absurd. There was no one within earshot, no one else mad enough to be in the sea that early on a weekday. So of course, no one could be speaking to him in such a soothing, deep voice.

'You are Neil Stevenson.'

He heard it for sure that time. Four words, clear and true, that he could no longer ignore. He stopped, still some distance from the buoy, his target every morning for years. His legs slowly bicycled, arms washing snake-like, as he turned in a circle trying to find the source of the voice.

'Hello?' said Neil.

'You are Neil Stevenson, your parents are Arthur and Judith Stevenson.'

There was something disquieting about the voice. Something other than it being disembodied and impossible. Something that made his skin crawl.

'Who is that?' Neil asked. 'Where are you?'

'Stop moving your legs, Neil.'

His legs ceased their kicking and he momentarily ducked below the water. He emerged, coughing and gasping seconds later. Why had he done that? He hadn't meant to, his legs had just stopped.

'Neil Stevenson.'

He was scared now. He turned back to the beach, kicking his legs out and driving forward, his little shoe and towel pile visible in the distance.

He would not make it that far.

'Stop.'

He stopped swimming and began treading water again.

'Please,' Neil begged.

'You are going to drown.'

'Why?'

'Because I say so.'

Neil tried to fight the voice, but he was a passenger in his own body. He thought about his wife as his limbs stopped kicking and he slipped below the water, lungs burning, brain screaming. Soon enough he gave in and opened his mouth, filling him with water, turning his body into an anchor. As he sank to the depths, Neil was sure he saw the ghost of something terrible beneath the water. A great dark shape, insubstantial, unreal, monstrous.

It smiled at him.

And then Neil died.

As she dressed that Tuesday morning, Detective Rita Hobbes had no idea she was about to take a tumble down the rabbit hole. That life as she knew it would soon slip away and be replaced by a hidden, dangerous world. A world that lived in the shadows and tip-toed behind the known; that skulked down secret streets and lurked within whispered rooms.

No, all Rita knew when she got up that morning was that she'd drank far too much the previous night, and now her head felt like the Incredible Hulk was using it as a stress toy.

'Christ on a bike,' she groaned as she surveyed her face in the mirror. Her eyes looked as though someone had used her face as a coffee table and left behind two dark rings. 'Never again,' she said, knowing there was every chance she'd break that vow before the day was done.

She didn't have time for a shower. Instead, she sniffed at her dark red hair, then her armpits, and grimaced before grabbing a can of deodorant and spraying herself from head to toe. Having half-arsed her ablutions, she padded out of the bedroom in desperate need of about two gallons of water and a bacon sandwich.

Rita was thirty-one years of age and liked to pretend she was much happier in her thirties than she had been in her twenties. She'd lived in Blackpool her whole life, and very much hoped she didn't die there. Rita was an orphan, passed from orphanage, to foster family, and back again, multiple times. The most oft-cited reason for the termination of her foster family placements had been the biting. She had bitten *so* many people *so* many times. Not just a nibble, no, she'd sunk her teeth in right up to the gums.

And that had not been the end of her youthful rap sheet. There had also been the fires. And the stealing. And that time she'd poisoned Jason Cooper, a fellow orphan, with pellets meant for rat traps. She'd done that after he'd grassed on her for drawing a penis on Maggie Karen's forehead while she took a nap.

Rita Hobbes had been marked down as a 'bad egg.'

Many had feared that all that lay ahead for young Rita was a life of crime, or perhaps a spell on the women's wrestling circuit, but instead she'd surprised them all by ending up on the other side of the law. Grown-up Rita hadn't wound up in jail, or face-down on the wrestling mat, instead she'd become a Detective Sergeant for the Blackpool Police.

Rita was stood in the kitchen of her house, gulping down her third glass of water, when she realised she wasn't home alone.

'Oh, you're still here,' she said as she turned to the kitchen table and discovered a man sat there in his underpants, eyes half-shut, hair a thick, dark, bird's nest.

'Yup, still here,' agreed Chris Farmer, Rita's sort of, but not really at all, boyfriend. She'd been quite clear on the terms of their relationship: they could go to the pictures to watch a film and then talk about the film over beer and pizza afterwards. They could also have sex, should they both feel so inclined. And that was as far is it went. No emotions. No sharing. No obligations. No sleeping over. But there he was. It was morning and there he was.

'Sorry,' he said, gnawing at a piece of toast that had clearly been left in the toaster a minute too long, 'meant to go, but I fell asleep after we had the sex. And now here we are.'

'Looks like it, yeah.'

'Don't mind, do you?'

Rita really, really did mind. Like, a lot. A more subtle soul would have put this across gently, or even pretended it was no big deal. But this was Rita Hobbes he was dealing with.

'Of course I bloody care, Chris, you know the rules. I told you to print off the list I emailed and pin it to your fridge so you wouldn't forget.' She sat opposite him and swiped a slice of toast from his plate. 'You'll remember to go home next time though, right?'

'Right.'

'It's not like we're bloody married.'

'Heaven forbid.'

Rita munched on the pilfered toast and spat crumbs as she spoke. 'Exactly. This is a very casual pleasure thing. As agreed. No point rocking the boat now.'

'We are on the same page,' he replied.

Rita chewed on the burnt toast as she eyeballed him. She wasn't entirely convinced that they were on the same page, or that they were in fact reading the same book.

'It's just, we are both very good at the sexy times business, right?' said Rita.

'No complaints here.'

'Good, so why ruin it by adding all the relationship stuff? The pretending to care about how each other's day went, the holding hands and throwing bread at stupid ducks, the his and her matching pyjamas and the simmering resentment. All that crap.'

'Those are your best examples of relationship things?'

'I'm telling you, a loving relationship is the best way to ruin a casual shag.'

Chris stood and took his empty plate over to the sink. 'Okay, okay, I get the message. I will never sleep over again, scout's honour.' He checked his watch. 'Shit. Shit it. I'm going to be late. The Guv will have my balls.'

Rita watched him scamper off to retrieve his clothes from upstairs.

Rita lived in a small, two-bedroom house on a street of identical looking houses. The rent was incredibly cheap as the place was riddled with damp and the electrics were, at best, massively dangerous.

Still. Cheap.

People had asked why she didn't just buy a place, but buying a place meant staying in Blackpool, and that was the last thing Rita wanted.

A car horn blared outside.

'Shit.' She knew who that was. 'Chris, stay out of sight, yeah?' she called upstairs.

'I'm the phantom shagger, got it. So, are we gonna meet tonight? Rita? Hey?'

Chris poked his head over the banister and looked down just in time to see the front door closing behind Rita.

'Good idea,' he said, 'let's play it by ear.'

Rita waved a middle finger in the direction of the car parked on the opposite side of the road. The smartly-dressed man with neat, sandy hair gave his car horn a further, very annoying, blast. This was DS Dan Waterson, Rita's partner, and ride to work that morning. She had a car of her own, but more often than not it stayed in the station car park, due to her habit of drinking too much to drive home after work.

'When you're ready,' said Waterson, before inhaling from his e-cig and blowing a cloud of vapour out of the window.

'Why do you always have to be in on time, Waters?' asked Rita, as she yanked open the passenger seat door and collapsed into her seat, rocking the car.

'Because that's what time we're paid to start.'

'Teacher's pet.'

'Man hands.'

'Coffee?'

Waterson smiled and reached down, grabbing a styrofoam cup of overpriced coffee and handing it over. It was as she sipped the coffee that she noticed the front door to her house open, and saw Chris Farmer emerge, blinking into the morning light.

'He does not take direction,' she grumbled as Waterson spotted him and turned to her with a shit-eating grin on his face.

'Well, well, well, is that young Chris Farmer I spy, beginning his walk of shame from your house of sin?'

'Why are you always so cheery in the morning, Waters?' Rita asked. 'It's your third most irritating trait. Why can't you be quiet and depressed like a normal person?'

'How many times do I have to ask you not to call me Waters? You know I don't like it, you know it annoys me, why do you still do it?'

'I think you just answered your own questions, Waters.'

Waterson sighed. 'Also, I thought you said you and him was a one-off?'

'It was.'

'And how many times have you enjoyed this one-off?'

'About fifty.'

'He's uniform,' said Waterson. 'It's like bonking the hired help; very unseemly, Rita.'

Rita gave Waterson the finger as she slotted her seatbelt home and the car pulled away.

The stone was slate grey; two metres in length, one in width, with rusty metal manacles affixed, ready for wrists and ankles.

The figure in the blood-red robe ran his hand across the stone's surface.

'It's time,' said the voice that only he could hear. The voice that had been with him, a constant companion, since he had been a child.

'At last,' he replied, and felt a tear run down his cheek.

2

Sometimes Jane dreamed about a man who wore a rabbit mask.

The mask was old and frayed, not made of plastic or rubber like a modern mask. No, this mask had history. Jane knew that if the strange man were to take off his mask then hand it to her, and she were to place the ratty thing over her own head, the smell from inside—ancient, rancid, an overpowering odour like despair and emptiness—would eject the contents of her stomach at once.

The dream had ghosted around inside of her sleeping mind ever since she was small. She would wake in the black with the imagined smell assaulting her twitching nose and she would shake, as though she were a dog attempting to throw off water after a frantic, deep plunge.

Often, Jane would forget what it was that had made her wake up with such an off-kilter feeling. Other times she would recall nothing more than the rabbit mask itself, or perhaps just its damp basement smell.

'Do you like my mask?'

She turned over in bed and kicked her legs.

'You're doing it again,' said Greg in a weary mumble, patting her flank with the back of one hand.

'No I'm not.'

'Oh, must be someone else then.'

'Do you like my mask?'

Jane smiled and turned on to her side, her back to Greg, and curled so that her knees almost touched her chest. She knew when Greg tapped her that she'd been having the rabbit mask dream, even if she couldn't remember it. Rabbit mask was the only dream that made her kick and squirm.

'Knock, knock,' said the man in the rabbit mask, *'it's time. Time to start, time to end. Time to send you round the bend.'*

That morning, as Jane stumbled from the bed to the shower to the kitchen to the couch, she had no idea that she would never have the rabbit mask dream again.

Never have any dream again.

Greg had already been up and out of bed when she woke, but she could hear him now, clattering around in the kitchen.

Jane grabbed the remote and flicked on the TV set. Static greeted her. 'Shit.' She pressed another channel. More static. 'Greg, is the telly broken?'

'No,' replied Greg. 'Everything is fine, fine, fine.'

Jane went from channel to channel, but all were gone. Finally, she discovered a channel that was working. On screen was a close-up of what looked like a mask, fashioned into a hedgehog's head.

It made Jane's heart judder.

It wasn't the rabbit mask of her dreams, but it was clearly of the same type. Old, tatty, wrong.

Jane jabbed at the remote and the TV changed channel.

The man in the hedgehog mask stared out at her.

She changed the channel over and over again, but there he was, there he always was, the mask filling the screen.

As her heart boom-boomed, Jane got down on to her knees and shuffled forward on the carpet, peering closer at the hedgehog mask. It seemed to her that its wearer was returning her gaze, which, of course, was impossible.

Impossible.

Jane could hear the person breathing, in and out, in and out, raspy, harsh against the mask. She had the strange fear that if she were to move any closer towards the screen, the hedgehog man would reach out and grab hold of her.

'You shouldn't sit so close you know,' said Greg, who had entered the room behind her. 'You'll get square eyes,'

'Greg, I don't think I like this TV channel.'

'No, it's fine. It's fine, fine, fine.'

She turned from the screen to look up at her boyfriend, who smiled down at her. It was an odd sort of smile, Jane thought, but that wasn't the oddest thing about Greg. No, the oddest thing was that he didn't have any eyes. Birds had taken up home inside his head, their small, sharp beaks poking out of Greg's eye sockets.

'Oh, I enjoy this show,' said Greg, pointing to the hedgehog-masked stranger on screen. 'Do I? I think I do. I'm sure I've seen it before and before and before.'

As she listened to Greg talk, Jane realised he didn't sound much like her boyfriend at all. The voice was too flat, empty of any colour or nuance. It was like someone had hollowed out his voice, and if she were to poke one of his words with her finger as he spoke them, it would collapse in on itself.

'Who are you?' she asked.

'I am Greg. Greg your boyfriend. We have dated for years and years and rent this house at a reasonable cost, all things considered. Shall we kiss?'

'No.'

'Okay,' said Greg, and he dug into his pocket, retrieving a fist of soil full of fat, wiggling worms. 'Everything is fine, fine, fine.' He began to pull worms from the soil clump and hold them before his eye sockets, the beaks snapping hungrily, until one found its target and pulled the worm from his fingers and hauled it into his head.

Jane wondered how he could see her with his eye sockets full of beaks. How could he think at all with a skull stuffed with feathers and talons and sharp, hungry squawks? She stood and began to edge away from Not Greg, as she now thought of him. Not Greg with his dead voice and his starving beak eyes.

'Where are you going?' asked Not Greg, feeding fat worm after fat worm to the snapping beaks.

'Nowhere.'

'Oh, that's not true. That's not true at all,' said Not Greg as she edged around the room, moving slowly toward the door. Not Greg turned from her, back to the TV set. 'Ah yes, I do remember this show, I knew I did. This is the Mr. Spike show. Mr. Spike is funny, you know. Or terrifying. Or silly. Something along those lines.'

Jane was three steps from the door, her eyes never leaving Not Greg as he stood transfixed by the non-moving person in the mouldy hedgehog mask.

'Once I met Mr. Spike on a road that didn't exist. He took off his mask and I pulled out my eyes so as not to see what was shown. I can laugh about it now, you know. Everything is funny, given time.'

A beak pierced the back of Not Greg's head and wiggled and fought until the bird's entire head poked through, slick with gore, and stared at Jane with black, blank eyes.

She ran from the room.

From the house.

From Not Greg and his head full of birds.

From the man in the hedgehog mask.

She raced for her car and started the engine, stomping the accelerator and leaving her house behind, but she found that the sound of the man in the hedgehog mask's breathing remained. Rough and guttural, constant and steady, as though he was in the passenger seat, leaning over, his masked face centimetres from her ear. Jane felt as though she could feel his hot, damp breath on her face, smell the rancid air blowing from his lungs, landing damp and sticky upon her skin. It made her feel like she wanted to lean away, even though the car was empty. Like she wanted to turn her face away and gag.

It was just another dream, that's all.

She thought she'd woken up, but she hadn't, not really.

That had to be the truth of it, because real life wasn't like this.

Or perhaps she'd gone mad.

It was all very strange and unreal and it made Jane feel all shaky on the inside, like her organs were bashing into each other like pinballs. Going batty had always been one of her greatest fears. Some yelped at spiders scuttling, others trembled deep down at the very idea of travelling by airplane, but the worry that sneaked up on Jane in her darker times was the fear of losing her marbles.

'Who are you, then?' her Granddad Thomas would say when she went to visit him in those final few years.

'It's me Granddad, Jane, your granddaughter,' she would reply, softly.

'Oh? Oh, no. No, I don't think so love, I'm only twenty-two, I haven't even had kids yet,' and he would look down at his wrinkled, brown-spotted hands in confusion.

'You're not mad, or dreaming, not at all,' said a man sat calmly on the back seat of the car.

He wore a rabbit mask.

The wheel turned sharply and the car tyres screamed in complaint as the world lurched round and round, until things came to a sudden stop and Jane bashed her head painfully against the door window and things turned into fuzz and sparks.

'My name is Mr. Cotton; I believe you recently met my good brother, Mr. Spike.'

Her world tilting, Jane fumbled at the seat belt with rubber fingers.

'Look at you now,' said Mr. Cotton, 'all grown up and ready for the chop. The first of a bad batch.'

Free of her seat belt, Jane pushed open the door and stumbled out of the car, now resting diagonal with a rear wheel up on the pavement. Her hands scuffed the ground as she made her escape, painting the tarmac red.

'Where are you going, Jane? It's time. Your time. He's waiting for you, rude to be late.'

Jane had felt scared many times in her life.

There was the time she was six and her dad had taken her to the local swimming baths. She'd thought she knew what she was doing, but soon enough she'd walked too far, and under she went, knowing there was no way she'd be able to get above the water again to catch her breath—

There were the times in class when the teacher was going from pupil to pupil and she knew she was going to have to stand

and speak in front of everyone and her mouth was so, so dry and her heart was fluttering—

There was the time she climbed over a fence to retrieve a ball, and just as she found it and picked it up she heard a low growl and turned to see the biggest dog that had ever been, baring its fangs, head down, drool pouring, and the fence was too far away and there was no way she was going to make it but she turned to run anyway—

But this wasn't like that, this was a deep down terror, primal and old and undeniable. It was *other* and it was *wrong* and it was *inevitable.* It was where she'd always been headed.

Jane felt like curling up into a ball and crying.

Instead she ran.

Ran down streets she didn't recognise, which she knew was impossible, because she knew every street in Blackpool like the back of her hand. She'd lived her entire life in the same faded seaside town, clinging to the west coast of England, shaking hands with the sea, and yet turn after turn took her deeper into confusion.

'Just one thing, just show me one thing I know,' but the strange and the new were all that she found.

This wasn't her home. This wasn't her town. She was lost and she was going to have to stop running because her body couldn't stand another step. Half crouching, half falling, she reached out to cushion the blow as she dropped to the ground and tore at the air with great, ragged breaths.

'There you are, I've been waiting for you.'

She looked up to see the man in the rabbit mask stood before her.

'You're not real,' said Jane. 'You're just a nightmare. You're not real!'

'It's true, I am a nightmare, but I am also very real. My name is Mr. Cotton, and this is my dear brother, Mr. Spike.'

The man from the television, the man in the hedgehog mask, stepped in beside him.

'What do you want?' Jane begged.

'I told you. It's time. The Magician is waiting.'

And then Mr. Spike took off his mask.

3

The man had been running for a long, long time.

It had started on the Underground—on the Piccadilly line—as the train shot rat-a-tat and shaky through the dark. His plan had been to change at Green Park, hop on to the Victoria line, and head for Oxford Circus.

The carriage was crammed with people heading towards the always crowded shopping hub of London, and the man was stood, gripping a bar, uncomfortably close to a cluster of strangers. Normally, the close proximity of a hygienically challenged man's ripe armpit would have driven him to distraction, but he had far worse things demanding his attention today.

He thought he'd been discreet, but Carlisle had discovered what he'd done.

He'd been drinking at The Beehive pub, sure his secret was safe, when an extremely unpleasant eaves who went by the name of Razor had delighted in telling him that his secret was, in fact, public knowledge. It seemed Razor had sold him out for a taste of magic, ratted on him to someone he knew who would pass on the information to Carlisle's ears.

The man had abandoned his three-thirds-full drink and fled the pub in search of sanctuary. Carlisle knew that the man had told the London Coven about what he'd been up to, and Carlisle was not the sort to let that go.

He knew people on Oxford Street, people who could squirrel him away, undetected. He had a feeling that he'd have to stay hidden a good long while; it was said that Carlisle had been known to nurse grudges for centuries. He was hopeful that he'd been tipped off early enough to make it into his hidey hole. More than hopeful.

He was three stops from Green Park when things started to go wrong.

The train lurched to a stop at Gloucester Road and belched up its passengers, who shoved their way out of the carriage before the waiting horde bundled on to the train after them, staking a claim to whatever small space they could find.

The man had a beanie hat pulled down so it almost covered his eyes, and was doing his best not to catch anyone's eye. Travelling on the underground was a dangerous gambit he knew, eyes were everywhere, but it was also the quickest way to get where he needed to be. So he'd taken the risk, shrinking under his hat and hiding within the folds of his large overcoat.

Over and over in his head he repeated the mantra: *see me not, see me not, see me not*. It was a weak type of perception magic. It didn't render him invisible, but it did make people less likely to notice him. Made people who might feed information back to Carlisle less likely to see him and take note of the direction he was heading in.

It would have worked, too. As long as Carlisle himself wasn't the one to see him.

The man felt eyes on him. He repeated the magical mantra over and over, but the sensation would not go away. The hairs on the back of the man's neck stood upright with alarm. His eyes darted back and forth until his gaze landed on a figure in the next carriage, staring at him through the window of the connecting door.

He saw a long, shadowed silhouette wearing a dark purple floor-length coat, ragged like an old shroud. A chalk-white face stared back at him with two black-circled eyes that burned like coals.

The man abandoned his mantra as his stomach turned and his heart slammed against his chest.

As the train shuddered to a stop at South Kensington, the door between the carriages opened and Carlisle stepped across.

Head down, the man bolted from the train, shoving aside complaining passengers that he neither saw nor heard. He didn't look back, he knew Carlisle had him pegged, and to even make eye-contact might be enough for his pursuer to bring him down.

He emerged on to the streets, his plan shot; a damp soap dancing from grasping hand to grasping hand.

'Hey, are you all right, mate?'

He didn't answer, didn't look to see who the concerned passerby might be, instead he ran and hoped a plan would come to him before he felt a cold hand grip his throat.

He ran wildly and indiscriminately. Who knew, perhaps having no clear plan or destination would throw Carlisle off.

Why had he even told the Coven about Carlisle's illegal happy pill business? Why had he told Stella Familiar, who ran the place now since the death of her three witches? Because of his own short-sighted greed, that's why. He'd been the messenger boy for someone who disliked Carlisle muscling in on their turf. Not only muscling in, but dealing in dodgy pills that were cutting down their clientele in ever-increasing numbers. Most of the gangs wanted to keep their customers alive, so when Carlisle started selling pills cut with who knows what—pills that had the unfortunate side effect of stealing years off a user's life—well, they took exception to that. It was bad for business.

Of course, they couldn't be seen to be dealing with the Coven themselves, so they offered him a fistful of cash instead, and the promise of more to come if he did the job right. But no one did the dirty on Carlisle and got away with it. He'd been stupid, and it was going to get him killed.

He ducked into a doorway to catch his breath, nervously glancing back to see how far ahead he was. Carlisle was nowhere to be seen. He felt a little hope twitch in his chest. Perhaps he'd been sharp enough to evade the great Carlisle? He'd always been fleet of foot when danger came a-knocking.

'Have you decided to stop? Oh good, running is so uncivilised.'

The voice was like velvet.

The man didn't turn to it, he just ran.

There!

There on the ground, a way out, an escape hatch to another place.

He pulled the metal sewer cover key from his pocket and fell to his knees, jamming it into the sewer cover, wrenching it up, and wriggling down into the dark to land with a wet thud several metres below. His eyes instantly became accustomed to the sudden switch from light to dark, glowing in the gloom, two large yellow beacons.

Even before the metal sewer cover fell back into place, he was away. His body begged him to stop, but the man knew he couldn't, not with death at his heels. And so he ran through the dark, his feet splashing through the damp trickle that snaked across the old stone floor of the sewer.

He knew the sewers well. He'd grown up down there, in the labyrinth network of tunnels that ran like veins under the skin of London. He knew every twist, every dark turn, every hiding place. He hadn't stepped out into the world above until he turned double figures. He felt better here. He was in his element in the sewer, and maybe, just maybe, it would give him the edge over the beast that stalked him.

It did not.

Something struck his ankles, twisting round and round and bringing him crashing to the slick, hard ground.

'No! No!'

His hands scrabbled at the rope that bound his legs together, but the rope only pulled tighter, like a python squeezing the life out of a dinner that had yet to accept its place on the menu.

'I'm sorry!' the man pleaded.

'I don't care,' came the reply.

Carlisle drifted out of the shadows, the other end of the rope in his black-gloved hands, his heavy boots splashing through the water.

'You told tales on me, sewer-born. I find that extremely rude.'

'They made me!'

'Oh?'

'Yes, yes, I had no choice!'

'The way I heard it, you sold me down the river for money. Tacky.'

'It was a lot of money.'

Carlisle threw his head back and laughed, his shoulder-length black hair dancing as his howls echoed around the stone tunnel.

'I hope you had time to enjoy your bounty young man, because now I am going to snap your neck.'

With a flick of his wrist, the rope that bound the man's ankles detached and coiled back into his hand. He opened his coat—the inside rippling and glowing as though the lining were fashioned from stars—and fixed the coiled rope to his belt.

The man scrambled backwards, unable to rise, unable to escape. But he still had one card up his sleeve. A rumour he'd heard that might yet save his life.

'You should be proud,' said Carlisle, 'most don't make it as far as you did before they find my hands on them. You're a nippy little whippet.'

He flexed his hands, his mouth a red slash across his pale face.

'I know where your artefact is!' said the man.

Carlisle stopped his advance, the corners of his mouth twitching down momentarily. 'And what do you know of my artefact?'

'I know three things,' the man replied, his back resting against the brick wall of the tunnel, heart beating almost to the point of giving out as he looked up at the figure looming over him.

'You have my curiosity, sewer-born. Please proceed.'

'I know you want it. I know you lost it.'

Carlisle raised an eyebrow.

'And… and I hear a rumour that it has been found.'

Carlisle reached into his pocket and pulled out a red apple. He polished it against the soft fabric of his purple coat, then took a bite. 'Temptation,' said Carlisle. 'Like the snake to Eve in the Garden of Eden, you sit there, tempting me with juicy, sweet information. But as you can see, I already have an apple of my own.'

'I don't… what?'

'What's to stop me beating the information out of you then killing you anyway?'

'Well… it's not good manners…?'

Carlisle chuckled and took another bite of his apple.

'So? Do we have an understanding?' said the man, rising slowly, his hands flat to the wall. 'My life for the whereabouts of your missing artefact?'

Carlisle took another bite of his apple, then bowed his head once in agreement. 'Very well, you have my word. Tell me the location and I will not kill you.'

The man felt a little relief wash over him. 'It's in Blackpool.'

'Blackpool?'

'Blackpool,' he confirmed. 'It is understood that your artefact is in the possession of a great magician.'

'I see. And who fed you this juicy morsel?'

'An eaves, who heard it from an eaves, who heard it from an eaves.'

The man felt Carlisle's eyes boring into him, interrogating him.

'So? Are we good?' asked the man.

'Good enough. Congratulations, you live to scurry amongst the rats another day.'

Carlisle tossed the apple into the air as he turned, caught it with his other hand, and walked away into the black.

The man held his breath, listening to Carlisle's footfalls as they drifted away and away, until he couldn't hear him at all.

His legs almost unhinged as the relief crashed over his body like an angry ocean wave against a crumbling cliff face.

He'd done it. He'd crossed Carlisle, been caught red-handed, and survived. He felt like laughing. Instead he turned and ran in the opposite direction from where Carlisle had disappeared, feeling elated, until finally he could run no further and slowed to a stroll, heading for a sewer cover that he knew opened up outside his favourite pub, where he could drink long and hard to celebrate his good fortune.

As he stopped beneath it and pulled out his tool to lever the cover open, his foot nudged something on the ground. The man looked down, expecting to see a stone, or the partially rotted corpse of a sewer rat. What he actually saw made his eyes widen and his stomach drop.

It was a red, half-eaten apple.

He felt the hands around his neck just long enough to realise that his life was at an end, then his neck was snapped and he crumpled to the ground.

'One thing you should know about me,' Carlisle told the lifeless heap before him, 'I lie.'

He placed his foot against the man's head and pressed down until the skull cracked beneath the heel of his boot.

4

The office at Blackpool Central Police Station that Rita had worked out of for the last five years smelled like old pizza and fried chicken. Officers weren't meant to eat hot food at their desks, but with the amount of hours they spent there—not to mention nights—it was more or less a daily occurrence.

Rita flopped into her chair, her nose wrinkling at the familiar background scent. She leaned back to put her feet up on her desk and almost kicked a teetering tower of overdue paperwork on to the well-worn carpet. She looked up at the ceiling, which had once been white but had long ago taken on a yellow hue from decades of detectives hunched at their desks, smoking. Not that they'd been able to smoke in there for years, but then the place was slow to spend money on touch-ups.

'What time d'you call this?' asked DI Collins, the question emerging from beneath a moustache several shades darker than his hair.

'Time your wife finally cleaned that shit out of her eyes and left your fat arse,' replied Rita, to a chorus of approving laughter thrown in Collins' direction.

'We're literally two minutes late, Collins, traffic,' said Waterson, 'by the way, I know it's you who blocked up the bogs last week.'

'You can't prove a thing.'

The whole office turned to eye Collins, who suddenly found his computer screen very fascinating.

'Hobbes, Waterson, in here,' said DCI Alexander Jenner, poking his balding, blonde head out of his office into the main space, cutting any further arguments dead.

DCI Jenner closed the door to his private office behind them as Rita and Waterson entered and stood before his desk.

'What was that about?' asked Jenner, thumbing over his shoulder as he made his way around to his chair.

'Men's bog, Guv,' replied Waterson.

'Collins admitted to blocking it yet?'

'No, Guv,' said Rita.

'Third time in a month. Someone seriously needs to look at that man's diet.'

Rita smirked. As far as bosses went, DCI Jenner could be a lot worse. Oh, he yelled, he expected way too much of them, and was just downright unreasonable at times, but somehow he managed to pull off the trick of being likable at the same time.

'Got something for us, Guv?' asked Rita.

'Woman. Jane Bowan. Her partner, boyfriend, says she's missing.'

'How long?' asked Waterson.

'It's been two days. Uniform have done the usual missing persons job, but family insist she hasn't just walked out. Here,' he tossed over a plastic folder containing all the information gathered so far. Rita snatched it up.

'No clothes missing, no bags or suitcases gone, her phone still on the bedside table, her bank account hasn't been accessed,' reported DCI Jenner. 'She just disappeared. So find her.'

An hour later, Waterson pulled to a stop across the road from the house Jane Bowan and her boyfriend Greg Nicol shared.

'Nice area, this,' noted Waterson.

'Yeah, for Blackpool. Let's keep things in perspective, Waters.'

'Water-*son*. Water-*son*. For my own sanity's sake, just try it out, please.'

Rita made a show of considering his plea, then frowned. 'Nah, sounds weird. Shall we?'

Waterson smiled and shook his head as they stepped out of the car and headed over to the blue door of the house.

Rita had been thinking about putting in for a transfer to London. To be truthful, she'd been thinking about it for the last four years, but this year, this was the year she was going to do it. She'd written up her transfer letter, printed it out, put it in an envelope, and sat it in the top drawer of her desk at the station.

Before the year was out.

She had to do it.

She'd been stuck in that small, shuffling town her whole life. It was time for something different. Something more. Her stomach ached at the idea of another year cooped up in that frayed little place, living on the edge of the world, if you could even call what she did living. She hadn't had the heart to mention her plans to Waterson yet. Sure, he heard her bad-mouth the place on a daily basis, but he had no idea she was actually about to go through with it and kiss the town goodbye.

Rita was actually a little worried about how he'd take the news. She and Waterson had been partners for years. Yes they bickered, yes they fought, but they were each other's rock. Best friends, really. She knew when she told him she was leaving him behind that he'd take it as a betrayal. He wouldn't say as much, he'd probably even wish her well, tell her congratulations on finally doing what she always said she would, but she knew, under the blather, the sense of betrayal, of abandonment, would cut deep.

But Rita didn't have a choice.

Blackpool was suffocating her. One more season spent in that small-minded, clapped-out town and she'd lose her mind. She needed to get out of there. To start over somewhere new.

A man answered the door; he looked like he'd had about a year's worth of rough nights, his eyes red and unfocussed, his skin pale.

'Mr Greg Nicol?' said Waterson.

He blinked as if confused, then slowly nodded.

'I'm DS Hobbes,' said Rita, showing the man her badge. 'This is DS Waterson. Can we come in?'

'Yes, right, of course.'

He turned and they followed him through to the front room. Greg sat in a chair, then hopped back up, dithering. 'Sit,' he said, 'please, down.'

'Thank you,' said Rita, as she and Waterson sat on the couch.

'So, is there news? Good news?' asked Greg.

'Not yet, I'm sorry,' replied Waterson.

Greg ran his hands through his mess of dark hair. For a moment, he looked as though he was about to crumple to the floor in tears, then reined in his emotions, nodded, and sat back in the chair again.

'We've been put on your case, Mr Nicol,' said Rita.

Waterson folded his hands in his lap. 'We're here to ask you a few questions that should help us get a picture of this from your perspective. You'll have answered these questions a hundred times I'm sure, but if you wouldn't mind going over your story one more time.'

'No, no, of course not. Happy to.'

Rita took out her pocket notepad and a pen, ready to scrawl down his answers in a handwriting that was legible only to herself.

'Can you take us through what happened?' asked Rita.

'Yes, of course. But like I said before, it's just… there's really not much to say. Practically nothing, it's all so bloody… so… I don't know what.'

Rita gave Greg Nicol her best "I understand" face. All police had that down to a fine art. One year they'd even given out an award for it at the office Christmas party. Waterson had won. Kept the little plastic trophy in his bathroom.

'Okay. Well. It was morning. I always get up before Jane, she likes to hit the snooze another couple of times, but I get up. Alarm goes off and I'm up. And, well, the thing is, that was the last time I saw her.'

'When you got out of bed?' asked Waterson.

Greg Nicol nodded.

'So you left for work and didn't see her again?' asked Rita.

'I heard her. Before I left, I mean. I heard her turn off the alarm and get up. Heard her moving around upstairs. I had a tonne of work at the office piling up, so I'd decided to get in early and get a good, quiet hour in before everyone else turned up. So I shouted goodbye up the stairs and rushed out the door.'

Rita nodded and took it all down in her notepad. 'Did you hear from her again? Phone call? A text message? Anything at all?'

'No. I sent her a text at lunch. I always do. Just a little "love you" text.'

'But she didn't reply?' asked Waterson.

'No. No, she didn't. That's not unusual—sometimes she leaves her phone turned off at work—so I didn't think anything of it.'

'I see,' said Rita. 'And how long was it before you realised Jane was missing?'

'About two hours after I got back from work, so just after eight. That's when I started to get worried. She wasn't answering my texts, or calls, and then I found her phone in the bedroom. I called Kate, her friend—they work in the same office—and she said Jane… she said Jane hadn't turned up to work at all. And she hadn't called in to say she was sick or anything, either.'

Greg Nicol bent over, head in his hands.

'Oh Christ. Oh Christ. She's dead, isn't she? Jane, she's dead. She's fucking dead.'

Rita stood and went over to Greg Nicol, patting him on the shoulder. It was meant to be reassuring, but came off more like she was patting a friend's pet dog that she didn't quite trust not to snap at her fingers.

'We don't know that, Greg,' she said. 'Let's assume not until we have reason to, okay?'

Greg looked up at her with red, bleary eyes, 'Can you find her?'

'We're going to do our best, Mr Nicol,' said Waterson.

'We were getting married,' said Greg. 'Been engaged almost two years.'

'When's the wedding set for?' asked Rita.

'It's in two weeks. *Was* in two weeks.'

Waterson gave Rita a look she recognised. He was thinking it was possible she'd ghosted him. Decided the marriage wasn't for her and cut out.

'Had she been acting strange at all?' asked Rita.

'Strange?'

'Just anything out of the ordinary,' she replied. 'Anything you noticed in her actions, or the things she said. Anything different about her behaviour that stuck out to you?'

'No, nothing. She was excited about the wedding.' Greg Nicol said this, then his brow furrowed.

'What is it?' asked Rita.

'Well, she'd been having bad dreams more often recently. She'd told me that.'

'Since when?' asked Rita.

'Just in the weeks leading up to her... to her not being here anymore. But it was just a few nightmares, what could that have to do with anything?'

Rita and Waterson left Greg Nicol and Jane Bowan's house and headed for the car.

'So,' said Waterson, 'bride-to-be gets the jitters as the big day looms, gets scared, gets stressed, starts having nightmares, then one morning she cuts out and holes up somewhere because she can't face telling her hubby-to-not-be that it's all over. That sound like a possibility to you?'

Waterson got behind the wheel as Rita looked back to the house, doubt itching at her.

'Yeah. Maybe.'

Razor liked London at night. It was the best time to skulk, and he prided himself on his skulking. He could spend hours surreptitiously moving his way from bar, to street, to library, to car park, his ears twitching at every conversation that came his way, searching for something useful. He knew by a person's body language, by their tone of voice, whether the information being shared was worth storing away for future use.

A little light rain began to spit, and Razor popped up the collar of his grimy leather coat, the bottom hem of which was tattered from where it met the ground. Razor was an eaves, and like all eaves, he looked a little like a person, and a little like a mutated mole. His eyes were beady, his ears pointed, hair coarse and close-cropped. And just like the rest of his kind, his mouth was full of needle-sharp teeth that could bite clean through a finger with little effort.

His snub nose twitched at the centre of a face that had seen better days. More than one fist, more than one blade, and more than one set of brass knuckles had left their mark upon what had never been the most aesthetically pleasing of mugs.

Razor dealt in secrets. In information. In whispered words. All eaves did. This was their role in the Uncanny world. If something was worth knowing, chances are an eaves had heard about it, and would be willing to pass the information on, for a price.

And the price they named? Magic. Just a taste. It nourished an eaves, and it kept them safe, which is just as well, as trading in secrets is wont to put a target on your back. Their dens, which twenty or more eaves at a time would call home, needed to be secure, else someone with a grudge creep inside and slit their throats.

So, with each new secret that was passed on, an eaves would swallow a portion of magic for nourishment, then hold the rest back to add new twists, dead ends, and meandering passageways around their den. Only an eaves knew how to traverse the impossible tangle of doors and streets they created – doors and streets that had no business connecting to one another. Only an eaves could navigate such a labyrinth.

Razor opened a door which, for anyone else, would have led to the inside of a fish and chip shop, but when Razor stepped through, he found himself inside an abandoned warehouse almost a mile from where that chip shop stood.

He marched across the open space, the metal roof creaking in the wind, before stepping out into the men's bathroom at a prestigious Leicester Square cinema. Razor snatched up the box of popcorn that a man who was urinating had left perched by the sink, then entered the third stall. He didn't break his stride as he found himself not facing a toilet, but walking across the roof of the British Museum.

As Razor munched the popcorn and headed towards the metal fire escape, he felt prickles shoot up and down his squat, thick neck, and spun round, dropping the stolen popcorn, fists clenched, ready for a fight.

A tall man in a long, dark purple coat was sat upon an incongruous comfy reclining chair, reading a book. 'Razor, I was wondering how long I'd have to wait for you to pass through.' Carlisle waved a book at him. 'A little over two hundred pages, as it turns out.' He stood and slipped the dog-eared paperback into an inside pocket of his coat.

'You got him then, did you?' asked Razor. 'The young sewer-born lad?'

'I briefly made his acquaintance, yes,' replied Carlisle, a large, easy grin spreading across his pallid face. 'In fact, if you'd like to say farewell to the poor soul, I do believe some of him is still attached to the bottom of my boot.'

Carlisle lifted his foot and waggled it in Razor's direction. 'No? Suit yourself.'

'What d'you want, Carlisle?'

'Oh, what does anyone want in this life? To feel free and happy, with a belly full of food and a song in one's heart.'

Razor was ready to rush him, as pointless as he knew that course of action to be. But Razor was a fighter, and if it came to it, he could take a lot of punishment before his life was given a brutal full stop.

'Oh, Razor, please, stop it. I mean you no harm, I promise; you may unclench your everything.'

'I know what your promises are worth.'

Carlisle laughed and clapped his hands together. 'Point taken. But no, I'm not here for any fisticuffs, I'm here merely for the valuable service that you and your kind provide to the likes of mine.' Razor shuffled as his brain tried to work out what Carlisle was on about. 'Information, my squat, muscular friend. Information.'

'Right. That I can do. And do I get a taste in return?'

'Now, now, you know that is beneath me, Razor. No taste, but you'll get to go home to your den without any new marks on that pummelled lump of meat and bone you call a head. How does that sound?'

Razor knew it was the best he could expect, and nodded,

hissing through his small, sharp teeth. 'I let you know about the sewer boy's visit to the Coven, what else d'you want?'

'You did, and I am most grateful, believe me, but in his final attempt to cling on to his woeful excuse for a life, he shared with me a sliver of information he thought I would be interested in.' Carlisle stepped forward, cupping Razor's head in his hands. 'And oh, dear, ugly thing that you are, it was information that fairly made me tingle from toe to nose.'

The silence crushed.

'I would've told you,' said Razor.

'Is that so?'

'Eventually, I would've. I just… I didn't know how legit the news was. Honest.'

'Now, let's not sully the moment with lies, Razor.' He released Razor's head and moved past him, stepping up on to the edge of the roof and looking out over the city, the surrounding office lights shining through the dark like distant stars. 'Is what the late sewer-born said true? Has my artefact been spotted in Blackpool, of all places?'

'Yes, so they say.'

'They do say a lot, don't they? Any name for me to hold on to during my travels up north?'

Razor grimaced.

'A name, Razor.'

'Formby. The elder eaves in Blackpool. He's been heard to mention your… your artefact, when he's had too many ales. Says that someone in that place has it. Someone in Blackpool.'

Carlisle turned to him and grinned. 'Not for long, they don't.' And without looking, he stepped off the roof and fell out of view.

5

Ellie Mason could have sworn it was the next right, then the next left, then on until the roundabout, but now here she was driving down a road she didn't recognise and the sky looked all wrong. It had a weird sepia tint to it, like a photograph in an old Western.

'Shit,' said Ellie. 'Shitty, shit, shit.'

Ellie had been to see a client two towns over and was now in a rush to get home to Blackpool. Her mum would already be throwing an epic shit fit. Ellie thought she had driven back the same way she'd travelled earlier, but now found herself driving up and down country lanes she didn't recognise, and of course the sat-nav had decided to go on the fritz.

There were no signposts, no other cars in sight, so she decided the very best thing she could do would be to turn around and retrace her steps. Sixteen minutes later she realised with a heavy heart that she was as lost as she had ever been.

She pulled to a stop and checked her phone again, but found it still had a stubborn lack of signal. Ellie swore and struck the steering wheel with the heels of her hands. She was late. She'd promised her mum she'd be back home in time for dinner, and now she was late and getting later.

It was just then that she saw the house.

Ellie had not noticed the house until that moment, which seemed altogether impossible as it was so large, and situated directly in front of her. How had she not seen it? There were no other buildings along the road that she could see; indeed she didn't believe she'd passed so much as a garage or a bus stop since she'd wandered off the path somehow.

Ellie got out of her car and strode toward the front door. The house looked old. Very old. Vegetation covered much of the crumbling brick frontage, and several of the upstairs windows sported jagged cracks. If this had been a movie, it would be exactly the kind of house the main plucky heroine should definitely not approach, but always would.

'Probably abandoned,' Ellie told herself as she knock, knock, knocked on the front door, kicking up a tsunami of dust. She waited, but there was no response. Ellie gave it one last knock and then, just as she was about to turn and make her way back to her car, the door opened.

Before her stood a man in a rabbit mask.

'Oh.' said Ellie, which was a reasonable response.

The mask encased the man's entire head, and was topped off by two large ears that pointed to the sky like antennae. The mask was not plastic or rubber, but covered with real, if tatty, fur. The man's outfit was no less peculiar. He wore an old suit of the sort that may have been fashionable when her great, great, great, great, great grandfather was young.

'Hello,' said the man in the rabbit mask.

'Hello,' said Ellie.

'Do you like my mask?' asked the man as he stroked his large ears and smiled. Ellie did not know how she knew the man was smiling, but she did.

'It was my mother's, father's, mother's once upon a time, when the mountains were small and the seas were song, or so the story goes. For a time it was lost to us, but I found it where I thought I would, in the forest, under a tree, and I dug, dug, dug it up.'

As the man spoke, Ellie felt a strange upside-down sensation in her stomach. She recognised that mask. She didn't remember her dreams most of the time, but this one dream—this one recurring nightmare that had poked and prodded at her for her entire life—this dream she remembered.

The dream of the rabbit mask.

'Now, Ellie, how may I help?' asked the man.

It was silly. Daft. Absurd. A coincidence of some sort, surely? Dreams didn't seep into the waking world.

'I wondered if.... wait, how do you know my name?'

'Because you look like an Ellie.'

'I do?'

'Oh yes, and I look just how you'd expect a Mr. Cotton to look.'

Ellie looked back to her car and wondered why she wasn't already running towards it.

'Are you going to a fancy dress party?' she asked.

'Oh, at some stage, more than likely,' replied Mr. Cotton and his large ears twitched. Ellie ignored that, because of course the ears were just part of a tatty old mask and so could not have twitched at all.

'I'm sorry to bother you, it's just I don't seem to know where I am and my phone isn't getting a signal. Do you think you could direct me back to the main road? I'm sure I could find my way again from there.'

'You would like to be put on the correct path?' asked Mr. Cotton.

'I'm running late and haven't a clue where I've gotten to. Daft of me, really. I don't know what happened, must have been daydreaming and taken a wrong turn or something.'

'So many wrong turns lurk where the right turn may be,' said Mr. Cotton, nodding. He clapped his white-gloved hands together and dust exploded, like a teacher slapping a chalk duster against the wall. 'I believe I would like to help, and I believe I will. My brother would also like to help.'

Ellie turned at the sound of someone breathing, rasping. Before her stood a second man, shorter than the first, but dressed just as anachronistically. This one, the brother, wore a tatty hedgehog mask. As Ellie watched, spiders began to crawl out of the eye holes of his hedgehog mask. Large, thick-legged spiders. Her breath caught in her throat.

'Don't worry,' said Mr. Cotton, 'my dear brother and I know exactly where you are going. Oh, we've known that for a long, long time.'

Ellie's mother called the police a little after nine that night.

6

Rita Hobbes and Dan Waterson were sat in the plush, warm front room of the house Ellie Mason shared with her mum. There seemed to be a numbers war raging between the amount of brightly-coloured pillows the room contained, and the amount of pictures featuring Ellie. The pillows were winning by one, as far as Rita could tell.

'Sugar?' called Janice Mason, Ellie's mother, from the kitchen.

'Two in one, none in the other, please Mrs Mason,' replied Waterson.

Janice Mason entered holding a tray with three china cups on it. 'Here we go, three lovely cups of tea.'

'Thanks,' said Rita, as Janice placed the tray on to the coffee table and retreated to a plump, bright yellow chair.

'So,' said Rita, 'Mrs Mason, you haven't heard from Ellie now in almost twenty-four hours, is that correct?'

'Yes,' she replied, her hands worrying at the hem of her cardigan. 'I know I waited too long. Too long to call you. But she always tells me not to fret so much. She's an adult, she says. But, you know, it's hard when you're a mum. Hard to give them space.'

In fact, she had only waited two hours after the time Ellie had said she would return home before calling the police.

Normally Rita and Waterson wouldn't be asked to look into a

case like Ellie's. At least, not so soon. She'd barely been gone twenty-four hours, and she was an adult. It was too early to know for sure whether anything bad had happened. But, as it turned out, Ellie Mason was the same age as Jane Bowan. Two females, of the same age, in the same town, go missing, without warning. Just disappear off the face of the Earth, without taking any of their belonging with them, and without using their phones, or their bank cards.

But those weren't the only common denominators.

No, it turned out that Ellie and Jane had known each other. Matter of fact, they'd been in the same class in school growing up. Both officers had decided to keep Jane Bowan's disappearance out of the conversation though. No sense upsetting Mrs Mason unduly.

'Could she have gone to a boyfriend's, or girlfriend's, without telling you?' asked Waterson. 'Could it just be a case of crossed wires?'

'No. No, no. We had a special meal planned, she would never forget that. And even if she had, why wouldn't she pick up her phone? I've rung, and I've rung…' Mrs Mason broke off, pulling a paper tissue out of the now half-empty box perched on the arm of the chair and dabbing her eyes.

'Sorry if any of our questions upset you,' said Rita, 'we know how broken you must be feeling, but we need to get as clear a picture as possible to help us find Ellie.'

Mrs Mason smiled and composed herself. 'Yes, sorry, just all a bit frightening. I'm just so worried that I'll never see her again. That something… that something very bad has happened to my baby.'

No one liked this part of the job—sitting with frantic or grieving family members, telling them bad news, or pushing them to answer a barrage of questions with their heads in pieces—but Rita had got used to it. Or as used to it as she could. She made it a rule to stay detached from people like Mrs Mason, otherwise the job would have driven her to a nervous breakdown years ago.

'Is there anything you can tell us about the days, or weeks, leading up to Ellie's disappearance, Mrs Mason?' asked Rita.

'Like what?'

'Anything, anything at all,' said Waterson.

'Okay, well, let me think on that.'

'A change in her habits,' said Rita, 'a change in her way of acting around you, or other people. Maybe she said something that seemed odd but you brushed it off.'

'I really can't think of much.'

'If anything comes to you, anything at all, let us know, okay?' said Rita.

'Yes, definitely, I'll wrack my old brain and try to… well…'

'Mrs Mason?' said Waterson.

'It's nothing. Daft.'

'Let us decide that,' replied Rita.

'It's just, well, my Ellie has always suffered with bad dreams, off and on.'

'Bad dreams?' said Rita, looking to Waterson.

'Yes. About a man in a creepy old rabbit mask. Probably from some old film she watched that she shouldn't have. It's just, in the last few weeks, she'd started mentioning how she'd been having the dream a lot more. Almost every day. But I mean, I'm not sure how that can help you at all.'

Rita nodded and wrote 'Rabbit Mask Dream' into her notebook. 'Thank you, Mrs Waterson.'

Ellie Mason opened her eyes.

Her throat was very dry, she ached, and she could feel the cold of the stone she was laid out on. She tried to get up, but found her wrists and ankles were attached to the stone; handcuffed?

Ellie felt terror. Deep down terror that robbed her of the ability to talk, to scream, to beg.

There was movement to her side.

Ellie lifted her head to see a figure step out of the gloom. The figure wore dark red robes. A goat mask covered his head.

Ellie tried to talk, croaked, coughed, attempted to regain control of her breathing, then tried again.

'Please…' her voice came out a thin whisper.

The figure didn't reply.

It was then Ellie noticed what he held in his right hand.

It was an axe.

A small hand axe, a wooden handle, a rusted metal blade.

'Thank you,' said the man in the robes, his fingers flexing around the axe's handle. 'Thank you so very much.'

Rita rolled off Chris Farmer as he panted and attempted to catch his breath, and looked up at her bedroom ceiling.

'Well done, you' she said. 'Gold star.'

'Yeah, thanks,' he replied.

Rita sat up and reached for the glass of water from the bedside table, taking a sip.

'So,' Chris began.

'So?' Rita replied.

'It's really getting late.'

'Yup. You'll probably want to be heading home, what with it being a school day and all.'

'Right. That's absolutely what I was going to say.'

Rita knew full well it wasn't, but she was in no mood to soothe his feelings. She was happy with their arrangement, especially as she was planning to fly the coop pretty soon. It wasn't her fault if Chris was looking for more. She had the feeling she was going to have to cut this sex-relationship off soon. Cut it off at the knees. It wasn't her fault. She'd never intended for him to fall for her. She never wanted to break his heart, especially as she'd still have to work in the same building as him. Awkward.

Chris leaned over and kissed her. 'Okay, I'm off, you cold-hearted, sexy, loveless thing, you.'

'Aw, that's the nicest thing I've heard all day.'

Chris laughed as he pulled his clothes back on, gave the side of the bed he'd just vacated a last, wistful look, then said his goodbyes.

As soon as Rita heard the front door close, she stood and threw on the ancient, oversized t-shirt she wore to bed. She climbed under the duvet and was about to turn off the bedside lamp, but a thought itched at her. It was something Mrs Mason said, about Ellie having nightmares. And Jane's fiancé, he'd talked about her having nightmares too. Of course, it had to be a coincidence... but when you added in the fact that they were in the same class together, suddenly it didn't seem like such a stretch to add it to the case file. It was another connection after all, no matter how crazy it sounded.

She checked the glowing digits on her phone. It was almost ten. Too late to call, really, but then this was about the case. She hustled downstairs, found the number in the file, and dialled. Four rings and then he answered.

'Greg? Is this Greg Nicol?'

'Hi, yes, I'm Greg, who is this?'

'Sorry to call you so late, Mr Nicol, this is DS Rita Hobbes.'

His voice wavered, obviously more worried he was about to hear bad news than good. 'Oh, hello, yes, hi, what is it? Is there news?'

'We have a number of promising lines of enquiry,' Rita lied.

'Oh.'

Greg obviously saw through that one.

'I just wanted to ask you a quick question, I think it might help.'

'Okay, what question?'

'You said Jane had been having bad dreams before she disappeared, right?'

'Yeah. She'd had them all her life, but she'd been having them a lot more recently. Well, not "them", "it", the one dream. It was always the same one.'

'Was it about a man in a rabbit mask?'

There was silence on the other end of the line.

'Mr Nicol? Greg, hey, are you still there?'

'How did… yes. Yes, she called it the rabbit mask dream. How did you know that?'

7

There were a lot of strange stories in Blackpool, and Formby knew them all.

He knew the true stories, he knew the pretend stories, and he knew the stories that were both at the same time.

Perhaps he knew those ones best of all.

Formby was an eaves. An old eaves. Some said he'd lived as long as any eaves ever had, though his exact age was unknown. He'd lived too long and outlived too many for anyone to keep score.

It gave him a certain celebrity in the Uncanny world, or perhaps notoriety was more accurate. Formby enjoyed it. Some people almost feared him. Said any eaves that had lived such an ungodly long time knew things, terrible things, that no living creature should ever know.

Well, there was some truth to that.

Formby held secrets that must never be told.

Truths that should always be denied.

But back to the stories...

Yes, Formby knew them all. It's an eaves' purpose to gather any and every bit of information that passed their large, slightly pointed ears. It all funnelled in and was stored in their memories. Everything they wanted to remember, and everything they didn't want to remember, was in there, and Formby, like any eaves, was able to access it when needed.

He knew the story of the Screaming Witch: a magical protector who fell for a demon and lost her mind. For laying down with a beast, the witch had been cast out of her coven—an unheard of thing—and was cursed to suffer never-ending torment.

It was said, when the night was cold and dark, that if you listened closely, you could hear the cursed witch's cries, weaved into the whistle of the wind. A normal person might miss the sound, as most were not attuned, but the witch's screams were why the dogs of Blackpool were known to act strangely during a storm. To cower and bark and hide. They could feel the pain, the fear, and they wanted no part of it.

If ever you took a walk on the beachfront alone after midnight and were *very* unlucky, you might even have seen the witch, staggering across the black sand, her face a mask of pain. Should you have the misfortune of crossing paths with the poor wretch, turn and head in the opposite direction, because if she were to lay a barely-there, icy finger on your skin, you would drop dead on the spot.

Formby knew that story well, and had met with the Screaming Witch on many nights. Sometimes she was able to talk, to share scraps of information, but mostly she just begged for her torment to end. But there wasn't anything Formby, or anyone else, could do to help her.

He knew the story of the Devil Tree, too.

In Carsters Park there was a giant, twisted oak, upon whose thick, gnarled limbs no vegetation ever grew, and no snowfall seemed to settle. Legend had it that a demon had been summoned in the park by a cabal of dark magicians, only for it to attempt to break free of their control. The dark magicians were forced to attack, to send the beast back to Hell, but part of the demon had remained. It sank into the soil and became part of an acorn that lay buried there, ready to sprout into an oak.

Young children who visited the playground in Carsters Park and escaped their parents' eyes would wander to the enormous tree and say they could hear it talking. Several of those children, after they grew into adults, said they never stopped hearing the tree. That its voice whispered and teased at them their whole lives, telling them terrible things and putting awful ideas into their heads.

More than one suicide note had made mention of the Devil Tree.

Blackpool was full of such black stories; dead things, awful things, pulled in by the tide and left beached on the sand. Sometimes, Formby wondered if Blackpool Tower's tacky light show was a beacon that attracted malevolence: drawing it in like ungodly moths with ragged wings, making them weave and dance before its fevered light.

And perhaps that was true.

Formby thought so.

Because above all else, he knew the story of the Blackpool Angel.

Formby stepped off the path, the wind blowing in off the sea, vicious and tugging at his coarse, brown hair, as though it were trying to rip chunks of it from his large head. His battered old boots sank a little into the sand as he watched the surf wash in, and then drag itself back out again, an endless waltz.

He wondered if everyone felt that sense of unease as they looked out at the water. How was it possible that anyone—Uncanny or not—failed to sense it? To have it itch at their flesh. To have it ball a fist in their stomach.

But still they came and built sandcastles and splashed out into the sea, screaming and laughing as they met the water's chilly embrace. For most it was just the ocean. They had no idea of the creature that had sat out there, imprisoned, before people had even walked across the land now called England.

Had no idea an Angel stood beneath the waves.

And not just any Angel, oh no, no. This was one of the original seven, hand-crafted by God Himself, to sit at His side. A creature of almost limitless power. A perfect, divine being.

But even the divine could succumb to temptation. Perfection could turn to boredom, after all. And so it was said that the Angel made a deal with the Devil. A deal for power, for independence, away from God's side. God, of course, discovered the Angel had turned dark, and unleashed His wrath upon the Blackpool Angel. A battle waged that cracked the Earth and shook the skies, until finally the Angel was brought low and chained beneath the sea, between life and death, never to rise again.

And there it waited still.

Was it the Tower, or was perhaps the Angel the beacon that attracted all manner of evil to Blackpool?

Formby shivered.

Rita followed Waterson into DCI Jenner's office and shut the door behind them. Jenner ignored them for a few moments as he peered at his computer screen and prodded warily at the keyboard with two fingers, as though it were the first time he'd ever used the thing.

Finally, he sat back and looked at the pair.

'Well?' he asked, as though they'd been keeping him waiting.

'Right, Guv,' started Waterson, 'here's what we know so far: two women have gone missing.'

'Yep, know that,' he replied, picking up a packet of mints and fiddling with it.

'Both women were the same age,' said Rita.

'The same age?' repeated Jenner.

'Yes, Guv,' said Rita.

'Huh. Bit of a coincidence?'

'Maybe,' said Waterson. 'Could be, but with only two missing so far, it's not enough to call it a pattern.'

'Go on.'

Waterson stepped forward. 'Neither of the women have been heard from or seen since they went missing. Neither have used their mobile phones, or accessed their bank accounts. Also, both went to the same school, Old Lane Secondary, same year.'

'Well that's not a big surprise, considering they were the same age,' said Jenner. 'Did they know each other? Were they friends?'

'We're going to look into that,' said Rita.

'Okay, good work, keep me updated, all right?'

'Right, Guv,' said Waterson.

As Waterson headed for the door, Rita dithered.

'You coming?' asked Waterson, hand on the door knob.

'There's just one other thing,' she said.

Waterson dropped his head and sighed. 'The dream thing?'

'Yeah, it's weird, okay?' said Rita.

'Yes, agreed,' said Waterson. 'But it's just dreams.'

'I'm sorry, what are you two babbling about?' asked Jenner.

'Both the missing women, Ellie and Jane, they were suffering from recurring nightmares.'

DCI Jenner's eyes slid from Rita, to Waterson, and back again. 'Nightmares?'

Rita felt her insides squirm. She knew how daft this sounded, and wished her mouth would just shut the hell up already. 'We were told that they were both suffering from nightmares, and that the nightmares had increased in frequency shortly before each went missing.'

'Right. So? People have nightmares. I have one about a clown who might also be my mum. It happens.'

'Yeah, but the thing is, it's the same nightmare. Both women were having the exact same nightmare.'

Rita turned to Waterson for support, but he seemed to have found the toe of his left shoe extraordinarily fascinating.

'Two women are missing, possibly murdered,' said DCI Jenner, 'less nonsense and more proper police work please, DS Hobbes. Hm?'

'Yes, Guv. Sorry.'

Waterson opened the door for Rita as she turned on her heel and strode out of Jenner's office, her cheeks burning hot with a cocktail of anger and embarrassment.

Every part of the Uncanny Kingdom has a place like Big Pins, the bowling alley come drinking hole, two streets away from Blackpool's beachfront. Big Pins was a private place, hidden from the rest of the population, where Uncanny sorts could gather, talk, and drink, without having to hide who, or what, they were.

Big Pins, like all of these places, was secreted down a blind alley. Most passers-by would not notice the entrance to the alleyway – to them it would appear nothing more than a continuation of the brick wall either side.

But Carlisle was not like most passersby.

He strode towards the secret entrance to the blind alley, his coat flowing back in the wind like a cape, his boots clomping across the cobblestones.

Carlisle did not like Blackpool.

He had paid the place a visit just once before, perhaps seventy years ago now, and vowed never to return. He found it a tacky backwater. A grim excuse for a town, with little obvious charm or reason to stop itself toppling into the sea. His opinion upon arriving for the second time was in no danger of changing.

He strode down the cobbled street of the blind alley, his skin tingling as he felt the wash of concentrated magic rolling around him. The world swims in magic, but in some places it is more concentrated than others. Here, in this alleyway, it made Carlisle's eyes dilate and the corners of his usually downturned mouth twitch into a smile.

He stopped and looked up at the slowly-blinking neon sign that announced Big Pins' existence, and sighed. He pushed his way inside, a fug of warm air and unfortunate smells rushing out to greet him.

As he stepped across the threshold, Carlisle felt an energy slide by him like the parting of a beaded curtain. Big Pins was protected by a magic-dampening bubble, and with good reason. Uncanny sorts gathered there to drink night and day, so the dampener acted as a safeguard. A safeguard against a drunken fight getting out of hand within Big Pins' walls; a fight that might otherwise lead to undue damage and loss of life. You were meant to feel safe inside such a place, so the dampening bubble gave all who entered—all who drank and bowled and gossiped—a little peace of mind.

Carlisle stopped as the door swung closed behind him, and took the place in. He'd visited Big Pins during his last visit, and it looked as though it had been renovated since then. Possibly sometime in the mid-seventies judging by the awful decor, which was a worn 1970s version of a '50s U.S. bowling alley. It was every bit as tired and tacky as it sounded, but that, as far as Carlisle was concerned, was Blackpool all over.

He made his way to the bar, past the venue's six ten-pin bowling aisles, all of which were in use by semi-inebriated clumps of flotsam.

As he passed through the place, Carlisle was pleased to note that certain clusters of people turned to shield their faces when they saw who had entered. It seemed his reputation preceded him. Carlisle smiled. He did enjoy engendering a sense of unease around him. A frightened man was a man on his back foot, and someone, potentially, to use.

Carlisle reached the sticky-topped wooden bar and took a stool. 'Barkeep, a pint of your least objectionable inebriation, please.'

A giant lunk of a man in a bowling shirt turned from polishing the optics and eyed the widely grinning Carlisle with small, hooded eyes set deep into a tombstone face. 'Huh. Back already?' asked Linton, the owner of Big Pins.

'And blessed do I feel to make your acquaintance once again, Linton my fine, fearsome fellow.'

Linton raised what was probably an eyebrow, but may have been a fistful of wire wool taped to his forehead, then grabbed a pint glass and began pouring a drink.

Carlisle turned as aisle four cheered a strike. 'I see you've decorated.'

'Yup. Decorated,' replied Linton, plonking the pint down in front of Carlisle and spilling a good quarter of it in the process.

'Yup,' said Carlisle, 'I don't like it.' He picked up the glass and took a mouthful. 'Now, this on the other hand, this is a step up from whatever swill you were serving during my last visit.'

'I do not expect any trouble in my establishment, Carlisle,' said Linton, placing a scarred baseball bat on the counter.

Carlisle eyed the much-used object and recalled his last visit, when the thing had made contact with the back of his head. 'You wound me with such suspicion, Linton, old friend.'

'I'm not your friend, Carlisle. I don't believe you have friends.'

'Well, they do say you can judge a man by his closest company, and I am fabulous company.' Carlisle offered up what would be best described as "a shit-eating grin", as Linton sighed and placed the bat back beneath the counter.

'So what is it then?' he asked. 'On your holidays?'

'Please, I do not holiday. Holidays are for the idle and simple-minded. No, no, no, I am here to speak to a gentlemen whom I believe makes frequent patronage of your fine, sticky-floored, rat hole.'

Linton crossed his thick arms across the broad barrel of his chest. 'He's not here.'

'You don't even know who it is I'm after.'

'Likes of you? You always want something. Information, most likely. And where do you best get information from but an eaves, and everyone knows which eaves you seek out first round here.'

'Linton, I do believe you've grown smarter in your old age. Did you go and read a book like I suggested the last time we met?'

'Drink your drink, leave, and I'll let Formby know you want a word with him.'

'So he's not here?'

'What did I say?'

'I see. Of course. My apologies.' Carlisle stood, finished his drink, and tuned to leave. 'Just one thing,' he said, turning back to the bar and pointing off to a darkened, far corner of Big Pins. 'Who is that ugly old thing over there, trying to hide?'

Linton's eyes twitched to the figure shrouded in gloom, then reached down to grab his bat.

'It's okay, Linton,' said Formby, leaning forward to reveal his face. 'He can ask his questions if he pleases.'

'Formby,' said Carlisle, 'you are here after all! Well, would you look at that, Linton, you big mountain of a man. Formby, that wretched old eaves, is here after all. What a stroke of luck!'

Carlisle turned from the bar and strode over to join Formby, taking a stool opposite, his long coat reaching down to the worn carpet. 'I take it you knew of my imminent arrival.'

Formby nodded and smiled. 'Not much escapes these old ears, your majesty.'

Carlisle raised an eyebrow to that greeting, but let it pass. 'Razor spread the word, did he?'

'That's so, aye,' replied Formby. 'Can I get you a drink?'

'That's okay, I like the look of yours.' Carlisle reached forward and picked up the pint Formby was halfway through, raising it to his lips and slowly consuming the remainder before gasping, smacking his lips, and placing the now empty glass back before the eaves.

'Well,' said Formby, 'that was a bit of a dickish thing to do.'

Carlisle clapped his hands together and laughed. 'Has Razor also informed you of the reason for my return to this godforsaken shit hole?'

'Aye, he has at that.'

'And is what he says true?'

Formby shifted on his stool.

'You will tell me,' said Carlisle.

'It's true enough.'

Carlisle smiled wide, though to Formby it did not appear pleasant, more like a shark readying itself for lunch.

'Well then, where is my artefact?'

'A magician has it.'

'A magician? Ooh. And would this magical practitioner be known to me, old timer?'

'Old timer? I understand you are even older than I, Carlisle.'

'Ah, you are old, ancient in fact, but I am timeless.'

Formby snorted. 'I might use that in future, if you don't mind.'

'So, this magician, who is it?'

'I don't know.'

The smile dropped from Carlisle's eyes, perhaps the shark would feast after all. 'You would not be telling me porkies, now would you?'

'I swear to it. I know the artefact was discovered, and I know that it is still here, in Blackpool, in the hands of a magician. But neither I, nor anyone I have spoken to, seems to know who this magician fellow is. Believe me, I have tried to find out. He has not mixed with the rest of the Uncanny world, it seems. Kept himself to himself all his years.'

Formby swallowed as Carlisle's eyes bored into him, and very much hoped the gloom of this corner of Big Pins was adequately hiding how much he was sweating.

'A magician,' said Carlisle, finally stopping his visual interrogation. Formby sagged back slightly in relief. Carlisle stood and flipped a coin on the table in front of Formby. 'For the drink.'

'Thank you.'

'If you hear any whispers on the wind about this magician, you'll send them to my ears alone, I trust.'

'Of course,' said Formby. 'You have my word.'

'The word of an eaves? Well, now I can sleep soundly.'

'There's one other thing,' said Formby.

'Go on.'

'Women are going missing. Some say the magician is involved.'

There was another drunken cheer as a fresh set of pins was cleared with one bowl.

'Christ, I hate Blackpool,' said Carlisle, then pulled his coat closed and headed for the exit.

8

The Old Dog was across the road from Blackpool Central Police Station, and as such, was always crammed with off-duty officers. It was a small, snug pub with an ancient TV set that was always tuned to one sport channel or another.

At that moment, as Rita was sat slumped and grumpy, nursing half a pint of lager and scowling at anyone daft enough to say hello, it was showing a snooker match. Rita closed her eyes and listened to the click-clack of coloured balls sliding across the baize.

'This seat taken?'

Rita looked up to see a beaming Chris Farmer, still in his uniform, already lowering himself on to the stool opposite her, drink in hand.

'Well, it looks like it is now,' said Rita.

'Oh. Well. I can always....'

'No, it's fine, you're there now, so.'

'Right. You know you're a very tricky woman to be around.'

'Aw, you sweet talker.' Rita grinned and winked as she took a drink.

'So, there was something I wanted to talk to you about,' said Chris.

'I thought we'd settled this already. No sleeping over.'

'No, not that, you've made yourself really, really clear on that one. I mean, really, really, incredibly, brutally clear.'

'It's not that I don't like you,' replied Rita, flushing a little.

'Look, it's not about me and you, whatever me and you actually is. It's about the case you and Waterson are on.'

'Oh? What about it?'

'I overheard Waterson and Benton talking. About you.'

'I do not like the sound of that.'

'Waterson was talking about some rabbit mask dream thing.'

Rita sighed and sat back, sloshing the liquid in her glass around.

'Yeah, he thinks I'm being an idiot. But both missing women had the same nightmare. I mean, the exact same nightmare. How can that not mean something?' She knocked back a slug of beer. 'You think I'm mental, right?'

'No. Well, a bit, but not because of that.'

'Thanks.'

'It's just… this dream, right. It was about a man in, like, a tatty old rabbit mask, yeah?'

'Yeah, why?'

'My cousin, Gemma... have I mentioned Gemma?'

'You've mentioned Gemma.'

'She used to tell me about a bad dream she had growing up.'

Rita sat forward sharply and clenched her pint glass so hard it was a wonder the thing didn't shatter. 'She had the dream? Gemma had the rabbit mask dream?'

'Yeah. That's a bit weird, right?'

Three people? Three women, all having the same nightmare? Rita felt a knot in her stomach. She was right. There was something to that dream. Something important that was connecting these people. It might be irrational—it certainly wasn't something DCI Jenner was going to believe—but it wasn't nothing.

'Chris, where did Gemma go to school?'

'Old Lane Secondary. Why?'

They left their half-finished drinks on the table as Rita headed for the exit, dragging Chris behind her, as Ronnie O'Sullivan settled down over the snooker table and attempted to pot a tricky green.

Greg Nicol opened his front door to see a strange specimen stood before him, grinning widely.

'Hello?' said Greg.

The strange man bowed slightly, then straightened up. He wore a long, dark purple coat that had seen better days, and his skin seemed as white as freshly fallen snow.

'And you must be one Mr Gregory Nicol,' said the visitor, his voice honeyed and posh. The voice was British, though for the life of him Greg was sure he'd never heard such an accent before.

'That's right,' said Greg. 'Can I help you?'

'Yes, I understand that you can. May I be granted entrance to your charming home?'

Greg must have agreed and let the man in, because a few short minutes later he found himself handing the man a mug of tea, though he did not recall actually agreeing, nor the man entering his house. It was the strain of Jane going missing, that was it. The lack of sleep, the lack of resolution. That feeling of being in limbo. No word, no body, alive or dead, impossible to say; Schrodinger's Corpse.

'I'm sorry,' said Greg, sitting down in an armchair, 'I'm sure I've already asked you, and you've already told me, but I'm not really on the ball at the moment. Who are you?'

'My name is Carlisle, and I'm here about the missing woman.'

'Are you police? A detective?'

'If you like,' said Carlisle, and reached into an inside pocket of his coat. As he did so, Greg caught a glimpse of the lining and was sure he saw colours dancing, stars twinkling.

'Here,' said Carlisle, holding up a piece of card, 'my credentials.'

Greg peered at the card and felt a little queasy. There was one card, but there were also two cards, and Greg's poor stomach churned as his eyes strained. One of the cards appeared to be a yellowed with age, and of course now useless, Blockbuster Video membership card. The second card announced his visitor as Detective Inspector Carlisle.

'My credentials,' said the man again, his voice warm as it

flowed into Greg's ears. He blinked and the sick feeling vanished, as did the Blockbuster Video card. The man, Carlisle, held only one card, and it showed he was indeed a detective here about Jane.

'Is there any news?' Greg asked warily. Any visit or phone call from the police made him worry that this would be when the bad news finally arrived and triggered his complete mental collapse.

'I have no idea,' replied Carlisle, taking a sip of tea.

'Oh. Right. So why are you here?'

'As you said when you greeted me at the door, you can help me.'

Greg was confused by this and again began to wonder about the Blockbuster Video card. Surely it had been that after all?

'What can you tell me about the disappearance of your partner?'

'Well, I've already told you lot everything I know over and over, I'm not sure I have anything else I can add.'

Greg looked at the man's clothes again. The strange, ragged coat, the big, scuffed, heavy boots, and thought it was a very strange way for a detective to dress. Greg now noticed with some concern that the man appeared to be sniffing at the air like a dog. 'What's wrong?' he asked.

'Something has been here.'

The man placed his cup of tea on a sideboard and fell to his hands and knees, sniffing at the carpet.

'Could I look at your identification again?' Greg asked.

The man slapped the floor with one hand then leapt back to his feet and strode towards him, causing Greg to back up until the wall stopped him.

'Something has been here,' said the man again, looking down at him. Greg was a reasonable height, but the man, Carlisle, towered over him.

'I don't understand what you mean.'

'Neither do I. Not exactly. But I can smell it. Taste it. Something to do with… dreams.'

Greg blinked.

'Tell me about dreams, Greg.'

'Well, it's like I said to the other detective—'

'Other detective?'

'Yes, DS Hobbes. Jane has always had these bad dreams. These nightmares.'

'Yes, yes, yes, that's it! Not just dreams, nightmares.' The man turned on his heels and headed for the door. 'What was the nightmare about?'

'Jane said she used to see a man in an old rabbit mask.'

The strange perhaps-detective paused in the doorway and glanced back, his brow knotted. 'I am very sorry for your loss.'

The words hung heavy in the air as the man left and the front door opened and closed.

Greg felt the words slowly become part of him.

Felt the truth of those parting words.

Loss.

He knew it was true.

Jane was never coming back.

Three hours later Greg was still curled up in a ball on the carpet.

Rita didn't like Gemma Wheeler's house. It was too neat, too orderly, too sparse. It was one of those homes that looked like nobody actually lived there at all.

'What's this about, Chris?' asked Gemma, who looked a lot like a chubbier version of Chris in a long, curly wig.

'This is Rita, my…' he looked to her for guidance.

'Colleague.'

'Right. Just my colleague and, sort of, acquaintance.'

'Okay. So…?'

'Gemma,' said Rita, 'have you heard about the two women who went missing recently?'

'Yeah. It's been on the local news and that, hasn't it. Terrible stuff. Makes you worry. Why?'

'Well,' said Chris, 'it's just Rita here's on that case, and I thought you might be able to help. Sort of.'

Gemma looked blankly at her cousin.

'Jane and Ellie, did you know them?' asked Rita.

'Yeah. Well, I didn't *know them* know them, if you get me. But they were in my year at school, so I knew who they were. We weren't friends or anything though. Spoke a couple of times maybe.'

'The couple of times you spoke, did the subject of dreams ever come up?'

There was that blank look again. 'Dreams?'

'Gemma, tell Rita what you told me about your nightmares. That thing you've dreamed about on and off since you were little.'

'Why?'

'Gemma,' said Rita, 'do you dream about a man in a rabbit mask?'

Gemma's face flushed and she took a step back. 'Why'd you tell her about that? That's private, Chris!'

'Jane and Ellie, they had that recurring nightmare, too,' said Rita, pressing on.

'What? That's... well, that's weird, isn't it?'

Rita and Chris both agreed that it was weird.

Gemma stepped back again, for a second Rita thought she might actually collapse, she'd gone so pale, but instead she slowly lowered herself down on to the couch. 'I don't like that dream,' she said. 'The rabbit mask dream. I don't like it.'

'What happens in the dream, exactly?' asked Rita.

'Nothing. Not really. At least nothing I can remember. I just have this person in a rabbit mask, and I don't like the rabbit mask, it's old and mouldy, and I know it stinks, and I can hear his breath in there.'

Gemma was starting to clench her fists, over and over, Chris sat next to her, trying to calm her.

'I can hear his breath rasping against the inside of the rabbit mask and I'm really, really scared he's going to take the thing off and I'll see what's underneath and I know if I see it I'm going to lose my mind. I feel like he wants me for something. Has always wanted me for something, and there's nothing I can do.'

'Okay, that's enough,' said Chris, as a tear began to roll down Gemma's cheek.

'How can the three of us have the same nightmare?'

'I don't know,' said Rita, wishing she had something soothing to tell the poor woman. 'The dream, the nightmare, have you had it more often recently?'

Gemma Wheeler nodded, and Rita began to feel very worried indeed.

Rita's phone informed her that it had just passed 2 a.m. and she wondered again just what the hell she was doing sat in her car staking out the home of Gemma Wheeler.

Chris had gone on shift, so for the last five hours, Rita had been alone in her car, waiting for.... well, waiting for something. It was fair to say that they'd worried Gemma with their visit, and Rita felt a responsibility. To what? To stop anything bad happening to Gemma? She realised that in many ways, this was crazy. That she'd taken it upon herself to become a woman's bodyguard because she shared a nightmare with two missing persons.

She'd already ignored two calls from Waterson—who was no doubt wondering why his partner had gone M.I.A—but how could she explain what she was doing to him, or to anyone else? It was clear he thought she was bonkers for deciding that the dreams were a line of enquiry worth pursuing. She couldn't say she blamed him. It *was* bonkers, but it also felt so completely and utterly right.

She thought about Chris, about how he'd come to her with information about his cousin and the dream. He'd not questioned things, hadn't said anything about it being a mad coincidence, he'd just picked up the thread and handed it over. Rita couldn't help but feel a little grateful, not to mention impressed. Chris had a more open mind, clearly, than many others on the force.

Oh God, thought Rita, *don't go getting real feelings for him.*

She didn't notice when her eyes grew heavy and started to droop, but at some point she realised she was no longer sat inside her car in the middle of the night, but was now stepping on to Blackpool beach, looking out at the sea.

There's something in there.

Beneath the waves.

Something dark and terrible and ancient beyond words.

It was out there, the thing, desperate to break the surface and step on to the land again.

What was it?

It wasn't a person, it was definitely an *it*.

'We fought it,' said a glowing man with great wings attached to his back and a halo shining so brightly it hurt to look at. 'We fought for centuries, the sky burning with fire. And we won. We stopped the beast it had become.'

Rita nodded like she understood. Maybe in the dream she did, for a moment.

Then she looked out to sea and saw something awful dragging itself out of the waves and rushing, screaming towards her.

Rita awoke with a start, reflexively pushing herself backwards before she realised where she was. She wasn't on the beach, she was in her car, and it was bloody freezing. It was now just past four in the morning, and Rita decided she'd had enough. She reached over to the car key and was about to turn it, when she noticed the face staring in at her from the passenger seat window.

Only it wasn't a face, not as such. It was a mask. A tattered old rabbit mask.

'Shit!' Rita jumped back, but the figure was gone. 'Shit, shit, shit!'

She looked around, out of every window, jerking her head this way and that, but she couldn't see the rabbit-masked figure anywhere.

'What the fuck?' she said quietly, and began to worry he'd just ducked down out of view. That he was crouched low and out of sight, ready to scare her again, or worse, grab her.

Maybe it was just a remnant of the dream? Yeah, that could be it. She'd been having a weird dream, and when she was still just half-awake, still caught in the dream's wake, she'd seen something that wasn't there.

But what if…?

She looked over to Gemma Wheeler's house.

The front door was wide open.

'Shit, shit, shit!'

Rita threw the car door open and half-jumped, half-fell out of it, racing towards the house, pulling out her standard issue baton and flicking it to full extension.

'Gemma!'

She ran through the open door, sprinting from room to room, but she already knew. Somehow you can just tell when a house is empty. You feel it, hear it.

Rabbit Mask *had* been there.

And now Gemma was gone.

9

DCI Jenner sat low in his chair and rubbed at his eyes. 'So, the man in the mask was there, and then he wasn't?'

'I know how it sounds,' replied Rita. 'I mean, it sounds mental. I sound like a mental person.'

'Agreed,' said Jenner, looking over to Waterson, who was stood mute at Rita's side. 'And did you see this incredible disappearing fancy dress man?'

'I wasn't there, Sir.'

'I was following my instinct on my own, Guv,' said Rita.

Jenner sat back in his chair and Rita could practically feel the weary annoyance emanating from him.

'With all due respect, a woman did go missing,' said Rita, steaming ahead, 'Gemma Wheeler, she's gone. She told me she had the same dream as the first two women, and now she's gone.'

'We don't know that yet for sure,' Waterson cut in.

Rita turned to him and tried very, very hard not to punch him in the face. 'I saw the man in the rabbit mask. Her door was wide open, phone and money left behind. Gemma gone, same as the others. On top of that, she's the same age, even knew the other two. Well, a little bit.'

Waterson raised his hands and eyebrows and took a step back. 'I agree, there's a pattern, but it's only been hours since she was last seen. That's not enough to write her up as a missing person.'

Rita may have said a swear word or two, then turned back to Jenner. 'Guv. They're linked. You must see that.'

Jenner sighed, then nodded. 'Yes. There's a link. An actual, solid link that you can follow. Same age. All women. All went to the same school. That's what you dig into, agreed?'

'Agreed,' said Waterson, making sure he was out of his partner's range.

Rita wanted to voice her complaint, but she could see she wasn't going to win that battle. Fine. If neither of these stupid men wanted to include the rabbit mask dream into the overall picture, then she'd include it on her own.

Clear of Jenner's office, Rita attempted to bore a hole through Waterson's head with her eyes.

'Hey, stop that,' said Waterson, swatting the imaginary laser beams aside.

'Thanks for the back-up, *partner*,' Rita spat.

'What do you want me to do? You're talking about dreams, Rita. We can't build a case on mask-wearing dream people. Dreams aren't taking these women, a person is.'

'Okay, it's weird, Waters, I get that, right, but it's *something*.'

Waterson dipped his head and sighed, then looked back up at her. 'Rita, I've followed you down some weird old paths, but I'm not gonna play the Scully to your Mulder this time. For one thing, I don't have the legs for a skirt.'

Rita glared at Waterson.

'Not gonna crack a smile at that, eh?'

She was not.

After the third furious round of drivers spanking their horns at her, Rita thought it best that she stopped driving angry and pulled over until she'd calmed down.

She yanked the wheel over, parked up, and stomped towards the beach. Rita had never really cared for the beach, to her it just highlighted the fact that she was on the edge of things. Away from anything interesting. Away from a better, new life.

Plus she'd had sex on the beach once and the sand had got everywhere. *Everywhere*. You don't forget that sort of chafing in a hurry.

She sat down heavily, dug her hands into the sand, and threw a great clump of it at the water. The wind caught it and threw it right back at her.

'Stupid, fucking wind!' she yelled, before looking around to make sure no one had seen her picking a fight with the wind.

She wanted to be angry with Waterson. No, actually, she wanted to be completely bloody furious at him. The problem was, she could see where he was coming from. DCI Jenner, too. She knew they were right. What use was it chasing a nightmare? It's not like they could lock the thing up. And apart from asking every woman in Blackpool of a similar age to Gemma and the other missing women if they'd ever dreamt about a rabbit mask, it was useless as a means of finding other potential victims.

And here was the main point: it didn't help her find those who had already gone missing. It was a link, a really bloody strange link, but it didn't help her get any closer to finding out what had happened to them, or where they were. Waterson was right. Not that she'd ever tell him that. But he was right. They had to work the other, tangible facts. Chasing phantoms wasn't going to save those women, or any others.

'DS Rita Hobbes, is that you?'

Rita jerked back at the sudden intrusion to see a tall, pallid man in a purple coat smiling down at her.

'Who's asking?' she replied, pushing herself up on to her feet and taking a step back to create a safer distance from the man, her hand ready to pull her extendable baton.

'We met at some police function or other, I think. Don't tell me you don't remember.'

Rita peered closer at the man and found herself caught by his wide, dark eyes. They seemed to almost shimmer. To draw her in. To make her not want to look away. 'Function?'

'Yes. Two years ago, perhaps? I'm DI Carlisle, do you remember me now?'

Rita shook her head, breaking eye contact. It felt like she'd taken four shots of vodka in quick succession. 'Two years?'

'That's right. We met and spoke, very briefly.'

Something seemed to tease at her memory. It was like she almost believed him. Almost. 'Can I see some I.D?'

The man's smile grew somehow wider, revealing more teeth than seemed possible for one person's mouth. 'But of course. Where are my manners?' He reached into his coat and pulled out a card. 'There, look, DI Carlisle.'

Rita looked at the card, then back at the pale, tall man, and then back at the card again. 'I see,' she said.

The man nodded and pocketed the card again.

The thing was, Rita really did see. And what she had just seen was not the identification of a detective in the police force, but a yellowed, useless Blockbuster Video card.

Was he trying some Jedi mind trick on her? Some Derren Brown style mentalist magic? Or maybe he was just some random nutter. Well, whatever he was trying to do, it had completely failed. Not that Rita had to let the strange man know that – better to let him continue his ruse and find out just what his game was.

'Sorry, I think I do remember you now, actually. At that police function.'

'That's right.'

'Yeah, names and faces, not my area.'

'Well that is unfortunate, considering your line of work.'

Rita laughed, or at least pretended too. 'So, what do you want, Inspector?' she asked.

'I understand you are in the midst of a most fascinating case.'

Rita's hand twitched towards the baton again. 'Yeah, it's an unusual one all right,' she replied.

'You see, I've been involved in a similar case down in London. Women going missing, men in animal masks, horrid situation, and I thought you and I could share everything we know so far, and perhaps assist each other. Now, doesn't that sound like a very good idea, Rita?'

She felt drawn to his eyes again.

'A very good idea,' continued the man, 'to tell me what you know.'

Rita wrenched her eyes away and staggered to one side, yanking out her baton. 'Okay, whatever it is you're doing, mate, you can stop, all right?'

The man raised an eyebrow and frowned, 'I'm simply trying to help out a fellow officer.'

'Really? I didn't know Blockbuster Video had its own branch of police.'

The man's eyes grew wide in surprise, then he laughed. 'Ah, you saw through my clever, clever ruse. I am impressed, Rita Hobbes. Most believe it with very little effort on my part.'

'Who are you and what do you know about the missing women? Are you involved?'

Rita began to slowly circle the man, a tactic she'd learned to keep the person off guard, off-balance, and keep oneself in control. Unfortunately, the man didn't turn, didn't seem the least bit concerned. Instead, he stood stock-still and perfectly relaxed. He seemed more amused than anything.

'I'm just another concerned citizen, looking to bring an end to this tale of tragedy.'

'Right, of course, and if I were to search that coat of yours, I wouldn't find a rabbit mask stashed inside, right?'

'Oh, I'm afraid if I was that wicked fellow and I was showing you my true face, you would no longer be standing, you would most likely have lost your mind completely.'

'I've seen him.'

The man turned now, curious. 'Oh?'

'The man in the rabbit mask. Just for a second.'

'Well. That's… unexpected. First the resistance to my charms, and now this. Aren't you full of surprises, detective?'

'Who is he?'

'You do not wish to know.'

'Who is he?' Rita demanded.

It was stepping forward in anger, losing control, that did it. As the red mist descended, Rita had just enough time to see a flash of bright, shining teeth, before the man's fist connected with her jaw and things went very, very black.

10

Rita woke annoyed and confused, which was not an uncommon experience.

'Sucker-punching bastard,' she said, sitting up and rubbing her aching jaw. She checked her phone. It didn't look like she'd been unconscious long, a minute or so at most.

Rita got to her feet, still a little groggy, and slowly made her way off the beach and over to her car.

The case just seemed to be getting stranger.

She slumped behind the steering wheel and reached for a half-drunk bottle of water that had been sat in the car's passenger footwell for a good week. The water was tepid and a little foul, but it helped drag her the rest of the way back into the light.

Nightmares, people in animal masks that seemed to be able to disappear in an instant, and now this man. This strange, pale man with his odd way of talking and eyes that made you want to believe things that were clearly untrue. Carlisle, he'd said his name was. Rita wondered if that was just another lie. She'd have to use the name for now. She reached for her notebook and began to scribble down the events of her beach encounter. This man definitely belonged on the strange column of this case. The column neither her partner or her boss wanted anything to do with, but a column that was getting crowded and impossible to ignore.

It was just as she was about to start the car and drive home that something caught her eye in the rear-view mirror.

It was a man, crossing the road, about fifty metres away.

The man's clothes looked very old-fashioned. Like something a gentleman might wear a hundred or more years ago. Oh, and he wore a rabbit mask.

Rita was almost knocked out for a second time as her head connected with the window of the door in her rush to exit the car.

'Shit!' she said, rubbing her head as she stepped out, eyes searching for the rabbit-masked man.

She couldn't see him. 'Shit, shit, shit it!'

Rita broke into a run, almost taking out a screaming cyclist as she did so, as she sprinted in the direction it looked like Rabbit Mask had been heading in. Chip shops and souvenir stands stuffed with cheap tourist tat flashed by as she hurtled forward, skidding to a halt at the corner, and glancing wildly around for any sight of her quarry.

'You!' she shouted, grabbing the shoulders of a startled, elderly man. 'Police! Me! I am police! Have you seen a man? Man in a mask?'

'What? What man? What are you—'

'Rabbit mask! He must have passed here, rabbit mask, rabbit mask!'

'What the bloody hell are yo—'

Rita cast him aside and carried on running. How could she have lost him? It wasn't as if he could easily just blend into the crowd, not with those clothes and the giant, bunny ears—

There!

Wait, it wasn't him, this one was different. He was dressed the same, and had a mask on too, but this one looked like a…. like a hedgehog?

Rita shrugged and ran in the masked man's direction as he headed inside a games arcade.

She stood, panting, a few feet into the garish, busy, and monstrously loud arcade. It was all claw games that you never won, penny-shove machines, and ancient shoot 'em ups. None of the so-called thrills on offer had changed since she was a kid.

Rita strode in, dodging the small, whooping children that scuttled by, almost bringing her down to the mangy carpet as she tried to squint past all the flashing lights and catch a glimpse of spines or rabbit ears.

A glimpse, that was all, of old, tatty fur, between the hustle and bustle, and Rita was off again, swerving through the public as though she were skiing a slalom.

'Oi, you, stop, police!'

She found herself outside a double door with the words PRIVATE stencilled on them, and didn't pause for a moment before pushing her way inside.

The dim room beyond was stacked high with dusty, broken games machines and large plastic bags full of soft toys, no doubt ready to replenish one of the machines in the arcade should anyone actually ever manage to win one.

Rita slowly pulled out her standard issue extendable baton and edged further into the room, cushioning the door with one hand as it swung closed, masking the noise. She needn't have bothered. It quickly became apparent that she was alone.

'That's not possible…'

She began to search the room, looking for another way out; a window, a door, a fire exit. But there was nothing. There was only one way out, and that was the way she came in. Rabbit Mask had come through here though, she was certain of it.

'Shit. Shit, shit.'

Rita sagged and leaned against the wall. It took a few moments to realise cool air was pooling around her ankles. Cool air that was emerging from the crack beneath the door she was leaning upon. A door that she was very, very sure had not been there moments ago.

Well, of course. Men in animal masks that come and go, and doors that appear by magic, Rita said to herself.

She stepped forward and placed her ear against the door, which looked like it belonged to an ancient, crumbling village church, and not the back room of a clapped-out seaside arcade.

Rita took a breath then tried pulling on the door's cold, brass handle. It swung open and the cold from behind it wrapped its arms around her. Shivering, her breath now a fog, Rita flexed her fingers around the baton and stepped past the door and into what lay beyond.

What lay there was a dank, stone corridor, the arched roof of which was a little too low for her to stand up straight. Slowly, she made her way towards the light at the other end, her boots squelching across damp, mossy ground.

'Okay, okay, nothing to be terrified about, all perfectly normal…'

She glanced back to make sure the door she'd entered through hadn't disappeared, and was relieved to see the piled up bags of soft toys still visible in the distance.

There were no other doors or windows in the corridor, just the opening ahead. A creepy stone corridor, leading to a mysterious chamber.

Rita began to wonder if getting sucker-punched had done her some serious brain damage.

The corridor came to an end and she found herself before the arched entrance to the chamber, the shadows of flickering flames licking across the ground towards her.

'Well, here goes something.'

Rita stepped into the room.

Rita wasn't sure what, exactly, she was expecting to find in the hidden room at the end of the stone corridor, but what her eyes took in as she shuffled into the chamber was certainly not it.

It was Gemma Wheeler, Chris Farmer's missing cousin, draped in a blood-red robe, chained to a large block of stone.

'Holy shit.'

Rita raced across to the woman, who was a little too motionless for her liking.

'Gemma? Gemma!'

Rita slapped at the woman's cheek, eventually rousing a groan. The woman's eyes flickered. She was still alive!

'Oh thank bloody Christ,' said Rita. 'It's okay, Gemma, it's me, it's DS Rita Hobbes, your cousin's, uh, friend. I'm getting you out.'

That turned out to be easier said than done. The chains were heavy, locked, and fixed firmly to the block of stone she was laid out on. Rita had seen enough Hammer Horror films growing up to know what this sort of situation was leading to: a blood sacrifice. But this was twenty-first century Blackpool for God's sake, not some backwards village in the middle-ages.

'Help… please,' begged Gemma, her words a slur.

'It's okay, Gemma, I'm here, nothing's gonna happen to you, okay?'

All well and good saying that, but she couldn't see how she was going to free the woman, not without leaving her alone and going for help. It was then that Rita noticed the stone altar, and what was perched atop it.

An axe.

A small, old, hand axe.

Rita snatched it up. 'Looks like you're going to be doing more saving than killing,' she told it, and made ready to bash the chains, free Gemma, and get the hell out of there.

But as she turned, she saw that she and Gemma were no longer alone.

'Shit!' she said, jerking back in shock.

Stood in the entrance to the stone tunnel was a tall man in crimson robes. He wore a large goat mask over his head.

'Game's up, you sick bastard! Take off that bloody mask, right now!' The man didn't move. 'Look, you're done, I'm police, all right? And this is the last woman you or your other mask-wearing sickos snatch, you got that? Now kneel down and put your hands behind your head or—'

Rita wasn't sure what happened exactly, but there had been a flash of intense light, and what felt like a car driving directly into her chest. She sat up from where she'd been knocked down to see the robed man walking slowly towards her.

Rita was in a horror movie, that's all there was to it, and this idiot was about to make her his latest victim.

'Not bloody likely,' she said, and grabbed the hand axe from where she'd dropped it, pushing herself back up and brandishing it. 'That's right, prick, you're nicked!'

As she ran at the man he raised his hands and seemed to mould a ball of crackling, bright white light, his fingers dancing as though he were playing the air like a piano. Rita pulled to a stop and gawped. 'What is that? Stop that!'

The man did not stop. Instead, he raised the crackling ball of energy and threw it at her. She should have leapt out of the way, but—acting on reflex—she swung the axe at the ball. Rather than sending her flying again, the ball ricocheted off the axe and flew back at the masked man, hitting him, and causing him to disappear in a puff of smoke.

Rita breathed heavily, staring incredulously at the spot the man had been only heartbeats before. She stared down at the axe in her hand, then back at the vacant space.

'Holy crap.'

'Help…'

Rita shook off the shock and ran back to Gemma. 'Okay, hold still,' she said.

She lifted the axe high, then swung it down at the chain clasped to Gemma's ankle. To her delight and surprise, not only did the strike cause the chain to break, but all of the chains attached to her shattered and swung free.

'Huh, talk about lucky. Come on, you.'

Rita levered the still mostly out-of-it Gemma Wheeler up on her feet and guided her towards the stone corridor. As she went, she cast one final glance to where the goat-masked kidnapper had been standing before the ball he'd conjured had bounced back at him.

'Yep,' she muttered, 'that beach bastard definitely gave me brain damage.'

11

Struggling under Gemma Wheeler's weight, Rita carefully weaved her through the games arcade and out on to the street, where she gently lowered her on a nearby park bench.

'Gonna... gonna kill... me...' Gemma moaned.

'It's okay, you're fine, he's not gonna touch you, love,' replied Rita, sliding the little hand axe into her belt and reaching into her coat for her phone to call for an ambulance.

'Emergency services, which service do you require, ambulance, fire, or police?' came the reply.

'This is DS Rita Hobbes, I require an ambulance,' she replied.

There was a silent pause.

'Emergency services, which service do you require, ambulance, fire, or police?' repeated the woman at the other end.

'Ambulance, I need an ambulance down at Archer's Old Arcade!'

Another pause.

'Hello? Can you hear me? What's the nature of your emergency?'

'Forget it!'

Rita hung up and shoved her phone back in her pocket. Blackpool's mobile phone coverage had always been spotty. Yet another reason to give the place the old heave-ho.

'Right, come on you, let's get you to the hospital.'

Rita pulled Gemma back up to her feet and steered her down the street and back to where she'd abandoned her car.

If Rita hadn't been in such a hurry, if she hadn't been more concerned with talking to Gemma, with keeping her awake, she might have noticed all the funny looks she was getting. The gawping stares from other drivers and their passengers as they sat together at traffic lights, or as she swerved past them at way past the speed limit.

But she did not notice.

Soon enough, the tyres of Rita's car screeched as she screamed to a halt in a vacant ambulance bay directly in front of the hospital's main entrance. She ran round the car, opened the passenger door, and attempted to get Gemma out and back on her feet.

'Gemma, come on, stay awake, stay with me, love!'

It was no use. It had been hard enough moving her around when she was only half with it, now she was practically unconscious, and the dead weight was too much.

'Help! Give us some help here!' Rita screamed at a man as he approached, bunch of flowers in hand, exiting through the hospital's automatic doors. The man didn't even glance at her.

'Bastard!' Rita spun back to Gemma. 'One second, I'll be right back.'

She ran into the hospital. 'Hey, I need help, I've got an unconscious woman in my car.' The doctors and nurses gathered in reception area ignored her. 'Oi!' Rita pulled out her I.D. 'Police, DS Rita Hobbes, I need help with a…'

Rita stopped. No one paid her the slightest bit of attention. In fact, a few of the nurses who had been huddled around a chart, turned and walked away.

'What is wrong with you idiots?' Rita cried.

She spied an empty wheelchair and grabbed it, pushing it through the automatic doors and back to her car. Through brute force, and a bit of colourful language, she managed to haul Gemma into the wheelchair.

'Right, you're okay Gemma, here we go.'

She wheeled her into the hospital's reception.

'Oh my God,' said the large, female receptionist upon seeing Gemma, slumped in the wheelchair.

'Nurse Baxter, I need help!'

The receptionist and Nurse Baxter rushed over to Gemma, the nurse taking a knee and opening one of Gemma's eyes, shining a pen torch into it.

'Hello, can you hear me? Can you hear me?' asked the nurse.

'Well, at bloody last,' said Rita. 'You're a bit oblivious in here, aren't you?'

'Who brought her in?' asked the nurse.

'What do you mean?' asked Rita.

'I didn't see anyone,' replied the receptionist. 'I looked up and she was just there.'

'Hello?' said Rita, waving her arms around, 'have you two gone completely mental? I brought her in!'

'I think she's okay, but we'd better get her through and do some checks,' said Nurse Baxter, continuing to ignore Rita, who watched with confused astonishment as the receptionist grabbed the wheelchair and began to follow Nurse Baxter out of the waiting area.

'What, in the fuck, was that?' asked Rita, shaking her head as she pulled out her phone again and dialled Waterson's mobile.

'Hello?' said Waterson, picking up on the third ring.

'Waterson! I found her, I found Gemma Wheeler! She's alive, I've got her over at the hospital and there's some really weird shit going—'

'Hello? Can you hear me?'

Rita swore, shook her phone, and walked outside, hoping the reception would pick up better.

'Waterson, it's Rita, can you hear me now?'

'Sorry, I can't hear you, I think we've got a bad connection.'

The line cut off.

Rita looked down at her phone, then back over her shoulder into reception.

She was beginning to get a really bad feeling.

Carlisle stood in the stockroom of Archer's Old Arcade, looking through the doorway into the stone corridor beyond. He ran a chalk-white finger along the stone surrounding the ancient wood of the door, then sniffed his fingertip.

'Impressive,' he said, then stepped into the stone corridor beyond.

This kind of magic was beyond your common, lowly magical practitioner. They'd managed to sandwich two different places, in two different times, right next to each other. Carlisle couldn't even see the join. Now, an eaves could do something similar, but not with different times, too. This was far beyond the ability of those wretched creatures.

Carlisle made his way down the old stone corridor, stooping low to prevent his head connecting with the arched ceiling. As he walked, he projected an aura of calm assurance, but inside he could not deny that he was concerned. He had hoped whoever had his property was some low-level fool—that retrieving it would be like taking candy from a baby—but this corridor told him that his quest would not be so simple.

Why did things always have to be so complicated?

He paused at the chamber's entrance and poked the toe of a boot at the chalk drawn on the flagstones in front of him.

It was a hex.

A booby-trap triggered by an unwanted visitor.

It was a chalk circle with all kinds of arcane symbols expertly drawn within. Carlisle crouched and peered at each symbol, each rune, each magical oath. If someone had walked over this, it should have killed them. Would have turned them to ash in an instant. The hairs on the back of Carlisle's neck told him that the hex had most certainly been triggered, but he saw no evidence of ash. No little pile of dusty grey to indicate the trespasser's final resting place.

The hex hadn't worked.

Or at least, not in the way it was intended to work.

'Curiouser and curiouser…'

Carlisle stood and stepped over the now useless hex, not that such a trap would have worked on him these days anyway. He had so many protections and totems sewn into the lining of his coat that it would take a magician of L'Merrier's heft to fashion a hex that would even cause him a tickle.

The chamber was stone, circular, with a small altar stood a few yards from a large block of stone. A place of sacrifice then. A sacrifice disturbed?

Carlisle sniffed at the air. Magic had been deployed within the space, and recently. A battle of some sort? Short, swift, and over in moments?

There was dried blood on the large, central stone. The sacrificial stone. More than one person's blood. He thought about the man he'd visited, what had been his name again? It didn't matter. The one he waited for was clearly long since dead. Murdered in the name of something.

Carlisle wondered just what that something could be.

But that wasn't why he was here. This was none of his business. He'd sacrificed more than one animal, more than one person, in his many, many years of life. Who was he to judge?

No.

His property, that's all he craved. It had been here. It had been used. He could feel it. Someone had removed it.

Something that didn't belong caught his eye, and he strode to one side of the chamber, crouching to pick up an item that had been left behind during the chamber's intrusion.

It was a black, standard issue, extendable police baton.

Carlisle lifted the baton and sniffed it.

'DS Rita Hobbes, I presume,' he said, with a smile.

The magician did not know where he was.

The world around him was indistinct shapes and colours and noises that he couldn't understand.

He tried to pull off the goat mask that encased his head, only to find he had no hands with which to achieve the task, nor a head to remove the mask from.

'Help me,' he pleaded. Or thought, or felt, or something else altogether.

How had this happened?

Where had he been?

The chamber!

She'd been in there. How had she found the entrance? No one should be able to find that door, that corridor, that chamber. But even if she had…

….had…

had….

….

His thoughts drifted apart like blown smoke. Was that all he was now? A scatter of thoughts? Smoke on the wind?

How had she survived the hex?

'I'm frightened!' he screamed, but how do you scream without a throat, a mouth, a tongue, an anything?

His own magic had been launched back in his direction.

Impossible and impossible and impossible, and…

The axe.

The tool of sacrifice.

She had it!

He was just a young boy, digging in the sand, when his plastic trowel had…

Taken it.

Hidden it.

'I am here,' said the Angel.

'I failed,' he replied.

'We cannot fail,' replied the Angel, its voice light and high, yet deep also, which was impossible and yet true and it filled the magician to the brim.

'Can you see it?' the Angel asked.

'See what? Everything is chaos and nothing…'

'Can you see it?'

The magician did see it.

The beach.

Blackpool beach.

And suddenly he was not nothing, he had arms to move, legs and feet to kick, and he was swimming, the sea water splashing cold against his face, the beach inching ever closer.

'I am here for you,' said the Angel, and finally the magician crawled out of the sea. The sand gripped between his fingers as he fell forward, the heavy sea water soaking the crimson robes that clung to his body.

'Alive,' he said.

The Angel had pulled him back from wherever his own magic had thrown him.

Limbs trembling, he slowly stood and gulped great gasps of crisp sea air. 'Thank you,' he said, through blue, cracked lips.

'The work will continue,' said the Angel. 'Must continue. So close, now.'

The magician nodded. 'She'll have taken her to the hospital. I can go in after dark, some simple perception magic to hide myself. Steal into her room, kill her.'

'No. The axe. You must use the axe, you know this.'

'Yes. Yes, the axe.'

'Find the woman, reclaim the axe, complete the sacrifice.'

The magician nodded as he took off his robes and folded them over one arm. This was just a momentary setback. The world would continue to spin. For now.

Rita had gone mad, that was the only explanation for it.

This time, as she drove towards the police station, she was very aware of the looks that were thrown in her direction. The shocked faces, the wide-eyed children tapping their dads on the shoulder.

For the thousandth time she looked at herself in the rear-view mirror.

There she was; wide green eyes, red hair. She was there.

She was there.

It was that knock-out punch, it must have been, things had gone all weird ever since then. Brain damage of some sort; temporary, hopefully. That could be the only explanation, because the other answer was impossible, and Rita Hobbes might be open to a little weird, but she did not mess with the impossible.

She screeched to a halt and burst into the station, rushing over to the duty sergeant at the reception desk.

'Arthurs, Arthurs, it's me, can you see me?'

Arthurs was stood with a polystyrene cup of tea in one hand and a newspaper in the other, perusing the football results.

'Arthurs!'

She gave him a shove and Arthurs swore as the hot tea spilled over his fingers.

'Bastard!' he said. 'Bastard, bastard hot.'

Another officer, Matthews, looked up and sniggered. 'Daft git,' she said.

'This is… this is…' *Impossible,* was the word Rita did not want to say. He hadn't seen her. Hadn't heard her. Even when she'd physically shoved him, he hadn't realised, hadn't noticed what had happened.

Rita turned and headed further into the station, passing people she saw every day. Not one of them acknowledged her. Not a "Hello", not an "All right, Rita?", not even a nod of the head. On any other day, not having to run a gauntlet of pointless greetings would have put a spring in Rita's step, but right then it felt like she was wading through treacle.

She made it up the stairs to the open-plan office she worked out of.

'Hey, I saved Gemma Wheeler,' she said. 'Found her, she was gonna be murdered, but I saved her. Rita Hobbes, super cop.'

She wandered over to the desk of DI Collins', the toilet blocker. He was exploring the grimy insides of his left ear with the blunt end of a pen, periodically pulling it out and sniffing the end.

'Oi, Collins, we all know it's you that makes a mess of the bogs, you know?'

DI Collins raised his eyebrows in an appreciative manner at his latest pen sniff, then slid the poor thing back into his ear canal.

'Hello! Hello!'

She swiped at Collins' hand, sending the pen flying across the room.

'Shit it,' mumbled Collins, before selecting a fresh pen from his desk and continuing his disgusting excavation.

Rita sighed and walked to her own desk, slumping in her chair as Waterson entered and sat behind his own desk.

'Hey there Waters, it's me, your best buddy and partner, fancy indicating that I exist at all? You'd really be doing me a favour.'

Waterson opened the drawer of a filing cabinet and started sifting papers, ignoring her.

'Be like that then. See if I care.'

Rita started as something clattered on the floor at her feet.

It was a police baton.

'Feeling sorry for yourself, Detective?'

Rita stood up sharply and turned to the voice addressing her. She saw Carlisle sat cross-legged atop a vacant desk, eyes fixed on her, sipping a cup full of vending machine coffee.

'You!'

'Correct, what a sharp deductive mind you possess, Rita Hobbes.'

'You can see me?'

'Another hit! The mean streets of Blackpool are in safe hands.'

Rita looked around at the rest of the office, all ignoring her, ignoring him, just carrying on with their day-to-day work, oblivious. She reached down and grabbed the baton, brandishing it angrily at Carlisle.

'Please, Detective, I give you back your property and you threaten me? What kind of a thank you is that?'

'What is going on? Suddenly no one here can see me, or hear me. What did you do? Did you drug me? On the beach? Is that it?'

Carlisle raised an eyebrow and smiled a horrible smile. 'I'm rather afraid that, as far as the dreadfully ordinary world is concerned, you no longer exist.' He raised a second cup, 'Coffee?'

12

There was a small boy.

He was on his knees on Blackpool beach, blue plastic spade in hand, wearing only shorts as the summer sun beat down, warming his skin.

This was the magician.

Would be the magician.

But for now, all those years ago, he was just a boy, digging a hole in the sand.

It felt good to dig, to concentrate on something physical. To dig and dig and dig and think only of the hole. Of deepening it. Widening it. To no end other than the pleasure of the work. To no end other than to stop himself thinking about the bad things.

The boy felt sweat prickle on his brow as his slender arms continued to power the spade. She was crying louder now but he didn't have time to pay attention to that. Couldn't pay attention. If he stopped to comfort his mother then the hole would never get dug. So she whimpered and sniffled and pulled out tissue after tissue and the boy kept his eyes off her and on the hole in the sand.

He blamed her. He shouldn't blame her, he knew that, but then who else was there to blame? She used to shout at his dad. Call him names. Make fun of him. Even at his age, he knew it was wrong to do that in front of him, but they'd argue anyway as he tried to concentrate on the TV.

He shouldn't blame her.

It wasn't her fault.

He realised he'd stopped digging.

Shit.

He looked up at his mum, sat on a towel with her legs folded beneath her, staring out to sea with red, raw eyes as if the answer to everything lay out there in the deep.

'Are you okay, honey?' she asked, without looking away from the waves.

He didn't answer, instead he went back to the task at hand. The hole. The ignoring her.

But it wasn't working anymore.

He dug harder, faster, but his cheeks were wet and his vision blurry.

Why did his dad have to go and kill himself? Why would he do something like that? Something so sinful? Bobby at school says it meant he'd have gone to Hell. Sinners went to Hell and there was no bigger sin than suicide, that's what Bobby's dad had told him. Bobby's still-alive dad.

His hands gripped the small shovel so hard it hurt. Hurt good.

His mum was crying louder now. He wished she'd stop. Wish she'd just shut up.

He dug, and his stomach hurt more and more as his anger grew, and he suddenly realised exactly who was to blame. Who he should be angry with. It wasn't his mum, or even his dad, who'd prepared the noose and placed his head through the thing.

It was God.

God should save. God should protect. His dad had been a God-fearing man. He went to Church every Sunday without fail. He'd read passages from the Bible aloud every day before the evening meal. And yet despair had gripped him so tightly that it had caused him to resort to the ultimate sin.

Where had God been?

Did all the praying, all the years of being good and holy and right count for nothing?

Did anything mean anything to God at all, or was his dad just an ant? Were they all just ants? Ants that God would one day burn away with a magnifying glass, just for His own amusement?

God had abandoned his dad when he'd needed Him most.

God had killed his dad.

The shovel hit something solid and the boy was pulled out of his thoughts. What had he uncovered? Treasure? Probably just a rock.

He scraped away the rest of the compacted sand. What he found was not treasure, nor was it a rock.

It was an axe.

It wasn't a big axe, like you might see someone on TV using to chop a tree down with. No, it was small, small enough for even a boy like him to use. He smiled and reached down, wrapping his fingers around the wooden handle.

'I hear you.'

The voice made the boy lunge back, and set his heart jumping. He looked around but there was no one else on the beach. Just him and his mum, and it hadn't been his mum's voice. Besides, she was still too busy crying to herself, not paying him any attention at all.

He shuffled forward towards the axe, then reached out, hand trembling, and picked it up.

'I hear you,' said the voice again.

The voice was faint, he could hardly hear it at all, but it was real. 'Who are you?' he asked.

'I am your friend.'

'Why can't I see you?'

'Because I must hide from something terrible.'

'From who?'

'From the most evil thing imaginable. From God.'

Years passed, and the voice grew stronger.

The boy had taken the small axe from the hole he had dug and hidden it in his bag. When his mum had finally stopped crying and decided it was time to go home, the axe had gone with them.

The axe and the voice.

He couldn't always hear it. Sometimes, at first, he'd go weeks without hearing a word. He'd go down to the beach, down to the exact spot where he had dug the hole, and ask the voice to speak to him again. To keep him company. To make him feel less alone. But the voice would say nothing. Then he'd be drifting off to sleep, and there it would be, tickling at his ear.

'I am here.'

He would sit up in the dark, a smile as big as Christmas, and wrap his arms around himself.

And as the years passed, the voice grew stronger. Less like a whisper, more like a friend was sat right by his side, speaking to him clearly.

The voice became more constant, too. No more days or weeks of silence, the voice could always be counted on. If the boy wanted to talk, the voice would reply, and the boy would feel the warmth spread over him.

But the voice was not just a friend. The voice was a teacher. It told him he was right about God. God was not benevolent. God did not care about the creatures that crawled over this planet. God was petty and cruel, and the idea of a small boy's father taking his own life in a room where he knew the man's son would find him, dangling like an abandoned marionette, filled God with glee.

'He laughs at us, at you. He laughs at your father,' said the voice. And the voice would know, because the voice was that of an Angel. An Angel that had tried to teach God the error of His ways, and had been cast out because of it.

'We are brothers in pain,' said the Angel, and the boy pulled his covers close to his chin, his face a scowl, mouth a tooth-clenched grimace, and he nodded.

Yes, the voice, the Angel, was a teacher.

It did not just tell him about the evil of God's ways, it opened up a hidden world to the boy. A world of delight. A world of colour. A world of *magic.*

It started small—simple card tricks that anyone could do—but soon enough the boy found himself able to do things he could not explain. The Angel told him the secret words, the secret shapes. Showed him the energy that washed all around him, around everyone, that most never saw. Could never understand even if they did. Great multi-coloured washes, like the whole world was sitting at the bottom of an ocean. But instead of salt water, they swam through magic.

Swam through the Uncanny.

If you could see the magic—if you could learn to command it using the right words, the right shapes—then anything might be possible.

It did not always go right. Not at first. There was the time he tried to cheer up his mum, still broken five years after her husband had killed himself. He put on a little top hat he'd made from cardboard and placed a box on the kitchen table. He told his mum he was going to make Nelson, their cat, disappear and then reappear.

He placed Nelson in the box and put the lid on top. He waved his hands over the box and said the words he'd been taught. Felt the magic in the room begin to move towards him, as though it were metal and he was now the most powerful magnet ever.

It soaked into him.

Into his skin, his muscles, his bones.

He said the right words, over and over, and then he opened the box.

Nelson was gone.

His mum had gasped, genuine surprise, genuine wonder. 'Oh my… how'd you do that, then? You're a little Houdini!'

The boy had smiled and laughed and his cheeks had flushed. He'd made her happy. Unfortunately, he hadn't been able to make Nelson reappear. He'd tried and he'd tried. He'd forced the magic into himself and said the words for hours and hours, until it felt as though he might sweat blood, but every time he opened the box it was empty.

His mum had got cross then. Couldn't understand why he was playing up so badly. Told him to get Nelson back or he'd be grounded, and no supper, and slapped legs. He tried to tell her he didn't know where things went to when he disappeared them, but she told him to stop playing silly beggars.

The boy found Nelson the cat a few days later, washed up on Blackpool beach, dead.

The boy fell to his knees and cried. Cried the tears he'd held back when his dad had died. Great, heaving sobs that shook his entire body. Tears that fell and soaked the very dead Nelson.

He didn't blame God.

Blame was too small a word.

Too insignificant a word.

'He doesn't care about you,' said the voice at his ear. 'He laughs at you.'

Yes, blame was too flimsy a word.

The boy did not blame God.

The boy *hated* God.

Hated Him with a white hot fury that dried up his tears in an instant and threatened to turn his teeth to dust as he clenched his jaw so tight.

'I have a plan,' said the voice. The Angel of Blackpool.

'Will it hurt Him?' asked the boy.

'Oh yes.'

'Good.' The boy carried Nelson away from the waves that threatened to reclaim him. Took him over by the groyne, the low barrier built to stop erosion, and began to dig the cat's final resting place.

'The evil He has done in the name of good,' said the Angel of Blackpool. 'The evil to you, to me, to Nelson. To everyone. He must be stopped.'

The boy nodded as he refilled the hole and hid the cat from his eyes.

'The axe. Sacrifice. We will grow strong. The axe will grow strong. Strong enough to free me. Strong enough to crack open the doors of Heaven itself.

'And what then?'

'And then we will kill God.'

The boy stood and smiled for the first time since he'd seen his Dad's purple face.

13

Rita ran out of the police station's reception and into the street beyond, hoping the cool outside air would whip some sense into her.

It didn't.

'This is mad. This is mad, this is,' she said, bending slightly, hands on her thighs, taking great gulps.

'Oh, this isn't even close to mad, I assure you,' replied Carlisle, gliding into the street. 'Why, I once visited a town where the laws of physics no longer applied. A great magician had gone mad with heartbreak and sought to take vengeance upon anything. Upon everything. Up was down. Cold was hot. Rocks had feelings that were easily hurt. All because a very plain woman refused his hand in marriage. Pathetic, really. Still, a knife to the neck put an end to that foolishness.'

'I'm sorry,' said Rita standing, 'can you just stop saying words, 'cause none of the mental things you're saying are helping me feel any better. Like, at all.'

Carlisle smiled.

'Would you like to know what has happened to you, Detective?'

'That'd be nice.'

'I'm rather afraid, my flame-haired justice seeker, that you have been hexed.'

Rita frowned and nodded. 'Right. Hexed. As in, you know, magic and that.'

'As you say, magic. And that.'

Rita began to laugh. 'You're off your rocker, mate.'

'I do hope so, the entirely sane are entirely boring.'

'You're serious? A hex? A *hex-hex*. As in a hex, a magical hex?'

'Please stop saying hex, the word is losing all meaning.'

'But that's... that's stories, and stuff. There's no such bloody thing as magic! There's chip shops, and there's dogs, and there's disappointing men. Actual real things that you can see and touch.'

'Then how do you explain all of this? Excuse me,' said Carlisle, stopping a woman who was passing by. 'What do you make of my young lady friend's haircut?'

The woman looked to where Carlisle pointed, his finger inches from Rita's head.

'She believes it flatters her face shape, whereas I say it drowns her delicate features. What say you, madam?'

The woman began to edge away. 'What are you talking about, you nutter, there's no one there.' The woman hurried away as Rita rather self-consciously fussed at her hair.

'Okay. Point made,' she said.

'You found the stone corridor in the arcade. Found the chamber.'

'Yes.'

'You should not have been able to do that. Not someone so... ordinary.'

'Well, aren't you the charmer?'

'Then again, you shouldn't have been able to tell I was lying when I presented you with a glamoured I.D. And yet you did. Curiouser and curiouser do you become, Detective Hobbes.'

Carlisle began to slowly circle Rita, sniffing at her every now and again.

'Um. Rude,' said Rita.

'You do the impossible, and then you double-down and don't die when you're supposed to.'

'Well, sorry about that, I'm always doing what I'm told I shouldn't.'

'The hex was a booby-trap, to prevent the unwanted stumbling into the magician's place of sacrifice. It would have reduced much higher beings than you to dust if they so much as put a foot upon it.'

'Well it didn't. It did whatever this is instead. People can't see me, or hear me. I can touch them but it's like they don't even register it. I'm some sort of like a ghost, but not.'

'It is as though you… short-circuited the hex in some way. Which for someone as insignificant as you are is, of course, impossible. And yet…'

'And yet what?'

'Well, I am not currently conversing with a small pile of ash.'

'Fair point.'

Carlisle paused in his slow circling and clapped his hands together. 'Detective, I believe I must now lick your face.'

'Come again?'

'For purely scientific purposes, you understand.'

'Yeah, that's a hard pass, but thanks.'

'It's the only way for me to ascertain just what the hex has done to you, and if it is possible to reverse it.'

Rita shuffled, then grunted. 'Look, fine, but if I feel like you're enjoying it for even a second, you're getting a knee to your soft bits, got it?'

'Consider it got.'

Rita shuddered as Carlisle gripped her face between his strong, icy hands, then bowed and licked her cheek.

'Well?' she asked as he straightened up and let go of her head. Carlisle rolled his tongue around his mouth with a look of disgust.

'Firstly, whatever face cream you are using in a vain and pointless attempt to halt the ageing process tastes horrendous.'

'It's forty quid a tube. What else?'

'The hex fought. It could not do what it was created for, but a good hex does not give in. The magic wiggled and strained and it did the best it could for its master, to prevent you from hiding. From looking for help.'

'That's why no one can see me? Or hear me?'

'Anyone ordinary, at least.'

'To stop me getting in his way by getting help?'

'And that is not all.'

'Great, what else?'

'Something beyond awful.'

'Oh, God.'

'I would most likely walk into the sea and drown myself rather than suffer this second thing.'

'What? What is it? I'm dying, aren't I? Is that it? Am I dying?'

'Worse. I'm afraid… you are confined to Blackpool. You can never leave this stain upon the British Isles. I am so sorry.'

Rita had to try very hard not to make good on her earlier threat to connect her knee with Carlisle's genitals.

Being the sort of person who liked to see evidence before believing something wholeheartedly, Rita got in her car and went looking for proof of Carlisle's claim. Carlisle folded into the passenger seat, his head pressed against the car roof. Rita fired up the engine and drove to the outskirts of Blackpool.

'Okay. Okay,' she said.

'You know,' said Carlisle, 'your vehicle could really do with a clean. I believe these seats have stains upon their stains.'

Rita ignored him. 'Let's say I believe that magic is real and a magician is murdering women in Blackpool.'

Carlisle opened the car's glove box and grimaced at the landslide of crap that spilled out. 'Good Lord, woman.'

Rita went on. 'Whoever was doing it—the magician in the goat mask and the fancy robes—he's dead.'

'Oh?'

'Yeah. Well, I think so. He chucked some magicky rubbish at me, but I twatted it back at him and he disappeared. So… he's dead, right?'

'No. I can… feel his presence still. It's like a sour taste at the back of my throat. He lives. He will return. His work is not yet done.'

'Right, great, fantastic. Aha,' said Rita, pointing at the sign they were about to pass that read YOU ARE NOW LEAVING BLACKPOOL.

'Brace yourself,' said Carlisle.

'For wh—'

Rita's response was cut short as the car slammed to a halt as though she had driven at speed into a brick wall. She was pretty sure she heard Carlisle giggling as she snapped forward and her forehead connected with the steering wheel.

'You're okay,' said Carlisle as Rita looked to him woozily.

'Bastard… airbag didn't work.'

'Again, supreme detective work, Miss Hobbes.'

Rita stepped out of the car, expecting to see the front end crumpled. Instead, her car looked fine.

'That's… what…?'

Carlisle joined her, smiling. 'You did not crash into anything, the car was just prevented from moving any further.'

Rita raised her arms and began to edge forward, as though moving through an unfamiliar room in the dark. As she reached the point the front of the car had stopped, she found she was unable to move any further. She could not feel a barrier, it was just suddenly impossible to go forward.

'Okay. Trapped in Blackpool. Crap.'

'Crap indeed. I've visited some piles of unmitigated refuse in my many years, but Blackpool is a whole new level of horrid.'

All Rita had thought about for years was making the big move to London. Running from the town she'd spent her youth, shuffled from orphanage to foster care and back again. A pile of paperwork, not a person. She'd ached to finally leave the place behind and start fresh, but she'd left it too late and now she was trapped. Literally.

Rita screamed the word 'fuck' very loudly until she ran out of breath and slumped down on to the side of the road.

'Eloquence and beauty,' said Carlisle, pulling an apple from his pocket and taking a bite. 'What a catch you are.'

'Okay, you seem to know a fair bit about me, so who the shit are you when you're at home?'

Carlisle smiled and swallowed, then tossed the half-eaten apple into the air, spun once, pulled open a pocket on his long, dark purple coat, and watched as the apple landed within.

'Allow me to make a proper introduction: my name is Carlisle, thief, liar, charlatan, murderer, and once and future King of Great Britain.'

Carlisle bowed deeply, then rose again, a grin no one would ever trust stretched across his angular, pale face.

'Bullshit.'

'Bull-true.'

'King?'

'Once and future.'

'Then why aren't you in any of the history books and that?'

'There is history, and then there is *history*. We Uncanny sorts do our best to keep off the radar of you… how to put this kindly… you human garbage.'

'I feel like there was a kinder way of saying that.'

Carlisle chuckled.

'So why are you here? To stop the murders?'

'Oh no, what business is another man's murders to me?'

'Then what's with the interest in my case?'

'I have come to reclaim my property. An item that was stolen from me a long, long time ago.'

'What property?'

Carlisle smiled. 'An axe.'

Rita stood, her hand moving instinctively to the small hand axe that was tucked away in her belt, under her coat.

'That's the one,' said Carlisle, slowly approaching her.

'It's evidence.'

'It is mine.'

'It's been used to murder innocent women,' said Rita, backing up, but finding she could move no further as she hit the Blackpool boundary.

'Murder innocent women? Are any of us truly innocent, Detective?'

'I don't care what mad shit is going on, I'm still a detective working a case, and this is the murder weapon.'

Carlisle stopped and nodded.

'Why d'you want it, anyway? I can point you to three different hardware shops where you can buy a brand new one. This one isn't even sharp.'

'It is mine. I will have it.'

'Why? Why's it so important to you?'

Carlisle paused, then looked Rita in the eyes. 'I will use it to reclaim my right. My throne. My crown.'

'Okay. How?'

'The axe is of Heaven. It provides certain… gifts.'

'Heaven?'

Carlisle nodded.

'Okay. Magic, magicians, Heaven. Fine. What kind of gifts?'

'The gift is unique to each person who wields it.'

Rita began to edge away from the impassable boundary and circle around Carlisle. 'I'm not going to give it to you. I told you. It's evidence.'

'Well, that is unfortunate.'

'Are you going to try and take it from me, because I will do you a lot of damage, scarecrow, believe me.'

'Oh, I do believe you,' he replied, but Rita didn't think her threat had caused him any concern at all.

'Alas, I cannot just take it from you, which is… irksome.'

'Why not?'

'The axe can only be passed on if the wielder gives their true consent.'

'Then you're shit out of luck, Casper the skinny ghost. Women are being murdered in Blackpool. The fancy dress man responsible used this axe to kill them, and I'm going to bring him down. Until that happens, the chopper stays with me, got it?'

Carlisle frowned, retrieved the apple from his pocket, took a bite, then nodded. 'A pact will be made, then,' he said.

'You what, mate?'

'I, Carlisle, true King of Great Britain, cruelly deposed, will help you stop this murderous magician who stalks the streets of your cesspool of a town.'

'And you'll get rid of this shitty hex on me, too, right?'

'Of course. When the magician is found, I will stop him, kill him, and the hex will be lifted.'

'Kill him?'

'It is the only way to end the hex.'

Rita wasn't sure how she felt about that. She was about justice, not murder, but maybe there was no other choice. She shook her head, they'd have to deal with that once they got to it.

'Okay, you help me stop this murderer, help me get back to normal, and I will let you have the axe, deal?' Rita spat into her palm and offered it for a shake.

Carlisle looked at the hand as though she'd just proffered a fresh pile of horse dung. 'Please consider it shook,' said Carlisle.

'Germaphobe?'

'Sane.'

'Fair enough. So then, what's first?'

Carlisle climbed back into the car and Rita followed.

'First? Why, first we must visit the Night Fair.'

14

Rita was trying to play it cool. More to the point, she was trying not to entirely freak out in front of the insane, scary man who resembled an emaciated Richard E. Grant auditioning for a new Tim Burton film. The one who had, only a few hours earlier, left her knocked out cold on the beach.

They were driving towards Blackpool Pleasure Beach, a large fairground, popular with tourists, pickpockets, and teenage boys looking to cop a feel of something soft on the ghost train.

'Why did you call it the Night Fair?' Rita asked.

'You'll see,' Carlisle replied.

'Or you could just, I dunno, go ahead and tell me?'

'You'll see.'

'Right, be a cock then.'

Carlisle smiled, or at least exposed his teeth. 'Always.'

So she'd been hexed. It happens. Not to real people in really-real life, but it happens.

Well, no, it doesn't, but it had happened, and Rita was now as certain as she could be that all of it was real. She wasn't mad, or brain damaged, and she wasn't going to wake up in bed and sigh in relief because it was all a dream.

Probably.

Unless...

Rita pinched her leg and jolted at the sudden pain.

'Afraid not,' said Carlisle.

Definitely not a dream. What she wouldn't have given for such a hacky reveal right about now. Magic spells, magicians, murder. It was all a bit much, but it didn't change the fact that she had a job to do. A murderer to stop. She'd just have to go with it for now, at least until she knew for sure that the killer had been stopped. It was only then that she'd allow herself to fully freak out, curl up in a ball, and gibber incoherently.

But not now.

For now, she was still a detective, and women were at risk.

Rita pulled to a stop and she and Carlisle got out. She saw a sign pointing them in the direction of the Pleasure Beach. They'd have to go on foot from here.

'Come along, Hobbes,' said Carlisle, and strode off ahead, Rita having to almost, but not quite, break out into a run to keep up with his long-legged strides.

'Oi, little slower would be nice.'

He moved like a predator, like a shark cutting through the water, knowing it had nothing to fear. Knowing that *it* was the thing to fear.

Rita placed her hand on the bulge of the axe, still tucked into her belt, hidden by her coat. A thing of Heaven? She wondered how much she should trust Carlisle. She touched her still tender jaw and knew the answer to that. He didn't care about the case, about women dying, he just cared about taking back what was his. For now, he was something she needed. He knew this weird world she'd fallen into, but she wouldn't let her guard down, because sooner or later, he was going to turn on her.

You never trust a wild animal.

You got an instinct for this sort of thing after spending that long on the force. People like Carlisle only looked after number one, and they didn't give a shit how many people got hurt because of that.

'I've got a question,' said Rita.

'Yes, your hair actually does compliment your face shape.'

'No. I mean, thanks, but not that.'

'Why did the axe bond with you if the magician did not give permission for it to do so?'

'Wait, can you read minds, too? If so, what am I thinking right now? I'll give you a clue: it's green.'

Carlisle sighed and shook his head. 'You are a prattling fool, Detective.'

'It was a bush. A bush.'

'It's a fairly obvious question.'

'And is there a fairly obvious answer?'

'No. I do not know why the axe agreed to become yours. It is… vexing. Not knowing is one of my least favourite pastimes.'

'Oi,' said Rita, as Carlisle veered away from the entrance to the Pleasure Beach, swarming as it was with tired-looking parents and sugared-up kids. 'That's the way in, the massive obvious entrance over there. There's even a sign that says "entrance" right next to it.'

'That's not where we're going,' replied Carlisle, not slowing.

'I thought we were going to the fair?' she replied, veering around a small boy with a face coated in candy floss and the wild eyes of a hopped-up junkie.

'Correct, but I do not believe I said anything about that fair.'

'Well, that's the only fair in Blackpool, and it's the one you had me park up in front of, so…'

'I said we were going to the Night Fair. The Night Fair shares the same space as your Pleasure Beach, but is not the same as your Pleasure Beach, understand?'

'Yep.' Rita stopped and thought about it some more. 'Actually, no, not even a little bit.'

'You do surprise me. Just follow my lead.'

Rita was not a fan of being a follower, but follow she did.

'Wait,' she said, standing at Carlisle's shoulder as he stopped, 'that's not supposed to be there.'

'Isn't it? How peculiar.' Carlisle walked towards the large, gothic, metal archway in the side of a wall – a large, gothic, metal archway that really, really shouldn't have been there. The metal was coated in rust, and the arch stretched from one fire-blazing torch to another. The flames did not burn yellow-orange, they burned blue and green and made Rita feel funny.

'I know this place inside and out—unfortunately—and that entrance doesn't exist.'

'Not for you, not yesterday, not even a few short hours ago, but now your eyes have been opened,' said Carlisle. 'Welcome to the Night Fair.'

Rita remained still for a moment or two as Carlisle strode under the archway and into the strange fair beyond. A strange fair that appeared to be much gloomier than the late afternoon sun should allow.

'It's dark in there. How can it be dark in there?'

'*Night Fair,* Detective. The clue is in the name. Come along.'

Rita looked back to the Pleasure Beach's entrance, where someone queasy from the rides was throwing up noisily into a bin, then to the twisted metal arch in front of her, beyond which lay the Night Fair.

'Right. Good. Night Fair. Got it.' Rita shook her head and ran to catch up with Carlisle.

It was indeed gloomier inside the confines of the Night Fair. Rita squinted up at the sky to see stars twinkling and a full moon hanging heavy in the sky. 'We're not due a full moon for weeks,' she noted.

'It's always a full moon at the Night Fair,' Carlisle replied.

'It's also night here. How is it night?'

'Am I going to have to explain everything in triplicate? Keep close, it's easy to get lost in a place like this, and things that get lost are often never found.'

'I didn't realised you cared so much.'

'Of course I care. If I lose you, I lose my axe. Now keep up.'

Rita kept up.

As they walked, Rita felt as though her head was spinning. This was nothing like the garish Pleasure Beach, this was older. You could taste the age, smell it even. There were no rides that she could see, but hundreds of stalls and tents crushed together as far as the eye could see.

At one stall, a large, fleshy man was waving in customers, taunting them, telling them there was no way any of them could toss one of his brass rings over one of the many trinkets laid out on a table, and for only a fiver a pop. Why anyone would want to win the prizes on offer puzzled Rita, as each of them looked as though they'd been fished out of a canal.

At another stall, what appeared to be a woman—but may well have been a large pile of rags that had swallowed a woman whole—was stirring a rusted pot of something that smelled so delicious it made Rita's stomach growl.

'Come on, then, Miss! Fill yer skinny belly! I've got everything in this pot of mine, from cat, to dog, to rook, to fairy, to them bearded dragon whatsit's! Enough to sate the appetite of the great beast himself!'

'Did you say fairy?'

'I did indeed, every pot 'as at least eight-percent real sewer fairy – that's a Lady Labelle guarantee, that is.'

Rita suddenly didn't feel quite so hungry.

The Night Fair was a chaos of noise, of people, of smells, and Rita was having to try very hard not to become overwhelmed by it all.

Carlisle stopped suddenly, causing Rita to bump into the back of him.

'Sorry.'

'The word "sorry" is for the stupid.'

'Okay. Why have we stopped?'

'Because we are here.'

Rita looked past Carlisle at the tent before them. Its ragged canvas might once have been brightly coloured, but was now varying shades of brown. A sign above the entrance flaps said FORTUNES TOLD.

'A fortune teller?' said Rita. 'Really? This is your big idea? How about after this we grab a paper and check our horoscopes?'

'Let me do the talking,' Carlisle replied, ignoring her shade.

'You know, technically I'm the one heading up this investigation. I have skills in this area. Actual, tested in the field skills and that.'

'How adorable. Follow me.'

They pushed through the entrance and left behind the gloom of the Night Fair for the much gloomier gloom of the fortune teller's tent. There wasn't much in the way of decoration inside. Straw covered the ground to stop the mud being churned up, and in the tent's centre was a table with a crystal ball on top. Sat behind this table, and giving Carlisle the evilest of evil eyes that

Rita had ever seen, was a woman who, if Rita were to hazard a guess, was older than the oldest thing you could imagine. The fortune teller was a strip of gnarled, wrinkled leather in a kaftan and fez, a small cigar clenched between lips so thin they seemed to blink in and out of existence.

'Fuck off,' said the fortune teller, her voice a wheeze.

Carlisle chuckled. 'Now is that any way to greet a customer, Madame Esmerelda?'

'You're not a customer, you're a lying piece of shit who should be dead and swinging from a post as a warning to other pieces of shit.'

Rita didn't need any of her training to feel the tension between the two, it was practically visible. 'I'm DS Rita Hobbes.'

'Do I look like I give a fuck, you tart?'

'Oi, I'm not a tart, you old bitch.'

'Oh? Not what the crystal ball is telling me,' she smirked, and blew out a cloud of noxious smelling smoke.

'I'm not gonna be slut-shamed by a strip of jerky, thanks.'

Madame Esmerelda threw her head back and laughed. It sounded like a hoover picking up gravel.

'I'm here for information,' said Carlisle.

The fortune teller stopped laughing and coughed so violently that Rita thought she might be choking to death, then spat out a thick glob of mucus that hit one side of the tent and slowly oozed down to the straw. As Rita watched, the glob crawled beneath the wall of the tent and away to freedom outside. Rita tried not to think too hard about that.

'Well, you're out of luck,' replied Madame Esmerelda. 'Last time I helped you I lost a leg.'

'An unfortunate turn of events,' replied Carlisle.

'You chopped it off!'

'It seemed appropriate at the time.'

Madame Esmerelda narrowed her eyes as a rather tense silence settled over proceedings.

'It's about a case,' Rita said at last, after it seemed like they might be stuck in an eternal silent staring contest.

'That so?'

'Women are being taken. Murdered. By a… well. A magician.'

'And?'

'And I believe by utilising your special skills,' said Carlisle, 'you might be able to point us in the right direction.'

'I suppose he's told you his sob story?' said the fortune teller. 'About being the rightful king and all that shit?'

'He did mention it in passing, yeah.'

'Load of old bollocks.'

'I am the rightful King,' Carlisle insisted.

'Only because you cheat at cards.'

'I never cheat.'

'You never tell the truth.'

'Regardless of how it came to be, I won the game and all that had been placed on the table was mine.'

'Right,' said Rita, 'so you're not actually royalty then. That figures.'

'Royalty?' screeched Madame Esmerelda. 'Him? I wouldn't wipe my arse with the bloke.'

Carlisle huffed and turned away from the fortune teller.

'So why is he helping you, then?' asked the fortune teller. 'He never helps anyone, not him. Not for no reason.'

'I have something of his,' Rita replied.

Madame Esmerelda peered into her crystal ball. 'Oh, so you've found it at last, have you?'

Carlisle grimaced and nodded.

'But she won't give it to you unless you help her out?' She began to laugh again.

'Will you help us or not?' asked Carlisle, irritated. 'Once I have regained my property, I can give you anything you please. A new leg even, if that's all it takes, you petty beast.'

'I'll not help you, your majesty. Why should I do anything that aids you in getting back that infernal axe of yours?'

'Because women are being murdered,' Rita cut in.

'Women die every day, you foolish thing, that's just the way of things. No, I'll not help you and I'll not help him. Now, get out of my tent.'

Carlisle turned on his heel, snapping his coat behind him, and strutted outside. Rita hovered at the exit. 'You're really not going to help? Not even try?'

'Bit of advice, dear: don't trust him. Those that do, end up dead or worse, understood?'

'I can take care of myself,' Rita replied.

'You're a fool.'

'And you're a fucking bitch, love.'

Rita turned and left the tent. She found Carlisle stood brooding, staring at a popcorn machine as fresh kernels bounced within.

'So, I might be reading between the lines here,' said Rita, 'but I get the feeling that the old bag doesn't like you.'

'I should have taken more than her leg,' he hissed.

'So that's it, that's your help? I'm really impressed here. Look at my face, look at how impressed it is.'

'I will not look at your face.'

'But you're missing my impressed face.'

Carlisle grimaced, Rita grinned.

She was about to ask "what now?" when something worrying caught her eye. It was there for a second and then it was gone, but she was sure she'd seen it. Rita ducked down and peered through the popcorn stall to see beyond, and there they were.

Rabbit ears.

Large and old and tattered.

'I see them,' said Carlisle.

'What is it? Is it the magician?'

'Look away, don't stare, just look away and follow me as calmly as possible.'

Carlisle turned, guiding Rita to do so with one hand on her shoulder, and began to walk away from the popcorn stall.

'But he's part of it, we should go and arrest him.'

'Good idea. I take it you're tired of living and are looking for a gruesome, horrifying death?'

'Well, no.'

'Well, in that case it's a really, really terrible idea.'

As they walked, Rita began to think she saw the rabbit ears everywhere. Poking into view from the side of a tent, reaching high from behind a man eating a hot dog, sticking up from the very ground itself. 'What's happening?' she asked.

'We have made a wrong turn,' Carlisle replied.

The ground before them split.

From the fresh crack in the earth sprouted a small figure in an old suit wearing a hedgehog mask.

'Run!' said Carlisle, and sprinted off.

Rita didn't need to be told twice. 'Wait!' she cried, as all around, every member of the Night Fair, visitor or vendor, was now either sporting a rabbit mask or a hedgehog mask. The whole place was becoming the pair.

Carlisle ducked around the side of a tent and pulled to a stop, Rita almost bashing into him. 'Who are they?'

'Mr. Spike and Mr. Cotton,' he replied.

'Right, and who are they when they're at home?'

'They are, quite literally, the stuff of nightmares.'

Carlisle dropped to the ground and crossed his legs, shutting his eyes.

'Now's really not the time for a nap, mate,' she said, peering around the edge of the tent to see the fair full of the masked pair, slowly walking towards them.

'At some point—most likely when we stepped from the fortune teller's tent—we walked into a dreamscape created by Mr. Spike and Mr. Cotton. This is how they operate. You step into their nightmare, into a world in which they control reality.'

'Okay, that sounds bad. How bad is it?'

'Oh, it could hardly get much worse.'

'Right. Good. And what do we do?'

'If you would stop interrupting me, you would see that I'm doing it.'

'Doing what?'

Carlisle sighed, then opened one eye. 'I am concentrating. All being well, I can persuade this place to create an exit point, and we can escape.'

'And if you can't?'

'Then we die horrendously, possibly several times over.'

'Awesome.'

Rita peered around the side of the tent again as Carlisle closed his eye. The many Mr. Spikes and Mr. Cottons were almost upon them.

'Not to rush you, but you have about eight seconds.'

'Then run,' Carlisle insisted. 'It is you they are after. Hopefully they will chase you and ignore me entirely.'

'Hopefully?'

'Run!'

'Fuck. Fuck, fuckity, fuck!'

And with that string of expletives, Rita burst from behind the tent and ran, only for the hundreds of rabbit and hedgehog mask-wearing people to charge after her, screaming.

'Shit! Shit, shit, shit!'

They were everywhere, and more were arriving all the time, arms bursting from the dirt like zombies crawling from the grave.

'Keep going, keep going,' said Rita, as the world around her leaned heavier and heavier into a terrifying horror movie. It felt like the whole Night Fair was pressing in on her; like the place itself was now alive, like she could feel the dirt throbbing with its heartbeat, and it was hungry to swallow her.

As Rita zagged a corner she found herself looking into the shiny glass eyes of a rabbit mask, and in her haste to stop, stumbled and fell to the dirt.

'Detective Rita Hobbes,' said Mr. Cotton, as Mr. Spike, in his hedgehog mask, appeared at his side, 'would you like to see beneath my brother's mask?'

'No thanks,' Rita replied, scrabbling backwards, yanking the hand axe from her belt and shaking it at the pair.

'Naughty, naughty, that does not belong to you,' said Mr. Cotton, reaching a white-gloved hand towards the axe.

'Then come get some, fuck face,' screamed Rita, swiping at his grasping fingers, staggering to her feet, and bolting once again.

'Come back, don't run. My brother Mr. Spike wishes to play.'

Every way Rita looked was blocked. There was only straight ahead, a rickety shack that proclaimed itself to be a WORLD OF MIRRORS.

'Oh crap,' she said, fingers white-knuckling the axe. 'Any moment now would be great, Carlisle!'

Rita ran, brushed aside the strings of hanging beads that hung over the House of Mirrors' entrance, and rushed inside. Both hands gripping the axe, she backed into the place, ready to swing the blade at the first Mr. Cotton or Mr. Spike to enter, as all around mirrors of every shape and size, some whole, some horribly cracked, reflected her image back at herself.

'Well?' she said. 'What are you waiting for? Come and get some, you masked dicks!'

Rita really, really hoped she sounded braver than she felt.

No one answered her challenge. Was it over? Had Carlisle done, well, whatever it was he was doing?

Rita soon got her answer as one of her reflections turned to face her. The reflection now wore a rabbit mask.

Rita reflexively lashed out with the axe, smashing the mirror, causing hundreds of shards to shower the ground.

'Shit!'

'Mirror, mirror,' came Mr. Cotton's voice. 'When you were six, you used to dream about a thing that lived in the walls of the room in which you slept, Rita. Do you remember?'

Rita did remember. Remembered tucking the blanket tightly around herself so no flesh was exposed as she shook in the dark and something scritch-scratched in the walls of her orphanage room.

'You do recall, and now your skin crawls. That is me, that is us. My brother and I within each shiver, within each goose-fleshed midnight.'

Another reflection turned, this one wearing the hedgehog mask. Rita swung, smashed, stumbled back.

'Scritch-scratch, and shiver shake, do you recall the night-mares we make?'

Now it wasn't just one reflection in one mirror, it was all of them. Every reflected Rita turned to face her, all wearing the hedgehog mask of Mr. Spike.

'Let my brother dear show you what hides beneath,' said Mr Cotton, and each of the hedgehog mask-wearing Ritas began to slowly reach up to their heads.

'Stop it!' Rita screeched, swinging wildly at each mirror, breaking as many as she could, but the shards now refused to remain as such, and began to run into each other, creating new mirrors, new reflections, and each was slowly removing a mask.

Rita ran for the exit, but now the shack seemed impossibly large, expanding and expanding, hiding the way out.

'Just look, Detective Rita Hobbes, look at my brother, he has a special smile for you.'

Rita dropped to the ground and tried to cover her eyes, but found she couldn't close them, couldn't place her hands over them.

'He wants you to see, he wants you to. Perhaps you will see the true face of the scritch-scratch creature within your bedroom walls at last?'

The hedgehog masks, all of them, hundreds of them, began to slowly inch up, and Rita's heart bang-bang-banged in her chest. Any moment, any second, she was going to see the face beneath the mask and she knew with a crystal clear certainty that when she did, she would lose her mind forever.

'Stop! Please, stop!'

A hand gripped her forearm.

'Exit,' said Carlisle, and the House of Mirrors cut to black.

15

Detective Sergeant Dan Waterson was trying to remember the thing he'd forgotten.

That's not what should have been at the forefront of his mind. He was sat in the front room of a woman named Allison Mackey, a classmate of the women who had already gone missing, hoping to tease out some information that might help with the case. But there it was. The forgotten whatever-it-was, itching at his brain like a creature trying to burrow its way out.

'Are you all right, love?' asked Allison, who had been sat in an uncomfortable silence for the last thirty seconds as Waterson starred glassy-eyed at the wall.

'Hm?'

'It's just, you sort of went properly quiet there for, you know, like just ages. Bit weird.'

'Right, sorry, just,' he tapped his temple with his pen, 'police brain, thinking things through. Making connections, you know.'

'Oh, like Columbo.'

'Right. Just like him. I've got a nicer coat, though.'

Allison laughed at that, and the sound of it made Waterson momentarily forget about the thing he'd forgotten.

'So, you can't think of anything that might connect the three women?'

Allison frowned and shook her head. 'No, sorry, nothing's popping up.'

'No enemies they might have? Someone they might have crossed in some way?'

'Sorry, love, it's a total blank. I didn't really know them that well. Only by name and sight, you know?'

Waterson nodded and handed Allison his card. 'If anything does occur to you, please don't hesitate to call me, okay?'

'Will do,' Allison replied, dropping the card on to the mantelpiece.

'Thanks for your time.' He stood and headed for the exit.

'Sorry I couldn't be any help.'

'That's okay.' Waterson paused as he reached the door and turned back to Allison, 'One more thing.'

'Yes, Officer Columbo?' said Allison, smiling.

'Have you been experiencing any bad dreams recently?'

'Bad dreams?'

'Yeah, nightmares. Any?'

Allison frowned and shook her head. 'Nope. It's all rainbows and unicorns up here.'

Waterson nodded. 'Right, thanks for your help, Miss Mackey.'

As Waterson drove away, he wondered why he'd asked his final question. What did bad dreams have to do with anything? But then asking himself that brought back the fact he'd forgotten something. As he pondered the forgotten thing once again, he realised he'd parked outside of a house. He looked at the ordinary terraced house, and wondered why he'd driven to that street, to that house, and parked. He'd intended to head back to the station to type up everything he knew about the case so far. But here he was, staring at a house he was pretty sure was somehow familiar to him.

Did a friend of his live there once, maybe?

That could be it, though for the life of him he couldn't seem to match a name or even a face with the place.

Waterson shook his head, turned up the radio, and drove away.

Rita was annoyed to see her hands were still trembling as she sat behind the wheel of her car.

She turned to Carlisle, sat in the passenger seat. 'What the bloody hell are those two freaks about?'

'I believe I already told you, Detective, they are the literal stuff of nightmares.'

'And they're working with the magician?'

Carlisle tapped a long, white finger against his chin and pursed his lips. 'Possibly. They are certainly on the same side at least. But Mr. Cotton and Mr. Spike are freelancers, the magician's aims are only their aims as that is the job they have been hired for. They are a selective pair though, they do not work for just anyone. If they are doing the bidding of this magician, he must be higher up the totem pole than I'd suspected.'

Carlisle looked to Rita, who tried to hide her shaking hands.

'Come,' he said, 'let us go and get a drink.'

'Best idea you've had so far,' replied Rita, and started the engine.

Big Pins was secreted down a blind alley, a side street hidden from the eyes of non-Uncanny folk, but now that Rita was of their stripe, she could see the narrow passage that had not existed to her the previous day.

'So, hidden alleyways. Cool,' she said.

'Hardly,' replied Carlisle, and strode into the blind alley towards the blinking neon sign of the tired bowling alley.

Rita followed cautiously. 'Okay, so hidden streets, bowling alleys that shouldn't be there, fairs that exist in the same place as another fair somehow; anything else?'

'Oh, lots and lots. For example, there's the Dark Lakes, or the City of the Dead underneath the streets of Manchester, ooh, and a rather nice bakery in Newcastle hidden down a nook that only eight people can see.'

'Okay, how much of that is real and how much is you taking the piss?'

'Well, where would the fun be if I told you the answer to that, Detective?'

Carlisle pushed open the door to Big Pins and stepped within.

As Rita followed, she felt as though she had just stepped through a soap bubble.

'Uh, what was that?'

'These sort of places—gathering spots for the Uncanny—are often situated within magic dampening bubbles. It's to stop the patrons from doing anything too dreadful to each other whilst on the premises.'

'Huh, you know that might be useful, well... anywhere booze is sold, really. We could take the idea on *Dragons' Den*, make a mint.'

'Must you prattle continuously?'

'Afraid so, Pasty Pete.'

Carlisle huffed and headed for the bar, Rita taking in the sights as she followed. As with the Night Fair, Big Pins seemed to be frequented by an eclectic bunch of people. Some looked positively regal, others would pass for homeless. In fact, she was sure she'd seen the ragged-looking man doing a little jig having bowled a strike. Hadn't she moved him along for begging in front of the cashpoint around the corner from the blind alley?

'So everyone in here is like you?' asked Rita, as she joined Carlisle at the bar.

'No need to insult me, Detective, there is nobody here quite like myself. But yes, all are of one Uncanny stripe or other. On my way through I spotted a vampire, three low-level magicians, a troll, and three dispossessed witches' familiars.'

'I'm sorry, did you just say vampire? Shouldn't we, I don't know, stab him in the heart with a stake or something?'

'Oh wonderful, a racist as well as a simpleton.'

The conversation was brought to a premature end by the giant of a barman who appeared behind the counter, eyeing Carlisle with what looked to Rita very much like undisguised hostility.

'Back so soon?' he asked.

'Couldn't keep away, Linton, the rare ambience of this place drew me back in like an angler's lure.'

Linton snorted and began pouring drinks.

'First the fortune teller and now this guy,' said Rita. 'Something tells me you make more enemies than friends.'

'You can always appreciate a man by the number of people who would call him their enemy.'

Rita accepted her drink from Linton and sipped as she nodded thoughtfully. 'Yeah, that sounds like bullshit to me, Pasty.'

'Please stop calling me Pasty.'

'Nope. Let's get a table.'

Rita headed for the nearest empty table as Carlisle tried to ignore the grin now plastered across Linton's face.

'Who's your friend? I like her.'

'She's a means to an end, nothing more.' Carlisle slid some cash across the bar and stalked over to Rita, his shoulders bunching as he heard Linton chuckling.

'I've got a question,' said Rita as Carlisle swept the tail of his coat aside and lowered himself on to a stool.

'Oh? You do surprise me.'

'If rabbit and hedgehog man can create these dream-wotsits-'

'Dreamscapes.'

'Right, those wotsits, how do we know we're not in one right now? Dreamscape inside a dreamscape. You know, *Inception* shit.'

'*Inception*?'

'What? Get stuffed, you must have seen *Inception*!'

'I will not get stuffed.'

'Dreamscape inside a dreamscape, how'd you know we're not?'

'We're not.'

'How do you know?'

'Is anyone sporting a rancid old animal mask attempting to do anything awful to us?'

'No.'

'There you go then,' said Carlisle.

They sat in silence for a few seconds as Rita peered around Big Pins, looking to see if any familiar rabbit ears were poking into view.

'Aha! There's the very fellow,' said Carlisle, waving at a man who had just entered Big Pins and, by the looks of things, was trying to slip right back out again before Carlisle spotted him.

The man, if it was a man—Rita was wary to jump to such

conclusions now—shuffled over. He wore distressed-looking clothes and fingerless gloves, and his face looked a little, well, *moley*. If you were on the bus and he got on, you'd have everything crossed that he wouldn't take the seat next to you.

'Carlisle,' said Formby, his sharp front teeth yellowed and jutting out.

'You've got, like, Spock ears,' said Rita, peering at Formby's pointed protuberances.

'You must forgive the woman,' said Carlisle, 'her keen detective eyes never sleep when faced with the blindingly obvious.'

Formby smiled a sharp-toothed smile at Rita and bowed his head a little. 'Detective Rita Hobbes, I am your servant.'

'Hey, how did you know my name?'

'I am an eaves, it is my business to know, well, everyone's business.'

Formby shuffled on to a spare stool and began to drink Carlisle's pint.

'This is Formby,' said Carlisle, 'his sorry ilk sell secrets for a sniff of magic. They have little loyalty and are, as you can see, quite uncommonly hideous to look at. Think of him as that rarest of things, a useful junkie.'

'As far as introductions go, that was about as rude as it gets,' said Rita.

'No, I refrained from mentioning his rancid odour.'

'Fair enough.'

'So, did you find your magician?' asked Formby.

'Not yet, though I did make the acquaintance of a couple of friends of his. You failed to mention the presence of Mr. Cotton and Mr. Spike in your fair town, eaves. A regretful oversight on your part, I'm sure.'

Formby shrank into himself a little. 'I don't like to say their names. If you speak of them too often they appear in your dreams.'

'Superstitious nonsense.'

'It's true!'

'If you know all the secrets of Blackpool,' said Rita, 'how come you don't know who this magician bastard is?'

'I don't know everything, I just know a lot, is all. Something must be spoken and shared from person to person for it to pass my ears, and no one who I mix with, pass by, or lurk close to has spoken anything of use.'

'Did I say a "useful junkie"?' said Carlisle. 'My mistake. Now if you'll excuse me, I must make use of the little boys' room.' He rose and strode across Big Pins towards the bathrooms.

'Carlisle,' said Rita, leaning over to Formby, 'what is he? I mean, he's not really a person, is he?'

Formby glanced over his shoulder to make sure Carlisle was gone, 'No, not a man. No one knows quite what he is, but he's not to be trusted. Never trust. Never never.'

'Unfortunately for me, I don't have much choice. Not until this hex bullshit is gone and the murderer's stopped, anyway. Then he can have his stupid axe back and I can get on with my normal, boring, awesome life.'

'Can I… can I see it?'

'See what?'

'The artefact. The thing he craves. The axe.'

Rita shrugged. 'Yeah, suppose so.'

Formby chittered his teeth together and clapped in excitement, his pointed ears twitching as Rita reached beneath her coat and discovered that she didn't actually have the axe anymore.

'Bastard... Bastard!' Rita sprinted to the mens' toilets, startling a man with three eyes as he relieved himself at the urinal. Carlisle was nowhere to be seen.

'Bastard!'

She burst back into the bar area, Formby there waiting.

'Told you, never trust. Never never.'

Formby scampered at Rita's heel as she raced across the room to the exit, ready to tear up the streets in search of the fleeing Carlisle, only to almost trip over him as she ran into the blind alley.

Carlisle was laid out on the cobbles, flat on his back, unconscious, the axe on the ground beside him.

'Sneaky bloody bastard!' said Rita. She walked back into Big Pins, collected what remained of her drink, walked back out, then poured the drink over Carlisle's face.

'Whugrnyuh,' said Carlisle, or at least something to that effect, as the beer shower snapped him back into consciousness.

'Morning,' said Rita, picking up the axe and sliding it back into her belt beneath her coat, as Formby sniggered.

'What do you think you were playing at?' she asked.

'Well, you just took it without being given permission by its wielder, I thought it might proffer me the same courtesy as a previous owner,' said Carlisle, pulling a hankie from an inside pocket as he stood and wiped at his foamy, damp face.

'And how did that work out for you?'

'Not well, apparently,' replied Carlisle, giving Formby, who was now almost bent double with laughter, the evil eye.

'Try that again,' said Rita, 'and the deal is finished, right? If we're partners in this, then we've got to have each other's back.'

'Well,' said Formby, almost unable to get the words out, 'his majesty here ended up *on* his back at least!' Formby threw back his head and cackled.

'That does not even work as a joke,' replied a sour Carlisle.

'On his back!' repeated Formby, tears streaming.

'Detective, please inform this foul, ugly creature that if he keeps on laughing I'll make earrings from his withered genitals.'

Formby shut his mouth and did his best to prevent any further smirks from escaping.

16

The Magician hated hospitals.

He was now twenty years old, and had spent more than enough time over the last few years sat within the walls of places like this. Pale corridors and tired chairs, disinfectant stink and the beep-beep of sad machines.

He shivered, or more accurately, he trembled. A tremor that turned his hands blurry.

'Be brave,' said the constant voice at his ear. Said the Angel of Blackpool.

His mother was dying.

He remembered the first time he'd heard the Angel's voice, knelt down on the beach, digging a hole in the sand, trying to ignore his mother as she cried. He'd give just about anything for there to be enough life left in her for tears.

The door to her room opened and a doctor stepped out. The Magician thought he looked like a bird. A pinched face and hook nose.

'She's not long left now,' said the doctor, and the Magician dug his nails into the palms of his hands to stop himself from smashing this bird in the face.

'Be brave,' said the Angel.

He smiled and nodded and the doctor walked off down the

corridor, the Magician's cold eyes watching him until he turned out of view.

'I could kill him,' he said.

'Yes. You could kill everyone in this hospital,' replied the Angel.

He smiled at that.

'Yes. I could send them one by one by one into the sea, just like Nelson. Someone would walk along the beach, with a metal detector maybe, some sad, useless old man full of life he's no use for, and he'd see them all. See all the bodies floating on the water's surface like grim lily pads.'

He walked to the open door of his mother's hospital room and paused, fingertips brushing against the door handle.

'Why don't I do that? Just send them all to sea and not go in this room at all.'

'Because that would be the end and you know we have much more important work. A destiny, you and I. We're meant for great things.'

The Magician nodded, then stepped inside the hospital room. His mother was laid out in the single bed, a thin cotton sheet over her. Her face was thin, cheeks shallow. She'd lost so much weight over the last few months that she barely looked like his mother at all. This was a stranger. A thing. Trying to think of her like that helped him not to scream.

He pulled a chair over to her bedside. He didn't look at her, instead he looked at the window in the far wall. He could see the sky through it; the brightest blue with barely a wisp of cotton floating through.

'Where is Heaven?' he asked.

'Not there,' replied the Angel. 'Not in the bright blue sky. Not beyond it either. Heaven exists elsewhere. Other. Aside from. Apart.'

His mother gurgled, a wet rattle in her throat.

First his dad, and now his mum, taken cruelly and before their time.

'God cares not for your tears. Cares not about the pain He has caused. An indifferent monster, that is what God is. That is the great truth hidden by those with something to gain from the pretence, in their houses of gold and shame.'

'When can we start?' asked the Magician.

'It's almost time. The first step we take today, at last.'

The Magician smiled, even as the beep-beep-beep of the sad machine became one long *beeeeeeeeeeeeeeeeeeeeeeeep* and the creature he could not believe was truly his mum finally ceased her nauseating, shallow-breathed gurgle and what lived in her left the cramped hospital room behind.

Nurses entered and attended her, said words to the Magician that he didn't hear. He stood and walked through the fog, down the hospital corridors, past room after room of those ignored by God. Left to die slowly in the terror building.

Soon, he found himself staring through a large window at a room full of new born babies, wriggling in their cots. New life. New death. More lambs to the slaughter before the chilling indifference of their creator.

In the room beyond the glass, the new born children were not alone. Two men were stood in old, dusty suits, facing the magician. One wore a rabbit mask, the other a hedgehog mask.

'Step one is here,' said the Angel in his ear.

'Who are they?' he asked, looking from Mr. Cotton to Mr. Spike, a shiver running down his spine.

'They are believers in our undertaking. They have gifts of their own, which, when combined with my power, can be turned to our advantage.'

As the magician watched, black smoke began to stream from the eyeholes of the masks. The black smoke weaved like snakes above the cots, moving from each, until six of the children were selected and the smoke wiggled into the children through their eyes, their noses, their mouths.

'These six,' said the Angel, 'they are anointed by me through Mr. Cotton and Mr. Spike. The magic placed inside of them, the taste of their dark dream, shall ripen as they age, and when the time is right, each shall be plucked with the artefact.'

The magician thought about his dad, about his mum.

'Why can't I take them now? I can get the axe and finish them.'

'Patience. I have huddled trapped beneath the sea for centuries. There is no rush. My touch, through Mr. Spike and Mr. Cotton's dark dreamings, must fuse with their souls fully over the coming years, or their sacrifice will mean nothing.'

The magician was impatient. His anger boiled within him. But the Angel was right. It never lied to him. He would wait. Their time would come. The time when he would take his axe to each of them. The time when he and the Angel of Blackpool would face God and punish Him for His sins.

17

Rita killed the engine as she and Carlisle pulled to a stop in front of a pleasant-looking semi-detached house.

'I think this is it,' she said, pulling out her notebook and double-checking the address.

'Must we?' asked Carlisle.

'Well, if you have any other leads like the fortune teller who hates your guts and won't tell us a bloody thing, let's go and see them, 'cos that wasn't a massive waste of time at all.'

Carlisle pursed his lips.

'Or we could do some proper detective work and start interviewing this list of known classmates of the missing women, how about that?'

Rita got out of the car. 'Oi,' she said, leaning down to see Carlisle, 'are you gonna keep sulking or should we get on with this?'

Carlisle huffed, then stepped out of the car. 'I do not sulk. I brood.'

'You also nick stuff from your partner and try to leg it away.'

'You realise I could pin you like a butterfly and pluck out your limbs one by one?'

'Yeah, and you realise I could take your axe and shove it up your arse?'

'Touché. Obviously this woman will not be able to see or hear you, so I shall take the lead.'

'Okay, but listen to what I have to say, right? I have actual training in this stuff.'

'I look forward to being wowed by your staggering interview skills, detective.'

Carlisle rang the doorbell.

There were 28 names on the list, including the three women who had so far gone missing. 28 classmates who moved through school together. Of the 25 who weren't the missing women, only ten had remained in Blackpool, and it was these ten that Carlisle and Rita intended to visit, one by one.

As luck would have it, they struck gold with visit number one. Wanda Radcliffe: a plump woman with a giant mane of dark blonde curls.

She'd peered at the card Carlisle offered, the card that was very definitely not police identification, and waved him and the invisible-to-her-eyes Rita through to the kitchen.

'Oh aye, I've heard all about it,' said Wanda. 'I'm still mates with a couple of people from school and we've been messaging non-stop on Facebook about it.'

'I'm sure it's all very exciting,' said Carlisle.

'Oh, it is! I mean, sad and that, obvs, but exciting too. You never think this sort of thing'll happen to people you sort of know, do you?'

Carlisle smiled thinly.

'Ask about grudges,' said Rita.

'I will,' replied Carlisle.

'What's that?' asked Wanda.

'The three women that have been abducted, do you have any information about someone that may have a reason to dislike them? A grudge?'

'Oh yeah, Mister Nolan.'

'Who's that?' asked Rita. 'Wait, you ask,' she said, nudging Carlisle.

'And Mister Nolan would be?'

'Oh, this perv of a maths teacher. Was always leaning over you, just a bit too close, you know? Looking down your shirt. He eventually made a pass at Jane. Jane Bowan. Squeezed her tit, so she said. Her and a bunch of her friends went to the Head and Mister Nolan got the sack. I'd say he's probably pissed off with them.'

'Ha! There we go, we do a bit of proper police work and we get an actual lead. Weird that, heh?' said Rita.

Carlisle ignored her smug smile.

Waterson was sat at his desk at the station, idly doodling on the edge of a newspaper.

'Oi, dickhead!'

Waterson looked up to see DS Nation, a colleague with a year round tan who swore he never went near a sunbed, waving at him.

'Hm? What?'

'For the third time, you coming down for a few pints later or what?'

'Right, yeah. Probably.'

'What's wrong with your face?'

Waterson sat up straight. 'Do you ever get the feeling that you're missing something? Something big?'

'Is this your way of confessing you've got one of them micro-dicks, mate?'

That got a big laugh from the office. Dick jokes always did.

'Yes. that's it. I thought you'd be the person to go to about it. Idiot.'

Waterson went back to his doodle. He was scritch-scratching a pair of rabbit ears. Over and over.

'Anything useful yet?' asked DCI Jenner, peering at Waterson's doodles. 'Hard at work, I see, Waterson.'

'Yep, sorry Guv, just, you know, thinking things through.'

'By drawing Playboy bunnies? What about the case? You got anything?'

'Not yet, but I've only been to see two of the other classmates so far. Something will turn up.'

'Hm. It had better. Upstairs is on me like a bastard about this.

They've got the press hounding them every two minutes, so give me something I can take to them and make it soon, right?'

'Yes, Guv, will do,' replied Waterson with more confidence than he felt.

As Jenner set off toward his office, Waterson stopped him and pointed to a vacant desk opposite to his own. 'Guv, whose desk is that?'

'Hm?' DCI Jenner looked at the empty desk and his brow creased. 'Well that's… um… I don't think anyone's used that for a few years, have they?'

'Nope,' said Nation, chiming in.

'Right. Of course. That's what I thought,' said Waterson.

DCI Jenner looked at the desk for a second more, then shook his head. 'Right, no rest for the wicked. Back to it Waterson. Get me something useful.'

Waterson looked at the empty desk, then back to his rabbit ear doodles. 'Yes, Guv. Will do.'

A ping from his computer caught his attention, a new email from Nation. 'SPURT: PILL GUARANTEES YOU AN EXTRA THREE INCHES!'

Waterson deleted the email and offered a middle finger to the guffawing Nation.

Mister Derek Nolan, former Head of Maths at Old Lane Secondary School, currently assistant manager at a local supermarket. The picture of him Rita had found did not make him look like a fearsome magician capable of consorting with dream monsters and chopping up innocent women with an axe. The picture showed a rather meek-looking man with thinning hair and a bushy moustache.

'What do you think?' she said, wagging the picture under Carlisle's aquiline nose.

'That one should never judge a book by its cover.'

After his third knock on the door failed to rouse an occupant, it became clear that Mister Nolan was not home.

'Come on, we can wait in the car,' said Rita.

'Or we can just go inside to see what might be found.'

'Yeah, that's sort of against the law.'

'Most of the best ideas are.' Carlisle crouched and placed the side of his face against the door.

'What are you doing? Can you hear someone in there?'

'I am attempting to persuade the door to unlock itself.'

'Course you are, you skinny nut-bag.'

Carlisle sighed. 'Could you please hush that mouth of yours for a few, short seconds? This is a delicate waltz I am undertaking, and it requires the utmost concentration.'

Rita put up both hands and stepped back. 'You go for it, weirdo, you sweet talk that sexy door.'

Carlisle closed his eyes and placed the palm of one hand over the lock. After ten silent seconds, at which point Rita had just about reached the maximum amount of time her mouth was willing to remain silent, the locking mechanism clicked.

'Et voilà,' he said, grinning and bouncing to his feet.

'Get to fuck. No way.'

Carlisle pushed open the now unlocked door. 'As I believe you moronic types like to retort, "*Yes, way*". Shall we?' Carlisle stepped across the threshold. Rita glanced over both shoulders to see if she was being watched, remembered that she was invisible, and was glad Carlisle hadn't seen her do it. She scooted into Mister Nolan's house.

Inside it was clear that Mister Nolan lived alone. The sort of man who would feel up a teenager's chest was rarely a catch for full-grown women. The rooms were sparsely dressed and worn. The decor had not been updated in at least ten years; everything was faded and tatty and Rita could almost smell the loneliness. That and the other man smells. He really needed to crack a window on that place.

'Do you sense it?' asked Carlisle, emerging from the kitchen, his eyes seeming to glow a pale yellow in the gloom.

'Yeah, this guy is bloody tragic. He needs to invest in some industrial strength air freshener, like, immediately, if not sooner.'

'Not the unpleasant, musty odour and general funk of tragedy; the magic.'

'Magic?'

'Oh yes.'

'And what does that feel like?'

'Like… potential.' He made his way to a small wooden door beneath the stairs. 'Down there. It is stronger down there.'

'What are you saying? Mister Nolan the boob-squeezer is magic?'

'No, I am saying that the magic within this house is not just the expected background amount, but that it has been used. Drawn upon. And often. So we investigate.'

Carlisle opened the small door and ducked inside. Rita took the axe from under her coat and followed him inside. She'd expected little more than a small, cramped cupboard, instead, she found Carlisle descending a set of worn stone steps. Not the kind of worn stone steps you'd find in a house, but the kind you'd see Indiana Jones descending, right before he was chased by a huge, rolling boulder.

'Okay, nothing to worry about here,' said Rita, fingers flexing around the wooden handle of the axe.

As she made her way down the steps, making sure not to fall too far behind Carlisle, she had a similar feeling to the one she'd had as she entered the stone corridor hidden in the arcade.

'This definitely fits with the other hidden place, hey?' she said.

'It is similar, I agree,' replied Carlisle, running a finger along a stone wall and licking his fingertip.

'Gross,' said Rita.

Carlisle spat on the steps.

'Grosser.'

'Hm, this is not the same level of magic, but it is, perhaps, still a little too coincidental.'

Rita joined Carlisle at the bottom of the steps and peered up to see the light from the house, still just about visible.

'If this guy is a super-duper magician, how much danger are we in exactly?'

'If he is the man responsible for the abductions, we could barely be in greater danger.'

'Great, thanks for the confidence booster.'

Carlisle walked forward, almost seeming to drift, his heavy

boots light on the stone floor. By comparison, Rita's own footsteps sounded like a heavy metal drum solo. The space at the bottom of the stairs was cramped, with flickering torches clamped to the rough walls.

'Atmospheric, eh?' said Rita.

'Magicians do like to set a scene,' replied Carlisle, as he approached the wooden door set into the far wall. He gripped the metal ring at its centre, glanced back to Rita with a nod, then pulled. The door creaked outwards, the noise setting Rita's teeth on edge as she clenched and re-clenched the axe.

'Behind me,' said Carlisle.

'No worries, if he's in there, you're welcome to get hit first, mate.'

Carlisle smiled, then stepped into the room, Rita wary at his heels.

Inside, there was not a dingy sacrifice chamber, like at the games arcade, but rather a giant study that would not have looked out of place at Hogwarts.

'Shit,' said Rita, 'I think we just broke into Dumbledore's man cave.'

The room was huge, with plush carpeting and fine wooden bookcases that stretched up for three impossible storeys, sliding sets of brass ladders giving access to the highest shelves.

'Uh, that's sort of not possible, right? If this place was as tall as those bookcases, it'd be jutting out the top of the house.'

'Bigger on the inside than out,' said Carlisle.

'Okay, so maybe it's Doctor Who's man cave.'

At the centre of the room was a large oak desk with a green, leather chair sat behind it. Dominating the table was a giant, ancient-looking book, its leather cover now ragged with age.

'What are all these books, then?'

Carlisle ran his fingers over the open pages of the volume on the table then peered at the shelves packed tight with book after book.

'Magical texts. Rare, some of them. If we took just a few I've spotted, we could make enough money to live like sultans for eternity.'

'Yeah, we're not on the rob, so keep your hands off.'

'Just an idle thought.'

Rita snorted and flopped into the leather chair as she took a look at the book open on the desk. It looked like the ancient bibles that monks used to delicately transcribe, but with much stranger pictures. Not of saints, or angels, but of internal organs, and animals with their throats slashed and their blood dripping into a cauldron.

'What language is that?' Rita asked. 'Latin or something?'

'Hm? No, that's a language much older than Latin. Much, much older, from a people you will not find mention of in any of your history books. A lost people who knew the power of words and sounds.'

'Why aren't they remembered?'

'Their island was lost beneath the waves millennia ago.'

'Wait… are you talking about Atlantis? Are these Atlantis words!'

'It's always Atlantis with you people. No, it's not Atlantis.'

'Aw.' Rita slumped back, sulking. It was then that she noticed the man stood in the doorway.

'Bastards!' said Mister Nolan.

'We'd like a word with you, magician,' said Carlisle. He opened his mouth to speak again, but was stopped by the purple lightning that burst from Mister Nolan's fingers and struck him in the chest, sending him crashing into one of the bookcases.

'Shit!' Rita ran to him, but Carlisle was already back on his feet and running for the door after the fleeing Nolan. 'Wait up!' she yelled, giving chase.

As she made it up the stone steps and out of the cupboard under the stairs, she was just in time to see Nolan pull a dagger out of thin air and toss it at Carlisle, who swept his hands to the side, somehow pushing the knife off course so that it embedded itself up to the hilt in the wooden door, two inches from Rita's face.

'Shitting hell!' she said, almost dropping the axe.

'You cannot run from me, magician,' said Carlisle, his long coat billowing out dramatically, even though Rita was pretty sure there was no wind coming from anywhere.

'Wrong,' replied Nolan, clapping his hands together, making the air behind him ripple and warp.

'Quick!' said Carlisle, grabbing Rita's arm and yanking her forward as Nolan leapt through the warping air and disappeared.

'Where'd he go?' asked Rita.

'Let's see,' replied Carlisle, pulling her into the strange, rippling air just as it collapsed.

It turned out that where Mister Nolan had gone was Blackpool Pier. Rita stumbled as the pier appeared around her, and she fell to her knees, the axe skittering across the ground as she dropped to her knees.

'I feel sick,' she said.

'Transportation magic. It can do that if you're not used to it,' replied Carlisle, who had stepped from the portal and on to the pier as elegantly as if he had stepped from one room to another.

Rita pushed herself up on to shaky legs and retrieved the axe. They were on the North Pier, the longest of the town's three piers, the one with a theatre crouched at its far end. Over the decades it had played host to any number of pantomimes, novelty acts, and mostly forgotten comedians. Rita had vague memories of being taken to see Cannon & Ball there once as a child, a comic duo briefly and inexplicably popular in the 1980s, who clung on to work in places like Blackpool.

'I think it's safe to say that our Mister Nolan has something to hide,' said Rita, gulping down a burp that tasted like the previous day's dinner.

'Reasonably safe, yes. If you are going to vomit, please do it over the side of the pier and into the sea.'

'I'm not going to vom—' Rita ran to the side of the pier and hung over the railings, loudly emptying her stomach.

'Are you quite finished?'

Rita straightened up, wiping the sleeve of her coat across her mouth. 'Better out than in.'

'You disgust me.'

Rita burped. 'So where's Mister Nolan?'

'He's here. I can feel him.'

Rita looked up and down the deserted pier. 'Actually, where is anyone? At all? There's always people on the pier.'

Carlisle walked towards the theatre, and Rita hustled to catch up.

'Well? Where is everyone? Actually, why can't I hear any birds? Normally you can barely think around here for all the seagull squawking.'

'It seems Mister Nolan has taken us to a moment between moments.'

'Yeah, what's that mean then?'

'He has made a jump into a pocket of stationary time where he believes he could hide until he was safe. Sadly for him, I was able to follow the path before it degraded.'

Rita patted him on the shoulder. 'Good work, partner.'

Carlisle stopped walking. 'Never pat me again.'

'You got it, creepy.'

Carlisle continued walking.

Inside, the theatre was not just silent; it was almost as though the entire place was holding its breath to avoid drawing attention to itself. The place was oppressively, noisily silent.

Rita looked at the dirty carpet with its cigarette burns and worn-in dirt. Carlisle sniffed at the air.

'This way.'

'Yes, Sir,' replied Rita, saluting and almost chopping herself in the face with the axe.

'Cretin.'

They made their way through to the theatre itself, with row upon row of empty seats facing the stage.

'Really?' said Carlisle, his voice projecting effortlessly around the large room. 'A little dramatic to stage a last stand on a *literal* stage, is it not?'

'Leave me alone, Carlisle,' came a reply.

'Mister Nolan?' said Rita. 'Why so nervy? We just want to ask you a few friendly questions.'

They moved down the aisle towards the stage, its red velvet curtain down.

'You broke into my home, and then into my inner sanctum.'

'Sanctum?' said Carlisle, snorting, 'a true magician's sanctum would not be stepped into so easily. But you're no true magician, are you?'

'He seems to know his stuff, to me,' said Rita.

'Yes, but you are a clueless buffoon.'

'Point to you, carry on.'

'Stop!' said Mister Nolan. 'No closer, Carlisle, or you'll regret it!'

'I see my reputation precedes me again.'

'I've heard the stories. The whispers. The accusations.'

'And we've heard accusations about you,' said Rita.

The curtain ruffled and Mister Nolan stepped out. Both of his hands appeared to be on fire.

'Holy shit!' said Rita.

Nolan raised a hand, then punched it forward, the flames rushing towards her and forcing Rita to dive out of the way, landing painfully on a row of seats.

'Bastard, ow.'

She scrambled up to see Carlisle rushing the stage as Nolan clapped his hands together and a multi-coloured glow formed around his fists, which then shot towards Carlisle.

'Watch out!'

Carlisle crouched and lifted his coat to cover his face, the magic-whatever-it-was struck the coat and deflected away, straight for Rita. No time to move out the way, Rita swung out at the ball of crackling, coloured light and struck it sweetly with the axe head and—

Rita blinked and was happy to see she was neither dead nor harmed. But something had happened. Something new.

She could feel it.

Feel what Mister Nolan had attacked Carlisle with, and what he'd deflected into her path.

Magic.

Rita could hear it talking to her. Could feel it prickling like static across her skin. Could taste it in her mouth.

'What spell are you?' she said or thought or felt or maybe screamed. The colours of the universe strobed across her vision and she could see the very fabric of the spell cast. Could see the stitches that bound it into the shape and purpose Mister Nolan had commanded of it. It wasn't a spell meant to kill, meant to destroy, rather it was a concussive blast meant to render Rita and Carlisle unconscious.

'You're mine, now,' said Rita to the spell, and she could almost sense it wag its non-existent tail in obedience.

'Rita?' said Carlisle, his voice distant, muffled, as the magic rolled and rushed inside of her, then rushed into the axe.

'Heads up, dickless!' said Rita, which wasn't exactly a standard wizard incantation, but it did the trick.

The spell now had a new master and a new destination. Rita swung the axe, its metal head molten for the blink of an eye, and the magic, a rippling spear of blues and oranges and colours that no ordinary person had ever seen, burst forth and shot towards Mister Nolan, whose face was wide with shock. The spell struck him in the chest, and Mister Nolan flew through the air, slid backwards across the wooden stage of the theatre then came to a stop, quite unconscious.

There was a silent pause as Rita looked from the prone Mister Nolan to the axe in her hands, and then to Carlisle. 'Well...bloody, bastarding, hell! That was amazing!'

Carlisle snorted and headed over to the out cold Mister Nolan, hopping up on to the stage like a cat.

'Oh come on! Did you see that shit? I totally caught his magic and twatted him with it! Somehow. Just like at the arcade! Only this time I really felt it. Really saw it!'

'The artefact. My artefact,' said Carlisle. 'I told you, it gives each wielder a different gift. It appears in your case that it allows you to take another's ability and use it against them.'

Rita grinned wildly, passing the axe from hand to hand, throwing in a few swings for good measure. 'Brilliant! Awesome! Ooh, so, if, like, someone is really good at piano, could I tap them with this axe and I'd suddenly shit all over Jerry Lee Lewis?'

'Is Jerry Lee Lewis magic?'

'He can play piano with his feet, so yeah, sort of.'

'Then perhaps.'

Rita scampered down the aisle and clambered on to the stage to join Carlisle, who was standing over the unconscious Mister Nolan.

'So what now?' she asked.

'Now we bind him, we wake him, and we interrogate him.'

'Right, good, on board with all that.'

'And then we shall kill him.'

'Slightly less on board.'

18

It had been thirty years since the Magician's mother had died, slowly and painfully, in hospital. Thirty years since he had watched as Mr. Cotton and Mr. Spike had stood over the new-born babies and infected them with darkness.

Thirty long, awful years.

'Our long wait is over, friend,' said the Angel of Blackpool, and the Magician hastily wiped a tear from his eye before it had chance to fall and draw anyone's attention.

'At last, at last,' he said under his breath, fingers stroking his calendar, the day circled in red.

'Revenge,' said the Angel.

'Revenge,' said the Magician.

He left work early, said his goodbyes as normal, and drove home.

Jane Bowan. She was going to be the first. The start. Step one to gaining the power to free the Angel and shatter the doors to Heaven.

Revenge.

The Magician realised he was actually whistling as he collected his bags and placed them in the boot of his car. One contained his robes, his mask, the other contained the axe. The axe he'd discovered on the beach so very long ago. The axe that would soon, oh so very soon, break them into Heaven.

He drove to the arcade, retrieved his bags from the back of his car, and wandered through, past the hordes of kids, tourists, and locals who were rushing around, moving from game to game, full of noise and flashing lights and chaos.

No one paid any attention to him as he slipped through into the stockroom. The staff at the arcade were so wishy-washy that a perception magic was probably not even necessary; he could've walked through, bold as brass. But now was not the time to risk arousing suspicion. The work was too important. Too longed for.

He made his way past the giant bags full of stuffed toys and opened the door that only he could see, stepping through into the coolness of the stone corridor beyond. The stone corridor led to a chamber. A point of power. Two times pressed together like the pages of a book. This point was a weak spot in reality, a tangling of mystical nerves, where the sacrifice to come would be impregnated with even more meaning, more power, more wonder.

Jane Bowan was waiting for him.

She was unconscious, laid out on top of a large, grey stone, her ankles and wrists manacled tightly to it so she could not leave, could not even move her arms or legs. Trapped. Pinned like a butterfly.

He moved to the back of the chamber and unzipped the first bag, retrieving the axe and placing it gently on the small altar.

'Can you feel it?' asked the Angel.

'I feel it.' And he did. The power in that room. The hushed, awed expectation of the journey they were finally undertaking. He'd had to wait so long. So long for the touch of Mr. Cotton and Mr. Spike, imbued with the Angel's magic, to fully bloom within each person chosen. It had wormed its way through their bones. Their muscles. Their souls. Infected even their dreams so that they had nightmares of the two that infected them. Fear was important. It might seem cruel, but fear leavens the sacrifice. It had all been explained to him.

Fear was important.

He remembered how scared he'd been when he'd heard his mother's anguished, animal cries when his dad's body had been discovered.

Fear was important.

The Magician opened the second bag and pulled out his scarlet robes. He marvelled at how the material seemed to shine beneath the flames that flickered at the torch heads.

He slipped the robe over his head, his arms, and let it fall into place over him. The soft material caressed his skin and almost seemed to sigh as he stroked his palms over it.

'This is the first,' he said. 'This is the first. There will be six. The axe will come down. And then we shall take what's His.'

'I almost wish God knew what was coming for Him. The fury. The anger. The power,' said the Angel, and it made the Magician smile. 'Knew the righteous anger that will lay waste to His kingdom of absence and scorch him from existence.'

The Magician pulled out the mask and looked into its empty eyes. He touched the goat skin that was stretched over it. Stroked the curled horns.

'I hide my face from God as I do this, not out of fear, but out of contempt.'

He placed the goat mask over his head and reached for the axe.

He felt the weight of it in his hand.

Felt the right and the might in his heart.

Revenge.

'Where... where am I...?' asked Jane Bowan, her voice groggy as she awoke.

The Magician didn't answer at first as he did not hear her. All he heard was the rasp of his heavy breath against the inside of the mask, and his own heartbeat thumping against his chest. A tattoo of anxiety.

He flexed his fingers around the handle of the axe. His hands were sweaty, he realised they were trembling.

'Fear is natural, fear is right,' said the Angel. 'Do not let it sway you.'

'Where am I?' repeated Jane Bowan, her voice now a scream of panic.

The Magician walked forward until he was within her sight. She shook and wriggled and fought against the chains, her eyes wide and rolling with panic. Terror. Disbelief.

Mr. Cotton and Mr. Spike had delivered her to him. Now it was his turn.

'Please! Please don't, please don't,' she begged.

The Magician felt his knees wobble.

'Do not falter. Do not weaken.'

'Is this… is this right?' asked the Magician.

'Let me go! Help! Somebody help, please!'

The Magician lowered the axe and walked away. Wanted to pull off the mask, needed to breathe a little freer. Didn't want his own hot breath bouncing back into his face.

'Listen to me,' said the Angel.

'I can't,' he replied, 'I'm sorry. I thought I could. I wanted to. This is… it's too difficult.'

'Please don't hurt me,' said Jane Bowan. 'Please. I'll do anything. You don't… you don't have to do this, I won't tell anyone, I won't, I promise, please.'

'This is not murder,' said the Angel.

The Magician felt the heft of the axe.

'This is not murder. This is a blessing. Her life will mean something. Something wonderful. Think of all the other people who perish because of God's neglect. Think of the other children who lose their parents in the face of His monstrous indifference.'

The Magician turned to Jane Bowan, his face a hidden grimace, teeth clenched, a high-pitched whine escaping from between them.

'Please don't,' she said, 'just, please don't.'

'It has to stop,' said the Angel. 'It has to. You know that.'

'I know that. I know.'

'This, in the end, is a kindness. A kindness to all of those that we will save. If she knew the truth of it, if it could be explained properly, she would thank you.'

'Please don't.'

The Magician straightened up, his teeth unclenched, his palms no longer sweating.

He saw the millions starving around the world.

'Please.'

He saw an earthquake that shook bridges and buildings and roads to dust, killing hundreds. Thousands.

'Don't.'

He saw his mother, laid out in a hospital bed, her face unrecognisable.

'We're going to make Him pay,' said the Angel. 'It's time to go to work.'

The Magician smiled. He'd faltered, but that was only because he was good and true.

He swung the axe above his head and brought it down in one swift, efficient move. The deed was done.

Jane Bowan was dead.

The Magician laughed. Just once. That hadn't been so bad.

Jane Bowan's spirit, her soul, sat up out of her body. It sparkled as though made of fairy dust.

'What's happening?' she looked down at her own dead body and screamed, fell from the stone, and scrambled backwards along the ground.

'One more swing,' said the Magician.

He stepped towards the soul of Jane Bowan and swung the axe at her. As the head met her insubstantial body, Jane Bowan twisted and rippled and shook, and was then absorbed into the axe itself.

And then it was all over.

He placed the axe on the altar and pulled off the goat head mask. The cool air felt good against his skin as he hung his head back and took deep, cold breaths of sharp air.

'I am proud,' said the Angel.

'For my dad. For my mother. I do this for you.'

'We do this for all. For every child who's ever wept in the dark because of *Him*.'

The Magician felt a tear running down his cheek, but it wasn't a tear of sadness or fear. No. It was joy.

At last, at last.

'We are so close,' said the Angel of Blackpool.

Revenge.

19

Mister Nolan's eyes snapped open as the cold water punched him in the face.

'Wakey wakey, Mister Gropey,' said Rita.

Nolan tried to stand, then realised he was tied to a chair in the front row of the theatre.

'Let me go!' he yelled, water spraying comically from his thick, greying moustache.

'Hush, or I will crack your skull beneath my boot,' said Carlisle, sat on the edge of the stage, legs dangling.

Rita pulled out her badge and waggled it in front of Mister Nolan's face. 'That's right, Magic Mike, you're nicked.'

'For what?'

'Well, for one thing, you threw all that magic stuff at me, a police officer. So that's assault.'

'You broke into my home!'

'Okay, true, but it was all in a good cause.'

Carlisle hopped off the stage and walked towards Mister Nolan, who attempted to push himself back through the solid chair at his approach.

'Women are being murdered in this dreadful town of yours, Nolan. Murdered by a magician.'

'What's that gotta do with me?'

'Jane Bowan,' said Rita. 'Ellie Mason. Gemma Wheeler. Any

of those names sound, ooh, I dunno, a little familiar?' Rita mimed groping in front of Mister Nolan's widening eyes.

'I… okay, yes, I know them, they were pupils of mine.'

'Pupils who assisted in your firing,' said Carlisle, 'and now a magician appears to be picking them off one by one, and would you look at this, a man who would have spent years blowing on the embers of his grudge to keep it nice and hot turns out to have developed into a rather basic but effective magician.'

'Quite the coincidence, that,' replied Rita.

'Oh, the word coincidence is written in ten-foot, flashing neon letters above his head, Detective.'

Mister Nolan glanced above his head, as if the neon letters might actually be there.

'Then again…' said Carlisle, who noticed the rather stupid glance upwards.

'Look, I'm innocent, honest! Yeah, I can't say any of them are my favourite people, but I don't want them dead or anything! I've moved on. I've got my hobby.'

'Magic is your hobby?' said Carlisle.

'Yeah. Turns out my great, great, great, great grandfather had a touch of the Uncanny. It took years of practice and effort, but I've finally been able to tap into it myself. Gives me something to do, you know?'

'It's not him, is it?' said Rita, dropping into one of the other chairs in the front row.

'It's definitely not him,' replied Carlisle, 'the man's a buffoon.'

'I told you! Wait, what did you call me?'

Rita sat up straight as her skin began to crawl. 'What's that? What's happening?'

Carlisle sighed as the air around them began to ripple and haze.

'Looks like our friend here sent out a distress call.'

'So he's what, called the police on us?'

'In a way.'

The theatre melted away, to be replaced by the inside of a cave. There were no windows, no tunnels in or out, no entrances or exits of any kind.

Stood around the edge were around twenty figures. Some

wore robes with magical runes and incantations stitched into the fabric with silver thread that seemed to glow white-hot, others wore smart, anachronistic suits, others sported chinos and casual shirts. All in all, it was quite an odd collection of people.

Mister Nolan stood, no longer tied to a chair, as the chair didn't exist in this space.

'You could brighten the place up a little,' said Carlisle. 'A few pictures for the walls, a sofa or two, make it a bit more homely.'

'You attacked one of our own,' said one of the gathered circle of men, and they were all men, Rita noticed. Clearly this was a bit of a boys' club.

'Actually, he attacked us, and by the way...' she pulled out her badge again and showed it around the circle, 'you just abducted a police officer.'

'A hexed police officer,' replied a second member of the circle, who had a piece of gold cloth covering his face.

'So what are you lot?' asked Rita. 'Some sort of magical police?'

'Pfft,' replied Carlisle. 'This is nothing more than a wizard social club. No doubt they get together, drink, tell tales, and attempt to impress each other with their latest tricks.'

'We also have karaoke nights,' said Mister Nolan.

'My apologies,' replied Carlisle, bowing slightly.

'She has the axe!' said one member of the circle, pointing to the handle poking out of Rita's coat. A burble went up as they all pointed and whispered to each other.

'She has *my* axe,' Carlisle corrected, 'and if any one of you party entertainers continues to make eyes at it, you may well find them plucked out and fed to a rat.'

'Look, can I just ask if we're in any danger?' asked Rita. 'I'd like to know if I can unclench or not.'

'You can... unclench,' replied Carlisle with a look of distaste washing over his pale face.

'Great. You know all this being in constant and surprising danger is doing wonders for my glutes.'

'Question,' said Carlisle, turning to the circle, 'a magician is murdering women in this area and you have done nothing to prevent it. Why?'

The circle shuffled their feet and avoided looking at Carlisle.

'Boys' club, isn't it? Freemasons. Illuminati. Protecting their own, right?' said Rita.

Carlisle approached one of the magicians and peered into his eyes. 'You don't know, do you? None of you?'

'He's not one of us,' replied a man with a long, pointed beard that reached down to his navel. 'All local wizards and magicians are known to us.'

'We reached out to the rest of the Uncanny Kingdom's magicians,' continued another, whose idea of 'magician' seemed to be 'guest at a yacht party in the 1930s'. ' We reached out to L'Merrier even, but no one knows who it is. Who it could be. It's a stranger.'

'Is there not some sort of magic you can do to spot him?' asked Rita. 'Izzy, wizzy, show me who he izzy. That sort of thing?'

'Yes,' replied Long Beard, 'but it doesn't work. Not on this magician. He's either beyond anything we've ever encountered, or he's being protected by something with immense power.'

'So, what you're saying is, you're all no help at all,' said Carlisle.

More foot shuffling.

'Well, we tried our best. Not our fault,' said Yacht Party.

'Goodbye.' Carlisle clapped his hands together and the cave and its occupants folded back and back until the three of them, Carlisle, Rita and Mister Nolan, were back on Blackpool's North Pier, stood outside the theatre as people bustled by, seeming not to notice the trio who had just appeared from nowhere.

'So what now?' asked Rita.

'Um, can I go home, please?' asked Mister Nolan.

Carlisle dismissed him with a wave of the hand and the former teacher scurried away down the pier.

'Damn,' said Carlisle, walking to the edge of the pier and leaning against the barrier, his jet-black hair whipping in the sea breeze.

'What is it? What's wrong now?' asked Rita, joining him.

'It seems our options have narrowed and I shall have to do something I really have no wish to do.'

Rita watched a pair of seagulls whirling in the sky above them.

'Sometimes I envy birds,' said Rita.

'What?'

'They can go wherever they want. Just flap off, no responsibility, no murder cases to weigh on their conscience. Just fish, the air, and a good old flap.'

'You are a very stupid person,' said Carlisle.

'I like you too, creepy. So what is this crap thing you're going to have to do?'

Carlisle turned his back on the sea and thrust his hands deep into the pockets of his dark purple coat, his face creased with concern. Rita hadn't seen him look so worried, and it made her feel uneasy.

'What? Tell me!'

'I believe I will pay a visit to Mr. Cotton and Mr. Spike and ask them a question.'

'What? Are you insane?'

'Yes, often.'

'Won't they try to kill you?'

'Very likely, which is why I'm not trembling with giddy excitement at the prospect of knocking upon their door. But alas, I see no other move to make. Nobody seems to know anything about the person we are chasing, but we know that frightful pair do.'

Carlisle reached inside his coat and pulled out a small, terracotta-coloured rectangle. It was the size and shape of a domino, and had swirling symbols scratched on to its surface.

'Here,' he said offering it to Rita.

'What is it?'

'Insurance,' he replied.

Rita took the small tablet. It was rough to the touch, and was much weightier than its small, thin size would suggest.

'What do you mean by "insurance" exactly?'

'If things go badly, if I need pulling out, it will let you know, and it will take you to me. Do not lose it. My life, quite literally, depends upon it.'

Carlisle turned, his coat sweeping, and strode away along the pier.

'What am I supposed to do in the meantime?'

Carlisle did not reply.

'Oh, nice, okay, well if this thing does start glowing maybe I'll just ignore it, how do you like them, you know, bananas?... Apples! Shit.'

Rita watched Carlisle step off the pier and disappear into the hustle of the street as she rolled the terracotta domino over and over in her fingers.

Carlisle was wandering the streets of Blackpool with a destination in mind, but no direction to follow. But that was okay. He knew that sooner or later he'd end up stood in front of the door to their house.

It was fair to say that Carlisle was annoyed. Annoyed that his efforts to reclaim what was his had so far been frustrated. Annoyed that he couldn't just brush the detective aside and take his axe. Reclaim his throne. Annoyed that—of course—the case that could lead him to reclaim it had to be so complex and have such heavy hitters on the opposing side.

Heavy hitters like Mr. Cotton and Mr. Spike, and whoever this mysterious magician was. A magician whose power seemed to outreach his own. But then Carlisle was rarely more dangerous than when on the back foot.

But still. He was annoyed. Here he was, voluntarily walking into guaranteed harm's way, having to trust that when the worst happened, a woman who knew barely a sniff of the Uncanny world would come to his aid. It made him not just annoyed, but nervous. Carlisle was never nervous, and the sensation made his stomach hurt.

He pulled an apple from his coat pocket and took a bite.

He'd had no direct altercations with Mr. Cotton and Mr. Spike, but knew well of their work. Of their abilities. Of the terror they could arouse in a person's mind. They could kill you, if you were lucky, or they could set up home in your head, forever. An endless nightmare.

After he had wandered aimlessly for long enough, Carlisle began to leave threads around him. Mental threads, from street to street.

'It's true, they were brothers, despite their obvious differences,' said Carlisle, imbuing each word with a call, a thread to follow, a lure to catch the eye.

'Mr. Cotton and Mr. Spike.'

He turned into a blind alley that hid a row of shops that had existed unseen by normal society for hundreds of years. A butcher's, whose window was full of meat that came from animals that were long since extinct. A shop that sold bottles of wine so intoxicating that they could slow time and warp reality around you. An antique establishment where, if you were to venture into one darkened corner and push aside a centuries old rug, and fight through the cloud of dust that erupted from it, you'd find the now blunt head of the spear of destiny.

'They lived in a house that did not exist.'

Carlisle exited the hidden street and entered a fish and chip shop, the smell of fried cod and batter swirling around him. He walked through and to the back, pushing open the fire escape and stepping into the alley beyond.

'And if you were to take a wrong turn one strange day,' said Carlisle, the words sparking and throbbing as they drifted around him, 'only to find yourself knocking upon this impossible home's door…'

Carlisle paused and closed his eyes. He was trembling slightly. He took a deep breath, then two, and brought himself under control. They would not see him shake. He was Carlisle, he was the one others feared. Life was a game and he was always three moves ahead.

He smiled.

'You would soon discover that there are many worse things in this world than being lost.'

He opened his eyes to see that Blackpool was no more. Behind him was a dusty road, rolling hills covered in sparse grasses, the sky a sepia wash. He turned back to the large, lone, dilapidated house before him. The brickwork crumbled and cracked, the glass in the windows impossible to see through, with jagged shatter-lines twisting this way and that. Vegetation hugged the building tightly, as if it intended to pull the entire dwelling below ground.

He had arrived.

Wherever this was. Wherever they lived. He had arrived.

He didn't bother knocking, or trying to sneak in to take them by surprise. He'd called to them and they'd let him in. They were expecting him.

Carlisle turned the door's handle and pushed it open, the hinges emitting a horror movie scream.

'Nice touch,' he said, loudly. His voice sounded even, strong, threaded with just a tinge of mockery. He wasn't afraid. He wasn't outmatched. He was Carlisle, and he was here for a friendly chat.

It was dark inside the house. The sort of dark that seemed alive. That seemed to press and squeeze Carlisle as he made his way, step by step, across the faded carpet, each footfall greeted by a cloud of dust.

'I like what you haven't done with the place,' said Carlisle. 'Shabby chic taken to the extreme.'

Mould crept across every surface. Carlisle wondered if the house itself was more of a vile, sprouting fungus than a real bricks and mortar dwelling.

'Welcome,' said Mr. Cotton, stepping into view. He did not walk from a room, or down the stairs, it was more like he simply stepped into reality from wherever he had been lurking.

Carlisle bowed slightly. 'We meet at last,' he said, and began to wander as nonchalantly as he could around the entrance hall, peering at the age-encrusted oil paintings that adorned the walls. 'Big fan of your work, by the way. Always nice to see someone at the top of their game.'

'You flatter my brother and I, Carlisle.'

'Oh, piffle, what's true is true.'

'Mr. Spike, brother of mine, has had a particular fondness for your antics over the centuries. I've wondered often when our paths would cross.'

'And here we are at last. Face-to-face, or face-to-mask, at least.'

The rabbit mask Mr. Cotton wore grinned at that, though of course it did not, as it was just a mask.

'By the way, where is that brother of yours?'

Mr. Spike stepped out of the dark and struck Carlisle across the back of the head with the fireplace poker gripped in his white-gloved hands. Mr. Spike, his breath noisy and excited against the inside of his hedgehog mask, stood over Carlisle's unconscious body. He raised the poker a second time and looked to his brother.

'No, no,' said Mr. Cotton to his disappointed brother, 'we have things to discuss.'

Mr. Spike threw the poker aside petulantly.

'Do not despair, brother of mine, when all is said and done, you will show him your true face, and all shall be screams.'

Mr. Spike clapped his gloved hands together gleefully.

20

It had been hours since Carlisle had left her behind on the pier, and Rita was starting to get worried.

She removed the terracotta domino from her pocket for the millionth time and rolled it around in her hand, traced the shape etched into it with her fingers, even held the thing to her ear in case it was supposed to make a sound, a magical alarm sound. But no. She hoped that, at least, was a good thing. She also wished the lanky, pasty git had told her exactly what his plan of action was, and what she was meant to do with the thing he'd given her.

Rita huffed, shoved the piece back into her pocket, and looked towards the main entrance to Blackpool Hospital. With nothing else to do, she'd decided to pay a visit to Gemma Wheeler, the cousin of Rita's sometimes night-time partner, and prospective victim number three of the magician.

She stepped into the reception area and waved at the woman manning the desk, 'Hey there, you! It's me again, Miss Invisible, don't mind me, I'm just gonna go and check on Gemma, is that all right? Completely ignore me if that's all right.'

The receptionist continued to chew on the end of her pen as she read from her gossip magazine.

'Brilliant, thanks,' said Rita, and headed, unseen, behind the desk, put Gemma's name into the system, found which room she was in, and went to find her.

It was weird how quickly she'd got used to being a ghost. To being neither seen, nor heard. To not even being noticed if she physically shoved someone. She hadn't felt a thing when she'd been hexed. As she'd found herself stumbling into that secret room where Gemma Wheeler was being held, about to be sacrificed using the very axe that now swung from her belt, tapping against her right thigh as she prowled the harshly lit corridors, avoiding oncoming orderlies.

Rita had taken it all in her stride, or at least pretended to. If she could just stay focused on the case, she wouldn't have to think about the craziness she'd fallen into. That had stolen her life from her. That had robbed her of her one chance to escape Blackpool, and her past. Concentrating on her job had always been Rita's way of ignoring her feelings. That and alcohol. When she needed to push down the tears and the loneliness of her childhood years, especially. That feeling of being unloved. A thing that nobody wanted to call their own.

Rita shivered and shook it off. Just think about the case, she told herself. That's all that matters. Find the killer, stop the killer.

Carlisle had assured her that Gemma would be safe. That the magician required the axe to carry out his sacrifice, and would not kill her without it, but still, Rita felt that they were being a little free and easy with the poor woman's life.

She found the room Gemma Wheeler was in. A uniformed officer was sat on a chair outside, scrolling through Twitter on his phone. Rita recognised him as Geoff Kinney, an officer she'd once seen drink whiskey out of his own shoe.

'Just popping in to say *hey* and *how'd you do* to the the almost-victim, Kinney,' said Rita.

The officer ignored her as she opened the door and stepped inside to find Gemma sat up in bed. Her erstwhile partner, Waterson, poured her a glass of water from a fat-bottomed jug.

'Oh, hi!' said Gemma, looking at Rita.

Waterson turned to see who Gemma was greeting, only, of course, to see that it was still just the two of them in the room. 'Yeah, hi,' he replied to Gemma, a little confused.

Rita waved her hands at Gemma then placed a finger to her lips. 'Shh! He can't see me,' she said.

Gemma pulled a face. 'What do you mean?'

'I mean, well, "hi", just that,' replied Waterson.

'Are you having a laugh or something? Can you not—'

Gemma's sentence was cut off as Rita placed a hand over her mouth. Waterson saw the woman pulling the strangest of faces, her lips all mushed.

'Um, here you go,' he said, handing her the glass of water. 'I'm just going to pop out and make a call, then I'll be back just to go over things one more time, is that okay?'

'Just say yeah,' said Rita, then removed her hand from Gemma's mouth.

'Just say yeah,' repeated Gemma.

'Right. Good.' Waterson took another curious look at Gemma, shook his head, then left the room.

'Okay, what the bloody hell is going on?' asked Gemma.

'You can see me?' asked Rita. 'Like, actually see me?'

'Uh, yeah, I can see you.'

'And hear me!'

'Yeah, I have ears. Why couldn't he seem to tell you were in here?'

Rita sat on the chair that Waterson had vacated and began toying with the terracotta domino in her pocket. 'Bit hard to explain. It's also complete nonsense. If you tried to tell me similar this time last week I'd have said you were a bloody lunatic, but you saw it. Or rather, you just saw him not seeing me, right?'

Gemma nodded slowly. 'Yeah. And?'

'How much do you remember about what happened to you? About how you got here?'

Gemma shrank. 'There was… two men. In masks.'

'From your nightmares, right?'

Gemma nodded. 'And then it's all, sort of, wispy. Not sure. I remember the arcade down on the front. I think I was taken somewhere in the back.'

'I found you, rescued you, and brought you here.'

'Oh. Cheers for that.'

'You were going to be murdered. Sacrificed. For reasons that, well, aren't entirely clear, but we're working on it.'

Gemma sipped her water. 'Okay, but that doesn't explain why he couldn't see or hear you.'

Rita wrestled with a way to explain things, then realised there was no best way, so just launched into it.

'Okay, so it turns out that when I found you I was hexed.'

'Hexed?'

'Hexed.'

'You've been hexed?'

'Completely hexed, yeah.'

'Right.' Gemma nodded as she mulled the information over. 'So what's that exactly then?'

'Hexed?'

'Yeah, what's a hexed when it's at home?'

'Magic. A sort of magic curse thing.'

Rita noticed the *oh-Christ-I'm-talking-to-a-loony* look spreading across Gemma's face. 'I know, I know, it's mental, but it's true, I mean how else do you explain me being invisible to people?'

'That maybe I'm suffering from some sort of trauma and I'm seeing things that aren't there?'

'Okay, fair answer, but I'm telling you the truth, honestly.' Rita reached out and pinched Gemma's arm.

'Oi, you bitch!' Gemma rubbed at the red mark on her arm.

'See? That hurt. If I wasn't really here then I wouldn't be able to pinch you, and you wouldn't be feeling pain right now. You see my point?'

Gemma scowled as she continued to rub at her arm. 'Fine. Okay. You're really here. But magic? Like, David Blaine?'

'No, real, actual magic. I've seen it, and not just what's happened to me. I've seen some crazy stuff. Ooh, even a vampire in a bowling alley.'

'Fuck off.'

'Swear to God.'

'Bloody hell. Well, how come can I see you and no one else can?'

Rita shrugged. 'Buggered if I know. Maybe because you're

part of all this too? Touched with the Uncanny stuff. Oh, did you know your old teacher, Mister Nolan, can do magic now?'

'Pervy Nolan is a magician? No way!'

'It's true. We thought he might have been behind it, like he had a grudge against you all for getting him fired, but he's innocent.'

Gemma bit her lip and toyed with the edge of her blanket.

'What's wrong?'

'I'm scared still, you know? What if they come back for me? Rabbit Mask and his brother?'

Rita reached over and took her hand. 'It's gonna be okay. Promise.'

'How do you know, though?'

Rita opened her coat to show Gemma the axe. 'For whatever reason, they need this to carry out the sacrifice, otherwise it's pointless. And guess what?'

'What?'

'They're getting this back over my dead body.'

Rita touched the terracotta domino in her pocket and wondered how much longer Carlisle would be.

Carlisle was in a lot of trouble.

He'd regained consciousness several minutes before but had kept his eyes closed and remained motionless. He needed to think. He needed to assess the situation before Cotton and Spike realised the game was back on.

He was tied to something. Tightly. He could feel rope cutting into his wrists, his ankles, his throat. The rope around his throat made it difficult to breathe—constricting his windpipe to half its usual diameter—but he did not panic. He continued to breathe slow and steady. All would be fine. He just needed to find the right things to say. He'd talked his way out of worse. Far worse.

Actually, that wasn't true, but he lied to others successfully on such a regular basis that he hoped to be able to fool himself, too.

He could not.

'How much longer will you go on pretending?' came a voice. Mr. Cotton.

'I take it the jig is up,' replied Carlisle, opening one eye to see Mr. Cotton sat in a brown leather chair, legs crossed, a couple of metres in front of him.

'You cannot fool us here, Carlisle. Nobody can, not even as adept a liar as yourself.'

'Well that seems hardly fair.'

'Oh, life isn't fair. Never has been. And nightmares? Nightmares are made from unfair. And fear. And pain. They are delicious.'

Mr. Cotton's mouth opened and a velvet tongue wormed out to lick his lips. Only of course it did not, as the mask was just a mask and that was impossible.

Carlisle opened both eyes and swallowed, painfully. He was roped to a chair. He began to test the ropes, hoping to slowly create some wiggle room. Some give. Some hope of escape. The ropes offered no hope at all.

'Why am I restrained?' asked Carlisle. 'Surely you have no need to incapacitate me? No need to fear?'

'We do not fear, my brother and I.' Mr. Cotton stood and held out a gloved hand. A second gloved hand reached out of the dark, out of the nothing, and took hold; Mr. Spike stepping out of the shadows to join them.

'You know, hitting a man from behind is not very gentlemanly behaviour, Mr. Spike,' said Carlisle.

Mr. Spike's shoulders shook and he made a wet, wheezing noise that might have been laughter. 'Why have you paid us a visit, Carlisle?'

'I have a question for you.'

'Oh? A question worth dying for?'

'Nothing is worth dying for.'

Mr. Cotton and Mr. Spike began to waltz together around the room.

'You do not usually help others, Carlisle,' said Mr. Cotton.

'I don't care about the detective,' he replied. 'I care only for what is mine.'

'Not yours. Not anymore. It is needed.'

Carlisle strained at the ropes, sweat running down his forehead and into his eyes. Just a little give. That's all he needed.

Mr. Cotton and his brother stopped dancing and turned to face Carlisle.

'See how he strains and struggles, brother?'

Mr. Spike nodded, shoulders shaking, as a giant centipede crawled from one of his mask's eyeholes.

'He has lived for so very long, and yet he demands more, regardless of the hopelessness of his situation. Tell me, Carlisle, do you ever have nightmares?'

'I do not sleep, nor do I dream.'

'Oh, you will find that you do not require sleep, to experience nightmares,' said Mr. Cotton, and his long ears twitched, but of course they did not. 'You had a question for us?'

Carlisle paused in his pointless struggle against the ropes, which seemed only to wind tighter the more he fought. He blinked his eyes clear. 'Who is your employer?'

'Ah. Now that is the question, isn't it? Who is the great and powerful Oz?'

'Tell me.'

Mr. Cotton stepped towards him, taking Carlisle's chin in his gloved hand and tilting his head up.

'Pray, have you heard tell of the Angel of Blackpool?'

Carlisle knew the story. He'd heard it whispered once, centuries before. 'It is a fantasy. A fairy tale.'

Mr. Cotton wagged a gloved finger in front of Carlisle's face. 'No, no, no, it has always been true.'

'Okay. So the Magician is this Angel?'

Mr. Spike wheezed his horrid laugh again.

'So the Magician is just working for the Angel, like the two of you? Thanks for the information.'

'Oh, is he not a blabbermouth, my brother?' said Mr. Cotton, patting Mr. Spike on the shoulder and dislodging a whorl of brown dust.

'Well, what is the harm?' asked Carlisle. 'I shall never leave here alive.'

'Never has a truer statement been uttered, your majesty.'

'So?'

Mr. Cotton looked at him with his blank, stationary face for several seconds.

The only sound in the room came from Mr. Spike's heavy, rasping breath. He nodded his head slightly. 'The Angel of Blackpool will rise, with our assistance.'

'And the Magician's,' replied Carlisle.

'Of course.'

'Why?'

'No, no. Too much.'

'Okay, then why do you help? What is your price?'

'We enjoy our work, my brother and I, but we are restrained from reaching our true, beautiful potential. We have been promised that these restraints will be removed. The world shall become one endless nightmare, and we shall feast, and we shall dance, and we shall frolic until our hearts burst with glee.'

Mr. Spike clapped his hands together excitedly.

A clock bonged in the distance and Mr. Cotton pulled out a pocket watch to check the time.

'Well, well, it seems that time has rather run away with us, and your visit is at an end.'

'But I have more questions,' said Carlisle.

'Brother, mine.'

Mr. Spike nodded and began to step towards Carlisle. He did not walk, he swayed, hands behind his back, each footstep a delicate, dancer's sweep.

'Maybe we can help each other out, form a beneficial understanding' said Carlisle. 'All I want, at the end of this, is what's mine.'

'Hear how he attempts to curry favour, to cut deals, to stab associates who trust him so, directly in the back. Tut tut, Sir, very bad form.'

'I can help you. Ask your Angel.'

'Thank you for paying our humble home a visit, we get so few willing visitors,' said Mr. Cotton. 'This has been a rare treat, especially to play host to such a distinguished, cruel, nefarious guest as your good self.'

Carlisle struggled and strained, rocking the chair back and

forth until it tumbled to one side. His head bounced off the carpeted floor.

'Wriggle, please do,' said Mr. Cotton. 'It makes this all the more delicious.'

Carlisle was beyond pretence now. Beyond saving face. Beyond dignity. He screamed and he shouted and he tried to close his eyes, even though they refused to do as he wished. It was no use. He was lost.

Mr. Spike crouched before him, cocking his head to one side, rancid air wheezing from behind the mask, dampening Carlisle's face with his putrid breath.

'Shall he show you true horror?' asked Mr Cotton. 'The face of every nightmare that ever brought a shiver?'

Carlisle did not answer. His body relaxed. He accepted his fate. To struggle any more was pointless.

'Brother, mine,' said Mr. Cotton.

And then Mr. Spike removed his mask, and Carlisle saw the face beneath.

And the world became screams and terror.

21

Rita pulled her coat tight as she looked up at the darkening sky, her breath forming like dragon smoke in the frigid air. She had spent another hour talking with Gemma Wheeler, but eventually left her to it with promises made that the case would soon be done, and that she'd be able to return home, safe.

Rita even mostly believed it.

'Carlisle, where the shit are you?' she muttered. He'd been gone close to four hours, and she was starting to wonder if she was ever going to see him again. Maybe he'd decided to bail on the case. Forget about the axe he claimed was his. It's not as though she had any good reason to trust him. Formby, that moley looking old man, had said as much to her. Carlisle was a liar. A dangerous cheat. And yet she was relying on him to help save Gemma Wheeler's life. To save her own life too, from the stupid hex that had erased her from everyday life. Okay, her everyday life might have been slowly suffocating her, but it was a heck of a lot better than her current situation, living in limbo land, a human ghost.

Before Rita had left the hospital, Waterson had briefly re-entered Gemma Wheeler's room to give her assurances that he was on the case. Rita would have given just about anything for him to have turned to her at that point, to have seen her, and delivered one of his usual withering remarks. Her partner—her best friend of years—and he didn't even remember her, let alone see her.

That stung.

She hadn't just been made to disappear, her very existence, her history, had been scrubbed out. She wasn't even a memory anymore.

Rita swore and rubbed at her eyes as she felt them growing damp and heavy. 'Pull yourself together, you daft tart.'

Detective.

Rita winced and clutched her temples as the voice, with that single word, seemed to burn inside her head.

Detective, find me.

'Carlisle?' Rita stood and looked around, but he was nowhere to be seen. He hadn't spoken to her, she hadn't heard his voice, she'd *felt* it. Reaching into her coat, she yanked out the terracotta domino and stared at it in wonder. The shapes, the squiggles and scratches, now burned a brilliant white.

Carlisle was calling to her.

'Hello?' she said into the thing, then placed it to her ear as though it were a phone, 'Carlisle, where are you? Can you hear me?'

There was no answer, but the domino continued to glow, and now it seemed to pulse in her palm, as though it had a heartbeat.

'Shit. How do I use this thing? I don't understand what I'm supposed to do, you lanky goon!'

And then the world bulged and stretched and warped, and a rip opened in the fabric of reality.

'Oh,' said Rita.

Peering through the impossible tear, she could see what looked like a room in an old house. She looked back to the hospital's entrance, down at the glowing terracotta domino, then through to the room beyond the tear.

'Okay, well, looks like I'm doing something dumb again.'

Rita pulled the axe from her belt, held out her domino-holding hand, and edged through the tear. She wasn't sure what would happen next, but very little did. It wasn't like she'd stepped through a rip in the world, it was as though she'd stepped from one room into another. No big deal.

She turned to see the rip in reality was still open. She could see a man in a dressing gown leaning against the hospital's wall, smoking a cigarette. She wondered how long it would stay open.

The domino pulsed rapidly in her hand, as if trying to get her mind back on the job, which, she assumed, was finding Carlisle. If that meant he was in trouble, that he needed saving, then what chance did she have? He knew this world inside out, he was part of it. He was clearly powerful in ways he wasn't willing to share, so if he was trapped, what chance did she have; a Blackpool copper with a magic hatchet?

She looked around the room she'd found herself in. It was, in a word, creepy. Or in three words: "Creepy as fuck". Rita's eyes drifted around the room. It was an old-fashioned bedroom for a child; piles of toys strewn around the floor, a small cot in one corner, a mobile hanging above it. It looked to Rita as though it belonged in some ancient Victorian house, the kind you'd see in period dramas on the telly, only this one had been left to go… rotten. Everything was faded, warped, degraded. Mould crept across almost every surface, and it seemed to Rita that unseen things watched her from the room's darkened corners.

She gripped the axe tightly and made her way towards the closed bedroom door. She turned the brass handle and the door opened with a sharp cry that made Rita gasp. She stopped and counted to ten, listening for any movement outside of the room, for any sign that the door had alerted someone in a rabbit or hedgehog mask that they had an unwanted guest.

All was silent.

Trying to control her breathing, Rita spoke to herself. 'Be brave, Detective.'

A man, if he was even a man, was in trouble, and this was her job. Protect. Take down the bad guys. No time for fear when duty called.

'Bad-ass. Bad-ass bitch.' Rita nodded and slipped out of the open door into the corridor beyond. It was, like the child's bedroom she'd entered through, brown and rotten. It was lined with paintings of figures in grand frames. Each painting depicted one or both of Mr. Cotton and Mr. Spike.

Carlisle had said that the pair were literally the stuff of nightmares, and if the stuff of nightmares lived anywhere, it would be a house like this.

Rita began to edge along the corridor, half-expecting the eyes in the paintings to follow her. For a hand to reach out of one of them and grip her shoulder with a dirty white glove.

Each footfall was greeted by the complaint of a rotten floor-board, and the corridor seemed to twist and sway as she made her way along it.

'How do I know where you are?' Rita whispered into the still-pulsing domino, its carved shaped blazing brilliantly.

She tried the first door she passed. It opened on another bedroom, though this one was not empty. Hundreds of tiny yellow eyes turned to regard her, every inch of the room swamped with large, black rats, their rotten teeth chattering at her.

'Sorry, wrong room,' said Rita, and made sure the door was very firmly closed as she hurried away.

At the end of the corridor was a rather grand staircase leading down to the ground floor.

'Carlisle?' she said, her voice a hiss, but there was no response. 'Carlisle, if you're close, make this domino throb hard twice.'

It did not throb hard twice.

Rita made her way down the staircase. The house stank of decay, and the air was thick with dust, making it hard to breathe.

At the bottom of the stairs, Rita took a right, only for the domino to stop pulsing.

'Okay, hot or cold?' She turned left instead and took a few steps, and the thing began its heartbeat pulse once again. 'Right, hot.'

She stopped in front of a door, waving the domino in front of it. It shone so brightly she couldn't look at it.

'Bingo.'

Rita opened the door.

Inside was a grand ballroom, far too large for what the house could realistically contain. A giant chandelier hung from the vaulted ceiling, every crystal contained within it cracked, or broken in two, or missing entirely. Long tables with yellowed table cloths crowded the room. Thick, grey cobwebs were strung from one silver candelabra to the next, and spiders lazily roamed the piles of rotten food, picking up fat flies that gorged on the oozing, rotten mess.

The stench was like a punch to the face, and it took everything Rita had not to stumble out of the room and vomit. She'd have liked to have done that, but something else was in the room. *Someone* else.

Carlisle.

He was laid on his side on the floor, roped to a chair.

Blood was soaked into the dirty carpet in a halo around his head, and dried tributaries of red ran from his mouth, his nose, his ears, even his eyes.

'Carlisle!' She ran to him, kneeling, patting his face. 'Hey, I'm here, your thingy worked, wake up!'

She hit him harder, shook him. He didn't wake, didn't make a sound. Didn't even twitch.

'Shit, shit, shit,' said Rita, feeling for a pulse.

No pulse.

Did he ever have a pulse? He must have done. And then something sparked in Rita's mind and she looked down at the terracotta domino in her hand, slowly pulsing away, one heartbeat after another.

'You've got to be kidding me…'

It had only started to glow, to pulse, when he needed help. When he'd died…? Rita was starting to put two and two together when something tapped against her foot. She looked down to a rat staring up at her, sat back on its rear legs, its front legs rubbing together.

'Sod off,' she said, and kicked the squealing rodent across the room.

Pocketing the domino, Rita hacked at the ropes binding Carlisle, and freed his body—his corpse—from the chair.

'Carlisle, mate, you're going to have to help me out here.'

He had always looked alabaster white, as pale as a ghost, but now his skin looked grey.

'How did you get here?' came a voice.

Rita spun around, but there was nobody there. She brandished the axe warily.

'Oi, who's there, then? Hey?'

A floorboard squeaked in a shadowed corner. Rita turned and swung the axe impotently.

'Stop messing around, okay? You don't scare me, I've faced worse on the job!' Worse than some nightmare monster who lurked in a house built from fear and rot who could apparently kill Carlisle with little effort? Yeah, she may have been bluffing just a little there.

'I asked you a question,' said the voice.

Rita turned again to see the carpet in one corner of the room ripple and bulge. The carpet tore, and up sprouted a pair of rabbit ears.

'Shit!' Rita grabbed Carlisle, sitting him up. 'Come on, you dead idiot, we've gotta move!'

'They always run and run and run but there's never anywhere to go.'

With a cry, Rita managed to lever the chair holding Carlisle back into an upright position.

Mr. Cotton rose fully into the room, a rat on his shoulder. 'You kicked Reginald. Reginald is not happy.' The rat squeaked furiously at Rita, then hopped down into Mr. Cotton's gloved hand. 'Sleepy time, Reginald.' The rabbit mask's mouth stretched wide into a Edvard Munch scream, and Reginald the oily, fat-tailed rat, hopped inside. The mouth closed behind him.

The exit, the tear Rita had stepped into this house from, that she could still hopefully escape through, was all the way upstairs. There was no way she'd make it, at least not carrying Carlisle's dead weight. That's if the thing was still even open.

Nope, Rita realised she was pretty much screwed.

Deciding she had no intention of going out on the back foot, Rita took a step forward and shook the axe at Mr. Cotton. 'Stay back, all right, or I'll twat you with this thing, you murdering, weird, bastarding bastard!'

'Oh, Reginald is not dead, I would never kill a rat.'

'I'm talking about Carlisle!'

Mr. Cotton's masked head tilted, 'Oh yes. That was fun. So brave to come here. In the end he screamed though. Screamed as my brother showed him true terror and his brain hubbled and bubbled and turned to naught but mush. A skull full of mashed potato.'

A gurgling, hacking sound alerted Rita to the fact that Mr. Spike had joined them. She swung around to see him stood behind her, shoulders juddering as the awful noise dribbled and rattled from beneath his hedgehog mask.

'Oh, that's funny is it?' asked Rita.

'My brother, Mr. Spike, does enjoy the lighter side of life, it is true. And now, the axe. I believe you shall give it to me so the work can resume, yes?'

Mr. Cotton reached out with one hand and began to move calmly towards Rita.

'Yeah, not bloody likely, you big freak,' Rita stepped back, swinging the axe to ward Mr. Cotton off, but Mr. Cotton did not pause.

'For shame. Such rude manners for one so fair,' he said.

Rita, heart smashing against her chest, looked back to see Mr. Spike guarding the door as his brother continued to advance.

'Stay back!' Rita demanded, swinging again.

'No, no, and no again. The axe is ours and nothing but nightmares upon nightmares shall be yours. I will show you everything that makes you shout and scream, over and over, and then my brother will show you what lurks beneath his mask. It will be delicious,' said Mr. Cotton, as Reginald the rat poked his snout out of one of the rabbit mask's eye hole and chittered his yellow, broken teeth together.

No way back without stumbling into Mr. Spike, and Mr. Cotton was almost upon her. Rita was out of options. She took a breath, stepped forward, and, with a war cry, swung the axe, missing Mr. Cotton completely and sending her tumbling to the floor.

'Tut-tut,' said Mr. Cotton. 'A swing and a miss.' He clicked his thumb and forefinger together and a tentacle burst from the rotten food piled upon the table. It wrapped itself around the struggling Rita's leg and began to drag her towards the table.

'Let me go!' she yelled.

'It looks like the food wants to play with you,' replied Mr. Cotton, and Mr. Spike gurgle-laughed once more.

Rita rolled on to her back to see what she was being dragged towards, the rotten food now a writhing, alive, thing. The spiders that crawled upon it were growing, and growing, their twitching, fang-like mouthparts dripping with blood.

Rita was terrified, but even in her terror, realised that this was what Mr. Cotton wanted. He wanted her fear.

'What dreadful delights we shall show to you, what scares shall we conjure.'

'Up yours!' screamed Rita, and swung the axe at the tentacle, severing it. The rotten food bucked and screamed, the tentacle thrashing, spraying the room with viscous black blood.

'Naughty,' said Mr. Cotton. 'You shall be punished.'

But Rita wasn't listening. As she struck the tentacle, she did not just sever the limb that was pulling her towards a horrific death, no: she connected to the magic.

To the nightmare power of Mr. Cotton, of Mr. Spike, of their horror house.

She felt it coursing through the axe.

It was just like with Mister Nolan, the gropey ex-teacher. The axe had connected to something Uncanny and was giving Rita access to its magic. Letting her understand it. Sense it. Control it.

She raised the axe in wonder, its head raging with sorcery, black and purple and deep red coiling around and through.

Mr. Cotton was rushing towards her, but she had nothing to fear. She felt the dark magic embolden her as she turned from him and struck out at the tables, at the rotting food, and made a demand.

Tentacles burst from the gross mass and rushed at Mr. Cotton, gripping his ankles, his wrists, his neck.

'You are a very bad house guest,' said Mr. Cotton, and then the tentacles tore him into pieces and pulled the wiggling bits into the disgusting mass of food and out of sight.

'Ha!' said Rita, staring gleefully at the axe. She turned to see Mr. Spike, his shoulders heaving, for the first time seemingly unsure about what to do.

'That's right, mate, think twice before rushing this bad-ass bitch!'

She felt elated, but not enough to get cocky. She had taken Mr. Cotton by surprise, but now Mr. Spike knew what she could do, it might not be the smartest thing to rush him. No, the best course of action was still to escape this place, but the portal was still all the way upstairs, and, furthermore, past Mr. Spike.

But then Mr. Cotton and Mr. Spike had control over this house. Over this dreamscape. Could create exit points. And Rita had access to that power. To instinctively understand it.

She swung the axe and buried the head into the floor, soaking up the Uncanny that made up the nightmare abode.

'Somewhere safe,' said Rita.

Rita looked down at the axe in her hands, to the blade that glowed fiercely, every colour imaginable strobing and coiling around it.

The colours of magic.

'Somewhere safe,' she said again, and then pulled the axe head from the floor and swung it until it connected with the fabric of the nightmare place's reality, and sliced open a gap. A way out.

Senses sharp, she heard ragged, angry breath and whirled around in time to see Mr. Spike, his hedgehog mask twisted into a furious snarl, his gloved hands reaching for her. Without thinking, the axe found its new target, sinking into Mr. Spike's head.

A sound like twisting metal erupted from Mr. Spike's mask as his body spasmed, and for a few seconds, Rita felt herself connected to his magic. Dark, horrible magic that soaked into the axe. Became part of it, ready to be unleashed.

She pulled the axe free, and Mr. Spike fell to the floor, his body exploding into a hundred screeching, writhing rats.

'Well that was… unexpected,' said Rita, as the rats scurried in every direction but hers.

Rita threw Carlisle's lifeless arm over her shoulder and dragged him to the exit she'd created in the room, her body crying out with pain as she bore his weight. She stumbled through the exit point in the dreamscape and fell to the floor beyond. As she collapsed to the ground, Rita rolled on to her back and found the exit point was already gone.

She'd done it.

She'd made it out.

She sagged back, the laughter of disbelief pouring out of her.

'Oh, it's you, is it? How's the case going, eh?'

Rita saw Formby, the ancient eaves, stood over her. She was back in Big Pins.

'Help me,' said Rita. 'Carlisle's dead.'

22

Waterson pulled to a stop on Blackpool's seafront and looked out at the water beyond the beach.

Watching the waves rush in and out always soothed him. Took his mind off his problems, at least as long as he just followed the water, like a metronome, in and out, steady as she goes, lulling him, calming him down.

Today it wasn't working.

He got out of his car and walked closer to the water, listening to the waves washing in and out, trying to force his mind to empty itself, just for a minute or two.

No good.

Maybe it was the pressure of the job finally overwhelming him. His mum had always been worried about him going into such a dangerous job. Into a job with such heavy expectations, mixing with the worst of the worst. He'd dismissed it though, he'd always known he was meant to be a copper, ever since he was five and had became obsessed with old black and white Sherlock Holmes films. The ones with Basil Rathbone.

Okay, he might not exactly be a modern day Holmes, but he was good at his job. Most of the time, anyway. And he felt good about the difference he was able to make to this place, his home town, but now…

The case was unusual for the area. Three women kidnapped, three women connected by age, by school, by… something else. *Rabbit ears.* Waterson shook his head and looked out to sea once again.

Out to sea.

Well, that hit the nail on the head. The case was unusual for sure, but it wasn't just the specifics of the case.

It wasn't just the mysterious rescue of the third abductee, who couldn't remember who had deposited her, unconscious, into a wheelchair in Blackpool Hospital. Someone who no one in the busy reception area had seen. Someone who wasn't picked up on the CCTV at all. No, one moment Gemma Wheeler wasn't present, then there was a momentary burst of static, and there she was, slumped in a wheelchair. *Ta-da!* A magic trick, minus the magician. Sure, that part of the whole thing was seriously off, and Waterson had no idea how to process it, how to account for it at all.

But then there was the other thing.

The forgotten thing.

The thing that churned his stomach and made the day feel like a foggy dream.

Waterson turned from the sea, frustrated, and looked over to the noise and riot of lights across the road. Archer's Old Arcade. The last place Gemma Wheeler remembered before waking up in a hospital room. Not that she remembered much, or why it was or wasn't significant. All she knew was that, at some point, she was there. She had the image of the machines, the claw games, the lights streaked across her mind's eye, like she'd rushed through, semi-conscious, her slurred memory taking an indistinct snapshot.

Or perhaps it meant nothing at all. A trick of a traumatised brain.

Well, it was all he had to go on. Gemma Wheeler had given them nothing else that he could try to gain a toehold in.

Waterson sighed and ran across the road towards the arcade, skipping past oncoming traffic, an angry food delivery driver honking the horn of his moped as he swerved past.

Of course, officers had already been here to question staff, managers, frequent visitors, anyone who spent more time than they should hanging out in the place. They brandished pictures of Gemma Wheeler and were greeted with head-shaking and shoulder shrugs. No one had seen her in the place. That did not mean, of course, that she hadn't been there. A lot of people crowded into that arcade on a daily basis, and no one was taking in faces – they were focused on screens, on grasping claws, on penny shove machines. Easy for someone to pass in and out unnoticed.

They'd searched the place, Waterson included, and found nothing. So why was he back?

Because the hairs on the back of his neck insisted he'd missed something. He liked to think he had good instincts as a cop, it was one of the things that gave him such a solid arrest record.

He'd missed something. They all had. But what? And would he recognise it even if he saw it?

He weaved slowly around the floor of Archer's Old Arcade, letting his eyes drift over every person, every machine, every surface, waiting for something to leap out at him.

He stopped by a claw machine. A young girl, no older than seven or eight, long blonde hair in bunches, tongue sticking out, was studiously maneuvering the grasping, metal claw over a pile of plush toys. These things were always rigged. It was almost impossible to win. The claw never closed enough for whatever toy it grabbed to make it all the way to the exit chute.

Down went the claw and the metal fingers closed, just enough to raise one of the soft toys away from the others. It just cleared the rest of the toys, swung back and forth, then tumbled out of the claw's grasp. The girl stomped her foot then fed another coin into the hungry machine. Out went the claw again, the girl steering its progress with the small joystick. Left, then right, then back, then the girl smacked the red button and the claw plunged again into the abundance of toys, grasping one, pulling it up into view.

There went the hairs on the back of Waterson's neck again.

A rabbit swung precariously from the metal claw, the scarf it had around its neck snagged on one of the fingers.

Rabbit ears.

'They all had the same nightmare,' Waterson said to himself. He wasn't sure why, but as he said it, he knew it was true.

He turned from the machine, from the toy rabbit, and followed his feet. Somehow, they seemed to know where they were going.

The stockroom.

This was where he'd had that feeling the last time he was here. That sense of missing something.

The door swung shut and the sound of the arcade became muffled.

He ran his hands over the giant plastic bags stuffed full of toys. A pair of rabbit ears poked out of a hole in one of the bags. Waterson reached out and stroked them.

'What? What is it?' he said, hitting the heel of his hand against his temple, trying to dislodge a blockage he felt sure was there.

He sagged and turned to leave, but stopped as something caught his eye.

It was a door.

The door had not been there the last time he was here, he was sure of it. Hadn't been there when he entered the stockroom this time, either. Perhaps it could have been hidden by stock bags the first time, and he just hadn't seen it, but not this time. This time it had been clear and the wall had been a wall, solid, no windows, no doors.

And now there was a door.

Waterson tried the handle; locked.

He ran from the stockroom and found the manager, pulling the befuddled man behind him and into the stockroom.

'What are you talking about?' asked the manager, as he was bundled into the room, almost piled into a bag of toys.

'Do you have a key for the door?' asked Waterson.

'What door?'

'That one!' Waterson pointed at the door, the air catching in his throat.

No door.

He raced over to it and began to frantically run his hands over the brickwork.

'Hey, are you… okay?' asked the manager.

Waterson turned to him, eyes wide, and didn't know what to say.

23

Despite his advanced age, Formby had the strength of a bull.

Rita watched in surprise as, with seemingly little effort, the ancient eaves grabbed the dead weight of Carlisle and tossed him over one shoulder.

'Follow me,' he said, hurrying past the gawping faces of Big Pins' regulars, and heading behind the bar. Despite the terrible circumstances, Rita still found herself giggling at the absurd sight of this short mole-man carrying Carlisle's long, narrow corpse, the knuckles of his white, elegant hands dragging a grim trail along the carpet.

Linton, the hulking proprietor of the Uncanny gathering spot, ushered Formby and Rita to a door behind the bar.

'Dead, is he?' asked Linton. 'Shame.'

Rita followed Formby and the late Carlisle into the back room, a small, shabby office stacked high with boxes containing bar snacks and bowling shoes. Linton yanked a cord and a bare bulb spluttered into life, casting a sickly yellow glow around the faded room. Formby headed for the sole item of furniture, a shabby couch, foam bursting from rips in its upholstery, and dumped Carlisle's body unceremoniously onto it.

'He better not leak any bodily juices and what-not on my

couch,' said Linton, before leaving them to it, closing the door as he left.

'Is he dead?' asked Rita. 'He's dead, isn't he? I mean, I couldn't feel a pulse or anything, so that means he's dead, right?'

Formby prised open one of Carlisle's eyes and peered at it.

'Did he ever even have a pulse?' Rita asked. 'He looked sort of like a vampire, like from a film—not *Twilight* shit, but a good one—so maybe he didn't have a pulse anyway.' Rita realised she was pacing in a little circle and flapping her hands as she spoke, so decided to stop doing that.

'Where was he?' asked Formby, levering Carlisle's jaw open with a knife and shining a small torch down his exposed throat.

'In a house. A creepy house. The creepiest.'

'He paid Mr. Cotton and Mr. Spike a visit?' asked Formby, turning to Rita as he asked, his eyes wide with surprise.

'Yeah. He said he wanted to ask them a question, about the case we're on. Wouldn't let me go with him.'

'Huh,' said Formby. 'Put himself in danger, did he? Not like him to go and do a thing like that for someone else.'

'Look, is he dead or not, because he seems pretty dead to me.'

Formby straightened up and turned off the torch, slipping it in the inside pocket of his dirty, grey coat. 'Oh yes. Dead as a dead person, that's what he is. The spark of life has spluttered its last.'

'Oh, Jesus,' said Rita, dropping to her haunches and scraping her fingers through her thick, red hair.

'Must trust you, then,' said Formby.

'What?'

'Trust you. He put his life in your hands.'

'Well, he's dead, so that looks like a bit of a mistake, doesn't it?'

Formby began to laugh. 'No, no, no, I'm talking literally. Life in your hands.'

Rita stood, feeling suddenly very tired indeed. Tired and now alone on a case that had erased her from normal life, and that now, without Carlisle at her side, she saw no way of solving.

'Stop talking in riddles, mole-face. I'm knackered, I'm angry, I'm sad, and I don't mind hitting you with this axe, okay?'

'Did he give you it?'

Rita sighed, 'Give me what?'

'His life?'

Rita was about to reply with a string of expletives when she remembered the terracotta domino with its elaborately carved patterns. She reached into her coat pocket and pulled it out. The thing glowed still, throbbing rhythmically.

'Oh. This is his life, isn't it?' asked Rita, holding the item close to her face, the light it cast warming her skin.

Formby nodded. 'That's right. Good bit of magic that, if you've got the knowledge of it.'

'He said it was an insurance policy.'

Formby clapped his hands together then reached to her. 'Give it over, then. The longer he's dead, the more painful it'll be when he's not dead.'

Rita moved to pass the piece to Formby, then hesitated. 'Wait, how do I know I can trust you? That you're not just gonna, I dunno, snap this thing in two? It's not as though you and Carlisle are best mates.'

Formby grinned, 'You do not know you can trust me, true. That is the Uncanny world you're in now. More often than not, you trust the untrustworthy.'

'Well, that's my mind put at ease.'

Rita handed the piece to Formby, who took it gingerly between thumb and forefinger.

'Right. Right then. I think I remember how you do this.'

Formby pulled the knife he'd used to open Carlisle's mouth back out of its sheath, raised it high above his head, then brought it down with a grunt of effort. The blade slid into Carlisle's chest like it were made of sponge, not flesh and bone.

'Jesus!' cried Rita, stepping back, as Formby waggled the blade back and forth, opening a small cavity in Carlisle's chest.

'There we go, fella,' he said, the glowing domino now slowly writhing back and forth like a fat slug. Formby lowered it into the gap he'd created in Carlisle's chest, then let it go. The terracotta domino wriggled its way into the hole and disappeared from view.

Then nothing happened.

'He still seems very dead to me,' said Rita.

Formby frowned and peered at the corpse on the couch. 'Yeah. He does a bit. Wait a minute.'

Formby spat on his hand, balled it into a fist, then bashed it against Carlisle's chest like he was the Fonz jolting a jukebox into life.

Carlisle was a corpse no more.

His eyes snapped open and he sat bolt upright, gasping for air, clutching his wounded chest.

'All right, all right,' said Formby, 'don't go fussing just because you've been dead for a bit.' He guided the twitching Carlisle into a foetal position on the couch and patted him on the head.

'Carlisle?' said Rita, stepping towards him.

'No, no,' said Formby, shooing her away. 'Wait out there a while, he'll need a bit of a sleep yet. You can't expect a man who's just been dead to be at his best right off.'

'He's alive. I mean, he was dead, now he's alive!'

'There's those keen detection skills again,' said Carlisle, his voice an arid whisper.

'Oi, you, hush,' said Formby, 'sleep now, rudeness later.'

Rita laughed in disbelief. She'd done it. She'd saved him.

Rita thanked Linton as he placed a second pint of ale in front of her.

'You know, you could've just left him for dead,' he said.

'Yes, you've already said that,' replied Rita, as Linton frowned and made his way back to the bar, where a patron was waiting to swap his dirty boots for a pair of bowling alley shoes.

It had been almost an hour since Carlisle had stopped being a corpse, and neither he nor Formby had emerged from the back room. Rita was itching to know what he'd found out. If he'd managed to get anything useful out of the terrifying masked pair before they'd murdered him.

She shook her head and took a gulp of her pint. A weird man had gone to a nightmare house to talk to monsters who had killed him. Only the death didn't stick because of some sort of magic nonsense. It was a wonder she hadn't gone mad yet.

She reached down and took out the axe, placing it on the table before her. It had saved her life again. It was weird, the effect it had. The way it seemed to connect her to the magic of whatever she went up against. How it seemed to make her understand it. *See* it. Know just how to wrangle it for her own needs. For as long as she needed it—for as long as she held the axe and it translated the spell—she wasn't a stranger to this bizarre world of magic. No, for a few brief moments, she was part of it. Connected to it. The master of it.

She stroked the blunt-looking blade with the tips of her fingers and felt a shiver of something run up her hand. Potential, that's what it was. There was magic still inside it. She'd hit both of them after all, hadn't she? Mr. Cotton and Mr. Spike. She'd used Cotton's magic to create an escape point, but Spike's magic still lurked, unused, inside of it.

Rita wrapped her hands around the handle and lifted the axe. It reacted to her touch. She felt as though the axe itself knew that the magic dwelled within it, and was waiting for her to tell it how to use it.

'Talking to you, is it?'

Rita pulled her hands away from the axe, her concentration broken by Formby, who sat down and availed himself of her partially-drunk pint of ale.

'There's magic in it. Right now,' said Rita.

'That so?' replied Formby, smacking his lips, foam from the ale spackling his rough beard.

'I hit them with it. Both of them, Cotton and Spike. Took some of their magic and used it, somehow, to come here.'

'That's handy,' said Formby, waving his hand at the bar to catch Linton's attention. Linton nodded and began to pull two fresh drinks.

'How is he? Carlisle?'

'Oh, he's been better, I expect. Though he's been dead before, of course.'

'He's what?'

'Got to expect it, the life he leads. Why he makes sure he has insurance when he needs it. He's not stupid. Nasty, untrustworthy, ruthless, murderous, but no, not stupid.'

Linton placed the fresh pints on the table and Formby licked his lips, reaching out with both hands to grasp his glass.

'He's not shat himself in there, has he?' said Linton. 'I've heard they do that, after being dead for a bit.'

'No, no, nothing wet has left his body,' replied Formby.

'Hm.' Linton turned and headed back to his bar once again.

'Apart from being alive, how actually is he?'

Formby frowned and considered the question. 'Well, tired, and weak, which is to be expected of course. Does nothing for your get-up-and-go, a bit of being dead, oh no. He's trying to put a brave face on it, but I seen it in his eyes.'

'What?'

'Well, they show you things, Mr. Cotton and Mr. Spike. Things to turn the sanest man mad. Kill you with the madness, they do. They showed Carlisle something, all right. Something that stopped his heart stone dead. I saw down his throat; red-raw from screaming in there.' Formby shivered and gulped his drink.

'But he'll be okay?'

Formby shrugged. 'Okay enough. In a while. Never quite the same I'd imagine, but alive.'

Rita sighed with relief and sat back. She'd rescued him, saved a life, even if she wasn't entirely sure how. That's what you did in the force, you had your partner's back. She thought about all the times she'd pulled Waterson's arse out of the fire and smiled.

'Suppose it's time I told you a thing or two,' said Formby.

'Hm? Sorry, what did you say?'

'Whilst his nibs is incapacitated out back, thought you might like to hear a thing or two I've heard whispered on the wind about you,' he said flicking his pointed ears and grinning, displaying his twin set of higgledy-piggledy piranha teeth.

Rita sat forward, wrapping her hands around the handle to her axe. 'There's whispers about me?'

'Whispers and words, and here's me, an old eaves with the ear-lugs to hear it and all that knowledge safe and sound in my brain meat.'

Rita wasn't sure she liked the idea of people talking about her.

People in this Uncanny world, at least. What was there to whisper about, anyway?

'Well? Go on then.'

'An eaves requires payment to share, you know.'

'Payment?'

'Fair's fair. Got to make a living, haven't we?'

'Okay, how much?'

'A promise of magic to feast upon. You have it coming your way.'

'Right, fine, whatever, just tell me.'

Formby clapped his fingerless-gloved hands together, the nails on each finger sharp and yellow.

'Then the transaction is fair,' he said. 'I did some digging. Went to the right places. Lurked and listened. No person living had anything of worth to say, but I found a few old ghosts in Friar's Cemetery, swapping stories, and up came your name.'

Rita blinked slowly as she took this in. 'I'm sorry, did you say ghosts? That there are ghosts, and that they're talking about me?'

Formby grinned and nodded.

'Good. Good to know. Not creepy at all, that. On you go then.'

'Carlisle wondered why his artefact, the axe, came to be yours without the wielder's consent, yes?'

'Yes.'

'It's simple, see? It is a thing of Heaven.'

'Yeah, you said that already, so what?'

'So, it is inclined to buddy up with other things of Heaven, understand?'

'Not at all, no.'

'Other things of Heaven, such as you.'

Rita nodded slowly. 'I'm sorry, come again?'

'Well, you are part angel, aren't you?'

Rita was quiet for quite a long time after that.

The Magician stood within his chamber, hands flat against the sacrifice stone, the giant lump of grey rock on to which each woman had been chained, ready for the axe.

He could not sense Mr. Cotton, nor his brother, Mr. Spike.

'What's happened?' he asked.

'I do not know,' replied the Angel of Blackpool, and this sent a shiver through the Magician.

'How can you not know? You always know.'

'They are… hidden from me, should they choose to be, whilst in their own dream realm. They do not allow me into their house. Something must have happened to them.'

'I need them,' said the Magician, feeling weak and foolish.

'No,' replied the Angel, 'all that we require is each other, and we will always have that. Their job was done, anyway. The important part.'

The Magician straightened up, feeling a little better. 'If they're missing, then it's up to me.'

'Yes,' replied the Angel. 'Mr. Cotton and Mr. Spike have served us well, but have failed to retrieve what we need.'

'The axe.'

'The artefact that will break down the doors to Heaven and allow us to take revenge on our cold, indifferent creator.'

The Magician knew what he had to do. It was time to step out of the shadows and take what was his.

For his dad.

For his mum.

For every single person who'd ever walked the face of the planet.

24

It was past midnight and DS Dan Waterson should have been in bed.

He'd tried to go home once he was off the clock, but had instead found himself driving around Blackpool aimlessly, unable to go home and climb into bed while the world was crumbling around him.

The door, in the arcade stockroom, it had been there, he was sure of it. He'd gripped the bloody handle and shook it, for God's sake. But then it hadn't been there before it had been. It had just been a wall, like it was again now. He leaned his forehead against the steering wheel of his car and scrunched his eyes shut.

A sharp tap at the driver's side window made him jerk upright.

'You okay there, mate?'

Waterson turned to see a familiar uniformed officer bent over and looking through the window. Chris Farmer.

'Yup, fine, just… past my bedtime,' replied Waterson, pulling the key out of the ignition and stepping out into the police station car park to join Chris.

'On lates, too, eh?' asked Chris. 'Hard lines.'

'Yeah. Actually, I'm off duty, strictly speaking, but you know how it is with some cases. They rattle around in there and won't let you rest.' He tapped at his skull.

'Not me,' Chris replied. 'The minute I'm done, I'm done. Lock it up in the back room and check back on it in the morning.' He grinned good-naturedly and Waterson attempted to oblige in return, but by the look of Farmer's expression, didn't exactly pull it off.

'You sure you're okay?'

'Rabbit ears, does that mean anything to you?'

'Rabbit ears?'

'Yes.'

'Well, yeah. I mean... well, it means rabbit ears to me. The ears of rabbits.'

Waterson nodded and headed towards the station building.

'Get some kip, Waters, you need it!'

Waterson stopped and turned slowly. 'What did you call me?' but Chris Farmer was already away, hands in his pockets, a carefree whistle on his lips.

Waters.

Nobody ever called him that. He hated it. An Uncle, Uncle Fisher, used to call him that. Used to call him a lot of things. Waters reminded him of Uncle Fisher so he stopped anyone calling him it. Why would Chris Farmer call him—

Waters.

Waterson winced and shook his head. For a moment the world tilted and he had to lean against the wall, but as soon as it started it was over. Waterson straightened up and made his way into the station, filling up a plastic cup with water from the machine in reception, nodding at the officer manning the desk, and heading up the stairs to his desk.

It was sparsely populated at this hour, just Annie Lark in the far corner, buried in paperwork. DCI Jenner looked like he was in his office, too. Lights on but blinds drawn. Waterson sat behind his desk and finished the water, dropping the empty cup into the bin.

He looked to the empty desk. The one no one worked at but he was sure someone had. He ran his hands over the paper he'd doodled rabbit ears on.

Waters.

Waterson stood up sharply, his chair tumbling back and crashing to the floor.

Annie Lark looked round from the other side of the room. 'You okay, Dan?'

'Someone… someone did use that desk!' he replied, stabbing a finger at the always empty desk.

DCI Jenner's office door opened and he stepped out. 'What's the fuss out here?'

Waterson pointed at the empty desk again.

'Aren't you off the clock, Waters?' asked Jenner.

Waterson staggered back like he'd just been punched in the brain.

'Red hair!' he said.

DCI Jenner looked, understandably, confused. He turned to Annie Lark, who shrugged her shoulders.

'She had red hair. Loads of it.' Waterson grabbed the chair to the always empty desk and shoved it at his boss. 'She had red hair and sat in this chair behind that desk and she was my partner.'

Jenner stopped the chair as it rolled towards him and began pushing it back to its desk. 'Who had red hair?'

Waterson opened his mouth to reply, but it wasn't quite there yet. It was almost in the open, if he just kept chasing it, he'd tease the whole thing out. He began to pace the office, arms outstretched, hands grasping. It was as though he were chasing a thread… a thread attached to an answer, a thread that—if he could only catch the end of it—would let him pull the whole bloody truth into view.

'I don't know, a woman! My partner, why don't I have a partner? I did have, I know I did, and she sat there and she had red hair and she called me "Waters" every bloody day because she knew it drove me mental. And the dreams, nightmares, there was stuff about nightmares and rabbit ears and masks and it was all there and then it was gone.'

Jenner frowned again and looked down at the always empty desk. 'Now you mention it… that does sound… familiar…' he winced and placed a palm on his temple.

'Yes!' said Waterson, face manic with delight. 'I'm not crazy, something's happened and we've all forgotten her. How could we forget her? How could I?'

'Forget who?' said a fearful looking Annie Lark.

Waterson pulled out his mobile phone and began scrolling through the contacts; and then there it was. A name. A name he was sure hadn't been there the last time he looked. He walked over to DCI Jenner and showed him the name on screen.

'Rita bloody Hobbes!' said Waterson.

Carlisle woke with a jolt.

He sat up on the threadbare couch and sniffed through his elegant nose.

'Big Pins,' he said, his voice a croak.

There was a bottle of water by his feet. He picked it up, unscrewed the cap, and drank the lot without pausing for breath.

Carlisle looked down at his open shirt, at the paleness of his chest, and feathered his fingers over the pink scar that shone like a neon light. He'd always been a fast healer. She'd retrieved him, clearly. Rita had retrieved his body from the home of Mr. Cotton and Mr. Spike and given his life back to him.

Carlisle tried to stand, to push himself up on to his feet, but his arms wobbled and then gave out, causing him to slump back and gasp for air.

He'd died several times in his long existence, and coming back to life never got any easier. His bones positively throbbed with pain. His eyes stabbed by every light, every colour. His mind a jangle of metal chimes caught in strong winds.

But he was alive. It made him uncomfortable, putting his life in the hands of another, especially the hands of someone like Rita Hobbes, but needs must on occasion.

He'd made his way to their home and he'd gotten them to tell him the truth. People, even monsters, were always more willing to share when they were sure the person they were talking to was about to die at their feet.

Carlisle smiled, but the muscles in his face hurt, so he stopped.

It had been a gamble, but one worth taking. Of course, he'd had no idea whether the detective would be able to retrieve him without stumbling into a similar fate as his own, but sometimes a roll of the dice makes life more interesting.

Outside, sat with Formby the eaves, Rita Hobbes was trying to take in the news.

'You are clearly bullshitting me,' she said.

'I am not, I do not bullshit. Actually, that isn't true, but in this case I don't.'

'So I'm an angel?'

'No.'

Rita felt like wrapping her hands around Formby's thick, bristly neck. 'You just said I was!'

'Well, you are.'

Rita let out a little scream.

'I mean to say, you are a bit. About 0.0003 percent of people are. Back in the day, angels used to come down here and fraternise, y'see. Like sailors on leave. Dirty sods.'

'So, you're saying some great, great, great relative of mine did the nasty with an angel, and a bit of that DNA, or whatever, has been passed on to me?'

Formby nodded and pushed aside his empty glass to reach over to take Rita's, only to be met with a slap on his knuckles.

Rita picked up her drink and took a mouthful. 'Well, this is huge. No, bigger than huge. Detective Rita Hobbes, angel.'

'A little bit angel.'

'More angel than you, sunshine.'

Formby spread his arms and nodded.

'Ha! Angel. A bloody angel. And Miss Havers at the children's home said I'd never amount to anything. Showed you, you saggy-faced old bitch.'

The door behind the bar opened and Carlisle walked out, slow and stiff.

'Carlisle,' said Rita, vaulting the bar to greet him.

'If you're looking for a thank you,' said Carlisle, 'don't bother. It was the least you could do.'

'You're welcome.'

Carlisle grimaced, then winced.

'Guess what?' said Rita.

'No.'

'I'm only a sodding Angel! Ha!'

Rita had never seen such a look of honest surprise spread across Carlisle's face. She rather enjoyed it.

'I beg your pardon?'

'Well,' said Formby, shuffling over, Rita's abandoned pint glass in his hand, 'little bit angel, from a long way back. Not much use, other than being able to handle weapons fashioned in Heaven, of course.'

Carlisle frowned. 'The axe.'

Rita grinned and held it aloft. 'The axe. You know, it's thanks to this bad boy that you're stood there now. Completely twatted both of those mask-wearing freaks with it. You should have seen me, complete bad-ass.'

'I'm... delighted for you,' replied Carlisle, wincing as he lowered himself on to a bar stool.

'Still coming round, eh?' asked Formby.

'I will be fine given a little time, this is not my first death.'

Rita snatched her drink back from a grumbling Formby, and downed the remainder in one. 'Bloody part angel,' she said, sitting next to Carlisle at the bar.

'Congratulations,' he replied, in a way that suggested he meant no such thing. 'No doubt it was that element of your being that also befuddled the hex so.'

'A lot of surprising stuff has happened recently, but me being a teensy bit angelic? That's definitely top of the pile.'

It was at this point that Rita's mobile phone began to ring. Rita, Carlisle, and Formby looked to her coat pocket, blankly.

'I think that's my phone ringing,' she said.

'It would seem so,' replied Carlisle.

'So what should I do?'

'I'm no expert,' said Carlisle, 'but I believe people usually answer them.'

Rita reached into her pocket and gingerly retrieved her ringing phone.

A name flashed on screen.

Rita pressed *answer*. 'Um, hello?' she said.

'Yeah, uh, hello. Hi. Is this… are you Rita Hobbes?'

'Maybe,' said Rita, heart beating like a speed metal band's double kick bass drum.

'This might sound weird, but… did we used to be partners?'

Rita smiled as she felt a tear race down her cheek.

25

It was close to three in the morning, the moon high, and Blackpool seafront was deserted.

'This is a bad idea,' said Carlisle, for perhaps the tenth time.

Rita pulled her car to a stop and killed the engine. 'It's Waterson, my friend, my partner.'

'And he should not know that you even exist. As far as ordinary people like him are concerned, you do not.'

'We were best friends, for years, isn't it just possible that some memory of me stayed lodged in there and he, I don't know, shook it free?'

Carlisle frowned, 'It is... possible. I suppose.'

Rita felt like a child on Christmas Eve. The hex, the stupid magic some murdering bastard in a goat mask had inflicted on her, had erased her from everyday life. The only chance to have it lifted being to, apparently, kill the person behind it. Rita wasn't a killer. She didn't think she was, anyway. She took criminals to prison. They didn't get the escape of death. They lived through their guilt with their liberty taken.

But then she'd never been hexed before.

Trapped, only "alive" in an Uncanny between world. Able to walk around the streets like everyone else did, but only as a phantom. A dream forgotten once awake. Her full existence for the Magician's life, that was the only chance she had, according to Carlisle, and maybe she'd have found herself having to make that choice, but now?

Now her best friend had called her and she was about to meet him for a chat on the beach. Maybe there would be another way after all.

As she stepped out of the car, the cold biting at her, she rested her hand on the axe, tucked into the belt of her trousers. Even through the material of her coat, she felt the tickle of the magic it held prickle her skin.

Carlisle let out a muffled noise as he stiffly got out of the car and straightened up, joints cracking.

'Are you sure you're up for this?' asked Rita. 'I've got the axe, I'm okay.'

'No, you are not. If anything happens and you lose that axe, then I will be very upset. So if you insist on this foolhardy venture, it will be with me at your back.'

'Aw, I'm starting to think you only love me for what I've got in my pants,' said Rita, patting the axe as Carlisle frowned. 'Come on,' she said, nodding for him to follow as she started towards the steps leading down to the beach itself.

As the two stepped onto the beach, Carlisle narrowed his eyes at the distant sea, pulled away by the moon. 'God, I hate this place so,' he said.

'What was it like?' Rita asked.

'Be more specific, Detective,' replied Carlisle.

'Death. What was it like, being dead?'

'Like talking to you on Blackpool beach.'

Rita mimed hysterical laughter. 'Come on, Pasty, I'm serious. You were actually dead. Dead-dead. What was it like? Can you remember? I mean, if there's a Heaven, then I'm assuming there's a place you go, so…'

Carlisle sighed but kept his eyes on the ocean. 'Death is different for different kinds of beings.'

'Well, what was it like for your kind of being?'

Carlisle frowned but did not reply as the wind toyed with the hem of his dark purple coat.

Rita sensed it best not to push the point any further. 'You still haven't said, by the way.'

'What I found out from Cotton and Spike?'

'You did find out something, right?'

Carlisle nodded, 'I did. I discovered whose hand is behind all of this.'

'The Magician? Well, who is it?'

'No. The power *behind* the Magician. The real power. There is a story, or a myth, or a lie, about a creature of pure darkness, imprisoned beneath the waves. A creature that raged and screamed and fought against its bonds. Bonds fashioned in Heaven itself. The creature could not be cowed or killed, so a prison it had to be. It would seem that this creature, this horror, is a reality. That it lives and it has, at last, been able to influence an ally.'

'Well, crap. None of that sounds good.'

Carlisle smiled, 'No. It is very un-good indeed.'

'So what is it, exactly? This creature?'

'One of the original seven angels created by God to sit at His almighty side.'

'An angel? Like me?'

'You are not an angel.'

'I am a little bit.'

'My calling you an angel would be like saying this beach was an angel, because six grains of sand that lay upon it were actually skin cells from a passing celestial being.'

'Well, I'm still more angel than you are.'

'Most are,' replied Carlisle, with a wry smile. The smile faltered. 'I believe he is here.'

Rita turned to see DS Waterson nervously approaching along the beach. She smiled and waved. Waterson raised a hand to return the wave, stopped, and shoved the un-waved hand into his coat pocket.

'Hey!' said Rita.

'Hi. Hello,' replied Waterson, his eyes drifting over to Carlisle, who was ignoring him, keeping his eyes on the sea. 'Who's that?'

'A friend,' said Rita. 'Well, not a friend, a person. Not a person. Sort of a person. He's someone I know.'

'Right.'

'It's... good to see you,' said Rita. 'And really good that you can see me. Obviously.' Rita felt daft, like she was sixteen and on a blind date.

'How is that you can remember her?' asked Carlisle.

'I don't know. I mean, I just remembered that I'd forgotten something. And it itched at me. And then, today, bang, there she was.'

'Bang, there I was,' said Rita, grinning.

'So, you were my partner?' asked Waterson.

'You don't know?' Rita replied.

'I know. I sort of know. It's all a bit foggy and unsure, but it's coming back to me, little by little. We were friends, right?'

Rita smiled. 'Best friends, Waters.'

'Well this is all very touching, but we actually have a case to solve. Impossible monsters to deal with, that sort of thing,' said Carlisle.

'The case,' said Waterson. 'This case, with the women, what happened to you, it's something to do with the case, isn't it?'

'Okay,' said Rita, 'this is all gonna sound like madness with a crazy side salad, but if you can accept that weird shit is definitely going on, then it's time we upgraded from Mulder and Scully to a pair of Mulders, right?'

'If you say so.'

Carlisle sighed and pinched the bridge of his nose. 'What has become of me? I once ruled a nation.'

'There's a magician, and a giant imprisoned angel, or something, and they're the ones taking and killing the women. Sacrificing them. Follow?'

'Follow,' replied Waterson.

'I got hexed saving Gemma Wheeler, and this hex, this magic, made me sort of disappear. No one could see me, or remember me.'

'Okay. Right. That is... a lot.'

'Yup.'

'So why are they doing all this? What's the point?'

'To get free, right?' said Rita, turning to Carlisle.

'In part. I imagine that is just step one, though.'

'So what's step two?' asked Rita.

'Perhaps your friend here, who can now conveniently both see and remember you, can fill us in on the remainder?'

Waterson shook his head. 'What are you talking about? All I know is what Rita's just told me.'

'How do I know you're not the secretive Magician in league with the Angel of Blackpool?' said Carlisle.

'Carlisle, he's not evil, he's my friend,' said Rita.

'Luring this gullible wretch out into the open to finally dispatch her, take what is rightfully mine, so that you and the beast in the sea can complete your gambit? Answer me, boy!'

Dan Waterson opened his mouth to reply, then his eyebrows scrunched and his jaw moved soundlessly.

'Dan?' said Rita.

Waterson looked to her, confusion rippling across his face. He coughed, and red trickled down his chin.

'Shit, Dan, what's wrong with—'

Blood burst from Waterson's chest as a thick blade erupted through his rib cage.

'Waters!' said Rita, stumbling back in shock as his blood splattered her front.

As the blade was pulled back and disappeared from view, Waterson staggered forward, his hands catching on Rita's shoulders.

'Shit,' said Dan Waterson. 'Rita, I think I've been…' And then he fell to the ground, stone dead.

Where he had stood there was now a figure in scarlet robes and a goat mask, a bloodied blade in a leather-gloved hand. He ran the blade across his robes, wiping it clean of Dan Waterson's blood.

Rita was frozen, crouched by Waterson's lifeless body. 'Come on, Waters,' she said, rocking his shoulder with one hand. 'Stop playing silly beggars.'

Waterson didn't reply, didn't move, didn't stand.

'Magician,' said Carlisle.

The Magician took off his mask, with its winding goat horns, and Rita looked up into a familiar face.

'Hello, Rita,' said DCI Alexander Jenner.

'Hey, Guv,' replied Rita.

26

Rita could still remember the first day she'd met Dan Waterson.

The awkward early chats as they got to know each other as partners, as friends. The endless stakeouts, the mockery of each other's often disastrous love lives. The good times.

Now he was curled up on Blackpool beach, dead, his blood splattered across her front, her hands soaked in it.

'So you decided to step out of the shadows at last?' said Carlisle.

The Magician, DCI Alexander Jenner, smiled and nodded. 'What did you do to Cotton and Spike?' he asked.

'Would that I could claim responsibility, but I'm rather afraid that it was your erstwhile subordinate here that has, for the time being, sent them into hiding. Your muscle has deserted you. They are gone to lick their wounds.'

'They are just tools. Hands.' Jenner opened his palms and electricity, forks of orange fury, danced from finger to finger. 'I have access to a far greater power.'

Rita brushed aside tears, the blood on her hands smearing across her cheek. She stood, teeth clenching. 'You. You killed those women.'

Rita was repulsed to see something close to regret, to shame, move across Jenner's face. 'It was… necessary.'

Carlisle could feel the power, feel the magic that rolled invisibly around and through Jenner. Power like he'd never sensed before. He should abandon this folly, he knew. He was no hero, this was the detective's fight. He was weak, still too close to his death to fight at full tilt, and even if he hadn't been, this man, this magician, was tapping into magic far beyond his ken.

He muttered a power word or two under his breath, and then he could see it. See a dark smoke trail that weaved lazily from Jenner and out across the waves.

An umbilical cord to the Angel of Blackpool.

The ageless, patient beast in its prison, feeding its strength to this mortal man. This ordinary thing without access to magic of his own. To the Uncanny world.

He should turn and run.

The Angel and the magician, they wanted nothing from him. All they wanted was for their work to continue, and for that to happen they required the axe. They would take it, and they would most likely turn Rita Hobbes into a grim confetti.

But it was *his* axe.

His artefact.

How he ached at the thought of holding it again. For it to accept him. React to him. To give him everything his hungry heart demanded. He had been someone with that artefact. Someone more than the liar, the feared, the untrustworthy criminal.

And so he stayed.

'I see your connection to the Angel of Blackpool,' he said, and touched Rita's shoulder. Now she she could see it too.

'We have a joint purpose. A great duty,' replied Jenner.

Rita looked, wide-eyed, at the black smoke that coiled and weaved around DCI Jenner. That stretched from him and away across the sea.

'You have no magic in you,' said Carlisle. 'You are nothing. Less than nothing. A duped fool. A hapless tool.'

Jenner stepped forward, fury twisting his face. 'No! I am *someone*. I am *important*! I will make God Himself tremble!'

Carlisle snorted contemptuously. 'And people say that *I* am full of myself.'

Rita threw her coat open and pulled the axe from where it hung against her leg.

'This what you want, is it?' she said, her voice a snarl.

'Be careful,' said Carlisle, the ache in his stomach throbbing, pushing him to make a useless grab for the axe. He resisted.

'Well,' said Rita, 'isn't this what you need, to carry on your "necessary" work?'

'Give it to me.' Jenner reached for the axe and Rita stepped back.

'No, no, if you want it, you murdering piece of shit, you're gonna have to take it from me. And the only way you're gonna do that is if I'm dead.'

'Okay then.' Jenner's eyes turned black, as though twin pools of ink had been dropped into them.

Carlisle felt the change in the air around them. Saw the smokey umbilical cord thicken, become denser, as more power was fed from prison to man.

'I see a dusting of Heaven in you,' came a voice from Jenner's mouth. It was not the voice of Jenner himself. It was rich and thick and it made Rita's hands tremble.

'We are now speaking with the Angel of Blackpool, I presume?' asked Carlisle.

'Hexed and hunted and attacked, and yet still she persists,' said the Angel, almost, it seemed to Rita, in admiration.

'Yeah, I'm annoying like that,' she said.

'And in countless other ways,' added Carlisle.

The world around them began to shimmer.

'Look,' said Rita, pointing out to sea. A great shadow hung over the ocean in the distance. A shape. A hulking, writhing beast. A thing of horror that made Rita's mind want to retreat. Want to deny.

'Perhaps we can speak in person,' said the Angel, and Jenner reached out to touch both Rita and Carlisle.

The world shuddered and moved out of focus and the sound of the beast gibbering in a million forgotten tongues filled the air.

And then silence.

Rita opened her eyes to find herself in a cold, vaulted chamber. Giant marble columns, thicker than ancient redwoods, stretched from floor to ceiling all around them, and millions of candles flickered, lighting the place. The space was perfectly silent, as though a sound had not been made within its walls for centuries.

'What is this? A church, a crypt?' asked Rita.

'No,' replied Carlisle, 'a prison.'

He strode forward, Rita catching up, their footfalls on the stone floor echoing. They rounded a column and found the Angel of Blackpool waiting for them.

It stood inside a glass box and wore brilliantly white robes. It had an easy smile upon its face, and its hair was thick and golden. It was the most beautiful thing Rita had ever seen.

'God could have provided a chair, at the very least,' said Carlisle, and the Angel laughed. It sounded to Rita like songbirds.

'Where is this?' she asked.

'Under the ocean,' replied the Angel, 'and between reality and reality and reality. Folded away. Forgotten. Ignored. Impossible.'

'Well, that clears that up,' said Rita.

The Angel unleashed its songbird laughter once again. 'What have you done to my friends, Mr. Cotton and Mr. Spike, I wonder?'

'What's wrong, aren't they picking up the phone?' asked Carlisle.

The Angel looked troubled, just for a moment.

'Ah, a limit to your power,' said Carlisle. 'You can't reach into their dreamscape, can you?'

The Angel turned its attention to Rita, who felt the warmth of its gaze. 'I had wondered why the artefact accepted you,' he said, 'and now I know. A weapon of Heaven, in the hands of the divine.'

'You should see me when I've had time to do my makeup properly.'

'You did not know of your ancestry for such a long time. Another of the creator's ignored flock. Tell me, what was it like to grow up alone, without family, with people paid to care? People who could not hide that they did not?'

'Ignore it,' said Carlisle. 'It is trying to get its hooks into you.'

'Carlisle,' said the Angel, 'I have often heard whispers of you. Oh, the things you have done, and yet you would judge me?'

'I judge everyone, it's sort of my thing,' he replied, grinning. 'Tell me, you've been imprisoned here for millennia, silent and alone—'

'So how did I make a connection with Alexander Jenner?'

Carlisle bowed his head.

The Angel smiled. 'It took… patience. Effort. Have you ever heard the story of the bird that sharpened its beak on the diamond mountain, until, after an eternity, the entire mountain was chiselled away?'

'No,' said Rita. 'I'm more of a soap opera girl, myself.'

'I tapped, and I tapped, and I tapped,' said the Angel, 'and finally, a little of myself broke through. Just a little, but enough. I reached out and found a sad little boy, wronged by God, and we became… friends.'

'Having to reach out to a mortal for help, you must have been desperate,' said Carlisle.

A snarl broke the Angel's beauty as it bashed its fists against its glass cage and the candlelight shook, casting nightmare shadows around the chamber.

'Do not mock me, thief.'

'You stand there, a thing of beauty, but that is not the real you,' said Carlisle. 'We saw the true shape of your soul out there, as we stood upon the beach. A thing of endless horror, casting a shadow of despair.'

The Angel's breathing slowed and it regained its composure. 'What you see as horror, I see as splendour. For what is a being realising its full potential, if not a thing of beauty?'

'Why have you brought us here?' asked Rita.

'Yes, I was rather wondering that myself.'

'I had hoped to appeal to your better judgement, Rita Hobbes.'

'Oh, right, then go right ahead, mate.'

'You have suffered, as have I.'

'I've had a few knocks along the way, yeah.'

'You, part Angel, and yet still punished by a creator who does not care for your pain. Your anguish. You fight against me, but I am not your enemy.'

'That right, is it?'

'You believe in justice.'

Rita looked at him with hooded eyes. 'Yeah. So.'

'Then help me get it. For myself. For Alexander Jenner. For yourself. For the whole of existence that has stood cold as its creator turned His back upon them. Every day, children die, and nobody cares. The innocent become sick and suffer slow, agonising deaths. Hurricanes sweep up unopposed and crash against the living, leaving anguish in their wash.'

Rita stepped closer to the glass cage.

'Rita,' said Carlisle, reaching out, but she batted his hand aside.

The Angel spoke. 'The elderly are abandoned and abused and He *does. Not. Care*. He is the true monster, and He must face the consequences of His inaction.'

'My life. My life has been His fault?'

'From conception to now. It could have been different.'

'It *should* have been.'

'Rita…' said Carlisle.

'Well It's right, in a way, isn't It?'

The Angel smiled.

'No, It's not. It's evil.'

'But then what does that make God?'

Carlisle shrugged, 'An arsehole?'

'The fear, the loneliness,' said Rita, 'feeling always unwanted and in the way. That was my childhood.'

'Yes, I know the sob story,' replied Carlisle.

'You see, you understand,' said the Angel to Rita.

'Yeah, I think I understand. And you know what I think?' asked Rita.

'What?'

Rita pressed her palms against the glass cage and grinned. 'I think you're so full of shit it's a wonder you're not drowning in there.'

Carlisle smirked, then caught himself. 'My apologies. Well, it was lovely to drop in for a visit; we really mustn't do it again some time. Detective, let us take our leave.'

'Sounds good to me.'

'You shall not leave,' said the Angel.

'Oh, we shall,' replied Carlisle.

'I do not allow it.'

'Not big on being told what to do, mate,' said Rita.

'I am taking us out of this sad place, to another, well, very sad place,' said Carlisle.

'Aren't we going back to Blackpool?'

'Indeed.'

'Oh. Right. Good one.'

'You are weak,' said the Angel. 'You have little power in you now. A strong wind would bend you double.'

'True, but I always make sure I have a card up my sleeve.'

Carlisle reached into his coat and pulled out a small pouch tied with string. 'Rita!' he reached out and grabbed her hand as the Angel raged within its glass cage. Carlisle knew this would cost him—that the effort would bring him to his knees—but he would have to take the risk.

'Is that a bomb?' asked Rita.'

'Quiet, fool,' replied Carlisle.

'Oh, very nice.'

Carlisle gathered up as much magic as his body could stand —his every nerve-ending screaming in agony—and muttered the incantation. He threw the pouch at the ground as the Angel began screaming in a million ancient languages, and the prison whipped from view. The world around them tumbled and twirled, but he held tight to Rita's hand as she screamed, because if he let go, she might be lost forever. Finally the whirl of reality slowed and they fell to the ground.

'Holy shit…' said Rita, sitting up.

Carlisle attempted to push himself up, the pain excruciating.

Rita rolled on to her knees and helped him up. 'Are you okay?'

'I'm fine,' he replied, sharply, then sagged. 'I'm not fine. It is too soon since my death, and that spell, that was some extreme magic.'

Sweat dripped from Carlisle's pale face. The whites of his eyes were now a blood-red.

'You're not going to die again, are you?'

Carlisle chuckled, then regretted it as his chest screamed in agony. 'I am afraid not, Detective, but the life in me is weak, the magic weaker still. We must retreat to safety until I regain my strength.'

Rita stood, helping Carlisle up to his feet. 'Can you walk?' she asked.

'Yes. I can walk,' Carlisle replied, though he wasn't sure how true that was.

Rita looked around to see where they'd ended up, and recognised the entrance to the Night Fair behind them. Carlisle's magic hadn't taken them far.

'So, we just had a chat with an evil angel?' said Rita.

'Indeed.'

'Well, they always say you can judge a person on the quality of their enemies.'

'They do.'

'And that thing is a shitting doozy. So well done us, I say.'

'You are a blithering fool, Detective.'

'Yes, I am,' she replied, grinning.

Carlisle took an experimental step forward and was delighted to find that his legs did not betray him.

'So, any ideas?' asked Rita.

'Always.'

'Okay, Mr Big Head, care to share?'

'The Magician, your erstwhile boss, is connected to the Angel of Blackpool.'

'The smoke thing?' said Rita, recalling the umbilical cord of black smoke that had stretched from Jenner and out over the ocean.

'That is what is feeding magic, feeding power, to the Magician.'

'So we've gotta find a way to cut the cord.'

'Precisely.'

'Okay, well, how'd we do that?'

He smiled and turned to Rita.

'We must—' began Carlisle, but his words cut off as a ball of fire struck him, and his body shot back and away.

Rita reached out to him, calling his name, but he was gone. She looked up to see Alexander Jenner, scarlet robes billowing, floating towards her within a corona of flames, his eyes still ink-black.

'What did you do!' she said, axe gripped in her hands.

'I asked nicely, now I will take,' replied the Angel within its Jenner puppet.

'Come on then you big… idiot!' Rita had hoped for bolder words, but that would have to do.

Jenner's face smiled and he rubbed his hands together, great swirls of purple and yellow and blue, crackling into life.

'Time to die, Detective.' He punched out a hand and the magic burst from it.

Rita leapt to one side as it struck the spot where she had been standing. Not pausing to look back, she rolled on to her feet and ran for the Night Fair's gate, only to find it locked. 'Great, a night Fair that closes when it's actually night!'

'There is nowhere to run to, Detective. Nowhere to hide. Not anymore. The end is here and the work must continue. God must be punished.'

Rita fell backwards just in time to doge another blast of lethal magic, which smashed into the gates, blowing them apart.

'Thanks!'

She raced through the shattered gates and into the Night Fair, darting from path to path between empty stalls, always taking the next turn, trying not to give Jenner, or the Angel piloting him, a clear line of sight. Not that this stopped it from continuing to attack, as spell after spell erupted from his hands and stalls burst into flames all around her.

'Shit, shit, shit,' said Rita, looking back over her shoulder and seeing Jenner floating into view, eyes pitch-black, a serene smile upon his face.

'I believe I will kill you slowly,' said the Angel through Jenner.

'No thanks,' replied Rita, right before she found herself at a dead end. 'Oh, bollocks.'

She turned, grasping the axe, as Jenner in his corona of flames hoved into view, blocking any escape. 'DCI Jenner, please, listen to me!' she cried.

The ground a few feet in front of her exploded, showering her with dirt.

'Come on, you're in there, you're a good man, you don't need to carry on with this!'

Light burst from Jenner's hand, and Rita instinctively swung out with the axe, connecting with the oncoming magic.

She felt its purpose roll through her. Magic meant to destroy. To hurt. To decimate. It was hers now, and as she swung the axe again, she sent it back to where it had come from. It shot from the axe head as she screamed, and struck Jenner in the chest, sending him flying backwards as if he was tied to a bungee cord.

'Eat shit,' she said, then ran back the way she'd came, escaping the dead end.

She wasn't powerless, wasn't helpless. This axe gave her power. Power to capture and to control magic, to understand it and turn it against the person who would use it against her. Rita smiled, almost laughed. She wasn't going to carry on running. Dan Waterson was dead, and the person responsible for that was in here, in the Night Fair, with her, and she was going to do her damndest to bring him to justice.

'Hey, big scary Angel, where are you? Come to mamma!' Rita sounded brave, bold, but her stomach still churned and her heart beat-beat-beat.

She whirled round to see Jenner walking towards her.

'Oh, decided to stop the flying bit, have you?' she asked.

'You are alone,' he said, the Angel's voice emerging from Jenner's mouth.

'A girl is never alone with a chip on her shoulder and a magic hatchet in her hands,' she replied, raising the weapon up, ready to fend off whatever came her way.

Jenner just smiled.

'You can repel an attack or two, perhaps even three, but I will get you. Beat you down. It's just a question of time, and I am immortal. I've all the time in existence.'

He flung another ball of crackling magic at her and Rita

gasped, swinging at it, taking control of it, and sending it back in the direction it came from. But Jenner, the Angel, was ready this time, and casually swatted the returned magic aside.

A food stand burst into flames. He was right. *It* was right. But Rita had no intention of standing her ground and seeing how many balls she could hit before she was out.

'The Magician, your erstwhile boss, is connected to the Angel of Blackpool.'

'The smoke thing?'

'That is what is feeding magic, feeding power, to the Magician.'

'So we've gotta find a way to cut the cord.'

She flexed her fingers around the hilt of the axe and searched for it. Called to it. Demanded it did as she wished.

There it was.

More magic flew at her, thrown contemptuously, and she returned it with a cry of effort.

Mr. Cotton and Mr. Spike, hidden in their dreamscape. That was her one hope. Her one chance.

'I have toyed with you long enough,' said the Angel.

Rita ignored it.

Instead, she began to speak with the axe, not in words, but in thoughts, in feelings, in understanding.

It held the magic still.

The magic she had taken when she struck Mr. Spike.

The magic she had not yet used.

It was dark magic, she could sense that. Magic from a bleak place of nightmares and pain. And it was hers to use.

The Angel lifted Jenner's arms and a storm of angry magic swarmed around him. Flames burst into life around him and he floated once more, levitating slowly into the air. He was laughing. That birdsong laugh, but it no longer sounded beautiful. It sounded wrong. It sounded cruel.

It was almost the end.

But not in the way the Angel expected.

Rita spoke with her axe, with the dark magic that raged within. She soothed it and it responded to her request.

It built a prison.

The flames around Jenner's body died in an instant, and he

dropped to the ground, crashing down to his hands and knees in surprise.

'It's over,' said Rita.

He looked up at her with wide, confused eyes. The eyes were no longer ink-black. 'What... wh-what have you done?' he asked in his own voice, his actual voice, not the Angel's.

'I've done my job,' replied Rita. 'I've caught the murderer and put him away.' She walked slowly towards him and Jenner fell back onto his rear, scrambling away from her, terrified, until his back hit against the side of a stall. He looked around, confused.

'Yeah, still the Night Fair,' said Rita. 'Well, sort of. It's not the actual Night Fair, this is one me and axe here made.'

'I don't... I don't understand...'

'I took Mr. Spike's magic, or a piece of it, anyway, and that pair, they can create little, like, dreamscapes. Little places cut off from the real world. So that's what I did. Quicker just to copy where we were in the first place. Now this is all there is for you. This Night Fair. There isn't anything past the fences, past the gate. Just this place.'

'Angel?' said Jenner, grabbing the edge of the stand's counter and pulling himself to his feet. 'Angel, talk to me. Please, talk to me!'

Rita almost felt sorry for him, he looked so pathetic.

Almost.

'It can't hear you. Can't get to you. It's reach doesn't extend into here, into a dreamscape, I'm afraid, Guv. The blabbermouth thing sort of let that slip. Careless, eh? But then arrogant twats like that always say more than they should. Can't help themselves.'

Jenner fell back to the dirt, tears streaming down his face. 'No... no... I need it... it's not in my head anymore, not in my head...'

'And neither is your connection to magic,' she said, crouching by him. 'That was all the Angel, now it's just you again. Sorry. Well, not sorry. Not at all, really.'

'You don't understand, I'm a good man.'

'And how do you work that one out, genius?'

'We were going to punish God. For killing my mum. My dad.

He deserves it.' Jenner made a grab for Rita, but she struck him on the forehead with the butt of the axe and he stumbled to the ground face-first, blood streaming from his forehead. He rolled on to his back, crying.

'Angel… please… talk to me… help me…'

'Those women. Dan Waterson. You're guilty, and this is where you'll rot. Hey, now you've got a prison, and your crazy Angel pal has a prison. Nice how that balances out, isn't it?'

Rita stood and walked to the Night Fair's gate.

'You can't leave me in here!'

'I bloody well can, Guv.'

And she walked out of the gate, and back into the real world.

27

Rita was lining up a bowling ball, one eye closed, scoping out the pins at the end of the aisle, when Carlisle walked through the door into Big Pins and joined her.

'So you're not dead?' he said.

'You neither,' replied Rita, then rolled the ball, swinging out her right leg for balance. It shot down the aisle and cleared the pins in one.

'Get in!' she said, giving herself a celebratory fist pump. Rita turned and sat opposite Carlisle, taking a sip of her drink. She could feel Carlisle's eyes on the axe as it dangled from her belt.

'What happened to you then?' she asked.

'Knocked out for a few hours. And how about you?'

'Just closed the case. Bad guy locked up. Connection to evil angel severed. And all was well in the world. Or Blackpool at least. For a bit.'

'You are still hexed.'

Rita frowned, then shrugged and took another sip from her ale.

'So the Magician is not dead?' asked Carlisle.

'I'm not a killer,' she replied.

'Then where is he?'

'In prison. Safe from the Angel's magic.'

'I asked where?'

'I told you. Prison.'

'Then you will remain in this state, trapped in Blackpool and hidden from the ordinary world.'

'Seems so.'

'I could kill him for you.'

'Yeah, but I'm not sure I'm cool with that, either. I want him to serve his time. His life sentence. That's justice.'

Carlisle snarled and swept the glasses from the table. 'We had a deal.'

'I'm sorry,' she replied. 'I can't just… he was being used. Influenced. Pushed. Ever since he was a kid.'

'Oh, so he lives because of what? Diminished responsibility?'

'Yeah. If you like. That thing, that Angel, used him. Moulded him. He deserves justice, he doesn't deserve death.'

'That artefact is mine. Give it to me.'

Rita placed her hand protectively on the butt of the axe. 'I can't.'

Carlisle flinched towards her, his face a mask of anger, and for a second she thought he might attack her. 'It belongs to me,' he said through clenched teeth. 'I helped you. I died for you. It is my property.'

Rita dropped her head then looked up at Carlisle, into his fierce eyes. 'Until I know how to get out of all of this, I need it. It's staying with me.' She gripped the axe's hilt. 'So, will you help me?'

Carlisle straightened out his long, dark purple coat, then turned on his heel and walked out of Big Pins.

Rita sagged back and blew, trying to get rid of the tension.

Formby shuffled over from a corner and joined her. 'May I?' he said.

'Sure.'

Formby took her drink and downed it.

'I thought you meant 'may I sit down', but okay.'

'You might have made yourself a bit of an enemy in Carlisle, Detective,' said Formby, scratching at his round, stubbled face.

'He'll come around,' she said. She wasn't sure she believed herself though.

'And the Angel. You cut off its access to the magician, but don't think that'll be that.'

Rita waved until she caught Linton's attention. 'Two pints here, mate.'

Linton gave a little salute and got to it.

'Then maybe that's what I've got to do. Take down an angel gone bad. It wasn't Jenner's magic that even did this to me, the hex. It was the Angel's magic. Maybe… maybe if I stop the Angel, the hex will go away and I can go back to my life.'

'Maybe. Wasn't much of a life to start with though, was it?'

'Oi! It was okay!'

'I hear lots, remember,' he said, exposing his piranha teeth with a big grin.

'Charming. You know, it was okay, actually. Bits of it. Sometimes.'

'Really?'

Rita stuck her tongue out at Formby and took her pint from Linton. She'd wanted something different. Something new. Anything new. And yeah, maybe she was stuck, literally, in Blackpool, but hadn't she got her wish? Sort of? Okay, it wasn't ideal, but what in life is?

Rita sat back and patted her magic axe as she sipped a pint within a bowling alley that catered to monsters and the magical.

Yeah.

This was certainly different to her usual.

The Angel sat with its legs crossed on the floor of its glass prison, and it concentrated.

It tapped. It tapped. It tapped.

This was just a minor setback.

It would take time, but more chances would come.

Yes, all it would take was time.

And the Angel of Blackpool had all of eternity on its side.

The End.

FATAL MOON

1

There was an angel.

It stood in a glass prison beneath the sea by a faded coastal town.

A story. A lie. A truth.

The Blackpool Angel.

Perhaps it had always been there, imprisoned, before the Earth had even formed. Perhaps the rocks and the trees and the seawater just happened to meet where the Angel's prison stood.

That is what some thought. Some of those that actually believed in the Angel. Believed in the prison and the reason the Angel was trapped within it.

Most who had heard the story did not believe it. To them, it was just a strange story to scare the children with on a bitter winter's eve.

The few that did believe were correct.

The Angel opened Its eyes and smiled as It contemplated Its prison. Contemplated the glass box It had been trapped within for so very, very long. Even for an Angel of the first order—one of the original seven created by God, to whom a millennia passed as nothing—the Angel felt the aeons It had been restrained.

It was to be punished for eternity.

That was God's will.

God's *justice*.

It had taken the Angel so very, very long to break through the glass box. To *tap-tap-tap* against the glass with the sharpened point of Its will. For just a little of Itself to be able to reach out and make a connection.

Alexander Jenner.

A grieving, angry child whose father had committed suicide. A tool to mould. To exploit. To ripen.

Mr. Cotton and Mr. Spike, too. Thugs. Monsters. The literal stuff of nightmares, available for a price.

They had heard and they had agreed and they had been used and all had been going well.

And then… the Detective.

But not to worry. Not to fear. The Blackpool Angel would not be so easily thwarted.

It lowered Itself down on to Its knees, the brilliant white robes It wore pooling on the cold marble floor, and It reached out.

It reached out, It strained, the effort almost making It break out into a sweat.

The Angel had a plan.

Always had a plan.

It had seen how the pieces had fallen, and It had looked ten steps ahead. Observed the final moves of the game. Seen them through the glass box of Its prison, through the cold marble room the prison sat within, through the sea that knew nothing of the Angel hiding beneath its waves, across the beach, and out, out, out.

The Angel's will extended, searched; an invisible root shooting through the soil, searching for nourishment.

Most heard nothing, but a few—a small, small few—heard. They heard, they listened, they spoke to others, and out it spread. A story. A message. A way out.

Carlisle and the Detective may have slowed things down, but the Angel knew.

Knew that soon enough It would step out of Its prison.

And then.

And then.

The Angel smiled and began to sing. Sing in a voice that

would have made the coldest of hearts weep with joy. Sing in a language that had not been spoken since the universe was young.

There was an angel.

And one day that angel would be free.

2

Rita Hobbes was feeling worse for wear. She tottered and swayed towards the front door of her house, digging through her coat pockets for the key, a magic axe patting against her right thigh with each stumbled step.

'Shit it,' she slurred, as she stared at the door's unfamiliar letterbox and realised she'd arrived at her neighbour's house. She leaned back against the door and looked up at the full moon, shining down on her from the black above. Returning her gaze to the ground, she pushed a snarl of red hair out of her face and tried to focus on a lamp post that seemed to be duplicating itself across the street.

Rita had good reason to be as drunk as she was.

Sure, there was the whole hex business. The fact that, after stumbling into the site of a sacrifice, she'd unwittingly triggered a magical boobytrap chalked on a stone floor. A magical boobytrap that had then proceeded to erase her from existence, or existence in normal society at least. Everyday people could no longer see her, feel her, hear her, and had, in all respects, forgotten she'd ever existed.

So that was one thing. A really pretty bad thing.

Then there was the fact she had been tossed at speed into a secret, Uncanny world of magic and mayhem. A world of wizards and living nightmares and monsters and just... well, non-stop weirdo crazy-balls stuff.

And then there was Dan Waterson.

Her friend, Detective Dan Waterson, her partner in the force for years, a man who'd always had her back.

And he was dead.

Murdered after he made the mistake of stepping into Rita's new world.

It had happened just hours ago. Rita had gone back to sit with his body after trapping DCI Jenner—her old boss, and Dan Waterson's killer—in a prison of her own creation. She'd sat alone with Waterson's corpse, crying as his blood soaked into the sand. She couldn't call for an ambulance thanks to the hex, and so she sat with her friend until a taxi driver waddled across the beach to take a piss, only to find himself distracted by a dead body at his feet.

After the ambulance had taken him away, Rita had headed to Big Pins, the bowling alley and drinking hole of the Uncanny of Blackpool. There she had drunk herself silly, trying to hide from what had just happened.

Just happened.

Rita rubbed her watery eyes with the heels of her hands and traipsed to the front door of her house. She let herself inside, slammed the door behind her, and made a wonky beeline for the stairs. She needed to sleep. To curl up in bed, pull the covers over her head, and shut out the world for a while.

But the world had other ideas.

Someone had redecorated Rita's house. Redecorated in a big way. Not one thing remained the same: not the wallpaper, not the furniture, and definitely not the pictures on the wall, which depicted a beaming young family; a mum, a dad, and a little boy with a bowl cut and missing front teeth.

All was different, all was new. The kitchen had even been knocked through to the living area to make a single, larger space. For a moment Rita wondered if she'd miscalculated and wandered into her other neighbour's house, but no, the key fit. This was her place.

She stumbled up the stairs, which had now been stripped

back to the wood and laid with a fancy runner carpet. She pushed open a door and looked inside the main bedroom. *Her* room. There, curled up in bed, were the man and the woman from the pictures, under the covers and sleeping soundly.

'Hey, arseholes, you're in my bed.' She shook the pair, but neither stirred. 'I said, hey, arseholes!'

She marched out of the room and went to the spare bedroom. There she found the gap-toothed boy, laid on his back snoring, covers corkscrewed around his legs.

Rita picked up the boy's teddy bear and pulled off its head. 'Oops.'

She staggered to the bathroom, had a pee—didn't flush—then made her way back downstairs and stepped out into the street, closing the front door behind her. She looked down at the keys in her hand. Yup, definitely hers. She sunk to her haunches. Apparently, the joys of the hex were going to keep on coming. It hadn't just made people forget about her, it had changed the whole fabric of reality. Made it as though she were never truly alive. And so long as she'd never existed, how could she have lived in that house?

She couldn't. Someone else had. Someone else *did*.

She wondered if she'd ever get it back. If the hex was broken, what would happen to that house? To the family asleep upstairs? It made Rita's head ache; the mind-bending paradox of it, along with the realisation that her life—a life she'd never much cared for but had grown accustomed to nonetheless—was really over. Or maybe the ache was just the first tickle of a hangover before it reached in and dug its thumbs into her brain.

She looked down at the house keys in the palm of her hand.

'Bollocks,' said Detective Rita Hobbes, as she hurled her keys down a drain and walked away from the house she'd never lived in.

Blackpool had known many strange visitors in its long existence.

There was the Angel, of course, trapped there, off its shore, long before people had settled upon its land. Since then there had been so many more. All kinds of Uncanny had decided to call the place their home; far more than should have, considering its relatively small size. Some said it was the influence of the Angel that drew so many. Its darkness radiating. A magnet for the bizarre.

Most dismissed that, as, of course, the Angel of Blackpool was just a story. A myth. A fantasy.

The Angel of Blackpool did not exist.

Of course.

Of course.

On that night, as Rita Hobbes found the place she once called home now belonged to someone else, Blackpool found itself welcoming a strange, new person into its embrace. She entered on foot, her weathered walking boots kicking up dirt as she walked forward. From her shoulder hung a backpack containing her humble belongings, a hand with long, delicate fingers holding its strap. Her hair was as black as the sky above, wound tight and pinned back, clear of her face.

Her name was Magda, and she hadn't come to Blackpool as a tourist. Hadn't come to walk on the beach, nor to enjoy the sea, nor to indulge in the many gaudy attractions that stretched out along the seafront. She hadn't come to idle on the piers, or ride the rollercoaster at the Pleasure Beach. She hadn't even come to take in the sight of Blackpool Tower—inspired over a century before by the Eiffel Tower—to rise up to its summit and take in the view of the town.

No.

Magda had come to Blackpool for entirely different reasons. She was hunting, and she was eager to begin.

3

January 1st, 1900, Hungary

Magda was seven years old when the Wizard paid her family a visit.

She was small for her age, skinny too, with a thick, unruly mop of jet black hair and eyes of ice blue. She was excited, as it was the first day of a new year. The first day of a new century.

'Don't go too far from the house,' said Magda's mother, as she skipped out of the back door, the forest opening up invitingly before her.

'Don't worry, I won't go far,' Magda replied, unsure as to whether she was telling the truth or not.

Magda lived with her family in a large farmhouse, a few miles south of Budapest. The forest hugged the left flank of the farm, the rest was acres of fields, full of wheat, of potatoes, of sugar beets. Her family was small and happy. There was her mother, a round woman who laughed easily and often, her eyes lined, evidence of a happy life. Then there was her father, a bear of a man who Magda believed to be the strongest person who had ever lived. He had once told her that he could pull a fully-grown tree out of the soil with nothing but his bare hands, and she had believed him with the certainty of innocence. And finally, her young brother, the most recent addition to the family, delivered by her mother just six months previously.

Magda ran into the forest, her heavy winter coat and scarf keeping her warm as the frigid winter air nipped as her exposed skin. The large trees of the forest had dropped their leaves months before, but this was how Magda liked them best. Their gnarled, twisting branches naked, reaching out like broken arms.

Magda and her family had lived on the farm for the past four years. Her mother said that before then they had lived in another country entirely. Not Hungary, but some other place. Some place Magda had never heard of, and she had heard of six or seven countries already. They'd had to leave that place. Magda had never got to the bottom of why, as her mother would always change the subject. Not that Magda cared. What did it matter? Hungary was home. The farm was home. The forest was home. Wherever she and her family were was home.

In many ways, they were a normal, happy, loving family. But there was, in fact, more to them than that. Much more.

Magda had been running around the forest for some time, and had stopped to catch her breath, the cold air burning her throat. She wrinkled her nose and realised her mother had not stepped out of the house to shout after her, to tell her to come back home to do her morning chores. That made Magda's stomach feel a little strange, like a hand was in her belly, wiggling its fingers. She'd always go out, running and skipping and climbing trees, and her mother would always, always call her back in far too quickly, commanding her to come inside and do her chores.

But not that day.

She ran back to the farmhouse, her imagination inventing all sorts of terrible things as she rushed to be back with her family. She had a sense for this sort of thing. They all did. People like her. A sense that would tickle at them when the worst was about to happen. Often this tickle had kept the likes of Magda and her family alive. Not that Magda knew that at this point. She had been too young to have the full talk. Her mother had wanted to, but her father had argued it could scare her, confuse her, too. Let her have some amount of innocence, he'd said. Let her have a real childhood, before the dark reality of what her life would be was thrust upon her.

He believed they had time.

Nobody knew where they were, *what* they were.

He believed they were safe for at least a decade or so, so what was the rush?

As soon as Magda stepped into the kitchen of the farmhouse, she knew for sure that something was very, very wrong. She could taste it on the air. That coppery tang of blood. Somehow she knew it would be a bad idea if she were to call out to her parents. If she were to ask where they were, whether they were okay.

She stepped quietly through the kitchen and into the corridor beyond. There was blood on the carpet. A big, wet, dark pool of the stuff. She fell to her knees and sniffed it. The blood was her mother's.

There was more on the stairs.

Stealthily, her heart fit to burst, she made her way up the staircase, keeping close to the wall so that a creaking step would not betray her presence.

She found her mother's dead body in the bathroom.

She was covered in blood. Some her own from her many injuries, some from another person. Not her father, or her baby brother, but a person she'd never met before. There was magic in the strange blood and it tasted sour to Magda.

There was no time to cry, or to fall to her knees and hug her dead mother's corpse. Instead, she made her way quickly to her baby brother's bedroom. He was asleep in his crib. Perhaps that is what had saved him. Had saved him from being discovered by whoever had slaughtered their mother.

She bundled her brother, Andras, up in his sheets and lifted him out of the crib. He snuffled and complained in his sleep.

'Shh, shh,' she whispered in his ear. 'Please, stay asleep, don't open your eyes.'

She carried him through to her own bedroom and laid him on the bed, quickly filling a bag with clothes and the small amount of money her father had always insisted she kept there. With that done, she hugged the bag and her brother to her chest and poked her head out of her bedroom, listening.

It was strange, like instinct was taking over. Like she'd been preparing for this her whole, short life. Perhaps it was just a part of her. Part of them. Part of the type of people that she and her family were.

Animal instinct.

She carried her brother and her meagre belongings downstairs and headed back the way she'd come, trying not to look at her mother's blood on the stairs, or on the carpet at the bottom.

She wondered where her father was. He would have drawn the attacker away from the house, away from her and Andras so that they might have a chance to escape. He would fight to the last to protect her, but it hadn't been enough to save her mother.

He was dead.

She knew it.

Was sure of it.

Somewhere, his eyes were shut, his body crumpled on the ground, bloodied, maimed, dead dead dead.

She wondered who had done this to them. Who, with sour magic in their blood, had stepped into their perfect life and torn it apart so viciously. So terminally. She would not get her answer for many years, and at that moment it did not matter. All that mattered was running. Was getting her brother away from that place. Getting them both somewhere safe.

But if your own home wasn't safe, where was?

Without looking back, Magda ran into the forest.

She would run for a very long time.

4

Detective Sergeant Dan Waterson was dead, and he wasn't enjoying it one bit.

He remembered dying. The actual, baffling moments that put an end to his life. Walking on Blackpool beach, going to meet his best friend, his partner in the force, who he and everyone else had somehow forgotten all about. She'd been scrubbed from his memory, from existence; Rita Hobbes, that funny, red-headed pain in the bloody arse. One second she hadn't existed, and then, just like that, it had all come flooding back to him. Her face, her voice, getting drunk together and talking rubbish, getting bored on stakeouts at three a.m. in the middle of a bitter Northern winter. Back it had all come, and with it the knowledge that the world was not quite as cut and dried as he'd always thought it to be.

He'd been stabbed.

That's how it had happened.

Stabbed with a big bloody sword. He knew it was a sword as he'd seen the business end of it thrusting out of his chest. A sword with a gold-coloured blade and his dark red blood running down its curiously-patterned metal.

He hadn't had a chance to do or say anything much after that, as death had come quickly, eager to claim him.

And then he'd sat up and found himself all alone.

A ghost.

Not that Dan Waterson believed in ghosts. Rita probably did, that was something he now remembered about the friend he'd briefly forgotten about. She was always willing to lean into the strange, to consider the impossible, so this malarky would have been right up her street.

Waterson knew he was a ghost, because after standing up and wondering where Rita and the strange, pale man in the long, purple coat had disappeared to, he'd looked down to find his corpse laid out at his feet.

He'd had a little bit of a panic attack after that, had DS Dan Waterson.

He'd done a bit of staggering, a bit of running in circles, a bit of screaming and wailing, before finally pulling himself together and acting like a detective. *Put the pieces together, Waterson,* he'd told himself. He'd gone to meet his friend, been stabbed from behind, died, and now he was a ghost.

Simple as that.

He didn't like the conclusion he'd arrived at, but he was at a loss to explain it any other way. That was definitely his corpse on the beach. He'd even tried to check for ID, just to be on the double-safe side, only to find he couldn't get to grips with the body. Couldn't hold it. Couldn't even touch it. The moment his hand met something solid, it was as though it turned to jelly and passed right through.

While Detective Waterson was busy getting to grips with this —or not, as it turned out—Rita Hobbes returned to the scene. She was alone this time, minus the strange, pale man with the untrustworthy face.

Waterson tried to catch her attention as she sat with his body. Spoke to her and yelled and waved his hands in front of her face. And then *through* her face. But it was no use, she could neither see nor hear him. It was all very frustrating.

'I'm sorry, Waters,' Rita told his corpse.

'Yeah, you and me both,' Waterson replied. 'Also, you know I hate it when you call me Waters, right? Maybe I should be over that now I'm a ghost, but nope, it still annoys me.' Waterson laughed. A laugh which turned hysterical and caused him to curl up on the sand in a giggling, shuddering, foetal position.

Shouldn't he be off to Heaven then?

Or an afterlife of some description?

He'd never actually believed in any of that stuff, though his mum was a devout Catholic and often loudly disappointed by her only son's failure to share her faith. Maybe this was all the afterlife was. No Heaven or Hell. Or purgatory even. Just this; wandering around, unseen, forever.

Bit depressing.

'Oh, shit,' said Waterson, sitting up from his giggle-curl. 'Mum.' His old mum—all alone since his dad had died seven years previous—and now she'd lost her only son. She'd hear about it soon enough. Her boy, dead. What would that do to her?

No chance of any more hysterical laughter now.

Waterson stood and walked over to Rita, who was still holding vigil over his body. 'You could've told me how shit my haircut was,' he said, seeing his head in a way he hadn't been able to in life. 'Some friend you were.'

An overweight man made them both jump as he let out a cry of surprise behind them. Waterson and Hobbes turned to find the man—who had stepped out of his cab to have a pee—looking past them, looking through them, down at Waterson's corpse lying on the bloody sand. Twenty minutes after he'd made a shaky phone call, the ambulance arrived, and they stretchered his body into the back.

Rita walked away then. Guard duty over.

'Well, what now?' asked Waterson, yelling after her as she wandered off into the night. 'Right. Great. Right.' He'd dithered a moment longer, wondering whether to follow Rita or, well, follow himself. Decision made, he hopped into the back of the ambulance to catch a ride with his corpse.

Sitting in the morgue for several hours while his dead body chilled in a cold drawer didn't do much to improve Waterson's mood.

It was weird. He didn't feel dead. Not as such. Not that he knew what death was supposed to feel like. But apart from being invisible, and not being able to properly touch anything, he still felt, more or less, like himself.

Waterson laid back on an empty mortuary slab and found himself giggling. *Christ.* Rita had always been the one to believe in strange things. She once told him about a UFO she'd seen, buzzing across the night sky over the Opera House. Swore up and down it was real. Waterson had poured some cold water on that and no mistake. And now here he was. A phantom. She'd bloody love that.

Good job she hadn't been able to see him, the smug look that would have spread across her face might have done him in for a second time.

The giggles turned to full throated laughter again, until his vision blurred with tears and he curled up on his side on the slab and slowly calmed down.

No long Mulder & Scully, now just a pair of Mulders, neck-deep in crazy.

It occurred to Waterson in that moment that he had no idea who it was that had murdered him. Or why. That was irksome. He sat back up, his legs dangling off the slab, and considered the possible hows and whys and maybes. It had to be connected to Rita's own weird predicament, that much was obvious. And as her predicament was connected to the spate of women going missing in Blackpool, it had to be linked with that, too.

If only he'd been able to turn around to see who'd stabbed him in the back before he croaked his last. That would be something.

Annoying.

The double doors to the morgue bashed open as two orderlies pushed in a trolley containing an occupied body bag.

'You seen the state of the bloke in there?' asked one of them, the taller of the two.

'Don't mind me, you two, I'm just a ghost,' said Waterson, waving at the pair as they stopped by a second slab and heaved the bag on to it.

'No, why?' asked the shorter orderly.

'That in there? Inside that bag? That is some disgusting shit.'

'How disgusting?'

'Give you nightmares for months, mate. Disgusting.'

The shorter orderly glanced to the doors, then at the body bag. 'Okay, I'm peeking.'

'You'll be sorry you did.'

'You've built it up. You want me to look, I'm looking.'

'Okay. But you'll be sorry,' said the taller orderly, smirking.

Waterson hopped off his slab and stepped over to stand by the shorter orderly as he gripped hold of the zipper and took a deep breath or two.

'Months?' said the short orderly.

'Oh, at least.'

He nodded and unzipped.

As its contents were revealed, both he and Waterson very much regretted their decisions.

5

If Carlisle hated Blackpool, he positively detested Birmingham.

He looked up at the Gaiman Theatre's crumbling facade and a grimace spread across his ghost-white face. The theatre had been a popular music hall venue in the first half of the Twentieth Century, playing host to all manor of stars: comedians, dancers, singers, and speciality acts. Arthur Askey, George Formby, Gracie Fields, they'd all faced the entertainment-hungry crowds at the Gaiman.

Carlisle had taken in a show at the Gaiman just once, in the mid-1950s. It had not gone well.

'Blackpool and now Birmingham,' Carlisle muttered to himself, 'I believe it is I and not the Detective who has been unjustly cursed.'

Carlisle shoved the wooden door off its hinges and walked through the dank entrance, sending a group of rats scattering into the gloom with chittering cries of surprise. The theatre smelled like urine and death. Carlisle headed past the mould-spotted ticket office and made his way into the theatre's auditorium. The Gaiman had last closed its doors in the late 1980s, and had been left to sag and decompose. A corpse turning to mulch.

More than one homeless person had made the building their home after its closure and abandonment, but none had stayed long, and most now knew to steer clear of the place. Better to huddle in a shop doorway than face the whispering dark within the theatre's damp walls.

The seats had once been a bright red, but as Carlisle walked down the centre aisle towards the stage, he saw now that they had turned varying shades of brown. Those that hadn't been torn up and tossed aside, that is.

The night Carlisle had spent inside the place, back in the 1950s, he'd sat in the front row, looking up at the turns as they performed their acts. Most had been doing the same thing, the *exact* same thing, for decades. The same few minutes, over and over for each new audience in each new town.

Most, but not Little Tommy Taylor.

Little Tommy Taylor was called Little Tommy Taylor because he was not in the slightest bit little. He was a mountain of a man, almost as wide as he was tall, with a head so large it was a marvel that his neck was strong enough to support the thing. Little Tommy Taylor was a comedian, but instead of telling the same tired one-liners night after night, his schtick was crowd work. Rather than trotting out pre-prepared gags, he would engage with the front row, mocking the people unlucky enough to be sat there for the amusement of everyone. Everyone except for those in the front row, of course.

Now, if there's one thing that ought to be known about the Uncanny world—and there are many things, but if there were just one thing to be known, it would be this—Carlisle Ignatius Huxley holds a grudge. He can nurse a grudge for centuries, keeping the embers gently burning should he ever find himself with a spare evening and the inclination to do something about it. He might have long since forgotten why the embers burned, but that mattered not. The fact that they still burned let him know that he was owed something. That a line had been crossed, and perhaps now might be an opportune moment to cut someone off at the knees.

Carlisle hopped up on to the warped stage and was almost surprised to find it was still able to take a person's weight. It creaked and complained, but the boards held.

'Where are you?' he cried, his voice echoing around the open space. There was no reply.

Little Tommy Taylor, a gap between his two front teeth you could shove your fist through, had spotted Carlisle early into his set and had zeroed in on him, on his paler than pale face, much to the amusement of the inebriated audience. Carlisle had sat there sour-faced, arms crossed, as Tommy stood at the edge of the stage, microphone in hand, an evil glint in his eye.

'What's the matter here, then? Eh? I've heard about sunburn, but this fella's got moon-burn! He's white! Ooh, he's white. How white is he? Is that what you rabble up in the birds want to know? How white is he? I'll tell you how white! Listen now, I saw 'im on the way in and thought he were a pint of milk! I did! Missus, you're looking at me funny over there, but it's the truth! I tell no lies. Don't ask the wife, but I tell no lies. It were only when I tipped him back and his wig got caught in me teeth that I realised! Oh, he's white! He is, isn't he? He's like someone drew a face on a stick of chalk. Hey, just how many ghosts have you seen there, my friend? All of 'em? Eh?'

If Carlisle hadn't had pressing business elsewhere after the show, he'd have dealt with the matter there and then. Instead, he had added the gap-toothed comic to his list of grudges and gone on his way. Unfortunately, Little Tommy Taylor had died less than fifteen years after Carlisle's roasting. Humans had a nasty habit of doing that. Dying before they could be murdered.

Now for most people, if the person they'd a grudge against died, that would be the end of that. You can't get revenge on the deceased, or at least that's the theory. For Carlisle, death was only a minor inconvenience.

The formerly grand orange curtain lay piled in a heap at the back of the stage as Carlisle prodded at it with the toe of his boot.

'I know you know I am here, comedian,' said Carlisle. 'You cannot hide from me, not even in death.'

Carlisle knew the real reason he was there, in the Gaiman Theatre, in dreadful Birmingham, and it wasn't to torment a long-dead vaudevillian. He was there because of *her*. Detective Rita Hobbes. She had his artefact—his axe—and refused to hand it over, despite everything he'd done for her. Despite the fact that he'd willingly, if briefly, died in her service. The sheer gall of the woman. It was *his* property. He needed it. Wanted it. Craved it. He'd done as agreed and still the axe remained at her side.

And so here he was, letting off a little steam as he pondered his next move.

Carlisle opened his purple coat, the lining flashing with stars and galaxies in the dark, and reached into an inside pocket to retrieve a stick of chalk. He looked at the chalk and recalled one of the dead comic's wisecracks. He sneered and sank to one knee, drawing a circle on the floorboards beneath him.

'If the phantom insists on hiding, then I shall just pull you from your hidey-hole,' he said, sketching arcane symbols around the perimeter of the circle.

Part of him wanted to snap the Detective's neck for her rudeness. To grip her narrow throat in his hand and squeeze until her eyes bulged out of her face and her tongue lolled from her mouth. He smiled as he worked on the chalk circle and pictured Rita's face as the veins in her temples throbbed and she slapped at him; crimson, ineffectual.

But no.

Sadly, that was not an option.

If he were to kill her, it was very likely that the axe would not return to him. It would choose its new wielder at random, and that might take years. Decades, even, and who was to say he would be able to take it from whoever found the thing in their possession next?

No.

He would have to find another way.

His work finished, Carlisle stood and slid the stick of chalk back into his pocket.

'Little Tommy Taylor, I command that you appear before me.'

Carlisle clapped his hands together and purple flames danced around the chalk lines of the magic circle.

'*Now*, if you would,' ordered Carlisle, and within the circle a figure materialised.

He was older than the man Carlisle recalled, but then he had perished a good fifteen years after that dreadful first meeting, and people were wont to wrinkle and bloat as the years pressed on.

'Here, what's this then?' asked the ghost in the chalk circle.

'This, you gap-toothed irritant, is your end.'

The ghost of Little Tommy Taylor scratched his chin, befuddled. 'What you talking about, mate? I'm already brown bread. Have been for donkey's years now. Pushing up the daisies, me. Stretched out for a long kip in me coffin.'

Little Tommy Taylor had been murdered by the husband of a woman he was having sex with in the dressing room of the Gaiman. He was almost finished when the dressing room door had opened and a surprised, then rather enraged, man entered. As Tommy shuffled around, his trousers around his ankles, the husband had beaten him to death with his rather sturdy walking cane. The murder had never been solved, and his spirit had remained within the confines of the crumbling Gaiman Theatre.

If he'd died of old age, or disease, or an accident, Carlisle would have had to scratch him off his grudge list. Lucky for him, Tommy's end had been a violent one. And yet there was more violence to come.

'Here, son, don't I know you?'

'You have a sharp memory, my friend,' Carlisle replied.

'Strike me pink, it's you! The pint of milk!'

Carlisle frowned. 'Indeed.'

'Well, what's this all about, then?'

Carlisle didn't answer. Instead, he began to make patterns in the air around him with his hands. His fingers left coloured trails behind them as he traced. As he conjured. As he persuaded the magic to do the thing he wanted. And the thing he wanted was to shred the late Tommy Taylor's very soul. To obliterate him entirely. And painfully.

Little Tommy Taylor screamed and grabbed at his transparent stomach, flopping down on to his knees.

'Please, don't.'

Carlisle laughed at that and continued on until the spell was complete and the moment was ready.

'I can take a joke, Mr. Taylor, but I do believe you overstepped the mark somewhat. Goodbye.'

'No, Guv, wait—'

But Carlisle didn't wait to hear the end of the ghost's sentence. Instead, he grasped the spell that hung before him and thrust it into the phantom's chest. The ghost warped and rippled and twisted and tore, his screams shaking the dust from the stage gantry above, causing it to fall like grey snow.

Within a few short seconds, the soul of music hall comedian and ladies' man, Little Tommy Taylor, was no more.

Carlisle sighed, content for a scant second or two, before the absence of his artefact weighed upon him once more.

'Shit,' he said to himself.

It was time to go and see a man about a spell.

6

April 19th, 1943, Berlin

They felt safest at night.

During the day, Magda and her brother, Andras, would stay indoors, in the basement flat they'd called home for the past six months. The owner didn't ask any questions, just took the rent and left them alone.

Magda and her brother were now adults, though they looked much younger than their age. That's how it went with their kind. They aged naturally for the first twenty years or so, and then the aging process slowed dramatically, allowing them to live for centuries. Unless they were found, of course. By the wizards who hunted them and their kind mercilessly.

'Soon,' Magda told her brother, who peered impatiently through the tiny window into the city outside.

'It's almost dark, why not just go now?'

Magda thought about her mother's corpse, bloodied and twisted. It was always there, whenever she blinked.

'You know why. Better to be safe.'

Andras snarled, his teeth growing long and monstrous.

'Stop that,' said Magda, and Andras crossed his arms, sulking.

Soon enough, night fell and the two emerged from their hiding place. In a city like Berlin, there were two advantages to only coming out at night: one, it was dark, and easier to move around unnoticed, and two, this was Berlin during the war. During the evenings, the allies flew overhead, dropping bombs, devastating the city piece by piece, which meant most hid in shelters from sundown to sunup. And while they huddled underground, Magda and Andras would roam the city unseen, scavenging.

They stalked through the remains of grand buildings, Magda imagining they were walking through the bones of a once-giant beast, poking through the creature's enormous rib cage for tasty, unpicked morsels.

'What was mother like?' asked Andras.

Magda smiled. He always asked that. Every night he wanted to know, and every night she would try to think of something new. Not only did it satisfy her brother, help him build a picture of the mother he had no memory of, it helped Magda keep hold of every piece of her. Helped the images, the sounds, the smells stay fresh and alive. As long as she could remember her mother so clearly, remember her father, too, they could never truly be gone.

'Well?' said Andras, down on his haunches, picking through a pile of rubble.

'She had these red cheeks,' said Magda.

'How red?'

'Like a fresh, rosy apple that has just been polished on your thigh.'

Andras nodded.

'It's the first thing I would notice, as I entered a room and she smiled, her cheeks full and shining so very red. Or when she would pick you up out of your crib and cradle you in her arms, gently singing you to sleep.'

It was a cold night. It was about to get colder.

It was Andras who first sensed something. 'Sister,' was all he said, but the tone of his voice told Magda all she needed to know.

They darted, feet dancing silently over unstable ground, until they found a half-fallen wall to duck behind.

Someone was following them.

'Police?' said Andras. 'Army?'

Magda tilted her head back and sniffed at the air. At first there was nothing, but then the wind changed direction, and there it was. That scent. That taste in the back of her throat. The same one she'd noticed mixed with her mother's blood.

The stranger's sour blood.

Magic.

'We need to leave,' she said. 'We need to leave Berlin right now.'

What remained of a doorway behind them erupted, showering them with shards of wood and brick. But this was no air raid. No bomb falling from the sky.

'There is no point in carrying on this game of hide-and-seek, wolf,' came a voice from the dark.

Magda peered over the edge of the wall they cowered behind and saw a figure drift out of the gloom. It was a man.

No.

Not a man.

More than a man.

A Wizard.

'I see you, girl,' he said, chuckling to himself.

The Wizard seemed like a giant. His head was entirely bald, the moonlight glinting off his bald pate, and he had eyes the size of fists. His crimson robes fluttered around his heavy frame in the wind, and the very air around him seemed to warp and crackle, boiling as it came into contact with him.

'Run,' said Magda, and she and Andras bolted from behind the wall, scampering like rats across the rubble, swift, surefooted, desperate.

That was him.

The man who had murdered their parents, and now, after all these years, he'd tracked them down, too.

'You can run, but eventually you will hit a dead end, children,' gloated the Wizard, amused by their desire to live.

The air around Magda shook, and before she knew what was

happening, she was upside-down and hurtling through the air. She came to a painful stop into a pile of shattered furniture that had once held pride of place in a family home; a family home that was now little more than the suggestion of a few walls.

No time for pain or discomfort, Magda flipped up on to her haunches, looking for any sign of her brother. He pulled to a stop a little way ahead of her, waiting for her to follow.

'Run!' she yelled, but Andras dithered. He wasn't going to leave his sister behind.

'Come on, sister!'

'Run, I will follow you, I promise!'

Their eyes met one last time, then Andras erupted in flames.

'No!' Magda fell back as her brother staggered to and fro, a roaring inferno of unnatural fire, a blaze of lashing tongues, black and purple. Finally, mercifully, he fell to his knees and flopped on to his front. The magical flames puttered out, leaving nothing but a shadow of ash where her brother had once stood.

'Vermin must be dealt with, even during times of war,' said the Wizard, who seemed not so much to step over the uneven ground, but glide.

Magda snarled, her eyes turning yellow, her mouth filling with large, sharp teeth as her hands transformed into wicked sets of claws. 'Kill you!'

The Wizard smiled indulgently.

It was suicide. Magda knew that, but she did not care. Her whole family now, gone, and the thing that did it was stood in front of her, a patronising smile spread across his wide face.

'Come here to me, child. Meet your end at last.'

Magda screamed as she sprang to her feet, ready to charge at him, ready to bite and slash and chew, ready to face her death at last, but death was not ready for her. The shattered remains of the building exploded around them, the concussive blast sending Magda flying back through the air again. This time it wasn't magic, wasn't the Wizard. Aircraft screamed overhead, RAF bombers delivering their nightly gift to Berlin. She staggered back to her feet, searching for any sign of the Wizard, but the ground he had stood upon moments before was now a blackened crater.

Magda glanced back to all that remained of Andras, her brother's death shadow, and fled the battlefield.

7

Jane Bowan remembered dying. Which was strange as she still felt very much alive.

'Hello? Anyone?'

She wasn't sure how long she'd been wandering aimlessly for, but it felt like a long time. Hours, days, weeks. Maybe forever.

She'd been chained to a big block of stone in a chamber, with flaming torches flickering shadows up the walls. Then there had been a person, in robes, with an axe, and…

And…

And…

Jane stopped and bent over, resting her hands on her knees, trying to calm herself down.

She'd been murdered.

A weird, sacrifice-like murder; the type of thing you might see in some old British horror film. A cheap one, at that. Probably featuring Christopher Lee, or Peter Cushing, or both. It was usually both.

'Hello?' she said again, and carried on walking.

The place she'd found herself in was very strange indeed. At times it seemed formless, like drifting through a vague fog. At other times it was like she was walking through empty rooms in an endless house. Occasionally, she was underwater, or in fire, or in space. All in all, it was a bit of a head fuck.

The rabbit mask dream.

That's what had started it all.

She'd always had the dream, well, the nightmare. That's what it had been. A nightmare. A nightmare of a man in a tatty old rabbit mask. Ever since she was little she'd had that dream, but it had occurred more often in her final few weeks. Almost every night, in fact.

And then the nightmare had become reality.

He'd called himself Mr. Cotton. This rabbit mask-wearing thing from her nightmares. She'd awoken one morning and he'd stepped out of her head and into her reality. And he wasn't alone. He had a brother, Mr. Spike, who wore a hedgehog mask and didn't speak. She'd known real terror then. More, even, than when her final moments actually came.

Mr. Cotton and Mr. Spike had taken her from her normal, wonderful, boring, amazing life and delivered her to the chamber. And then that was that and here she was. In this place. This bizarre, empty, full, never-ending place.

'Hello?'

Jane stopped. That hadn't been her voice.

'Anyone? Hello?'

There was someone else here, another woman.

'I hear you!' Jane called back.

The voice sounded familiar.

'Where are you?' asked the new voice.

'I'm here, just follow my voice. Ooh, I'll stand still and clap my hands over and over and you can sort of zero in on me.'

'Right, okay.'

Jane clapped, and shortly, out of the indistinct world Jane found herself in, a woman appeared.

'Oh, it's you,' said the woman.

'Ellie?'

Ellie Mason grinned and rushed forward to hug Jane.

'Oh God, I thought I was gonna be alone forever!'

They knew each other. They'd gone to school together, been in the same classes for much of it.

'Do you remember what happened?' asked Jane.

Ellie bit her lip and nodded. 'He killed me. The man with the axe. I think he killed me.'

'Me too.'

'So where are we, then? Is this, like, the afterlife or something?'

'I don't know. I suppose it must be, yeah.'

'Hey.' A third voice, another woman.

Jane and Ellie looked around for its source.

'We're here!' cried Jane.

'Where are you?' asked Ellie.

A figure faded into view, more indistinct than the two of them. She had long, red hair.

'What? It's you two,' said Rita Hobbes. 'How can it be you two?'

A cheer from one of Big Pins' bowling lanes roused Rita from her slumber. Her eyes opened with great reluctance, and she took in the place where she'd spent the night; the back room of a scummy bowling alley. She unfurled her aching body, which had spend the night curled up on a heavily-stained, rank-smelling sofa. Her head felt like someone had snuck inside her skull and stuffed it with rancid meat. She wiped a crust of dried saliva from her chin and groaned.

How did she get here? She replayed the events of the previous night, or at least the ones she could recall. She remembered going home, only to find out that it wasn't her home anymore. She remembered the strangers sleeping in her bed. And with nowhere else to go, she remembered coming here, to Big Pins, a '50s style bowling alley and Uncanny gathering place.

Linton, the owner, had agreed to let her use the back room as a temporary home, as long as she kept the place tidy. Rita looked around at the room, with its disgusting, nicotine-stained ceiling, threadbare carpet, and creeping damp, and wondered just how much worse Linton thought she could make the place.

She sat up and realised she'd been hugging the axe. The enchanted axe. The axe that gave her the power to take the magic of someone else and use it herself. She'd been dreaming as she hugged the axe. Dreaming about the two women DCI Jenner had murdered, Jane and Ellie. It would have been a third if she hadn't had rescued Gemma Wheeler, who was still in hospital and under police guard. Because although Rita knew the case was solved—the killer incarcerated in a dreamscape prison of her own making— there was no way for the police to know that.

Jane's boyfriend. Ellie's mum. Waterson's mum. All left hanging. All left in the dark. But at least she'd brought Jenner to justice. At least she'd stopped him, and that creepy bastard of an Angel.

Rita stood, slid the axe into her belt, and made her way into Big Pins proper. She saw the cause of her awakening, a group of drunk women, bowling on lane one. They looked like perfectly normal women, but Rita knew it was best not to take anything in Big Pins for granted. Maybe they were witches. Or vampires. Or vampire witches.

Rita slumped down on a stool at the bar, her eyelids heavy, her throat dry as cotton.

'Morning,' she said to Linton, as he slid a glass of orange juice her way. 'Thanks, big man.'

'How was your rest?'

'Your couch stinks.'

'You are welcome.'

'So does this place ever close? It's, like, seven in the morning, and that lot over there are already mullered.'

'Why would we close?'

'Places close.'

'They do?'

'Yeah, obviously.'

'Not this place.'

Rita sipped at her orange juice. A plate was placed before her. On it sat a bacon sandwich. At that moment, it was the most beautiful thing she had ever seen. 'Linton, I'm pretty sure I love you.'

'Thank you. I don't love you.'

Rita chowed down on the sandwich as though she hadn't eaten for days. She realised that she possibly hadn't.

'Hello, Detective,' said Formby as he took a stool beside her. Rita mumbled a hello around a mouthful of thick, white bread, bacon, and brown sauce. Formby grinned, exposing his set of sharp little piranha teeth. Teeth that could bite through bone. Formby was an eaves, a type of Uncanny creature that looked a lot like a man-sized mole. Eaves traded in secrets, in whispers, in overheard knowledge.

'Seen anything of Carlisle?' asked Rita after swallowing a payload of greasy deliciousness.

Formby gestured for Linton to provide him with a drink as he shook his large, scarred head upon its short, thick neck. 'He's left. Gone.'

'What? Gone where?'

'Birmingham way as I hear it.'

'Why?'

Formby shrugged. 'Buggered if I know. Terrible place is Birmingham.'

Rita sagged. She'd upset Carlisle by not handing the axe over to him, but she still needed his help. If anyone was going to find a way to dispel the hex that had been placed upon her, it would be him. Besides, it's not like she wanted to keep the axe from the guy, she just couldn't give it up as long as she was stuck in this stupid situation. She needed it. For protection. 'He'll be back,' she said, and patted the axe dangling from her belt.

'So. You,' said Formby. 'Still here, still hexed. Still cut off from your life and your people. Very sad. Very, very sad.'

'Yeah, thanks for the cheery pep talk, love,' replied Rita.

'What're you going to do?'

Rita mulled the question over and shrugged. 'Not sure, to be honest.' A burble of conversation at a table by the door caught Rita's attention. 'Sounds like some early-morning excitement.'

'One minute,' said Formby, hopping off the stool.'

'What are you doing?' asked Rita.

'I'm an eaves. I'm doing eaves stuff.'

Rita carried on with her sandwich as Formby shuffled over to the animated table and started poking his snub nose into their conversation.

'You should be careful,' said Linton, spraying a pair of bowling shoes.

'Should I?' asked Rita.

'Carlisle, he's not a man to play with. He'll get what he wants, one way or the other.'

'Don't worry about me, big man,' replied Rita, 'I've dealt with worse. Not to toot my own horn, but I twatted an evil Angel yesterday. I'm hot shit, me.'

Linton raised an eyebrow and continued to de-stink bowling shoes.

Formby arrived back at the bar, clambering up on to his stool and continuing to enjoy his drink. Rita looked at him in silent expectation. 'Well?'

'What's that?'

'What did you find out? What were they talking about?'

'Oh. Just murder.'

'They're planning a murder?'

'No, no. Maybe. Wouldn't put it past the buggers. But no, someone's been murdered. Body was found last night.'

Rita turned fully to Formby. 'Who? Not a "normal" person, I take it, if that lot's interested?'

'He was a wizard. Dead wizard now, course. Ha! Big news, that. Dead wizards is always big news.'

Rita looked over to the table, then stood and made her way over. 'Hey, you lot, what's this Formby tells me about a murder?'

'None of your business, hexer,' said a remarkably ugly little man with dark, green skin. He looked like Yoda cosplaying as the Green Goblin.

'I'm a detective, murder is my business,' replied Rita, well aware of how bad-ass that sounded. It wasn't the first time she'd said it.

'Not one of us, though. Not properly,' replied Yoda Goblin.

Rita sighed and opened her coat, revealing the axe in her belt. 'Know what that is, love?'

Yoda Goblin nodded.

'Out with it then, tell me what you know.'

Yoda Goblin looked at his drinking companions, who were all leaning away from him as if he was nothing to do with them.

'Don't know anything. Just a dead wizard was found in Blackpool. Killed horribly. Taken to the morgue, now.'

Rita took out her notepad and jotted the details down. 'And that's all you know, is it? All any of you know?'

Yoda Goblin and his companions nodded, Rita flicked the notepad closed and pocketed it. 'Thanks Greeny, if you hear any more, let me or Formby know, right?'

Rita headed back to the bar.

'What you doing there, then?' asked Formby. 'Not your business.'

'You asked me what I was going to do. Well, I want this hex lifted. I want my life back. But who knows how long that will take, or if it'll happen at all. In the meantime, I'm going to do what I've always done. I'm going to be a detective.'

Rita sat and realised she was smiling, just a little.

There was a new mystery to solve.

8

May 10th, 2006, Scottish Highlands

She was going to tell him.

Magda rolled over in bed and looked at the face sleeping soundly beside her. Jamie McAlister. The first person outside of her family that she'd ever loved. Ever allowed herself to love. Love was a weakness, letting someone into her life was a weakness. Because her life was danger.

She sat up, setting the bed in the cottage she'd called home for almost two years creaking.

Two years.

She hadn't stayed in one place for that long since she'd run off into the forest, cradling her sleeping baby brother.

Death shadow.

That was her dominant image of Andras now. Not his smiling face. Not his dark, brooding eyes. Not the way his mouth would look when he hunted, full of beautiful, sharp teeth.

No.

The ash afterimage.

The death shadow in that bombed-out house in Berlin.

She'd left Berlin without returning to their basement home to collect her belongings. She ran from the Wizard, from Germany, and kept on running. From country to country. From city, to town, to countryside, never staying put for longer than six months at a time. Everywhere was her home, and nowhere too. Always moving forward, looking back over her shoulder, fear keeping her sharp. Keeping her alive.

And it had worked.

She had not seen the Wizard again, not since that night in Berlin. She often wondered if the bombing had killed him, though she thought that unlikely. That night, face-to-face with him, she could feel how powerful he was. Her skin had tingled and itched with the magic boiling off him.

No, he'd survived, but she'd stayed off his radar, for decades, because she'd learned how to hide.

Oh, she'd encountered other wizards. They loved to hunt her kind. Saw it as their duty to cull their numbers, like they were nothing. Like they were animals to put to the slaughter.

Magda was not an animal.

Not in the way they thought.

She was regal. She was strong. She was beautiful. All of her kind were.

A warm hand on the small of her back made Magda jump as it broke her train of thought.

'Morning, my lovely,' said Jamie, all sleepy-slurry.

'Morning,' replied Magda, leaning over to plant a kiss on his lips. She stood and enjoyed the way Jamie's eyes roamed over her naked body. She smiled and dressed.

'Aw,' said Jamie, jutting out his bottom lip.

'I believe you saw quite enough of me last night, my dear.'

She was going to tell him. Couldn't lie to him anymore, couldn't keep the most important part of herself from him. No, she was going to tell him.

She never got the chance to.

Jamie sat up and pointed past Magda, to the wicker chair in the far corner of the room, and asked, 'Who are you?'

Magda turned to see the Wizard sat with his eyes closed, like he was meditating.

She darted for the door, but it slammed closed on its own, and a heavy wardrobe slid across the floor, sealing it shut.

'No, no,' said the Wizard, opening one eye, 'you have done very well, wolf. Be proud—if your kind can be proud—but all good things must come to an end.'

Jamie hopped out of bed and grabbed a boot, brandishing it at the oversized interloper.

'All right, man, I dunno how you just did that, but you can piss off out of here before I call the police!'

'With your shoe?' replied the Wizard.

Jamie looked at the shoe, then back at the Wizard. 'No, this is to hit you with.'

'I see.' The Wizard clicked his fingers and the shoe shot from Jamie's hand and landed in his own.

'Don't hurt him,' cried Magda.

'He threatened to shoe me, wolf.'

'He's not like me. He's just, he's normal. He's a normal man.'

'What d'you mean,' said Jamie, 'what am I not like?'

The Wizard mock-frowned at Magda. 'Keeping secrets from your mate? Tut-tut, wolf, is there no end to your wicked ways?'

It was all falling apart. Her life, her love, her happiness. At long last she'd felt secure, felt happy, felt her heart open up, and here he was. The Wizard. As though he'd allowed her this time just to make its end all the more shattering.

She'd let herself get weak. She would not allow it again.

'Do you two know each other?' asked Jamie, self-consciously pulling on a pair of jeans.

'Oh, we go a long, long way back, don't we Magda, dear? I killed her family. Her mother, her father, her poor young brother.'

Jamie looked from the Wizard to Magda, dumbfounded.

'Magda is not what she appears. She is a monster. She is a thing of the dark. She has a touch of Hell in her, which is why I am here to take care of her, for the safety of all.'

'I haven't harmed anyone. Not in years.'

'But you will. You know you will. Perhaps, most of the time, the ache is not so bad, but every full moon, how it must itch and ache. The desire to run wild. To bite, to chew, to feast, and to turn the helpless into beasts to run at your heel, under your black command.' As the Wizard spoke, Magda's body trembled, sweat prickling her body. 'Sooner or later, you will succumb. It is inevitable. It is your animal instinct and it will not be silenced.'

Magda realised she was growling.

'Okay, what is going on?' demanded Jamie.

'Tell me, what do you know of werewolves?' asked the Wizard.

Jamie blinked twice, the silence thick. 'I beg your pardon? Did he just say werewolves?'

'I did, for they are real. Magic exists and so do monsters, and your lady here is very much a monster. A master werewolf, able to control her lycanthropy and turn others with a single bite. That is, if she doesn't kill and eat them.'

'You're insane,' said Jamie. 'I'm calling the police, I've had enough of this.' Jamie reached down to grab his phone, but the Wizard clicked his fingers and the phone melted through Jamie's fingers. 'Shit. Shit!'

'Magic is real. Monsters are real. Show him, beast.'

Magda sank to her knees, trying to fight it. She could control it. She was a master, not a slave to it like the people she chose to turn. She sank her fingernails into the palms of her hands until she felt the blood flow.

'You cannot fight it. Let it out. I command you.' The Wizard balled his fists and placed them to his temple. 'I command you! Show yourself, hound!'

There was a flash of blinding light and Magda felt it overcome her. Felt the wolf emerge. She strained, she struggled, she tried to hide it, but as she looked up, she saw how Jamie was looking at her. The real her. The wolf had been let out of its cage.

'Don't look at me,' said Magda, her voice rough, deep, guttural.

'Magda?' Jamie stepped back, horror etched deep into his face.

She leapt to her feet, hands claws, and screamed at him. 'Don't look at me!'

He'd spoiled it. The Wizard had spoiled it. If she'd only had a chance to explain. To tell the truth, to show him how beautiful she really was, how beautiful her kind were, how she was nothing to fear, how she would never hurt him, everything would have been fine. She knew it. But not now. Not now. He'd wrecked it. He'd torn down her family, and now this too was ruined.

She rounded on the wizard, her sharp teeth bared. 'Kill you!'

She rushed him and the Wizard flicked one hand, wrenching Magda off her feet and tossing her against the wall.

'Don't,' said Jamie, quietly, 'don't hurt her.'

The Wizard clapped his hands together and Jamie was gone, sent elsewhere. Magda knew she would never see him again. She leapt to her feet, her heart full of rage, of hunger, of violence. 'Why must you always come? Why?'

'As I told you in Berlin, you are vermin, and vermin are dangerous. Vermin are diseased. You are of the dark, you taint this beautiful Uncanny world, and I shall send you back to the Hell you came from.'

Lightning fast, Magda grabbed the wardrobe that blocked the door and threw it across the room at the Wizard. He punched out a fist, sending out a ball of boiling magic that obliterated the wardrobe, part of the wall behind it, and much of the floor below, sending Magda, the bed, and the bedside drawers, tumbling down to the room below.

Magda landed hard, the wind knocked out of her, but she recovered fast, hopping back to her feet. She didn't look for where the Wizard was, or consider going on the attack. It would be useless, she knew that, and she wasn't ready for death. She wanted to live. No, she wanted more than to live, she wanted revenge.

Now faster than she ever could be in her normal form, she bolted from the house, running directly through the front door, turning it to splinters, and ran into the thick forest of the highlands.

Running again. Running through a forest from the bad man. The Wizard. How many times was her life to repeat the same story? A story of hiding, of death, of pain, of looking over her shoulder.

No more. She could not allow it to happen again.

This was the last time Magda would run.

The last time any wizard would cause her heart to break.

9

Rita Hobbes entered Blackpool Victoria Hospital unnoticed. Well, unnoticed apart from the half-witch sat in the reception area, whose senses were attuned to the Uncanny. Not that it mattered. The half-witch didn't realise she was the only one who could make Rita out, and in turn, Rita didn't realise that the woman looking her way could see her. So Rita slid between the doors of the hospital as good as unnoticed.

Rita often wondered how anyone could work in a hospital all day. The lighting, the smells, the palpable tang of despair. It was all a bit depressing. Obviously the saving lives thing came into it, but the other stuff far outweighed that in her mind.

She slipped through the corridors, heading for Gemma Wheeler's room, entering unseen by the half-asleep officer on guard.

'Blackpool's finest,' muttered Rita. It was a good job that the man who had wanted to chop Gemma to pieces was banged up in a dreamscape.

Gemma glanced up from the trashy magazine she was reading and smiled as she saw who her visitor was.

'All right, spooky?' said Gemma.

'Hey,' said Rita. 'I'm in for something else, but I thought I'd stop by and see how you're doing.'

'Not bad,' Gemma replied, sitting up in bed. 'A lot better for knowing the shit that wanted to kill me is locked up.'

Rita did a curtsy. 'You're welcome, m'lady.'

'You still, you know, magically invisible, or whatever?'

'Yup. Still hexed up to my tits for the time being.'

'Shit. Bummer.'

'You said it.'

'Chris doesn't remember you at all, you know.'

Chris Farmer. Gemma's cousin and former casual sex buddy of Rita.

'Well he wouldn't do. It's like I didn't exist. Better that way, anyway. I'd only have broken the poor sod's heart.' Rita grinned, and decided to ignore the little ache in her heart. No, she hadn't been going to get serious with Chris, in fact she'd intended to leave Blackpool for a new life, and taking him along was not part of the plan, but still. She'd liked him. Enjoyed him. And it hurt to think he'd have no memory of that.

After a few more minutes of chat, Rita excused herself and continued on her mission: paying a visit to the morgue's latest tennant, the dead wizard. As she pushed her way inside and the double doors closed behind her, she had no idea that she'd missed sharing the mortuary with the ghost of her ex-partner, DS Dan Waterson, by just minutes. Not that she would have seen or heard him if they had crossed paths, of course.

After a little grim trial and error as she checked a few drawers, she discovered the one that contained the wizard's corpse.

'Okay, let's see what there is to see.'

Rita took a breath or two, then unzipped the body bag.

You never really get used to seeing a dead body, no matter how many of them you come across. And you certainly never get comfortable looking at the corpse of someone who had been murdered. But the contents of that drawer, of that body bag, well, that was something else altogether.

After almost a minute spent on her knees, gripping a metal bin and dry heaving, Rita pulled herself together and got back to her feet.

'Okay. Right. Some nice nightmare fuel. Great.' She grudgingly made her way back to the murder victim and forced herself to take another look.

It was, without a shadow of a doubt, the worst dead body Rita had ever seen. The wounds were many and large. The face had been torn off, one arm and both legs detached from the torso, and the intestines had been yanked out of the abdomen. It looked as though the man, the wizard, had been used as a chew toy for an extremely pissed off grizzly bear.

'Jesus. Jesus Christ. What could have done that?' she said.

'What indeed?'

Rita whirled around to see that she had been joined in the mortuary by Carlisle.

'Back from Birmingham, then?' she said.

'As perceptive as ever, Detective. I wonder how the Blackpool Constabulary are coping without your finely tuned investigative skills.'

Rita saw Carlisle's eyes drift to the axe hanging from her belt, saw him lick his lips in anticipation. 'You still can't have it, mate. Not yet.'

'You're quite set on that, are you?' he asked.

'Pretty much. I sort of need it.'

'As you wish.'

Carlisle reached into his long, purple coat and retrieved a small pouch.

'What's that then?' asked Rita.

'A little concoction. A gift.' Carlisle threw the pouch at Rita's feet. It exploded with a puff of smoke as it struck the ground.

'Uh, what the fuck?' asked Rita, understandably.

'You will give me my artefact,' said Carlisle, fussing at the cuffs of his coat.

'Yeah, not happening, sorry.'

Carlisle smiled and fixed his dark eyes upon hers. 'Detective, you will grant me the axe.'

Rita opened her mouth to argue, but heard the following words emerge: 'Yes. Of course.'

Carlisle chuckled as Rita—straining to defy her own limbs—reached down to the axe and pulled it from her belt, proffering it towards Carlisle.

'I give this axe to you. You shall now wield it.' Rita struggled and strained against herself, but nothing she wanted to do happened, nothing she wanted to say came out.

Carlisle sauntered over and took the axe from her. 'The wise choice, at last, Miss Hobbes. I am most grateful. And now, I believe our association is at an end. Good luck.' Carlisle grinned, turned towards the mortuary's exit—

Then fell back hard to the tiled floor as though a giant had punched him squarely on the nose.

Rita strolled over to the prone Carlisle and retrieved the axe. 'Still mine, I reckon.'

Carlisle sat up, grimacing at her. 'Damn.'

'Seems like this baby knows when you're cheating, Pasty,' said Rita, waggling the axe as Carlisle slowly rose to his feet. 'Whatever hoo-doo you chucked at me was making me say that stuff, but I didn't actually mean it.'

'So it seems,' he replied, brushing down his coat.

'Aw, you look a little embarrassed there; almost a hint of colour in those ghost-cheeks of yours.'

Carlisle snarled and stepped towards Rita, who found herself taking a wary step back. 'Do not overstep your mark, Detective.'

'Okay, let's both just relax before I have to chop you in half with this thing.'

Carlisle looked at the axe in Rita's hand, at his artefact. He felt the ache in his stomach for it. The craving. The *need*. 'This hex of yours, it must be lifted,' he spat, turning away so as not to look at the axe any longer.

'Well, duh. Agreed there, mate.'

'You will take me to DCI Jenner so I may snap his neck and rid you of this curse.'

'Um. No. We've already gone over that. Plus I don't even think that would do the job.'

'Trust me. When I twist a person's neck, it always does the job.'

'Okay. Disturbing. What I meant was, it wasn't his magic that fed the hex, was it?'

Carlisle raised an eyebrow.

'And you think I'm slow. Jenner isn't Uncanny, is he? It was that Angel. The Angel of Blackpool, acting through him. Feeding that magic to him. Which means…'

'Which means to lift the hex on you, we must deal with the Angel of Blackpool.' Carlisle pulled out a chair, sat down, and placed his head in his hands.

'I'm going to take it that what you're doing there isn't a good sign,' said Rita.

'You have met the Angel of Blackpool, do you believe dealing with It will be a simple task?'

'No. But that's where you come in, right?'

Carlisle stood and walked towards her, causing Rita to slowly back up. 'This isn't some rank and file angel we are dealing with, woman. There are a hundred different ways to kill an angel, but the Angel of Blackpool? That is one of the original seven, created before everything, before matter, before time, with God's own hands, to sit at His side.'

Rita ceased her retreat as the wall blocked her way. 'So what are you saying?'

'I'm saying it's impossible.'

'Don't like that much.'

Carlisle smiled, 'Luckily for you, I do not believe in the impossible. At least, not when it is standing in the way of what I want.' He licked his lips and his eyes darted briefly to the axe Rita clung to with both hands.

'That's… good?' said Rita.

'Oh, there's nothing good about it, Detective.' He clapped his hands together and turned to leave.

'Where are we going?'

'*We* are going nowhere. I am going to London to pay a visit to an old friend.'

'It's nice to keep up with old mates, but haven't we got more pressing stuff to deal with?'

'We do, and I am.'

Rita flapped her arms ineffectually. 'Okay, so, what do I do?'

Carlisle gestured at the wizard corpse. 'It looks like you have a little pet project to keep you busy. Leave the real work to me.'

'Okay, you're not going to help me out with a tip or two?'

Carlisle walked over to the exposed body and took a look, his eyes slowly roaming over the mess of meat and bones. 'No,' he replied, turned on his heel, and left the mortuary.

'Right. Thanks, mate.'

Rita sighed, but couldn't help but smile. Carlisle was going to help get her life back, and Carlisle was a powerful ally.

10

All Ben Turner really wanted to do was go home, watch some TV, eat bad food, and go to bed early.

It was "hump day", as Janice from H.R. insisted on calling it, each and every Wednesday morning. 'Welcome to hump day! It's bloody hump day again!' she'd announce, and she'd laugh each time she said it.

Ben was not a mean person, but he had fantasised more than once about Janice slipping at the top of the building's staircase and tumbling head-first down all five flights.

'Hump day?' he'd say, looking down at her battered body. 'More like *lump* day!' He wasn't really good at one-liners.

Ben was approaching his mid-thirties, was a little softer around the middle than he'd like, and had short, neat, brown hair. He hadn't always. It wasn't so long ago that he'd had a wild, untamed mane that reached past his shoulders. Sally had liked it that way, or at least she had before she left him for a Deliveroo driver.

Ben was an accountant at Briers & Travers, and dressed exactly how you would picture an accountant to dress. He knew his work was, to most, about as dull as dull could get, but he enjoyed getting lost in the numbers. What could be more beautiful than a spreadsheet where everything added up just right? The world around him would fade to background noise as he focussed in and bossed those figures around, filing them into their little cells like a diligent prison warden.

He looked up from his desk and realised the office floor had almost cleared. It was an hour past closing time already, and his less professionally-minded colleagues had long since escaped.

'Ben,' said Steve, adjusting his thick-framed glasses atop his freckled nose, his hair a copper crew-cut. 'Hey, Earth to Ben, come in Ben.'

'Hm?' Ben replied, stretching back in his expensive office chair, which he'd lobbied Janice in H.R. for, to give his back some extra lumbar support. He didn't need it, he just knew it annoyed Janice when someone asked anything of her.

Especially on hump day.

'You on for a pint? Carly, Phil, and Jonno are already in The Goose wetting their whistles.'

Ben made an 'Urgh' sound, accompanied by a 'Not feeling it' face.

'Give over, mate,' said Steve, reaching around and turning off Ben's computer.

'Hey! I hadn't saved that.'

Steve started to laugh, 'Well, that's what you get. Come on, you're practically a shut-in at the moment.'

'I had a drink with you last week,' Ben groused.

'No, that was last month.'

'Oh. You're sure?'

'It happens so rarely these days that it stands out. Trust me.'

Ben made another 'Urgh' sound, but he knew he was on to a loser. His couch, his TV, his bed, they were going to have to wait.

'All right, all right, but just the one, right?'

'Scout's honour, mate,' said Steve, crossing his heart.

'You were never in the scouts.'

'No, but I was in a girl guide or two.'

On cue came Ben's third 'Urgh' exclamation, which delighted Steve no end.

'Okay, I'll see you down there and get you one in. And a chaser, yeah?'

'No, no chaser!' said Ben to the rapidly exiting Steve, who

waved off any complaints without turning. 'Just the pint. A half even would be fine. Steve? Steve!'

Steve was gone.

Ben sat back and sighed again, looking at the black, blank monitor. He considered turning the computer back on and getting another quick twenty minutes in, but realised Steve would only return and, possibly, toss the computer out the window this time. Ben grabbed his coat and headed out of the office.

As the lift descended, he looked at his reflection in its mirrored interior. He still wasn't used to being clean-shaven. When he was with Sally he'd had a beard bushy enough to hold a pencil, if you slid one in. She'd called him her nerdy mountain man. He'd liked that. He'd shaved it off the day after she dumped him.

'Full moon again,' said Alan, the building's security man, as Ben signed out at the front desk.

'Yep,' replied Ben, not wanting to get into a drawn-out thing. Alan loved a drawn-out thing.

'We'd be up slack alley without the moon, you know,' said Alan, seemingly only fuelled by Ben's utter disinterest.

'Yeah. Suppose so.'

'No suppose about it. I saw a documentary about it the other day. Slack alley. That's where we'd be. Fascinating stuff, space and all that stuff up there, don't you think?'

'Absolutely,' said Ben, quickening his step to the automatic doors.

'Right up slack alley,' repeated Alan.

Ben sighed with relief as he stepped out of the building and the doors hissed shut behind him. The Goose was across the road from Ben's workplace, and was one of those empty, falling-to-pieces pubs that should, by rights, have long ago had to close its doors. But open it stayed.

Ben stepped in, the warmth of the place embracing him, to see Steve and the others, almost the only drinkers inside. Steve waved, then held up a pint and a whisky chaser. Ben very nearly said 'Urgh' yet again, but instead shrugged off his coat and made his way across the faded, filthy carpet to take his place at the table.

'Told you the shut-in was coming,' Steve told the rest.

'Close thing though,' said Ben, 'Alan collared me on the way out, wanting to talk about the moon and space.'

'Oh, Jesus,' said Carly, grimacing, 'I got trapped for twenty minutes with him once, talking about the best way to run a salmon farm.'

'Probably because you smell like fish, love,' replied Steve, who got an elbow in the ribs for his troubles.

Ben had only meant to stay for the one, but as the first whiskey chaser slipped down, he felt himself relax. Almost two hours and several more rounds darted by after that. It was fair to say that Ben Turner was, by now, a little drunk. He needed this. If he'd gone home alone again he'd only have ended up thinking about Sally all night. He was thinking about her now of course, but this was different. Now she was in the back of his thoughts, while he was out and about, being sociable. This counted as a step in the right direction.

He wondered if he should text her. Just a quick 'How's things?' He even reached into his pocket and touched his phone, before he realised how stupid an idea that was.

It was done.

Long, long, long since done. She was with that other person now. That man whose name he'd tried not to remember. He'd seen the pictures on her Facebook. Arms around each other, smiling. He almost envied her. Here he was, still glum and boo-hoo, whilst she was out there living her life.

'One for the road?' said Steve, snapping Ben out of his introspection.

'Hm?' Ben looked up to see he was now only sharing the table with Steve. 'Where'd everyone else get to?'

Steve laughed, almost falling off his stool. 'Christ, you're wasted, mate.'

Ben realised he really, really was. His head was going to feel like someone had stomped on it in the morning.

'One more?' asked Steve.

'Nah. No. Thanks. I'm done.'

'Suit yourself, I'm going to piss off then.'

'Yeah, I'll see you. I'm just gonna, you know, use the Men's.'

'It was good you came out, Benny. That cow was too good for you.'

'Don't you mean "I was too good for her"?'

'No mate, she was a proper ten out of ten. You're a six at best.' Steve laughed and swayed towards the exit. 'See you in the morning, Benny Boy!'

Ben smiled and waved, then pushed himself on to his feet, bracing himself against the wall for a moment as the room turned wobbly. It was after relieving himself in the Men's room and returning to the bar, ready to weave his inebriated way home, that he collided with the most beautiful woman he'd ever seen.

'Shit, shit, sorry. My fault. You okay?'

The woman smiled back at him and Ben felt his stomach explode with butterflies.

'Don't worry, I'm fine,' she replied, with an accent he couldn't quite place, though it sounded a little Eastern European.

Ben wanted to reply, but found his mouth flapping soundlessly as he took in the woman before him. Her thick, black hair shone, her blue eyes seemed to sparkle, her smile wide and inviting.

'Ben!' he said, much, much too loud.

'Hello, Ben, I'm Magda.'

She held out a hand, which Ben stared at for far too long. It was pale, with long, delicate fingers.

'So, are you going to shake it, or…?'

'Yes! Right, shaking it,' he took her hand in his and shook. Her hand was warm, his was sweaty. 'Nice to bump into you.'

Magda laughed, it took Ben a few seconds to realise he'd inadvertently made a joke.

'Are you leaving?' she asked.

Ben eyed the door, then looked into Magda's amazing eyes again.

'Uh. Yes. No. Well, I don't know.'

'You don't know?'

'I mean, I do know. What are you going to do?'

'I thought I might get a drink before heading home. Would you like to join me? I hate drinking alone.'

Ben accepted and bought her a drink, not realising that this was the longest he'd gone without thinking about Sally since she dumped him.

After their drink, and another couple after that, Ben offered to walk Magda home. He'd been drunk as a skunk before meeting Magda, but now, even after a few more drinks, he felt focussed. Clear. Happy. Without noticing how or when it happened, Ben realised, as they took a midnight stroll along Blackpool beach, that Magda was holding his hand.

Christ, he was happy Steve had talked him into going to that pub.

The happiness wouldn't last much longer.

'This is crazy,' he said.

'What is?' replied Magda, smiling at him.

'I've never connected this quickly to anyone in my whole entire life. Definitely not a woman.'

'We're connected?'

'Yeah! Well… shit. Sorry. That's a bit much, isn't it? Ignore me, I'm drunk. I'm a drunk idiot.'

Magda stopped walking and Ben worried he'd already blown it. It was only when she leaned forward and pressed her full lips against his that he realised he hadn't.

'Where are you from?' he asked, breathlessly, when she finally pulled her mouth away from his.

'Oh, all over the place. But I'm from here for now.'

Ben Turner had never felt so lucky. If he hadn't gone to the pub. If he hadn't gone to the toilet before leaving the pub. If Sally hadn't have dumped him all those months ago. Fate was a crazy thing.

'When can I see you again?' he asked.

'Oh, very soon.' she replied, and Ben noticed that her eyes had changed colour.

'Hey, how did…?'

'What?'

Her eyes weren't blue anymore. They were yellow. Which nobody's eyes were.

'You will be part of my family now,' said Magda.

'Your teeth...' said Ben. They'd changed, just like her eyes. They were longer now, sharper, more like a animal's than a person's.

Magda leaned in again, but not for a kiss this time. This time she sunk those strange new teeth into Ben's neck. He screamed and pushed away, falling back into the sand, a hand to the gushing wound on the side of his neck. He looked up to see Magda smiling above him, serene, her teeth dripping with his blood.

'Listen to the full moon, Ben,' she said, looking up at the night sky. 'Soon every night will be a full moon and we shall run free, beautiful, wild.'

She tipped her head back and howled at the sky as the world slipped away for poor Ben Turner, and the black rushed in from all sides to take him.

11

It seemed that the case of the dead wizard was going to be something of a solo investigation for Detective Rita Hobbes. That was okay though. She had years of experience under her belt already, not to mention a magic axe, and some first-hand experience of the Uncanny waters she was wading through.

It was morning, and Rita was hitting the street, looking for leads. The previous day she'd gone through the hospital's records for any additional info, and hung around listening to the morgue staff to see if any of them knew anything extra that wasn't in the system. The investigation had come up frustratingly short though.

The nightmare-inducing corpse had no ID on him, and his face was too mashed up to get any dental records from, so as far as the hospital was concerned, the wizard was a John Doe.

After wasting hours at the hospital, Rita headed to Blackpool Central Police Station, her old place of work, and went through a similar process as she had at the hospital. Annoyingly, she learned nothing new. Nobody had any idea who the wizard was or what could have done that to him, and no missing person had been reported. Rita was looking at a big fat zero. All in all, a frustrating first day on the case, but she wasn't out of options yet. There was still another lead to investigate.

Collins was a local supermarket, unique to Blackpool and its surrounding area. The one Rita entered that morning was the largest of the five-shop "empire". She wasn't there to sample their unrivalled selection of fresh fruit and veg though, nor to see what delights the cheese counter had to offer. No, she was at Collins Supermarket to have a word or two with its assistant manager.

Rita found him in a cramped back office, looking at a bank of small TV sets that relayed images from the supermarket's security cameras. Derek Nolan. Low-level wizard and former Head of Maths at Old Lane Secondary School, fired for fondling a student.

'Hey there, Mr. Gropey!' said Rita, as she shut the door behind her.

'You!' Derek hopped up out of his chair and backed up. 'I told you and Carlisle already, I don't know anything about the Magician!'

'Oh, that's old news, I caught him already, keep up,' she replied, plopping herself down into a swivel chair and turning to look at the wall of TV sets, one of which seemed to be looking down at a woman in the staff toilets taking a pee.

Derek grabbed a remote and turned off the sets.

'Okay, I'm going to be tearing that camera down on my way out, you dirty little perv,' said Rita. 'And I'll be making regular visits to sweep the place for any new cameras, understood?'

Derek nodded, looking down at the floor like a toddler who'd just had his favourite toy taken away. 'It's a sickness,' he mumbled.

'Then get help,' she replied.

'Why are you here?'

'I'm here because the bloody remains of a wizard are in a body bag back at the hospital morgue, and I want to know what you and your little boys' club of local wizards know about that.'

Derek looked up at her, blinking dumbly. 'What?'

Rita stood and moved her coat aside so he could see the axe hanging from her belt.

'Hey, no need for that! I don't know anything about a body, not anything, this is the first I'm hearing about it.'

'There must be talk. I can't imagine a hotter topic in the club house.'

'I haven't been since I took you and Carlisle there. And even if I had, I'm nobody. I'm a junior member, they don't tell me everything. Honest to God.'

Rita walked over to Derek slowly, making him back up until the wall blocked his way. 'You'd better be telling me the truth, Gropey. I might be hexed, but I'm still the police, and I will take you down if you lie to me.'

'Understood. I don't want any trouble.'

'Good. Then take a message to the others. Tell them I'm on the case and I expect their cooperation, because I'm gonna have questions. Understood?'

'Absolutely. I'll tell them. I can't promise anything, but I'll tell them.'

'Then also tell them this is not a manner for debate. Police, remember?'

Derek nodded.

Satisfied, Rita turned and headed for the door. 'And if I catch you perving again, I'll make sure you spend the rest of your life looking at the inside of a cell, got it?'

Derek flopped down into his swivel chair as Rita left, shaking all over. After a few minutes to catch his breath, he turned on the wall of security cams to see the one that he'd hidden in the ladies toilets a few weeks previous now only showed static.

'Bollocks,' he muttered.

Ben Turner woke that morning twisted in his sheets, head pounding. He dragged himself out of bed to silence the alarm, which he always placed on the other side of the room so he'd have to get up to turn it off; a trick he learned a long time ago that helped him wake up. A trick Sally had taught him.

He didn't have any recollection of getting home the previous night, but there were things he did recall. Things that seemed like a dream that was turning to smoke in his mind. He stood in the shower for a while, head hung as the water battered down on him, trying to grasp hold of the fading memories. There had been a woman in the dream that may or may not have been a dream. Mary? Maggie? Something like that, he was sure of it. She'd been tall, and sleek, with eyes that had just pulled him in.

Eyes that had… changed?

God, she'd been beautiful. So completely beautiful. And then terrifying.

He remembered her attacking him as he stepped out of the shower, and wiped the mirror clean so he could examine his neck. He leaned in closer and craned his head to one side, exploring the exposed skin with his fingertips, searching for any sign of being bitten.

Nothing.

He towelled off, dressed, and wandered into work on legs made of rubber.

'All right, mate,' said Steve plopping himself down on the edge of Ben's desk. 'Jesus, you look like shite.'

'Yeah, thanks.'

'That's the problem with ducking out on so many nights at the pub, your tolerance goes down.'

Steve laughed and headed back to his office, leaving Ben wondering if he was right. He felt like re-heated crap, and his head was trying to convince him that a beautiful woman had grown big, sharp teeth and munched on his neck. Which, of course, was crazy. More than crazy. And if it wasn't crazy, then where was the evidence? No bite, no wound, nothing. He'd just gotten pissed, that was all. Someone had probably spiked his drink—Steve more than likely—and left him wandering around Blackpool, tripping balls.

The woman though… he was so sure that part was real. Magda! That was it, that was her name. There was no way he'd just imagined her. Well great. A beautiful, sexy, incredible woman had been interested in him, right until the point a Mickey kicked in and left him on his ear. She must have thought he was a complete maniac.

Ben downed a bottle of Evian and shuffled to the kitchen for a refill.

He wondered if he'd bump into Magda again.

He wondered how long it would be before he was throwing up in the toilet.

Rita passed beneath the ornate, twisted brass archway of the Night Fair, and pushed open the gates to reveal the stalls within. The Night Fair was a place Uncanny types went to for a little fun in Blackpool. It was called The Night Fair, as no matter what the time of day was, within its boundary, the stars were always out, pin-pricking the darkness.

Rita wasn't at The Night Fair to browse its weird food stalls, or wander through its house of mirrors, she was there to step into the *other* Night Fair. The dreamscape copy she'd created using the stolen magic of Mr. Cotton and Mr. Spike. The magic she'd used to imprison DCI Alexander Jenner.

Rita pulled out the axe and swung it, cleaving a tear in reality, and opening the dreamscape just a little. Enough for her to step inside of.

Jenner was sat in the dirt, his head resting against the side of a stall.

'Hello, Guv,' said Rita.

Her former boss did not look up. 'I can't hear It. I can't hear my Angel.'

'Yeah, that's for your own good, you big sack of crazy. Believe me, if others had their way, you'd be dead as MySpace.'

'And this is better?' spat Jenner, a snarl across his face, body tense as piano wire.

'Easy now, Guv. Don't make me spank you with my good friend Ms. Axe here. She'll leave a mark.'

Jenner sagged then curled into a ball.

'Here,' said Rita, and tossed him a bag full of food and water. 'Go nuts. Well, more nuts.'

Jenner didn't move. Rita sank down to her haunches and looked at her old boss. The Guv. The man she'd trusted and respected for years, at least until she found out he was kidnapping and murdering women because an Angel told him to.

The man who'd killed Dan Waterson.

To see him now, so broken, so pathetic… this wasn't the Alex Jenner she'd called her boss. She wanted to hate the man. Wanted to feel a white hot fire in her stomach. Those women deserved her anger. Waterson deserved it. But all she felt was pity. Pity for a man who'd been used by a thing he could never truly understand. Plied and manipulated, ever since he'd been a vulnerable young boy. Jenner wasn't who Rita directed her anger at. No. That hatred belonged to the Angel of Blackpool.

Speaking of which.

'A wizard was murdered in Blackpool, Guv.' Jenner ignored her, trailing a finger round and around in the dirt, making mud circles. 'Did you hear me? A wizard was murdered. And not just murdered, torn to pieces. I've never seen a vic like it.' Jenner did not answer. 'Guv? Alex? Come on, you're free of It now. We can talk. It won't know what you've said. Is this anything to do with the Angel? This murder?'

Jenner sat up and looked at Rita with empty eyes. She shivered. Could he be saved? Was there anything in there to save at this point? Was she going to have to keep him here forever? A prisoner to look after until the day she died?

'They're in there,' said Jenner, so quietly that Rita almost missed it.

'What? Who's in where?'

'We took, and we chained, and I chop, chop, chopped, and took what was needed.'

Rita looked at the axe in her hand. 'Jane? Jane and Ellie?'

'I took their souls. I killed them and I took their souls and they are in there still, waiting. The others will join them. You'll see.'

Jenner stood, a grin on his face that made Rita step back.

'Don't move, Guv, I don't want to hurt you.

'They're in the axe,' Jenner growled, slowly walking towards her.

'I'm warning you, Guv!'

'Two have fallen, their souls captured, and sooner or later, the others chosen shall join them, and then—

Rita stumbled back. 'Last warning!'

'—and then the Angel will step free of Its prison and Heaven will tremble!'

The dreamscape closed behind her as Rita fell back on to the grass, the entrance to the actual Night Fair before her once again, the flames of torches flickering either end of the rusted metal archway.

'Shit,' said Rita, standing and brushing the dirt off her rear. She walked away from the Night Fair, from the dreamscape, as the full moon shone down.

'Hair of the dog?' said Steve, slipping his coat on.

Ben didn't hear him. He was slouched in his chair, the monitor before him an indistinct blur.

'Oi, pisshead, it's home time,' said Steve. 'D'you fancy a couple to sort yourself out?'

Ben turned to look at Steve, who seemed... well, wrong. It was like Ben was looking at him through a weird prism.

'What?' said Ben.

'Christ, maybe you need to go right to bed, mate.'

Ben wanted to answer, but Steve wasn't there anymore, nobody was. He wondered how long he'd been sat there, slack-jawed. How long it had been since Steve had spoken. He squinted up at the clock on the wall. An hour had already passed since clocking-off time.

He stood, then yelled out in pain as his guts twisted inside his belly, folding him in two. He fell to his knees. 'Help. Somebody help.'

The words snuck out weakly, but even if he'd screamed them, it wouldn't have done him any good – the building was empty apart from himself and Alan at the front desk, three floors down.

Ben wondered if he was dying. Was this a heart attack? The pain had been in his stomach, but now it was in his chest, too. It burned. Worse than burned. More than burned. It every-kind-of-pained.

His dad had died of a heart attack only a few years older than the age Ben was now. Was it his turn? Was it—?

He threw his head back and screamed as he felt his bones *crack*.

Not a heart attack. Not a heart attack.

Oh Fuck. Oh Christ.

It felt like his whole body was being torn apart. Body hot, skin burning, Ben tore off his sweat-drenched shirt, just in time to see the flesh on his chest pull apart.

Alan Crowther had worked security at Briers & Travers for going on eleven years now. It suited him. He liked the uniform, the little bit of power, of authority. Plus, he was a people person, and everyone had to come past him on their way in or out; lots of opportunity for connections and interesting conversations.

His current conversation topics all had to do with space. The universe. The cosmos! He was binge-watching all sorts of interesting space docs on YouTube while he sat at his desk. It was good to learn new things. *Never stop learning,* that was his motto. *The longer you learn, the longer you live,* that was another of them. He loved a good motto. He'd often thought about putting together a coffee table book of all the mottos he'd collected or thought up over his life. He had a notepad full of them.

Alan Crowther wandered over to the locked doors of Briers & Travers and looked up at the night sky.

'Full moon again,' he said to himself. 'Last full moon of the cycle. Four days and done. Sea'll be getting a good old tug tonight.' He blew his nose, checked the contents of his handkerchief, pocketed it, then made his way back to his chair whistling *Space Oddity* by David Bowie.

Alan's wife had left him three years previously for her pilates instructor. He'd paid for that instructor, too. Linda had always been moaning about how much weight she was putting on, so he'd forked out the cash for a bit of one-on-one training.

Well, she certainly got the one-on-one.

He'd seen her just the other week, walking down London Road with him. Alan had been on the top deck of the bus, but to him it didn't look like Linda had lost any weight. Put a bit on, if anything. She looked happy though.

He didn't hold grudges, not Alan. What's meant to be was meant to be, as far as he was concerned, and the universe had called time on his and Linda's marriage.

'C'est la vie,' he said to himself, then checked his watch. Yup, it was about time to do his first walkaround of the building.

'No rest for the wicked, laddo,' he said, and set off for the stairs. Sure, he could have taken the lift, but he liked the exercise. Linda might have put on a few pounds, but he was determined to stay trim. Security was a physical job, and besides, he couldn't afford to outgrow his uniform, not with his ex taking half of his earnings.

The first floor was clear, though it smelled badly of fish and chips. Someone had been eating at their desk again by the stink of it. Dirty bastards.

Alan remembered his and Linda's first date. They'd both been twenty-six and they'd sat on the beach sharing a cardboard cone stuffed full of fat chips, doused in salt, vinegar, and ketchup. He'd let her use the little wooden fork the bloke in the chip shop had given him. She'd done her nails all nice and Alan didn't want her to get grease on them. He was a gentleman like that.

The second floor was clear, too. They were always clear. In all his years there, he'd never actually found someone where they shouldn't be after lock up.

'Tell a lie,' Alan said to himself, stopping as he was about to make his way back to the stairs. He *had* found a couple in the building once. On the same floor he was on now, in fact. First month on the job he'd found them, in a corner office; bloke and a bird going at it, hammer and tongs, her with her skirt hitched up and her blouse on the floor.

Alan grinned in the dark.

Ellen, that's what she was called. She'd left a few weeks later. Wouldn't look Alan in the eye on her way in or out in those final few weeks. Bloke still worked there. Top floor now, though. Brian Meeks. Vice president. Always nice to Alan, Brian was. Alan could've caused a bit of a stink, as it had been Brian's boss's daughter Alan had found him ploughing over the desk.

Soul of discretion, that's what Alan was. Plus, Brian had bought him that nice case of whiskey. Good stuff, too. Single malt, aged eleven years. No rubbish.

Alan was halfway up the stairs to the third floor when he heard a noise. He paused and looked up towards the door that lead on to the floor, cocking his head to one side to hear better.

There it was again. A sort of low growl or something.

Blimey, had someone brought a dog in and forgotten to take it home with them? Daft bastards. You weren't allowed to bring animals into the building. Alan hadn't seen anyone bring a dog in, but then he'd only been on shift since four. Jeff had been in during the day, and Alan wouldn't have put it past Jeff to let stuff like that slide. Soft, he was. Sometimes he didn't even wear his tie.

Alan huffed to himself, took out his little hand baton, and headed to the third floor. He wasn't supposed to be armed—in fact, he'd been expressly told not to bring weapons into the office after the knuckle duster he bought off eBay fell out of his jacket pocket and went clanging across the lobby—but Alan wasn't having any of that. Security could be a dangerous game, and danger needed to be met with extreme prejudice.

'Here, doggy, doggy, come to Uncle Alan.'

Alan flexed his fingers around the baton. He didn't want to hit a dog, but the thing sounded jumpy, mewling and growling. Probably scared, being left behind like that. Alan knew that a scared animal could be a hostile animal. Even the most placid of doggies could bite if they felt cornered.

'Well, blimey,' Alan said as he looked around the open plan area of the office.

There were a few monitors smashed on the carpet, the desks they'd stood on completely wrecked. Alan shuffled forward and prodded at a little pile of torn clothes on the floor. Trousers, shoes, a shirt. It looked like whoever they belonged to had exploded inside of them. Alan frowned and scratched at his head with the baton. What on Earth was going on here?

A low growl behind him.

Alan spun around to find out exactly what kind of dog could

have caused such destruction. Only it wasn't a dog. It wasn't a dog at all.

As it rushed howling towards him, all claws and teeth and fury, Alan Crowther, security guard and amateur astronomer, felt strangely calm. He pictured Linda on Blackpool beach one last time, smiling over the cone of hot chips, steam coiling up, her blonde hair almost glowing.

And that was the end of Alan.

12

If there was anyone in the Uncanny world with a larger, more well-tended ego than Carlisle, it was Giles L'Merrier.

L'Merrier was a wizard, and by far the most powerful of his ilk in the Uncanny Kingdom – a fact that he would make known with some regularity. L'Merrier's Antiques was located on a side street off Portobello Road, London, not far from the market. Outside, a wooden sign bearing the shop's name in hand-painted cursive squeaked in the wind.

Carlisle had travelled to London to ask the great L'Merrier how he might go about killing an Angel. If anyone knew, Carlisle was sure it would be him. L'Merrier had the reputation of a know-it-all. A dangerous and extremely vengeful know-it-all.

Carlisle straightened out his coat and pushed open the door, setting the shop bell tinkling as he stepped into the establishment's mote-laden interior. The shop had an atmosphere all of its own, a stillness, a sense of knowing and of secrecy. Carlisle wandered the shop floor, swatting aside the thick dust that swirled before him. The shop was dark, hushed, and bulged with all sorts of strange antiquities. Some were of the very ordinary variety. A chipped cabinet that had once belonged to British Royalty. Faded oil paintings depicting tranquil countryside scenes. A complete collection of promotional tea mugs for Tetley Tea from the 1970s.

And then there were the other things.

On a shelf next to the counter, Carlisle spotted a glass eye, perched next to a set of ivory dominos. The eye was as big as a tennis ball, its iris bright red. As he peered, the eye twitched, ever so slightly, to look at him. Carlisle turned away. The last thing you wanted was to make prolonged eye contact with a Seer Stone; it might drain you of every memory you've ever had before you had a chance to blink.

In one corner, draped in shadow, was a set of quite unusual armour. In many ways it appeared to be Roman, but it was not. Not quite. No Roman ever wore this set of armour. The armour was small, standing only as high as Carlisle's thigh and missing its helmet. Carlisle knew the creature that had once worn it: a small, fox-like creature, brave and loyal, hunkered down in another reality. A warrior, waiting for battle in the Dark Lakes, ready to join an undead army, ready to obey the command of the Magic Eater.

Giles L'Merrier had lived a long life, striding across this earth and others, this reality and more besides, and had taken tokens from each, and here, within his shop, these strange things had come to rest.

'Are you going to hide in the shadows for my entire visit, tubby?' asked Carlisle.

A velvet chuckle rolled out of the dark, followed by the corpulent but gliding frame of the shop's proprietor. He had a giant, entirely bald head and eyes that danced with mirth, with confidence. His huge barrel of a body was entirely hidden by luxuriant, scarlet robes, upon which had been embroidered all manner of magical shapes, words, and names. The mighty Giles L'Merrier, the most powerful wizard still to draw breath.

'Carlisle, little one, what an entirely expected pleasure to host you within my humble house of wonders.'

Carlisle continued his slow perusal of the shop, making a show of not turning to properly greet L'Merrier. He hoped the momentary tensing of his jaw muscles caused by L'Merrier's "little one" crack had not been noticeable in the murk of the shop. 'Oh, so you were aware I might be paying you a visit?' he asked.

'I hear things, you know. I am a spider and all manner of stories and movements are fed to me, twitching the fine silken threads of my web.'

As a rule, L'Merrier was not a fan of people paying him a visit. He had been known to become quite violent upon that point, so Carlisle was relieved to see that he seemed to be in a good mood for once. 'I suppose you heard about my reasons for leaving London recently.'

L'Merrier grinned and rested his fat hands upon the steep hill of his stomach. 'Ah yes, I believe there were two reasons, were there not? Firstly, fear.'

Carlisle spun on his heel, his eyes narrowed. 'Fear?'

'I do believe you had been running a rather naughty, and ultimately lethal to your customers, business. A business that the London Coven had heard tales of. No doubt that put you on Stella Familiar's list of people to punch.'

Carlisle snorted. 'Please, I am not frightened of a familiar, regardless of her affiliation. I am Carlisle, I am the one who is feared. Generally.'

L'Merrier chuckled. 'Yes, I suppose some do fear you. It takes all sorts, does it not?'

Carlisle frowned and shoved his hands deep into his pockets, rubbing a thumb along an enchanted knife hidden within one and momentarily wondering what sort of sound L'Merrier might make if he were to shove it into his neck. 'Two reasons?' said Carlisle.

'The artefact.'

Carlisle nodded.

'You know, I actually had the artefact here for a short while, oh, many decades ago now.'

'Impossible,' Carlisle shot back. 'I would have known.'

The darkness around L'Merrier seemed to thicken for a moment. 'You think I could not hide it from one such as you? I am Giles L'Merrier. I walk this hunk of rock a titan. A wonder. I have more magic in my piss than you do in your entire body. I could turn your flesh to dust with a single thought should I wish to. Would you care for a demonstration, little one?'

There followed a heavy, strained silence as the two men

glared at one another, each daring the other to make a move. Carlisle was the one who finally broke, turning to continue his perusal of the shop's antiques. Firstly, as he had come to see L'Merrier for reasons other than a fight, and secondly, because Giles L'Merrier was quite right, Carlisle was no match for him. Not that he would admit that to his face.

'I have a question,' said Carlisle.

'I, no doubt, have the answer,' replied L'Merrier. 'I have all of the answers. All that is required of you is to ask the correct question.'

'The Angel of Blackpool.'

If L'Merrier had any eyebrows, they would have risen at this point. 'Repeat yourself.'

'The Angel of Blackpool. You know of It?'

'Of course,' huffed L'Merrier. 'What beast, fair or foul, of this Uncanny land is there that I, the mighty L'Merrier, do not know of? That I have not met, have not shaken hands with, or sunk my sword up to the hilt in?'

'So you know It?'

L'Merrier smiled.

'It is real,' said Carlisle. 'I assumed it was nothing but a tale, a child's spook story, but It is real. I have spoken to It.'

'Have you indeed?' L'Merrier replied.

'I have walked through the vaulted halls and stood before the glass cage It is trapped within.'

'And you still live.'

Carlisle twirled, his purple coat fanning out, revealing the lining, flashing with light, with stars, with wonder. 'I live.'

'I am… impressed.'

Carlisle smiled and bowed slightly. 'It is not such a simple job as you may believe to put a full stop to my life, L'Merrier.'

L'Merrier returned the slight bow. 'Noted, little one.'

'The Angel of Blackpool is real and It rages. I fought against It, now I wish to destroy It.'

L'Merrier frowned. 'So you come to me and ask how one might go about killing an Angel of the first order?'

Carlisle smiled, 'Aren't I a wicked one?'

L'Merrier burst out in huge, concussive laughter. The shop

itself seemed to tremble, and the Seer Stone rolled from its shelf and shattered on the wooden floor.

'I do hope that wasn't expensive,' said Carlisle.

'You come asking questions about how to kill an Angel? Well, well, is this not a coincidence?'

'It is?'

'Why do you wish the Angel dead?' asked L'Merrier.

'To complete an obligation and reclaim my artefact.'

'You know, there are other artefacts of Heaven, I have some here inside this very shop.'

'No!' Carlisle realised he'd taken several steps towards L'Merrier before he had regained control. He stopped and scrubbed the feral expression from his chalk-white face.

'Tetchy, aren't we, Carlisle?'

'I… apologise.' He turned and walked away, creating an illusion of safety, as though L'Merrier couldn't reach across the shop with his thoughts and pluck him from where he stood if he so chose.

'Apology accepted,' said L'Merrier. 'This once.'

Carlisle shoved his hands into his pockets again and frowned. The hold his artefact had over him. The need. The craving. The all-consuming desire to hold it in his hand and wield its power once more. He knew it was an addiction. That it affected who he was, his thoughts, his actions. That he was almost a slave to it. But he did not care. Because when he had that axe, he was really, truly, who he was meant to be. And when he had it again, he would never have to apologise to anyone.

'You will help me?' asked Carlisle, quietly. Imploringly.

L'Merrier studied Carlisle, his eyes roaming over him, into him, through him. Carlisle could feel the interrogation, it was as though he were being jabbed all at once with a million blades and it *hurt*. Finally, the blades stopped their stabbing and Carlisle took a step back, gasping slightly.

'I have heard whispers, of late,' said L'Merrier.

'Whispers? Of what?'

L'Merrier clicked his fingers and the shards of the Seer Stone leapt into the air, reformed into the sphere with its blood red iris, and took its place back upon the shelf.

'There is talk of a man. Perhaps he is a man. He certainly has the form of one, at least.'

'This man,' said Carlisle, 'he knows how to kill the likes of The Angel of Blackpool?'

'So the chitter-chatter goes.'

'Where can he be found?'

L'Merrier smiled. 'Tell me, Carlisle, what do you know of the City of the Dead?'

13

Ben Turner tasted blood in his mouth.

His eyes opened, just enough to be pierced by daggers of morning light.

'Jesus...'

That taste in his mouth. He reached out to grab his glass of water but pawed at thin air. No glass? He always put water there before going to sleep, even if he got home blind drunk.

Ben threw the covers back. He would have screamed at what he saw, but his throat tightened and cut the sound down to a thin squeak.

He was naked and covered in dried blood. Great washes of it painted his entire body. It caked his hair, it soaked the covers and the mattress. It led across the wooden floorboards towards the bed in big red footprints.

Ben leapt out of bed and turned again and again in sharp circles, examining his body for any sign of where the blood might have come from. He couldn't find anything, not even a paper cut. He ran to the wall switch and turned the light on, darting towards the full-length mirror on the wardrobe, trying to find a wound, a gash, that he hadn't been able to see.

Nothing. The blood in his bed, the blood on his body, the blood in his mouth. It wasn't *his* blood.

Ben staggered backwards and flopped down on the edge of

the mattress as his calves hit the bed base. He realised he couldn't remember getting home. Just like the night before, when he'd gone to the pub and met Magda. He remembered how awful and long the working day had felt. How sick and sore and out of sorts he'd been, wishing he'd called in sick. He had a vague memory of Steve, talking to him at the end of the day, perched on the end of his desk. And then…

And then…

Morning and the taste of blood in his mouth.

Somebody else's blood.

'Shit. Oh shit, shit, shit…'

Could whatever had been put in his drink at the pub the other night have still been in his bloodstream? Could it have affected him again? Drugs can stay in your bloodstream a long time, he knew that.

But so what? Even if that was true, it didn't tell him who all the dried blood belonged to and why he was painted in the stuff.

Psychotic break.

Sally, his ex, had always said he was moody. That she wouldn't be surprised if he had a breakdown at some point, just like her dad had. Could that explain things? He had been depressed a lot, ever since the break-up. Maybe this was how it was expressing itself. Finally, too much to take. Blackouts. Blackouts and what? Had he attacked someone?

'Jesus, Jesus, Jesus.'

The police might be after him. He should check the news, see if there was anything on there about someone being attacked. He looked at all the blood again and wondered if someone lost so much blood, would they survive? How many pints of the stuff was slopped around his bedroom?

'Jesus.'

He'd killed someone. Had he? He must have done.

'Maybe it's a cat's. Maybe I just killed a cat.' He laughed, a single, high-pitched laugh that shot out, only for him to cover his mouth to stop any further eruptions.

That could be it though. Maybe. A poor family cat, out for a midnight stroll.

'Just a cat. A cat, a cat, a cat. Please let it be a cat. Holy shit and please, please God, let it just be a cat, or a dog, or a fucking fox, even!'

'Hello again.'

Ben let out a scream and fell off the bed. There was a woman in the doorway to his bedroom. He recognised the woman. She'd bitten his neck two nights previously. In his imagination. Right?

'Magda?' he blurted.

She smiled and nodded.

Ben was suddenly very aware that he was naked, and pulled the bedcovers over his crotch.

'How did…? Did we meet again last night?'

'How do you feel?'

'Not entirely amazing.'

'The first time is always confusing once you've been turned. But you have been made beautiful.'

She walked towards him, her hips swaying, and Ben found himself once again captured by her piercing blue eyes.

'I dreamed that you bit my neck. Like a vampire.'

'I am not a vampire, Ben,' she replied, stroking his matted hair.

'No. Of course not. I know. No such thing as vampires.'

'Oh?' she replied, and leaned down to kiss him on the lips. 'You taste… delicious.'

'Whose blood is this?' he asked. 'It's not a dog's, is it?'

Magda smiled and shook her head.

Rita looked up at the dull concrete facade of Briers & Travers. It was the building's security guard who'd discovered the scene. A Mr. Jeff Saunders. Right now he was sat in the open doors of an ambulance parked up in front of the building. He had a foil sheet over his slumped shoulders and a shocked look on his face.

Formby nudged Rita. 'See, told you. I heard it sharpish. Another one.'

'Stay here while I take a peek,' replied Rita, and Formby shuffled off down an alley to keep out of sight.

Rita walked to Jeff in the ambulance, who was being attended to by a plain clothes officer she knew well, DI Collins; a lump of a man with a moustache that should have been removed with extreme prejudice several decades ago.

'Here you go, pal,' said Collins, handing Jeff a Styrofoam cup of coffee.

He accepted it gratefully with shaking hands. 'Thanks.'

'No bother. What you stumbled on in there, give anyone the flaming heebie-jeebies.'

Jeff nodded and sipped the coffee, then swore as the scalding, dark liquid burnt his top lip.

'Morning, Collins,' said Rita. 'Blocked the bogs back at the station lately?'

Collins didn't hear her, of course.

Jeff's legs dangled pathetically from the back of the ambulance. 'I knew something was up, you know? Alan, he always texted me when I was on after him. Especially if he were on nights. I'd wake up and turn me phone on and there'd be five or six messages. Usually a link to a video or two he'd found online, you know? Filling the night hours. But today… nothing. Not a single message.'

Collins nodded but wasn't paying attention, instead he was scrolling through pictures on his phone.

'Top work, Collins,' said Rita. 'And to think you used to wonder why the Guv overlooked you for promotion. Idiot.'

'I messaged him myself, I did, Jeff continued. 'On the way in. No reply. I knocked on the doors for him to let me in, but no sign of him. So I let myself in, and he weren't at the desk. Couldn't find him anywhere. And then…'

Jeff stammered to a stop and blew on his coffee.

'And then…?' said Rita waving her hands at him to carry on. But of course he couldn't see her hands. Or hear her voice. So that was a bit pointless.

'Oi, Collins, help a woman out,' she said, and shoved Collins, causing him to fumble his mobile and drop it on the ground.

'Shit it!' he barked, and bent over to retrieve his phone.

It was weird, how the 'normal' people she interacted with, those that couldn't see past the hex, didn't seem to notice her even when she did something as blatant as pushing them. They feel it, because they move, and in this case, drop their phone, but the hex must cause their brain to ignore the cause. She wondered what would happen if she hit Collins in the stomach with her axe; would his mind try to shrug it off even as his intestines unravelled at his feet?

It seemed as though Jeff was done with talking, so Rita left them to it and passed a second ambulance and a huddle of police cars to make her way into the building. Most of the officers were in the reception area, chatting, letting the forensics mob do their bit, so Rita tagged along behind a woman with blue plastic gloves on and baggies over her shoes.

The crime scene was on the third floor. *All over* the third floor.

'Well, shit in my mouth…' said Rita, slowly taking in the gross tableau before her. Much of the office furniture had been destroyed. The chairs, the computers, the tables. It looked as though someone had taken a sledgehammer to the lot.

And then there was the blood.

And the chunks of Alan Crowther's body.

It would not have surprised Rita if she found out that he'd gone up there, stuck a stick of dynamite up his rear end, then lit it. Such was the explosive distribution of his body.

The forensics woman crouched and began taking pictures of Alan Crowther's decapitated head, his eyes still wide open.

'Jesus…' said Rita. The wizard in the morgue, this was the same. Well, this was even more… extreme than that, but it was clearly connected. Something savage, something evil, was killing people in Blackpool.

A second forensics officer took pictures of a section of the wall. Rita made her way over to see several large gouges had been ripped through it. It looked, to Rita, like a claw mark. And there was a footprint on the carpet beneath it. A bloody footprint.

Rita took out her phone and snapped a picture of the footprint. It looked like an animal's, but it was huge.

Minutes later, Rita hustled out of the office and across the road to the alley where Formby was still waiting.

'So what's to see?' he asked.

'A lot. Take a look at this.' Rita showed him the picture of the bloody paw print.

'Oh.'

'Is he a wizard?' asked Rita. 'Was Alan Crowther a wizard?' That would add to the pattern, if true.

'Hm? Oh, no. Not him.'

'You're sure?'

'Course.'

'Right. Damn.' Okay, so perhaps whatever was doing this wasn't just miffed at wizards.

'So?'

'So what?' replied Formby.

'The picture! The bloody, massive paw print. I'm taking it that it's bad news, right?'

'Oh aye,' replied Formby, sucking in some air. 'Very, very awfully bad.'

14

The employees of Briers & Travers each had a little card that they swiped across a small, wall-mounted scanner on their way in and out of work each day. When doing her rounds of the crime scene, Rita had decided to check the records for the previous day, and it turned out two people had scanned in, and failed to scan out. One was the murdered security guard, the other was an employee named Ben Turner. Ben Turner also, it turned out, worked on the third floor. The same floor that the security guard's insides and outsides were now slopped liberally around.

Rita had found Ben Turner's address in the system and decided his house would be her next port of call. She pulled to a stop across the road from his home, a small, terraced house on a nondescript Blackpool street. She killed the ignition, double-checked the house number, then headed over.

She did not head directly for the front door, instead she made her way down an alley, vaulted the fence, and kicked the back door in. She might be invisible, but booting in a back door would still draw less attention than forcing the front door. Rita was there to snoop, to see if Ben Turner had anything to hide. It didn't matter if he was home, or if he heard the forcing of the door, as the hex meant he wouldn't notice her.

That was the idea anyway.

As she passed through the kitchen and into the corridor, a flash of something caught her eye as it swung towards her head.

Rita ducked down, the object crashing against the stair bannister. Rita dived forward and rolled to create some distance between herself and her attacker, then spun, still crouching, to face her assailant. What she found before her was a wide-eyed man, his hair a mess, gripping a cricket bat with white-knuckled fingers.

Without waiting for him to take a second swing, Rita yelled and rushed the man. He suddenly wasn't as brave as he had been when her back was turned, and cowered as she charged. Rita grabbed his arm, twisted it up behind his back, and shoved him face-first into the wall. 'Drop the bat!' she screamed.

'Dropping the bat!'

'Drop it!'

'Dropping it!'

The cricket bat clattered to the floor and Rita back-heeled it out of reach.

'Name?'

'Ben. Ben Turner. You're hurting my arm.'

'Count yourself lucky it's not broken, mate. Yet.'

'Oh, shit.'

'Okay, I'm going to step away from you now and I want you to stay facing the wall.'

'Fine, fine.'

'If I think you're going to do anything I'm not okay with, I'll twat you with my magic axe, understood?'

'Sorry, your magic what?'

'I said, understood?'

'Yes, yes.'

Rita took a step back and released Ben Turner before taking a further three steps and pulling the axe from her belt.

'See, not turning,' said Ben. 'I am not turning.'

'Good, because I don't like getting blood on my—' it was at this precise juncture that Rita realised something she'd been missing. Ben Turner could see her. Hear her. Everything her.

'Okay then, what are you?' she asked.

'I… how do you mean?' asked Ben, craning his neck to look at her, confused.

'Don't mess about, I know about all the Uncanny crap now, I'm tits deep in it, okay?'

'If you say so.'

'So you can see me, despite the hex, which means you're something. Some Uncanny thing. So what is it? Are you magic? A wizard?'

Ben was a bit quiet then.

'Answer me!'

'Yes! Sorry, I will. Do you mind if I, sort of, turn around? Just a bit?'

'Go for it, but remember, magic axe.'

'Right. Yes.' Ben Turner—very slowly, arms raised—turned to face Rita.

'So?' she said. 'Are you going to go ahead and tell me what you are?'

'I'm… well, I'm an accountant. Mostly.'

Rita narrowed her eyes and took a step towards him, and was pleased to see Ben shrink back against the wall. He was a pretty big bloke, handsome too, in a very conservative sort of a way.

'A man was murdered at your office.'

Rita saw the information land. The body language, his change of expression. He was either a damn fine actor, or this was the first he was hearing about it.

'Who?'

'Security guard. Alan Crowther.'

'Shit. Oh, shit.'

He wasn't acting. When you'd been a detective for as long as Rita had, you got a feel for it. For knowing when someone was play-acting.

'So you don't know anything about it?' she asked.

'No, I don't. Why would I?'

Rita could see he looked on edge. 'Why didn't you clock out of work yesterday?'

'Well…' Confusion rippled across Ben's face. 'I don't… I don't actually remember leaving, to be honest. I was sick and…'

Rita peered closer at Ben, there were dark red stains up his arm. Blood. She pointed the axe at the stains.

'What's that then? Tomato ketchup?'

Ben looked at his arm, then at Rita. He shook his head. 'What's happened?' he asked. 'What's happening to me?'

Rita slid the axe back into her belt. 'Sorry, mate, but it's not good news.'

'How not good?'

Well,' Rita sighed, 'I think there's a good to very good chance that you're a werewolf. That or a wild bear escaped from the circus and went on a rampage around your office.'

Ben cycled through six or seven silent facial expressions.

'Oh, I hear you, Benny boy.'

It wouldn't take long for the police to find their way to Ben Turner's house and ask questions, so Rita thought it best that she got him out of there, and fast. After he showed her the state of his bedroom though—the blood-stained sheets—she paused just long enough to black-bag anything gory and stuff it into the boot of her car, and to scrub the carpet and flip the mattress. It would only pass a cursory investigation, there wasn't enough time to linger and do a thorough job.

'A werewolf?' said Ben for the sixth time as the pair exited his home.

'I know. Mad, isn't it?'

'I don't even like dogs,' said Ben. 'More of a budgie person.'

'Funny, you don't look like a mad old lady.'

'Thanks.'

'I did mention the fact that you probably murdered a man, right?'

Ben flushed red and frowned. 'I don't... maybe it wasn't me. You don't know. I'm not even sure I believe you, anyway. Werewolves aren't real. Generally.'

'Neither are magical hexes, but it didn't stop me triggering one. And don't forget all the blood in my car boot, none of it yours.'

Ben frowned, nodded, and slid into the passenger seat.

'Where are we going?'

'Bowling,' replied Rita.

Ben nodded again. At this point, he thought it best not to ask more. Rita started the car and pulled away.

'So,' said Rita, 'the cricket bat. Why did you attack me?'

'I thought… I thought you might be her.'

'And who is "her" when she's at home?'

'Magda. She's called Magda.'

'An ex?'

'No. I sort of chatted her up two nights back. Or she chatted me up. Things have been weird ever since then.'

'So you thought you'd cave her skull in?'

'No! Well, maybe just knock her out.'

'Why?'

'She bit me. Bit my neck. Or I dreamed that she did. I think maybe my drink was spiked, because I don't have any bite marks, look...'

Ben leaned over, yanking at the collar of his jumper. Rita scanned his neck, but there were no wounds.

'I was starting to think I'd made her up, but then… I woke up this morning and I couldn't remember getting back, and there was all that blood and she was just… there.'

Rita had seen enough movies to put the pieces together. Assuming real life functioned the same way as the movies. Not that this was real life as she knew it, of course. Christ, it made Rita's head spin trying to rationalise this stuff.

'So she turned you. If you're a werewolf, she must have been the one that turned you. Bit you, right?'

'I'd quite like to wake up now,' said Ben. 'I don't like this dream at all.'

Rita laughed. 'Yeah, you get used to it. Well, not used to it, just not as bewildered. Actually, that's not true either. So this woman, Magda, what did she say when you saw her again?'

'Just, random stuff. That she'd made me beautiful. That we were bonded now. That our time was coming.'

'And then?'

'And then she left.'

Okay, things weren't going too badly. If you ignored the dead wizard and the dead security guard. Here she was, Rita bloody

Hobbes, Uncanny newbie, with no assistance from that unhelpful bastard Carlisle, and she'd already nabbed a werewolf and gained a lead on some nutty woman turning people into werewolves. Policing the Uncanny world? Piece of piss.

15

The late Detective Sergeant Dan Waterson was at a bit of a loose end.

Ever since he'd peeked inside the black body bag in the morgue—the one containing the shredded remains of a wizard—Waterson had taken to his heels and gone on a bit of a restless wander.

'Shit,' said Waterson, for potentially the one-millionth time since his premature death.

Was this going to be his afterlife then? Just endless solo-strolling, feeling sorry for himself? Hadn't he lead a good life? He'd helped people, it had been his job to. If there was to be an afterlife, you would have thought he'd have accumulated a few brownie points there. Have pushed him a rung or ten up the afterlife ladder. But here he was, wandering around feeling sorry for himself.

He needed a plan. A purpose of some sort. A reason to carry on.

'Shit,' he repeated.

The dead detective sighed, hands deep in the pockets of his blue chinos, then looked up, to see he'd circled Blackpool and found himself back at the beach. He walked across the sand and looked up the beach to where he'd been murdered, a few hundred metres to the left of where he currently stood. He didn't fancy revisiting the scene of his demise, so he turned right and trudged off in the opposite direction, the sea at one side, the town at the other, Blackpool Tower piercing the sky in the distance.

There was something poking out of the sand.

It caught Waterson's eye as the sun was glinting off it. Breaking off from his journey, he made his way to the object, which was partially concealed by waves lapping over it. He could see part of a hilt, part of a blade. It was a sword. There were strange, ornate symbols carved into the blade. If Waterson's eyes weren't playing tricks on him, the symbols seemed to glow with a black and purple haze the closer he got to it.

He knew that sword.

He hadn't seen the whole object that had been shoved through him, he'd been too busy blinking with dumb surprise and then doing the whole dying thing, but he had seen part of the blade as it thrust up and out of him.

He reached out to take hold of the sword, to yank it out of its grave, but of course his hand passed right through. No matter how many times he tried, or how hard he concentrated on making his hand more like meat and bone and less like fog and nothing.

'Shit!' said Waterson, the word fast becoming his catchphrase.

As he sank back on to his knees further, he noticed something else. Something besides the glowing sword. He noticed twin tendrils of black smoke twisting out of the sea and snaking at speed toward him.

Waterson uttered his catchphrase again as the smoke snakes hit him, twisted round him, then yanked him off the sand out, screaming over and into the sea.

Waterson was still screaming when he realised he was no longer moving and that he was no longer on the beach, or over the sea, or even in the sea, but someplace else entirely. He stopped screaming and opened an eye. There were candles. Lots and lots and lots of candles. Way too many candles. It looked like someone was trying to get rid of a giant surplus of wax.

Waterson opened both eyes and stood. He was in a large, vaulted chamber of some sort. Marble floor, marble ceiling, giant, thick marble pillars at regular intervals, and everywhere, lit candles. In candelabras, large and small, on the floor, affixed to the sides of the pillars. The multitude of flickering flames threw dancing shadows across every surface.

It was all a bit spooky.

Maybe this is actually Heaven, thought DS Dan Waterson.

Yeah, that bit before, the aimless wandering, that was just him waiting for his number to be called. For his table to be free. And now here he was, picked up and delivered to the entrance to Heaven. That made sense. Even more sense when he turned the corner and met the Angel.

'Hello?' said Waterson, wary, edging slowly towards the figure in the brilliant white robes who was on his knees, head bowed, encased within a large glass cube.

'Hi, I'm Dan. Is this Heaven?'

The Angel laughed. It sounded to Waterson like songbirds. 'Hello, Daniel,' It said, lifting Its head to look at him.

'Oh,' said Waterson, as he took in the full beauty of the figure before him. 'Wow.'

The Angel stood and smiled.

'You *are* an angel, aren't you?' asked Waterson.

'I am. One of the originals. Divine.'

'Wow,' said Waterson again, though that didn't really mean anything to him. Still, he was talking to an angel, and that was pretty wow-worthy. 'So, is this Heaven? Or, maybe, a gate leading to the main house, maybe? Also, you seem to be in a glass box. Any reason, or…?'

'I am in prison.'

'Oh.'

'You are going to help me escape this prison, Daniel.'

'Am I?'

This was all taking a bit of a turn, as far as Waterson was concerned. All he wanted was to enter a place of eternal happiness, and instead it seemed like this Angel was about to give him chores.

'Quite lucky, really,' said the Angel.

'Yes. I suppose so. What is?'

'Your death.'

Waterson frowned and nodded, mulling that one over a bit. 'Come again?'

'After he lost the axe, I gave the Magician, Jenner, a sword with which to dispatch anyone who tried to stand in our way. Upon the sword was a hex that would pin any soul taken to the physical plane to Blackpool. That way they would not find themselves in Heaven and tell tales where I do not wish tales to be told.'

'Right. Sorry if I'm not completely up to speed with all this sort of thing, but it's really Rita who was into the weird stuff. Me, I like snooker and beer. I also babble like this when I'm scared. Though should I be scared? I'm already dead, I can't be deader, surely?'

The birdsong laugh again. 'Oh, there are worse things than being dead, Daniel. I can show them all to you.'

Waterson swallowed and dithered, wondering if he could leg it in the opposite direction.

'No, you cannot,' replied the Angel, reading his mind.

'Good. Not a big fan of running, anyway. Tight hamstrings.'

'The hex also gives me control of you. Which means, without access to my other tools, I shall now pick you up. Use you.'

'You know, for an Angel, you don't seem very nice.'

'Hush now,' replied the Angel. Waterson opened his mouth to reply, but found that he could not.

He staggered back, passing between hundreds of candles on the floor, their lit ends weaving as he passed over, but remaining bright. Waterson raked at his throat with his fingers, tried to force the words out, but none came.

The Angel laughed.

16

Rita really enjoyed the faces Ben Turner pulled as she lead him to Big Pins.

There was confusion; that was good. Shock and surprise; those two played a big role. Childlike wonder; that came into play once, too. Rita saw it wash over his face, and she drank down each and every expression with glee. This time, she wasn't the tourist, wasn't the new kid in town. No, this time, Rita was the one who knew the secrets and was able to share like some seasoned, nonchalant pro. Swaggering ever so slightly, she lead Ben down the blind alley – the alley that wasn't there, that Ben knew wasn't there and did not (and never had as long as he'd lived in Blackpool, which was his whole life) exist. Until it suddenly did exist and he was walking down it, gawping in disbelief.

'How? How, how, how, I mean…? This is crazy.'

'Hm?' replied Rita, scuffing a worn cobble under her shoe. 'Oh right, yeah, hidden streets. They're dotted about. Here and there. No big deal.'

Ben hopped out of the blind alley, back into a street he knew existed, and then hopped right back into the blind alley once more.

'Ha! This is… wow!'

Rita grinned, enjoying the gleeful shock.

'You're telling me this alley has always been here? I mean, always-always?'

'Yup. Pretty cool, eh? A secret, invisible alley. Those of us in the know, know of course.' Rita sniffed and leaned against the wall, buffing her nails on her coat.

'So it's true. You were telling the truth. There's a whole hidden world people don't know about?'

'Oh yeah, all sorts of magic guff all over the place. Hidden streets, vampires, ghosts, all kinds of crap. I'm also a teensiest bit related to an angel.'

Ben blinked at her. 'You're… you're an angel?'

'Yeah. Little bit.' When Rita said "little bit", she was vastly overestimating.

'Amazing. You know, I thought you looked, sort of… well…'

Rita raised an eyebrow. 'Sort of what?'

Ben's cheeks flushed. 'Sort of… nice. Angelic. Sort of.'

'Well, aren't you the charmer?'

So much blood had rushed to Ben's cheeks that Rita worried he might pass out.

'Come on,' she said, letting him off the hook, 'lots more to see down here, love.'

Rita pushed open the door to Big Pins, its neon sign coughing and spluttering above, and lead Ben inside.

'Why is there a dodgy looking 1950s ten pin bowling alley in a secret alley?' asked Ben. 'If that's not a stupid question.'

Rita stopped at the bar and waved at Linton so he'd pour a couple of drinks.

'Not stupid. If you were a bunch of secret weirdos, you'd want a secret place to hang with other weirdos being weird, right?'

'Right, yeah. I suppose you would.'

'So you get places like Big Pins. Just because you're a wizard, doesn't mean you don't like beer and bowling.'

Rita and Ben took their drinks to a spare table.

'That guy behind the bar…'

'That's Linton. Yes, he's big, yes, he's scary looking, no, I don't know what he is either. Other than big. And actually a lot nicer than you'd think. Lets me kip in a back room for free.'

Ben nodded and sipped his drink. His heart beat a little too fast and his eyes darted around the room at the other patrons.

'It's okay, you're safe here,' said Rita. 'Well, probably.'

'Thanks, that makes me feel much better.'

Rita waved at the small, round figure of Formby as he shuffled into Big Pins, hands clasped together. He hurried over and took a seat at the table.

'Good timing,' said Rita. 'Anyone would think you were following me.'

Formby ignored the insinuation. 'Any news, then?' he asked, nose twitching, eager as all eaves are for fresh information.

'Yup, this is Ben Turner,' she replied pointing to Ben, who stared warily at the strange person who had sat down next to him.

'Is he… what is he?'

'This is Formby. He's an eaves.'

'That I am,' said Formby, grinning, exposing his twin set of sharp little piranha teeth and holding out a grubby hand to shake. Ben took the hand, grimacing.

'Yes, Ben, Formby is what we might have thought of as a monster.'

'I'm a nice one though. Mostly.'

'Oh, I'm sure,' said Ben, slowly sliding his chair away from Formby in a not at all obvious manner.

'Honestly,' said Rita, amused, 'he's a mate, okay? He might look like a thumb with sharp teeth and Spock ears, but he's a good guy.'

Formby nodded and supped his drink, which had, only moments before, been Ben's drink.

'He will nick your drink though,' said Rita.

'My drink, now,' said Formby, smacking his lips.

'Think I might just… pop to the little boy's room,' said Ben.

'Sure thing,' replied Rita, pointing to a far corner, 'that way.'

'Thanks,' said Ben, turning to make his way over. Rita leaned over and grabbed his arm, turning him back.

'Don't think about wriggling through the window and legging it, okay?'

'I wasn't thinking about doing that,' Ben replied.

Rita raised an eyebrow. 'I'm a copper, I know a flight risk when I see one.'

'Okay. Sorry. It's just all a bit...' Ben gestured at Formby, at Linton, at the thing with leathery wings lining up a bowling ball, ready to take down a spare.

'I know. I understand. I'm only a few days into this myself. But you're part of it now. And not a good part so far. The best place for you is with me and my magic axe, okay? Trust me on that.'

Ben looked up as the winged person swore at the still-standing pin, then nodded at Rita and headed to the Gents.

'So he's the killer, then?' said Formby.

'Shh!' said Rita, peering over Formby's shoulder to make sure Ben was out of earshot. 'Yes, I think so.'

'Then why so friendly? Werewolves get put down, not patted, in my experience.'

'It's not his fault. And he didn't kill the wizard.'

Formby cocked his head and frowned. 'You sure?'

'Yeah, he only got turned two nights back, after the wizard was murdered, so it couldn't have been him.'

'But he did kill the security guard.'

'Okay, sure, that's a strike against him, fair do's. But someone has done that to him. He wasn't in control. A woman made him into a monster and he knows her name and what she looks like.'

'Probably a master werewolf.'

'A what-the-what?'

'Master werewolf. Your pissing friend is a plain old werewolf. Gets turned and then every full moon he turns and goes on a kill rampage. A master werewolf, they're pure lycanthrope. They can control the change. Can change whenever they want. Can turn others, others like Ben, to be their pet, too.'

Rita nodded, noting everything down in her pad. Ideas, information, evidence. 'So they're bad news, I take it?'

'Oh aye, bad lot, master werewolves. Not many of them left these days mind you, so she's a rare one.'

'And she's the one I have to find. Directly or indirectly, she's the one responsible for all this. For the wizard, for the security guard, for Ben. She's the criminal, she's my target.'

'Then best be careful. Vicious they can be.'

'Oh, werewolves can be vicious? Who knew?'

Formby frowned at her, not in the least bit amused. He opened his mouth to reply when the conversation was halted by the sight of Ben bursting through the toilet door and into the room with gusto, stumbling to the faded carpet.

'Ben?' said Rita.

A hulking shape with dark green, leathery skin and two sharp tusks jutting up from his lower jaw exited the toilets after Ben.

'Oi, ugly, what's your game?' said Rita, standing and throwing her coat open, resting a hand on the axe.

'He stinks! Stinks!' said Tusk.

'He could do with a shower, but he's not that bad,' replied Rita.

Tusk grunted and began to stomp towards Ben, who stumbled to his feet and rushed back until he was behind Rita.

'He just attacked me! I was washing my hands and suddenly he was behind me, sniffing.'

Linton stepped out from behind the counter, baseball bat in hand. 'Okay, what's the noise about?'

'Him!' said Tusk. 'Stinks. I smell what he is.'

'And what's that?' asked Linton.

'Werewolf.'

The other patrons of Big Pins were all ears now, and Rita could feel the ripple spread out and around. Apprehension, fear, violence, all bubbling together and getting ready to explode.

'You brought a werewolf into my place?' asked Linton, slapping the bat in his palm.

'I'm okay, I won't do anything,' said Ben.

'Yes, because I kill you now,' said Tusk, stepping towards Ben.

Rita pulled out the axe and held it high, heart thudding. 'Back up there, toothy, or I'll hack those gnashers right out of your gob.'

'Kill the werewolf, kill the werewolf,' the low chant began to circle round and round Big Pins. Rita was starting to get the impression that these Uncanny types were not overly fond of werewolves.

'Take him away,' said Linton.

'Linton, wait,' pleaded Rita. 'Yeah, he's a werewolf, but is it currently a full moon?'

'No.'

'Then what's the rush?'

'Vermin. Kill vermin,' said Tusk.

'Yeah, I think we all know your take on this, uggers,' said Rita. 'Linton, I'm on a case, there's someone bigger than Ben at play. A master werewolf in Blackpool.'

Rita looked around Big Pins and saw that new bit of information had hit home.

'That's right,' she continued, 'a master werewolf, not your mindless creature like Ben here.'

'Thanks,' said Ben.

'This werewolf here is under my protection until he helps me bring the master werewolf to justice, got it?'

Rita looked to Linton for support. He frowned, then nodded, turning to Tusk and pressing the baseball bat against his chest. 'You will not hurt him.'

Tusk growled, 'Can't protect always, sooner or later I will—'

The rest of the sentence was cut short as Linton swung the end of his bat at Tusk's forehead and knocked him out cold.

'He's barred,' said Linton to the rest of Big Pins, who all nodded and made a great show of going back about their business.

'Thanks, Linton,' said Rita.

'Yes, thanks. Thank you,' said Ben, stepping out, shaking, from behind Rita.

'For her, not for you, wolf,' replied Linton, grabbing Tusk by the foot and dragging him to the exit.

'Well, that was all a bit exciting, eh?' said Rita, slipping her axe back in her belt.

Ben didn't seem so cheery. He sat and put his head in his hands. 'Christ. What am I? What have I done? What has she turned me into?'

'Monster,' replied Formby, who was now finishing off Rita's drink.

'Don't worry,' said Rita, 'everything is going to work out just fine. Trust me.'

Ben nodded and Rita wondered if she'd just lied to him.

17

Derek Nolan—the low-level wizard, ex-teacher, and current assistant manager of a local supermarket—arrived home from work at a little after two in the afternoon.

'Here puss-puss,' he cooed, as he closed the front door behind him and shrugged off his coat, hanging it on the hook on the wall and depositing his keys into the bowl that sat on the table beside it.

'Alfie. Daddy's home,' said Derek, making little kissy noises to try and rouse the fat cat from wherever it was dozing. Derek had never thought of himself as a pet person, but for the last year or so an old stray had started turning up in his back garden, and Derek had found himself growing attached to the thing. Eventually he had let the cat, now christened Alfie, into his house, and the cat hadn't taken a step outside since. It knew when it was on to a good thing.

Derek went through to the kitchen and lifted Alfie's empty food bowl from the floor and placed it on the table before heading over to the buzzing fridge to grab some of the leftover cold cuts he'd put on a covered plate the previous evening.

'Alfie, got some tasty meat for you, boy,' said Derek, pulling off the shrink wrap and depositing the meat into Alfie's bowl. With no sign of the lazy cat coming to feast, or even just to greet its master, Derek grabbed a bottle of beer from the fridge and headed for the door under the staircase.

All wizards have a sanctum of some sort. A secret place wherein they can study, practice, and generally do wizard-y things safe from the curious eyes. Derek's was under the stairs. Quite a long way under the stairs. He opened the small wooden door and stooped slightly as he shuffled into the space beyond. Stone steps led into the gloom.

Derek sipped from his bottle and began to make his way down to the impossibly large room that lay at the bottom. His sanctum. A library far too large to actually be hidden beneath his modest-sized house. The walls were lined with towering bookcases that seemed to stretch up and up until you lost sight of the top. A large wooden desk and green leather chair were the only other items in the sanctum. Apart from the mini-fridge, but the mini-fridge was currently empty as Derek had yet to do his big shop for the week.

That was twice now that Detective Rita Hobbes had come to him recently, looking for answers. Neither time had he had the answers she was looking for. Derek slumped in his chair and threw his legs up on the desk. Why was she always coming to him, anyway? He was nobody. Not really. A minor-wizard at best. It wasn't fair, being hounded. What had he ever done to deserve that?

Well, yes, there was the groping incident that had lead to his dismissal as a teacher several years back, but he'd not groped anyone since. Not unless he'd paid them first. He was an honest groper these days. A regular pillar of society.

It took several more minutes of self-pity before Derek Nolan, honest-groping minor-wizard, noticed the splatter of blood on the floor to the right of his desk. Derek frowned and sat up, placing his bottle down on the desk. Was it blood? It looked like blood. Derek leaned to the side to investigate, and discovered the reason why Alfie had failed to appear. Even after he'd put out food for him.

It was Alfie the fat cat.

His small, plump body lay on the floor of Derek's secret sanctum, poking out slightly from under the desk.

'Alfie?'

Derek went down on his hands and knees to peer under the desk and get a good look at Alfie. Maybe he was just injured. Been in a fight with another cat, or that noisy dog from two doors down. Always barking and gnashing its teeth at any passing mog, that one. Had he sunk his teeth into poor Alfie, only for Alfie to wriggle free and make his way down here to keep safe until Derek's return?

'Alfie, you okay, mate?'

Alfie was not okay. As Derek peered closer, he saw that his adopted cat was not just dead, but torn into four different pieces. His guts were wrapped around his neck.

'Oh, Christ! Oh shit in my mouth!' said Derek, scrambling away from the gruesome find. What could have happened, and how did Alfie get down into his sanctum after it had? He couldn't have done, not in that state. Which meant…

'Oh…'

Which meant it had happened within the sanctum itself.

Derek stood slowly, noticing the second figure for the first time.

'Took you long enough, wizard,' said the woman perched nine shelves up on one of Derek's over-stuffed bookcases, full as they were with all manner of magical texts.

Derek's eyes darted to the door, to the stone steps that led up to the house. The woman clicked her fingers and the door slammed shut, the desk in front of Derek scraping across the floor and stopping in front of the door to block his escape.

'I don't think so,' said the woman, her piercing blue eyes glowing sharp through the gloom of the sanctum.

'Who are you?' asked Derek, shaking from head to toe.

The woman frowned and considered the question. 'Well, to you, I am death.' She hopped down from the high shelf, landing soundlessly upon the ground. 'You can also call me Magda.'

'This… this is my sanctum! You've breached my sanctum!' said Derek, trying not to sound as scared as he felt.

'Yes. I also killed your cat.'

Magda approached, slowly, playfully, and as she moved closer. Derek could see dark blood smeared across her mouth.

'Did you…? You killed him with your teeth?'

The woman smiled. 'Yes. He did not taste good. Try him, if you don't believe me.'

Derek decided it best to take to his heels. With the way blocked, the easiest way out was a little simple transportation magic. One of the spells he was, for some reason, most adept at. Not bothering to say goodbye, Derek willed the magic in the sanctum into himself and demanded it obey his command. Demanded it take him from this place and deposit him somewhere safe.

The air around him swirled with colour and Derek readied himself to depart. Only it didn't happen. The colours crackled and fizzed and then puttered out.

'Problem?' asked Magda, smiling.

Derek tried again, and again, a sweat breaking out across his brow with the effort, until he finally fell to his knees, defeated.

'Not… not possible…' said Derek, gasping for air.

'I am not stupid, wizard,' said Magda. She wandered over to one corner of the sanctum and crouched, running her finger across the floor and holding it up for Derek to see.

Chalk.

Magda had cast a holding spell, so that no one was able to magic their way out of the place. Derek had walked into a cage.

'You were the one who killed the wizard,' said Derek.

'Yes. And I feasted upon his flesh, and upon his magic. I enjoyed both.'

Derek staggered up to his feet, his heart racing. No way to jump out, he was going to have to fight for his life. He already feared he knew how that was going to turn out. He looked down at dead Alfie.

'You're a werewolf,' he said.

'Not so stupid, are you? But I'm not just any werewolf, I'm a master werewolf.'

Derek thought about what he'd witnessed. The door, the desk; that was magic. The spell keeping him contained, the chalk symbols would need magic fed into them to bring them to life. But a werewolf, master or not, wasn't able to use magic. It was beyond them. They didn't have it naturally, and could not be taught. Could not master it. The only magic in them was that of their own curse. What Derek was seeing was impossible.

'You can't do this. Any of it. You're not magic, not properly, not like me. How are you doing it?' asked Derek, curiosity vying with his fear for pole position.

'Viciously,' replied Magda, and in the blink of an eye, her face turned monstrous, her mouth full of large, sharp teeth, her eyes yellow and bulging, her features a hungry snarl.

Magda tore into Derek, who barely had time to scream before he expired. Magda then feasted upon some of his flesh until her stomach was satisfied. After that, she suckled upon his magic, drinking it all down, feeling her own connection to the Uncanny growing stronger with each mouthful, her grip on magic ever surer. She was strong enough now. She was sure of it. She was ready.

Magda took what was left of Derek Nolan—small-time wizard, ex-teacher, and former supermarket assistant manager—and laid it out on the beach for all to see.

18

February 14th, 2012, Somewhere in Wales

Hell is not just one place, it is many places.

Think of Hell like a fungus, buried deep under the Earth. Though, of course, it is not below the Earth at all, just as Heaven is not above. Such terms are meaningless when it comes to such places, but they serve as handy tags to those with a flat understanding of the universe.

So think of Hell like a fungus.

There is the main body of it. A fist of dank despair. And squirming from this central, rotten mass are millions of rancid tendrils. Roots winding through rock and dirt and sea and reality, until they hit fresh air.

A little piece of Hell in the open.

A fissure. A rift. A crack.

An exit, an entrance, a meeting place.

Most of these seams to Hell are beyond reach for anyone who walks upon the planet's surface, Uncanny or not. They simply do not exist in a way they could be found, seen, or understood.

But still, enough of them do.

In a cave perhaps, high on the side of a mountain. At the

bottom of an unused, dry well by a family home in the English countryside. And then there is the one Magda found, under the arching roots of an ancient oak tree known as the Creeping Oak. The Creeping Oak stands somewhere in a desolate, beautiful area of Wales. It is best if the location is kept vague.

The tree itself has stood for many centuries, and its roots jut high from the dirt, as though arching their backs like a cat. Locals said it was because the tree used them to creep across the countryside, using its roots like a spider would its legs, but that of course is impossible.

Of course.

Magda had been searching for some years for a place like the Creeping Oak. Most who claimed to know the location of such a place, of a direct line to Hell, were more often than not lying, or at the very least ill-informed. Many of those that did actually know were unwilling to give up the information for any price, for such a place could be as precious as it was dangerous.

So Magda had searched. As she had kept her head down, attempting to keep off the radar of any wizard with a taste for her blood, to keep off the radar of that one wizard in particular, Magda had visited numerous Uncanny gatherings late at night and made her desires known.

Eventually, she had met an eaves who claimed to know the location of what she was after. In return for a taste of magic, he would tell her where it was hidden, and she agreed. The eaves told her, and Magda tore his throat out with her teeth and ate his heart.

The Creeping Oak stood alone upon a small hill, overlooking a barren valley. Winds tore at it as though trying to rip the tree from the land and deposit it far, far away, but the Creeping Oak stood strong against the winds, barely shaking a branch.

The wind bit into Magda, but she did not feel it as she crested the top of the hill and walked towards the giant tree. Its trunk was at least three metres wide, which was much wider than any oak Magda had come across in her long life. She took in its gnarled roots, thrusting out of the ground, reaching high above her then shooting back beneath the soil. Each root was as thick as her arm.

Magda reached out and touched one of the roots. She could feel the life in it. It throbbed, it twitched, it writhed. She walked towards the trunk, where several roots could be seen feeding into the tree. Magda placed her hand flat against the tree trunk and closed her eyes.

'Ahka Hyula Fa'Lach.'

The wind dropped in an instant, and the world held its breath.

For several seconds, nothing happened.

Magda began to suspect she had been fed false information, before she had fed on the information's source.

Then the tree beneath her hand cracked.

Magda opened her eyes and stepped back, afraid about what might happen next. Afraid, but determined.

A jagged crack appeared up the tree trunk and the tree opened.

Magda took a breath or two to calm her jumping heart, and then she walked into the tree. Rather than smack straight into the tree's interior—or at the very least the other side of the trunk—Magda instead began walking up an iron staircase. She looked past her feet to see it twisting down and down for eternity, but she knew she was meant to go up. Each step she took, the ancient staircase swayed and shook, and it felt to Magda that at any moment, with any footstep, the brittle staircase might collapse and send her falling down forever.

She found the creature at the top. Found the demon.

A little old lady, white of hair, plump of cheek, rotten of teeth, wiping her fat hands upon the stained gingham apron she wore.

It was not how she had expected a demon to look, but then demons have no set form. They can and do look like all manner of things.

'Hello, hello, do come in, I get so little company,' said the Demon. The top of the Creeping Oak—if that's where they were, and Magda was not sure how they could be—looked like the kitchen of a cosy old cottage.

'Milk in your tea, dear?' asked the Demon.

'Yes. Thank you.'

Magda, wary, made her way to the large wooden table and took a seat. Something that might have been a dog opened an eye from its sleeping place by the open fire, grunted, then closed it again.

'Here we go then, can't beat a nice cup of tea, eh?'

The old woman—the Demon—handed Magda a fine china cup full of tea, then took a seat opposite to her.

Magda eyed the cup with suspicion.

'Oh, it's just tea and milk and hot water, dear, on my honour!' and the Demon laughed at the idea of it having any honour. 'I heard you was on your way, you know. The soul of a very disgruntled eaves passed this way and I cocked an ear to hear what it was making such a fuss about.'

'He would have told others about me,' Magda replied. 'Sooner or later, people would have found out and come after me.'

'Oh, no need to explain to me, dear, I'm a demon, after all. Rotten shits all of us, you know. I'd sell my own granny out for ten bob. If I had a granny, which I don't. I'm a demon. Demons don't have grannies.'

Magda nodded and sipped her tea. It was good.

'Told you,' said the Demon. 'Just normal tea.'

'Tastes better than normal tea.'

The Demon grinned and shook her head, coyly.

'Okay then, so what's it to be? Selling your soul, is it? The usual?'

Magda nodded.

'Yep, yep, people always selling their souls. Seems like they can't wait to get rid of the things. A soul for me and a wish for you, that's how it goes. You're sure you're willing to pay the price?'

Magda was sure.

'What you after then?'

Magda sipped her tea again, then looked the Demon in her watery, red eyes. 'Magic. I want magic.'

'I see.'

'I want to be able to access it. Take it. Use it. Master it. Then I will never have to run in fear from those who wield it ever again.

I will never cower before a wizard. They will cower before me. Cower and beg and scream and die.'

'I see,' said the Demon. 'Well, it's good to have a hobby.'

'Can you do it? Can you give me magic? Can you give me what they have?'

The Demon nodded, finished her tea, and stood, taking Magda's cup from her hands.

'I haven't finished,' said Magda.

'You have. And it's done. The deal is fair.'

'It's…' Magda looked at her hands, looked at the air around her. 'I don't feel anything.'

'You will. Now you have what your heart desires, and when your number is up, I'll be there to take mine, understood? No getting out of it. We've made a trade, fair and square.'

'Yes.'

'Good.'

Magda said goodbye and made her way back down the swaying iron staircase, and stepped out of the Creeping Oak. She turned to see the entrance into the tree no long existed.

Magda buttoned her coat and walked down the hill.

19

Manchester is an English city well known for two things. There is the sporting heritage, home as it is to two giants of the footballing world: bitter rivals, Manchester United and Manchester City. Then there is the music. Manchester is a city of music. Many famous bands and musicians plied their trade in that northern city, from the aching, lyrical sadness of The Smiths, to the swaggering, fist in-the-air confidence of Oasis.

But these are just the everyday things the city is known for. In the Uncanny world, it is known for much more...

It is the birthplace of Ivner the Mighty, the first Wizard in recorded history, who perished laying low the eternal dragon, and whose bones are said to rest still somewhere within the boundary of Manchester, awaiting resurrection.

There is the invisible river that runs like a great, winding snake half a mile above Manchester. It is, as the name suggests, invisible, but its waters are said to contain healing properties. If you were able to actually find it.

And then there was the reason Carlisle found himself in Manchester, purple coat flapping in the bitter northern breeze. He was here to find the City of the Dead.

Carlisle had, of course, heard of the place, and knew something of what it was. The City of the Dead, lurking somewhere beneath Manchester itself. A place where things that could not be killed ended up when they died. Which did not seem to make any sense. How could that which could not be killed possibly die? But this was the Uncanny world, and sense did not always count there.

According to Giles L'Merrier, the key to killing the Angel of Blackpool could be found in the City of the Dead. A man, or a thing that looked like a man, that might be persuaded to kill an Angel of the first order.

Carlisle walked the streets until he found a place that felt right. He reached into his coat and pulled out a piece of white chalk. He stepped towards a red brick wall—the outside of an ordinary building—and drew the outline of a door. Having done that, he placed the chalk back into his coat and placed the palm of one pale hand against the rough brick at the centre of the pretend door.

'I request access,' he said, and forced magic into the door's chalk outline. Satisfied, Carlisle lowered himself to the ground, crossing his legs and closing his eyes. For twelve hours he sat, he waited, he did not open his eyes. Even when people began to drop change at his feet, taking him for a beggar, Carlisle remained perfectly still, eyes shut, and concentrated on the rhythm of his breathing.

His chest expanded as he inhaled, and lowered as he exhaled, and that's all he thought about for twelve hours. Just the simple act of inhaling and exhaling. Of his lungs inflating and deflating. A hypnotic cycle that rolled on and on and on.

Finally, his concentration was broken by a polite cough.

Carlisle opened his eyes and spun on his rear end to face the source of the cough.

He was stood in a doorway. A doorway that had not existed before Carlisle drew it. He was a monk, dressed in billowing, brown sackcloth, a large stick—taller than the monk himself—gripped in one hand. Dangling from the stick were tiny bones, hanging from pieces of string. Carlisle recognised the bones as finger and toe bones. Human finger and toe bones.

Carlisle hopped up gracefully on to his feet and bowed. 'Delighted to meet you,' he said.

The Monk frowned, then sighed. 'Come on then, if you're coming.' He turned and walked back into the doorway. Carlisle smiled and followed, the doorway disappearing as he did so, now just the side of a building with chalk lines drawn on it once more.

Derek Nolan's eviscerated body had been found on Blackpool beach, his blood soaking into the sand, turning it a dark red. He had been murdered, according the records Rita snooped at, after she had met and taken Ben Turner into her own protective custody. Thanks to this forethought, and much to his relief, Ben did not have another death to add to his tally.

'He wasn't killed here,' said Rita, as she made her way back to Ben from the taped-off area of the beach where Derek had been found.

'How do you know that?' asked Ben.

'The way he was posed, looked like he'd been laid out to be found. And he was killed in the day, so if that amount of damage had happened to him on the beach, with the sun up, there's a good chance someone would have spotted that, don't you think?'

'Right. Good point.'

They climbed into Rita's car and set off for Derek's house. Rita had been there once before, just a few days earlier, with Carlisle, whereupon they had discovered he was a wizard.

'What are you thinking about?' asked Ben, who had taken over driving duties.

'Hm?' replied Rita, glancing at him.

'I haven't known you long, but you always seem to be talking.'

'Oi, are you calling me gobby?'

'No. Well, a bit.'

Rita laughed. 'Fair play, I do have a mouth on me. I was just thinking about a friend of mine called Carlisle. Well, not a friend exactly. Maybe an enemy, in a way. I dunno.'

'Okay. Sounds… complicated.'

'Hm. He did for me what I'm doing for you. He broke me into

the Uncanny world, held my hand as I took my first few steps. And now he's off God knows where looking for a way to kill an angel.'

Ben nodded thoughtfully. 'I beg your pardon?'

'Long story. Basically I'm hexed and there's an evil angel trapped under the sea that we have to stop to, well, un-hex me. Carlisle is trying to sort that out. I think. Hopefully.'

'So, you want to go back?' asked Ben. 'To your normal life?'

'Of course. I mean, I think so, anyway. Don't you?'

'Yeah. But my situation is a bit different. I turn into a monster and kill people with my teeth.'

'That is true, you definitely have it worse.'

Ben laughed, but it quickly passed. 'He called me vermin, that monster back at Big Pins.'

'Did you see the state of him? If anyone's vermin…'

'They were scared of me. Even that big bloke behind the bar. Scared of what I become. I don't want to carry on if I have to stay like this.'

'Woah now, less of that sort of talk.'

'Rita, I won't be a monster, okay? I won't kill anyone else.'

Rita went to argue again, then caught sight of Ben's eyes. He was right. She wouldn't want to live a monster either. She patted him on the leg and turned the radio on. *Hungry Like the Wolf* by Duran Duran was playing. Ben had to pull over as he and Rita burst into a hysterical fit of laughter that only passed after about five, tear-streaked, belly-aching minutes.

Rita had not known Derek Nolan well, and what's more she hadn't liked him at all, but he was still a person she knew who had been murdered. A face she recognised, a name she knew, a voice she could hear clearly in her head. Which brought the case closer to home. Made it feel more personal. She had only been rattling his cage the day before, and part of her wondered at that coincidence. Could her visit have prompted his murder somehow? Did this Magda Ben mentioned have eyes on her?

They drove past Derek's house and found two police cars parked up outside, and several officers and forensics marching in and out of the place. They parked up on the next street so as not to arouse suspicion.

'What are you going to do?' asked Ben.

'I'm going to do my Miss Invisible bit and have a nose around. Those bods in the blue boiler suits tells me this is the murder scene.'

Rita went to step out of the car, then stopped. 'You know, funny thing.'

'What?'

'So far, the only dead people are wizards.'

'Well, Alan, the security guard, he wasn't a wizard. Was he?'

'No, but she didn't kill him, you did.'

'Thanks for the reminder.'

'Let's assume this woman, this Magda, killed the first wizard, and killed Derek, too. Well, she didn't kill you. She turned you.'

'So?'

'And you're not a wizard. Three attacks from her that we know of, and the two that were on wizards are fatal. You, she didn't want to kill. You she wanted to turn. Maybe there's a reason for that.'

'Maybe she has something against wizards.'

'We think so,' said a third voice.

Rita and Ben turned to see a man leaning down to look in the car at them. He wore a snug, dark blue suit and had a pinched face.

'Uh, who are you?' asked Rita.

'I'm Ulner, I've been looking for you,' he replied, and then he clicked his fingers.

Rita blinked and found she was no longer sat in the passenger seat of her car, parked a street away from Derek Nolan's house. Ulner had used magic to move her. She turned to find a bewildered Ben Turner still at her side.

'What just happened?' he asked.

Rita looked around and found she recognised where they had been taken. They were inside of a cave. There were no windows, no tunnels in or out, no entrances or exits of any kind, and gathered around the edges of the space were a variety of men, some dressed normally, some dressed in robes and other strange outfits. Wizards. It was the gathering spot for local wizards that she had visited once before, with Carlisle.

Ulner waved at her from his place amongst the gathered wizards.

'You know this is an abduction?' said Rita. 'And the abduction of a police officer at that. Serious business, boys.' Rita opened her coat and rested a hand on her magic axe.

'You wanted to speak with us,' said Ulner.

'Yeah, about that. See, a normal person approaches another person and they agree to go somewhere together. That's how it usually works, but I suppose you fellers aren't used to asking for permission, are you?'

The gathered wizards grumbled quietly to each other.

'Sorry,' said Ben, 'but what's happening now? I know everything is generally insane, but it would be nice to know.'

'That was a wizard, and these are more wizards. The first wizard magicked us to this place, where all the local wizards meet up for a natter.'

'Right.'

'Don't worry, there's nothing to be scared about. That is correct, right?' she asked the gathered crowd.

'Of course,' replied a wizard no taller than four feet, dressed in a robe with a collar that stood almost half his height.

'I suppose you've heard about Derek Nolan, then?' Rita asked.

'We have,' replied Ulner. 'We believe that something impossible is happening.'

'That more or less seems to be the case every hour these days,' said Rita.

'Do you know what a master werewolf is?' asked Ulner.

'Of course,' said Rita, as if Formby hadn't given her the gist of it only a couple of hours earlier. 'There's werewolves, and there's master werewolves. The masters can control their wolfy-changing thing, and can turn others with a bite. That about it?'

The gathered wizards burbled their agreement.

'So what's the impossible bit?'

'Werewolves, master or not, do not have access to magic. Should not be able to take down a wizard. It appears, somehow, that this one does and can.'

'Right, and you're all shitting yourselves, eh?'

Ulner looked down to the little wizard with the high collar, then back to Rita. 'More or less.'

'Look, no need to worry, your girl Rita is on the case. I already have a name and a description, and an eaves keeping his eyes and pointy ears open for me. I'll solve the case.'

'But how many more will die before you do?' asked Ulner.

'Look, if you have any way of helping out, believe me, I'm open to suggestions.'

'Rita,' said Ben.

'Yep?'

'I don't… I feel wrong…'

Rita looked at Ben. His skin had turned pale, waxy.

'What is happening? What is he?' asked Ulner.

'No one. A friend. It's fine,' said Rita, flapping a dismissive hand in Ulner's direction as she put a hand to Ben's shoulder. He was trembling. 'Ben, what's wrong?' she whispered.

Ben bent over, gripping his stomach, sweat breaking out across his brow. 'I remember this… I remember this pain… last night.'

Rita took a step back. Last night? Last night had been a full moon, but that was last night, the four day full moon cycle was over, it couldn't be a full moon again, not so soon.

'Ben, I think you're just having some sort of panic attack.'

But it was no panic attack. Ben fell to his knees and screamed, throwing his head back, his mouth now full of large, sharp teeth.

'Werewolf!' cried Ulner. 'You bring that beast here!'

'But, it's not a full moon!' said Rita. 'How can he be changing?'

The cave was in chaos, Ben screamed in agony as his body bucked and tore, and his bones cracked.

'Ben, stop, please stop.'

His screams made Rita shake.

The gathered wizards did not stay to attack, they fled, disappearing one by one until the cave faded from view and Rita found herself in a back alley, alone with the rapidly transforming Ben Turner.

She looked up into the darkening sky. The moon looked back.

'That's not right,' said Rita. 'That can't be right.'

The moon was full again, for a fifth consecutive night, and Ben Turner was now a beast.

20

Watching someone turn into a giant, hairy, wolf-beast was not something Detective Rita Hobbes was about to forget in a long time. That is, if she managed to get out of the situation she found herself in without being killed horribly.

'Ben?'

The thing Ben Turner had turned into had its back to Rita. It was down on its haunches, the dark, coarse hair of its bulging body showing through torn rags of clothing. Rita slowly took the axe from her belt and flexed her fingers around its wooden handle, trying to fool herself into believing she wasn't terrified.

'Ben, can you hear me?'

Ben Turner threw his head back, let loose a piercing, bone-shaking howl, and bolted from the alley.

'Shit!'

Rita ran in pursuit. She had to keep up with him, but he was already out of view by the time she ran out into the street. They'd been deposited in town, and the street was busy with people on their nights out, weaving from pub to pub. Although Ben had already run out of sight, it was pretty easy for Rita to work out which direction he was heading in. All she had to do was follow the screams.

Gasping for air as she pounded after him, Rita wondered exactly what her plan was going to be if she caught him. Would she be able to sweet-talk him into being a nice doggie? That seemed unlikely, which made her only other option the axe in her right hand, and she really didn't want to hurt Ben, or perhaps, even kill him. No, she didn't want that at all.

There was chaos everywhere as she ran, shocked people scattering and screaming in the wake of the nightmare beast that had rushed past their disbelieving eyes. Many of them were no doubt already trying to reconcile what they'd seen with a story that their mind could make sense of.

Rita finally pulled to a stop, hands on her knees, gasping for breath. There was a low growl to her left. She stood up sharply and turned to the sound, axe gripped in both hands. It was an alleyway, its length shrouded in shadow.

'Okay. Monster in a dark alley. Awesome.'

Rita took tentative steps into the alley.

'Ben?' said Rita, walking slowly down the alleyway, trying to will her eyes to pierce the dark that surrounded her and reveal the black bulk of the werewolf Ben had transformed into.

'Here… boy…?'

Rita stopped as she reached the end of the alley. The dead end. There was nothing there but a brick wall blocking her way. No way out that end, so where was he?

A deep growl from above. Rita looked up to see two large, sodium-yellow eyes glowing in the dark. He'd clambered partway up a fire escape that clung to one side of the alleyway. To get back out of the alley, Rita would have to walk under and past him. Werewolf in front of her, solid wall behind her. Rita wasn't in a great position, and her knees chose this moment to turn partially to jelly, just in case she was in any doubt as to how scary a situation she now found herself in. What had she been thinking, chasing after a murderous, mindless monster with giant claws and even bigger teeth? She'd been thinking of saving Ben. Of saving him from killing anyone.

Well, now it looked like he was going to kill her.

Ben dropped from the fire escape and rose up on his hind legs. He towered over Rita. Ben had been close to six foot before, but now, in his transformed state, he must have been closer to eight. Thick saliva hung in great strings from his hungry maw.

Even in her terror, Rita found herself able to marvel at the creature looming before her.

'Ben, it's me. It's Rita. You can hear me, can't you? You recognise me.'

Ben took a step towards her, the claws on his feet scraping against the stone ground.

Rita stepped back, but she had nowhere to go, she was already almost pressed up against the dead end.

'Ben, you're not a monster. You don't have to be. Fight it. Your name is Ben Turner. Ben Turner.'

There was no recognition in his eyes. Ben Turner wasn't in there, only the beast.

He reached out a paw and Rita screamed, swatting it back with the axe, drawing blood with the blade. Ben growled and stepped back.

And then she felt it.

The axe, the one she'd taken after triggering the hex, it afforded her, its wielder, certain abilities. Each wielder got something different from the axe, from the artefact. For Rita, it allowed her to rob some of the magic from anything Uncanny it touched. In this case, she'd drawn blood from a werewolf, and the axe had tasted Ben's curse.

Normally, Rita could translate the magic that soaked into the axe. She could see it, taste it, smell it, understand it. She could conduct a conversation of sorts with it, and have it do as she demanded. But this magic, this was something different. Magic is there to be used, to be controlled, but not lycanthropy. Not the kind of changeling power that coursed through Ben Turner's veins. That was a wild, dark, powerful magic with one purpose. To submerge. To control. It was not to be used, to be willed, to be given orders. No, this magic overwhelmed. Took over. Infected.

Rita fell to her knees, shaking, as the thing that Ben Turner had become stepped back, recognising instinctively what was happening. This was no longer food, this was a thing like him. This was family.

Rita fought. She wanted to drop the axe but her fingers wouldn't let her, wouldn't release. And even if they had, it was already too late. The magic was in her now. It was taking over. The full moon was high and it knew what it had to do.

Rita screamed and fell to one side, curling in a ball, shaking, sweating, her body in agony. It was tearing through her body, the magic, tearing through her mind. She could feel her sense of self, her thoughts, her memories, her desires being pushed away and away and new thoughts, new wants, blooming.

She looked at her hands, they sprouted thick hair before her eyes, her nails turning long and sharp and strong.

'No!'

Ben threw his head back and howled with joy at the moon above.

Rita wanted to…

Wanted to run…

She just wanted to run.

She knew she could run forever and never get tired. She was so strong, so agile, so alive. The world around her was full of smells now, everything so potent, and she knew each smell.

Blood.

She could smell blood. It was close. Blood meant food meant flesh meant the kill.

She hopped up on to her feet. On her hind paws?

'Stop!' she said, but she didn't mean it. She was going to kill. Going to tear the flesh from people's bones with her teeth and eat and eat and eat and—

The spell broke. All of a sudden the thoughts, the pain, the desperate need to kill dropped away. She looked up to see the moon faltering. It was full, then it wasn't, then it was. Like some sort of strange special effect, two frames hopping back and forth.

She could feel the magic in her clinging on, unsure, ready to submerge her again if the moon stayed full. But the strange flickering stopped, and the moon was no longer full. It was as it should have been.

Rita slumped back against the wall, the axe falling from her grip, and she gasped for breath, her body aching. Throbbing. Trembling.

'Christ…'

The magic was gone. The thing that had tried to overtake her

—almost had—had drifted away. All used up. She wasn't infected. The axe had given her access as a one-time deal, and now that the moon was back to what it should have been, the transaction was over.

Shaky, and wondering if she might throw up at any moment, Rita pushed herself to her feet. Even in her traumatised state, she was happy to see that she hadn't gone so far that her clothes had ripped before the moon had faltered. Praise the Lord for small mercies.

Ben was curled up on the ground before her. He was no longer the beast, he was plain old Ben Turner again. And he was unconscious. And naked. Rita only briefly looked before draping her coat over him and taking out her phone to call for help.

21

Carlisle followed the Monk in silence for hours.

They stooped through low stone tunnels. They walked along the banks of an underground river, ignoring the Roman Legion that was camped out on the other side of the bank. A lost legion, cursed to roam beneath the Earth for eternity. They walked through the sewers, swatting away bothersome fairies that buzzed around their heads.

'How much further is the city, exactly?' asked Carlisle. 'Which isn't to say I'm not enjoying the silent drudgery of this seemingly never-ending walk.'

'Soon,' replied the Monk, gruffly. 'Soon we'll arrive at the Maze. Get through the Maze, and we'll be there. Don't get through, and that'll be that.'

The Monk opened a door to reveal a giant cavern, its curved ceiling glittering with crystal seams. In the cavern was a lake of jade green water, and tied to a jetty in front of them was a small boat. The Monk stepped aboard and Carlisle followed, taking a seat as the Monk drove his stick into the water and propelled them across.

'This Maze you speak of,' said Carlisle, 'is there any reason to believe I will not make it through?'

'Can't trust a Maze,' replied the Monk. 'They have a mind of their own. Some of them, at least. Proper ones. They choose who they let through unscathed. Most are lost in there still. Taking turn after turn, never finding the true path.'

'Lucky for me I have an unwavering sense of direction. I always end up where I am supposed to be.'

The Monk grunted, then spat into the water. 'Heard that before.' He pulled out a brass key that hung around his neck on a thin strip of leather, and held it to his forehead.

'What is that?' asked Carlisle.

'The key. The way in, the way out, it's never the same, but this leads me true.'

As they left the crystal-topped cave, all turned black. The only sound that could be heard was the lake's water sloshing around them as the Monk navigated through the gloom. He turned briefly to look at his companion; Carlisle knew he had as he saw the Monk's eyes glowing in the dark.

'Normally, we do not allow the living into our city,' said the Monk. 'But you… you are thrice dead, at the very least.'

'Yes, it doesn't tend to stick with me. Not a fan. May I ask how you know that?'

'I know. I can see the damage it's done each time. See the death in you. It's part of you now, always will be. A hollow itch that can never be scratched.'

Carlisle frowned and placed a hand to his chest. It was true that ever since his first death he'd felt an emptiness inside. And each time he had come back it had got worse. As though he had left something of himself behind each time. Taken something out of him that he could never get back. Carlisle shook off the thought; he did not like the path it was leading him down.

The boat came to a stop, buffeting against an unseen bank, and the Monk took Carlisle's arm, leading him from the boat, on to the bank, and away. The Monk clicked his fingers and the head of his walking stick bloomed with a blue light that cut through the black.

'You might have done that a little earlier,' said Carlisle.

'Yes, I might have, but I didn't. Nearly there, then.'

Carlisle pulled his arm free of the Monk's liver-spotted hand, smoothed down the line of his coat, and followed on.

With a grunt, Formby shrugged the still-unconscious Ben Turner from his shoulder and on to the floor of a cellar beneath Big Pins.

'Thanks,' said Rita. 'Heavier than he looks, that one.'

Linton stood in the doorway, bat in hand, with a not-at-all happy look on his face. 'This room is solid. Door, too. If he changes, the thing won't be able to get out.'

'Thanks, Linton,' said Rita.

Linton grunted and left them to it. Rita sighed and hunkered down on her haunches, running her hands through her thick, red hair. She realised her hands were still shaking, a little residual fear and adrenaline from the chase. From what she'd experienced as the lycanthropy magic had fought to submerge her beneath its black hold. She knew it would have, too. She hadn't been able to control it, to speak to it so that it would listen. If the moon had stayed full for even a minute more, she would have been gone, turned completely animal, and who knew what carnage she would have caused. How many deaths she and Ben would have been responsible for as they ran through Blackpool, feral, desperate for blood and flesh between their teeth.

'Okay, are you?' asked Formby, patting her on the shoulder.

'Yup, just a little shit up is all.' Rita stood and shivered, trying to get herself together. She looked down at Ben, still wearing her coat to cover his modesty. 'It was horrible. I mean, worse than horrible. To see him turn, and scream, and then become that… that thing.'

'Aye,' replied Formby, chewing on his knuckles. 'The sight of a change, especially to one you know, is not for the faint of heart. Or even the strong of heart.'

Rita ran a hand across the handle of her axe. 'I felt it. The magic. The werewolf magic.'

'Tried to take you, did it?'

Rita nodded. 'Through the axe. I got a taste of it. It didn't taste good. Formby, how could the moon have been full again so soon? Its four day cycle was already done. And how could it then just change?'

'Powerful magic, that. I could sniff it as I was out on my rounds. Could smell it on the wind. Someone doing something powerful. Testing themselves. Flexing new muscles. I'd say we can expect more full moons from now on. Maybe even every night, I reckon that's the goal.'

'So this Magda, she's wanting to turn every night into werewolf night?'

'Seems so. Makes sense.'

'Was it everywhere, the full moon?'

Formby shook his head. 'A local trick. Only Blackpool, only where she is.'

A groan from the floor caught their attention as Ben came to, pushing himself up on his elbow. He looked as though he was waking from a monster drinking session.

'Where am I?' he croaked.

'Big Pins,' said Rita. 'Do you remember what happened?'

He scrunched his face up, then shook his head.

'Went all wolf, you did,' said Formby.

'What? But I thought that only happened on a full moon?'

'Aye. Had another one. Magic moon.'

Rita helped Ben up to his feet, the coat he was wearing—her coat—flapping open to reveal his naked form beneath.

'Shit,' said Ben, quickly pulling the coat closed. 'I'm naked.'

'Yup,' replied Rita with a grin. 'Honestly, I barely looked. A couple of seconds at the most, just to get the basic idea of it.'

Ben smiled, but the expression faltered. 'Did… did I hurt, or, well, kill anyone?'

'No, don't worry, you didn't harm anyone. The spell broke and the moon changed before you got around to hurting anyone. Myself included, by the way.'

Ben made his way over to a chair and slumped down, head in hands. 'I can't keep doing this. Keep putting people in danger.'

'Don't worry, from now on, until we sort this, you're going to stay in this room at night. Just to be on the safe side.'

'Can this be sorted? And please be aware that I'm very, very scared about what the answer to that question might be.'

Formby clapped his hands together. 'Yes. Curse can be broken on anyone bitten.'

Ben almost burst into tears with relief, and Rita knew first-hand how he must be feeling. To have that inside of him, ready to take over, to make him destroy. Terrifying.

'How do we do that?' asked Rita.

'For the bitten, all you have to do is kill the master werewolf who turned them. Kill them and the curse is broken. Any they bit, any they turned, will be free.'

'Okay,' said Ben. 'So we need to find Magda, and, well…'

Rita nodded. 'And kill her.' Rita didn't like the sound of that. She was no killer. But what were her options? Allow Ben to suffer just so Rita didn't feel bad about herself? This was different to the last case, different to her old Guv, to Jenner. This wasn't her neck on the line, it was the safety of others. And not just those Magda had cursed with her bite, but all those they would go on to hurt, to kill. Could she really allow her own moral compass to get in the way of stopping that?

'Are you okay?' asked Ben, noticing how deep in thought Rita had fallen.

'Oh, always great, me. It's all flowers and jaunty music up here,' she said, tapping a finger to her head.

Ben nodded and rubbed at his eyes with the heels of his hands. 'Christ, I feel like something took a dump in my brain.

'Formby,' said Rita, 'you've been doing your sneaky business like I asked, right?'

Formby grinned, revealing his mess of sharp little teeth. 'I asked, I listened, I lurked. I am a good eaves.'

'Okay then, this woman, Magda, what have you got for me?'

Formby sat and closed his eyes, then nodded and smiled. 'There is talk of a wolf with magic. Impossible thing, but it's happened. There are whispers of piles of dead wizards in Belgium. In a small town in Germany. In a village in Holland. The wizards do not like talk of it because it makes them look weak.'

'So that's Magda?' asked Ben.

'Must be,' replied Formby. 'Wizards hunt her, now she hunts them.'

'Why do the wizards hunt them?' asked Rita.

'Snooty bunch, wizards. Think a lot of themselves, they do. They see themselves as masters of all magic. Can speak to all the Uncanny and mould it, use it, control it. Better than anything else. But the wolf magic is dark magic. Magic they cannot understand, cannot grasp, cannot use. They see it as an insult. An affront. If there is magic they cannot use, then there is danger, and it must be stamped out.'

'So what? They're jealous?'

'Jealous and scared,' replied Formby. 'Not that they would admit to it, mind. Not a snooty, big-head wizard.'

A master werewolf with magic, killing wizards, turning others, making the moon shine full when it shouldn't. Rita had the description, the name, the motive. All she needed now was Magda's whereabouts so she could take her down. She wished Carlisle was with her to help, because she knew that what came next would not be easy.

As Rita made that wish, Carlisle was cold and annoyed.

'Not wishing to sound like a child in the back seat of a car, but are we nearly there yet?'

The Monk stopped. 'Yes. We are here.' He held up his shining staff to reveal a lattice doorway; wrought iron with vines weaved through its fretwork.

'This is the entrance to the Maze?'

'Yes. This is where you must go, and we shall either meet on the other side, or we shall not.'

'Are you not guiding me through?'

The Monk turned to Carlisle and smiled. 'What would be the point of that? I do not need to navigate the Maze, I am of the City.'

'Could you not just take me your way?'

The Monk laughed, and then in the time it took Carlisle to blink, was gone.

'Well, that is just rude,' said Carlisle. Sighing, he approached the Maze entrance, nudging experimentally at the metal frame with the toe of one boot.

'Okay then,' said Carlisle, straightening his coat and stepping through.

He was not usually a man to be worried by the unknown—the unknown, paradoxically, was the world he knew—but he had to concede that on this occasion he felt some trepidation. He teased at some of the protections he had sewn into his coat. Small objects, runes, secret words and phrases sewn to the fabric in fine thread. When you encountered danger as often as Carlisle, you made sure you had as many points in your favour as possible.

Carlisle moved forward. The Maze was very much what he expected. Narrow passages with topiary walls that reached high above his head. Carlisle attempted to force his hand into one of the walls to see if he could push his way through the vegetation and make his own route, but found that the wall would not yield to so much as a single finger.

The slow route it was.

The very slow route, as it turned out.

Carlisle was not sure how long he had been walking for, but his legs grew tired and his patience short. Each time he found the end of a path, he would have two choices, left or right. He chose randomly, as each path seemed identical to the last. Carlisle began to suspect—so identical was each stretch of the Maze—that some trickery was being employed that forced him to walk the same path over and over.

He turned right.

Perhaps madness was the Maze's aim. Only those who could walk and walk and endlessly walk and yet keep their mind together would find themselves at the exit.

He turned left.

Or perhaps there was no exit, perhaps this is what the Monk did to all who attempted to gain access to the City of the Dead. Those who attempted to arrive whilst still drawing breath.

Carlisle turned right and found a man sitting in a chair, a book in hand. The man was dressed in a long purple coat and had a chalk-white face. The man was he.

'Ah,' said Carlisle Two, sliding the book into his pocket and rising to his feet, bowing with a flourish. 'You've found yourself at last, then? You took your time, I must say.'

Carlisle stepped towards himself, eyes roaming, looking for any signs of what might happen next. 'I apologise,' he told his doppelgänger, 'I do hate to be kept waiting.'

'I do, don't I?' said Carlisle Two with a thin smile.

'So what is this? What is the purpose?' asked Carlisle.

Carlisle Two opened his long, purple coat, the lining flashing with stars and magic, and revealed something that made Carlisle's pupils dilate.

'Recognise this?' asked Carlisle Two, removing the artefact—the axe—from where it hung from his belt.

Carlisle felt his heart skip, his lips grow dry, his breath quicken.

'You believe yourself to be lacking without this, do you not?' said Carlisle Two.

'It is… my right. My property. I will hold it, wield it, again.'

Carlisle Two tossed the axe from hand to hand, trails of light, purple, red, green, blue, streaking from the blade, leaving trails of magic in its wake. 'You are nothing without this.'

'I am Carlisle.'

'A thief, a liar, nothing more. But with this artefact… with this you can command armies. With this you can sit upon a throne and belong there.'

'It is my right.'

'A sewer-born such as you?'

Carlisle stiffened. 'I am Carlisle.'

'You are a nothing, dressed up and doused in perfumes to hide the sewer stink. A collection of lies and half-truths. A thing running from its birth. You were born in the dark, in the filth, and did not see the light of a day until you were almost ten.'

'No. I am not like them. I am like me and me alone. I am Carlisle.'

'A sewer-born with aspirations, nothing more. You even sneer at your own kind. Have done all sorts to yourself to make you something other. So little of what you were born with remains as you search, search, search for more.'

Carlisle noticed that the two of them were no longer alone. A third person had joined the circle. A woman.

Carlisle stepped back.

'Get out of my mind,' he hissed, as the woman in damp rags, mouth empty of teeth, skin covered in dirt and warts, stepped towards him, arms outstretched.

'I died and you did not visit. Ashamed, ashamed, ashamed.'

'I am what I create. I say I am Carlisle, I say I am the true King of the Uncanny Kingdom, and that makes it so!' Carlisle realised he had fallen to his knees.

The woman stopped before him and ran her filthy hand lightly across his cheek. 'I forgive you.'

'You will not,' he replied, pulling his head away from her. 'I do not seek forgiveness, and I will not accept it.'

'How long has it been since you pictured this woman in your mind?' asked Carlisle Two.

'She is nothing,' Carlisle fired back. 'She is nothing and nothing and nothing. I am my own. I created myself.'

The woman fell to the ground, clutching her stomach, and rats appeared, gnawing at her feet, her arms, her face.

'Left to ruin by ungrateful fruit,' said Carlisle Two, who raised his axe and swung it down into the woman's head, her legs twitching for just a second before life left her.

'No one shall miss the likes of her,' said Carlisle.

'Such heartless self-regard.'

'Is this going to go on much longer?' asked Carlisle.

Carlisle Two smiled and held the axe aloft. 'You are nothing without this. Empty.'

Carlisle snorted, but his palms sweated.

Carlisle Two grinned and the axe in his hand burst into flames.

'No!' Carlisle rushed at his mirror image, tackling him to the ground.

Carlisle Two laughed, and the axe flew from his hands and skittered across the ground, coming to rest by a topiary wall. The vegetation caught alight and the flames rushed in all directions, the entire Maze erupting in fire.

Carlisle Two continued to laugh as Carlisle watched his artefact turn to ash before his eyes. Anger took hold, pain, anguish. Carlisle stood and reached into his coat to pull out a leather whip. 'Monster!'

He lashed out at Carlisle Two, but screamed out in pain as the wound he caused on his twin bit into his own flesh. Twice, three times, four, the whip snapped down and each time Carlisle staggered and grunted and cried out as blood gushed from wounds that tore open his own body.

'I am Carlisle! I create myself, I create myself!' The whip dropped from his hand as the blazing Maze swamped him with smoke and the blood ran in rivers from his many wounds.

'You are nothing,' whispered Carlisle Two as he watched him falter and fall to the dirt. 'Born of the sewer, only to return to it. I see your future.'

Then all was black and silence.

22

Tina Burrows hated surprise parties, especially when she had to pretend she had no idea one was coming.

She was sat on the bus in one of her best sparkly dresses. Just the normal sort of thing she'd wear to a run-of-the-mill night at the pub. Obviously. She pulled out her phone and checked her make-up as Brian, her boyfriend, made small-talk about work like he wasn't leading her to anything but a quiet pint or two and a bag of chips on the way home.

'Marion was getting it right in the neck from Colin about the Myers account,' he said.

'Oh dear,' replied Tina, putting her phone away.

'She says she's gonna go to HR about it. I mean, I don't like telling tales to teacher, but Colin was well out of order.'

Tina was turning thirty-five in two weeks' time, so by holding the party early, Brian and their friends thought they were being clever. Of course, Ellen had crumbled and told Tina everything a week earlier. Never could keep a secret that one. A liability.

Brian rang the bell and the bus pulled to a stop across the road from the bar they'd hired out for the night. It would just be Tina, Brian, a bunch of their friends, and the staff. Many might call Tina miserable for feeling so put out at her friends' thoughtfulness, but she just didn't like a fuss being made. Not about her, anyway. Never had. Didn't like being the centre of attention. It was one of the main reasons she was dreading the day Brian plucked up the courage to ask her to marry him. She loved him, of course she did, but being the bride at a wedding was maximum centre of attention. You couldn't get more centre of attention than that. It made Tina sweat just to think about it, and a sweaty bride was not a good look.

Maybe Brian would be up for hopping on a plane to Las Vegas. Just the two of them and an officiate dressed like Elvis. Now that she would be up for.

'Here we are then,' said Brian, barely able to conceal his giggles as he held open the door. Tina put on her best smile and stepped into the pub.

'Surprise!' yelled all twenty people who'd gathered, pulling party poppers and cheering.

'Oh my God!' said Tina, looking around with very realistic-looking surprise. Marion waved at her from the throng. 'Brian, is this down to you?'

'Guilty,' he said, and kissed her.

At first, the extra guest went unnoticed.

The music was turned up and the alcohol was replaced as each glass was emptied. Tina went from person to person, chatting, laughing, dancing. She hated to admit it to herself, but she realised she was having a good time. It really was sweet of Brian to organise this, even if he did know, and ignore, her feelings about this sort of thing.

Yeah, there was no way he'd agree to Las Vegas. But what the hell, Tina would marry the annoying goof anyway.

It was Marion who first noticed the woman sat in one corner, quietly drinking a glass of wine on her own.

'Hi! I'm Marion!' said Marion, flopping down next to her, drunk and a little out of breath from the energetic dance moves she'd just unleashed to The Killers' *Mr. Brightside*.

Magda smiled. 'Hello.'

'Nice party, isn't it? Tina deserves it though, don't you think? She's such a love.'

Magda nodded and sipped her wine.

'How d'you know Tina, then? From work or something?'

Magda shook her head.

'Oh. It's just, this is sort of her party. Oh! Did you come as someone's girlfriend? Are you Mike's new partner?'

Tina could see Marion talking to the woman she didn't recognise. She assumed she must have come with someone else. Something about the woman made her uneasy. It was her eyes, that was it. Piercing blue eyes that didn't seem to blink.

'Brian,' said Tina, taking her boyfriend's arm, 'who's that over there with Marion?'

Brian peered past Tina and frowned, shaking his head. 'No idea, love. Do you want another glass?'

Tina nodded and Brian headed off to the bar. The woman with piercing blue eyes stood and wandered to the centre of the room, stopping close to Tina. She was smiling.

'Excuse me,' said Tina, 'who are you?'

'My name is Magda. Soon, we will be very good friends. No, more than that. We will be family.'

A lot of confusing things happened after that.

The woman, Magda, raised her hands above her head and ribbons of colour began to dance through her fingers. At first, people thought it was an act of some kind and clapped, but soon the clapping subsided, to be replaced with shouts and screams.

They tried to leave, to get out, as the woman's mouth became full of sharp teeth and her hands sprouted claws, but for some reason the doors wouldn't open and the chairs refused to break the glass in the windows.

All around was panic, but Tina stayed calm, almost resigned to it somehow. One by one, Magda moved with grace and speed around the pub, sinking her teeth into the flesh of the party guests, washing the floor with blood.

Tina was last.

She watched as Magda pulled her bloody face away from Marion's neck and allowed her to drop, unconscious, to the floor. Magda's eyes weren't blue any more, they were bright yellow.

'It's my birthday party,' said Tina, shell-shocked, as Magda slowly padded her way. 'I never did like my own birthday parties.'

'This is a kindness,' said Magda, 'a gift from me to you. Watch how we run.'

Tina felt the teeth sink into her neck.

Heard the scream escape from her mouth.

And then it was over.

23

It was night again, and Ben Turner was nervous. Rita watched him fidget, then sit, then stand and pace the basement under Big Pins, before attempting to sit still once again.

'This is bloody torture,' he said for possibly the hundredth time since the sun had dipped.

Rita thought back to how she'd felt as the lycanthropy magic had almost swamped her, and knew the fear Ben must have been feeling. At any moment, the woman who had bitten him—Magda—could cast whatever spell she'd tossed out the previous night and turn the moon full again, causing the beast inside him to tear its way back out.

'Don't worry,' Rita said, 'if it happens, you'll be safe in here. Linton says there's no way you'll be able to break out and hurt anyone.'

'Yes, apart from me. I don't remember much about, you know, when I've turned, but I do have flashes of actually changing. It hurts. It hurts like my whole body is being ripped apart; bones and joints popping, my skin tearing.'

Rita went over and hugged him, feeling his body shivering against hers. Rita was not a hugger, but she felt the situation called for it. 'I'll be here,' she said. 'I'll be here all night in case anything happens, all right?'

Ben smiled and nodded, and as their eyes met up close, Rita

had the sudden urge to lean in and kiss Ben on his very nice mouth. Instead, she stepped back and turned away. Now wasn't the time for that sort of thing.

'You know, for a second there I thought, ha, I thought you were going to kiss me.'

'Fat chance,' said Rita, 'I'm not that desperate.'

'Oh. Right. Yeah, me neither.'

Rita's stomach tightened at the hurt in Ben's voice. She'd never been the most professional of police detectives, but she drew the line at snogging the civilians in her care. Especially if they had a habit of turning into flesh-eating monsters. Even if they did have a very nice face and a bottom lip that she wanted to bite.

The next few hours dragged. The night is long when you have to sit through it, waiting for the worst to happen at any moment. Ben, probably drained by all the nervous energy he'd spent, eventually drifted off to sleep on the couch Linton had dragged downstairs for them to sit on. Rita stayed awake and watched over him. She didn't want him to be alone if he started changing. She wanted him to see a friendly face before it took over fully and she had to dart from the room and lock the door behind her.

The police must have been looking for him. If she'd worked out the clocking in and out of the office thing, no doubt someone else would have too, especially as he would have appeared to have dropped off the face of the Earth. They would have paid his house a visit and found it empty of him, but full of evidence as soon as they took a closer look, they'd only had chance for a quick tidy and scrub.

Rita looked at Ben as he slumbered peacefully. She wondered if he knew that no matter how this turned out, there was no way back for him. Like her, he was trapped in this Uncanny world now. Unlike her, the "normal" world wanted to catch him and lock him up. Even if she managed to deal with Magda (and she still wasn't over the moon at the prospect of having to kill her) and the lycanthropy magic weaving though Ben was purged, he still wouldn't be able to go back into his life. His home. His job. No matter what, he was the man responsible for the death of Alan Crowther. Ben Turner's life as he knew it would never be the same again. He'd spend the rest of his days a fugitive. But better that than a monster.

The door to the basement opened and Linton ducked inside.

'Morning, Lurch,' said Rita, stretching.

Linton grunted. 'Sun's up.'

No full moon that night. Rita wondered what Magda had been up to that had distracted her from casting the moon spell again. Whatever it was, she was thankful that Ben had been spared for one night.

While Ben Turner showered and had breakfast, Rita left Big Pins to stretch her legs.

It was a little after dawn, and the streets of Blackpool were more or less deserted. Just invisible Rita, eyes heavy from lack of sleep, ghosting her way around town. She needed to work out the next step. Well, she knew exactly what the next step needed to be, she just had to figure out how to take it.

She needed to locate Magda.

The woman behind all this was holed up somewhere in Blackpool, but Formby had so far been unable to sniff her out. The grapevine was empty of whispers. If she couldn't be found, that meant more deaths, more people being turned to werewolves, and more long nights as Ben holed up in a locked room to see if he was about to become a monster.

Rita needed to figure out some way to flush Magda out into the open.

Fortunately—or unfortunately as it turned out—Magda was also keen to make Rita's acquaintance.

'It is a fine morning, Rita Hobbes.'

Rita jumped slightly. She had taken a seat on a bench by the beach and had started to nod off when the voice slapped her back to reality. Rita turned to see a woman sat next to her, gazing out at the rolling waves with the most beautiful blue eyes she had ever seen. On a scale of one to ten, this woman was a twelve.

'Whu?' said Rita, sitting up and rubbing at her eyes.

'I prefer the night,' said Magda, 'of course, but even I cannot deny the beauty of a new day's first hour.'

The woman had an accent Rita couldn't quite place. Eastern European perhaps, but muddied, like she'd travelled a lot and called many places her home. Rita was in no doubt as to who she was speaking with.

'Magda,' she said.

'We know each other's names. We are friends now,' said Magda, smiling to reveal a set of perfect, bright white teeth. Rita wondered how many different people's blood had stained those perfect teeth over the years.

'So you're the big bad, then, eh?' said Rita. 'Nice leather jacket. Very cool. Very Fonzie.'

Magda laughed. 'Big bad? Is that what I am? There are many worse things than me. I've met them. They have hunted me.'

Rita slid a little further down the bench, trying to create a little distance, her hand resting on the axe hidden beneath her coat. 'Well, you do eat people, I'm told.'

'That is true.'

'And you turn people into big, mean wolves against their will.'

'I make them better,' said Magda. 'I make them beautiful. We become family.'

'Not everyone gets on with their family.'

'I do. Did.' Magda turned to address Rita directly for the first time. 'I had wondered what you were.'

'Well, a bad arse, that sort of goes without saying. Oh, and the detective who's going to stop you.'

'I saw you through Ben's eyes. When they turn, when they flourish, they are part of me.'

'Nifty trick, that.'

'I saw you handling the magic. I had thought you were perhaps a wizard. So I decided to kill you.'

'Thanks.'

'But the moment I sat next to you on this bench while you slept, I realised you are no wizard. You are just a woman.'

'First of all, I was just resting my eyes, and second of all, I'm not just a woman. I'm Detective Rita Hobbes, angel... about a million times removed.'

'Lucky for you,' replied Magda.

Rita stood and took a step back. Magda remained seated, relaxed. Too relaxed for Rita's liking. This was not a woman who was worried, or intimidated. This was a woman who had nothing to fear, and that made her very, very dangerous.

'Why are you killing wizards?'

'Should I not?' said Magda. 'They hunt me. My kind. They murdered my whole family.'

'Your family?'

'I was just a child and a wizard paid my home a visit. Slaughtered my mother, my father. I ran with my little brother cradled in my arms. One day they killed him too. Should I not seek revenge for their deaths? For all the pain I have suffered?'

'I'm sorry,' said Rita.

'I do not ask for your sorries, Detective. They think me vermin? Then I shall act as such. I will infest, I will kill. I tried to run, tried to hide, to live a quiet, humble life, but they would not leave me be. Any pain I unleash, they brought upon themselves. Tell me they do not deserve it.'

Rita saw pain flash across Magda's perfect face, just briefly. It was enough to read years of sorrow, of anger. She could understand why she might want to attack wizards, but that didn't change a thing. A murderer was a murderer, regardless of motive. Rita ignored the thought that came next. The one telling her that to stop Magda, she would have to become a murderer herself.

'Look, I get it. Revenge, cool, what could be better? But even if I could overlook that, there's the other stuff. Ben, for example.'

'I told you, I have made him better, made him beautiful.'

'You've cursed him.'

Magda stood, snarling. 'Cursed? We are not a curse. What I give is not a curse! We are beautiful.'

Rita stepped back and pulled out her axe. 'Calm down there, lovely face, let's keep this civil.'

Magda began to walk slowly towards her, causing Rita to back up. She realised that the axe in her hand might be a futile weapon. What if she struck Magda with it and her lycanthropy transferred, like it had with Ben? It would remain in there, waiting to infect her the next time the moon was full, which could be any night of the week thanks to Magda's cosmic interference.

'They have hunted us almost to extinction, and we hid, we cowered. Not anymore. I won't do it. I can't. We have been persecuted. Never again.'

'Or you could be the bigger woman?' suggested Rita. 'Forgive and forget and go live undercover in the arctic on a strictly vegetarian, no-biting people diet?'

Magda unfurled a fist and a ball of flame ignited in her palm. 'Now I have what they have, and more, and we shall no longer hide in the shadows, ashamed. We shall walk proud.'

The ball of flame erupted, blinding Rita for a moment. Before she knew what was happening, Magda was on her. She felt hands, now claws, gripping her, digging into her flesh.

'Don't,' was all she managed to say before she felt Magda's teeth sink into her neck.

24

Ben was a monster.

He sat at a corner table in Big Pins, while on the other side of the room, various shady-looking characters played ten pin bowling, like all was normal and ordinary, and magic and murder and werewolves weren't anything to worry about.

A werewolf.

That's what he was.

It was ridiculous. Completely absurd. And yet he knew it was true. He could remember the pain of starting to turn. The full-body agony. The sense of his own self being pushed aside for something *other*. Something terrible.

He was a thing from the movies now. A made-up creature from a scary story.

Ben sighed and leaned forward, cradling his glass of orange juice. He wondered where Rita was. When she was around, he felt a little better. A little safer. A little saner. Without her, he was just a lone weirdo cast adrift in this strange underworld of creatures and magic that he didn't believe in, but was now neck-deep in.

Christ, he missed his life of just a few days ago. What he wouldn't give just to be that lonely, vaguely depressed guy going from home to work to home, trying his best not to think about the woman who dumped him. Ben realised that was the first time he'd actually thought about Sally since this had all begun. He supposed that was progress.

But it didn't stop him being a murderer.

That felt weird. And terrible, of course. It was hard to think that he was the one responsible for Alan's death. He was and he wasn't. It was the beast that had done it – he had no memory of it, no control over it. That didn't assuage his guilt much. In charge or not, changed into a beast or not, Alan was still dead because of him. Because he'd gone for a walk with a strange woman, because he'd shrugged the night off and gone into work the next day, even though he'd felt like shit.

If only he'd phoned in sick. He should have done. Work didn't like sick people going into the office and spreading their sickness to others, but Ben was the sort of person who tried to work through any sickness. And now, because of his bone-headedness, Alan—boring, nice Alan—was laid out flat in the morgue.

But then what would have happened if he had phoned in sick? Night would have fallen, the moon would have risen, he still would have changed into that… into that *thing*. Did he seriously think he would have stayed in? That the wolf would have stretched out on the sofa and caught up on a bit of TV? No, someone would have died regardless. Whether he'd gone to work or not, someone would have died. It was a miracle it had only been one person.

Ben Turner sipped his orange juice and looked to see how many hours were left before night fell.

Rita opened her eyes.

She was laid out on the ground, looking up at the sky. She blinked in confusion and sat up. The beach was to her right, a bench to her left.

'Shit!'

Her hand jumped to her neck, to the place she remembered Magda's teeth sinking into her, but there was no wound. Her heart hammering, Rita wobbled up and slumped on the bench.

She bent down and collected the axe at her feet. How long had she been unconscious? She checked her watch. It was already early afternoon. She'd been out for hours.

Had that actually happened? Had she been bitten, or had Magda just knocked her out?

Rita's hands went to her neck again. She couldn't feel a wound, but it was tender to the touch. It *had* happened, she was sure of it. Like Ben, the wound had healed at an accelerated speed, but she'd been bitten alright.

Which meant…

Which meant nothing good.

She checked her watch again, her arm shaking. Only a few hours before night fell. Would Magda pull her full moon trick again? Was Rita going to turn into the thing she'd seen Ben transform into? Into the thing she'd felt almost overwhelm her when the axe had transferred some of the lycanthropy into her?

Rita stood and began to run. It took her twenty minutes before she stumbled up the blind alley and crashed into Big Pins, looking around wildly for Formby.

'Rita?' said Ben, approaching her with concern.

'Formby, is he here? Have you seen him?'

'Hey, woah, what's wrong? Are you…' Ben's words faltered and he sniffed her.

'What? What are you doing?'

'I don't… have you been bitten?'

Rita bit her lip and nodded. 'She found me. Magda. You weren't kidding about how beautiful she was. Well, we had a nice little chat and then she infected me, so. All good. Great. Not panicking at all here.'

'Shit,' said Ben. 'Shit!'

'Yep, fully agree with you there, Benny Boy.'

The entrance door opened and Rita spun around to see a grinning Formby shambling in. 'Hello,' he said, before shrinking back as Rita rushed him and grabbed hold.

'Formby! Good! Back room!'

'Time for a drink, I'm parched.' But Formby found there was no time for a drink as he was hustled—his feet barely touching the rank carpet—into the back room that doubled as Rita's bedroom.

Formby staggered in and flopped on the couch, looking up at Rita and Ben with confusion. 'I didn't do it,' he said. 'Whatever it is. Probably.'

'I met her,' said Rita. 'I met the master werewolf lady.'

'Oh? That's good.'

'Yeah. Except the cow bit me. Well, wolf. Cow wolf.'

'Oh. That is not so good.'

'So now you're invisible, forgotten, *and* a werewolf,' said Ben. 'That's a terrible run of luck.'

'Yeah, thanks for pointing that out, chuckles,' replied Rita.

'Hm? Sorry, just… thinking out loud.' Ben wandered over to the tatty couch and sat on the opposite end to Formby as Rita began to pace back and forth, chewing her nails. 'This is fucked. I'm fucked! I'm fucked, aren't I?'

Formby nodded, then a thought seemed to bubble up in him.

'What?' said Rita, seeing his expression change. 'What is it? Is it something good? Please tell me it's something good.'

'Not night yet,' he replied.

'Yep, I already know that.'

'Wolf curse doesn't stick until after you turn for the first time.'

Rita stopped pacing. 'Okay. Okay, that's good. Is that good? Tell me why that's good.'

'It's good because if we can get you cured before the moon rises, before you change, then you won't ever change into a big dog.'

Rita leapt at Formby and grabbed him by the cheeks, planting a big kiss on his forehead. 'Formby you beautiful, mole-faced sex god!'

Formby grinned and blushed.

'Okay. A few hours left until nightfall, when—we have to assume—Magda will pull her full moon magic trick again. Okay. Okay. Good. So how do we get this out of me before it beds in? Aspirin? Sweat it out in a steam room? Leeches?'

'No, not leeches. Leeches are good in a stew, though.'

'Wait,' said Ben, 'Linton gave me a bowl of stew earlier. Did that…?'

Formby sniggered.

'Great.'

'Ben, Formby, focus; what do I need to do?'

'Simple,' said Formby. 'Just need to find an exorcist.'

Rita sat down between Formby and Ben. 'Right. Of course we do. That was going to be my first guess.'

Magda sat in the sewer chamber, below the streets of Blackpool.

This was the sort of place she'd been forced to call home more times than she cared to remember. Out of sight. Beyond the eyes of anyone who might want to kill her, like they'd killed her family.

She snarled as she remembered the wizard who had taken everything from her. The same one who had taken it upon himself to wipe her family line from the map. She did not know who he was, but it did not matter. She was the hunter now. All wizards were guilty, and she would slaughter them all. Sooner or later, she would cross paths with the one who had blighted her life, and she would rip him limb from limb.

She pulled her bag from its hiding place and unzipped it, pulling out a dog-eared black and white photograph of Andras, her brother. He'd been so alive. So vital. None had enjoyed the hunt as much as he had. The wind in his fur, the scent of blood in his nostrils. This was all she had of him now. All she had of any of her family; she had no pictures of her mother or father in her bag. Just this. Just one old, faded picture of Andras. It was creased multiple times, brittle and faded. Sooner or later, that would be gone too.

Even her memories would fade, with time.

Magda realised her cheeks were damp, and angrily brushed the back of her hands across her face, wiping away the tears.

So many tears shed for her family. So many years of weeping. Well, this would be the last time she cried for them. Now she would make them proud. Now she would have revenge upon all of wizard-kind.

No more tears.

No more hiding.

No more nights spent hiding beneath the ground.

She had grown stronger with each wizard she had killed, suckling on their magic as they died. Her grasp on the Uncanny only grew with each wizard's death. She would kill all of the wizards in this area. She would turn all of the town's inhabitants into her kin. She would make the moon rise full, every night, wherever she was from now on. She could do it. She had the power now.

No more skulking in shadows.

No more testing of the water.

It was time to walk loud and proud.

Tonight.

Tonight it all began in urgency.

Tonight the moon would be full, and the wizards would fall.

Magda wasn't crying when she put the picture of Andras away. No, she wasn't crying, she was singing.

25

Carlisle was not a sunny bunny. As a matter of fact, he wasn't the sort of person who'd even use the phrase "sunny bunny", so when he returned to consciousness and found the hateful words forming in his head, he was already peeved.

'You're awake, then?' asked the Monk.

'Evidently,' replied Carlisle, sitting up from a small cot lined with a thin, damp mattress. He began to pat himself down, his coat, his pockets.

'Do not worry, nothing has been taken from you. We do not need anything you may have.'

'Forgive me if I do not take your word on that, Monk,' said Carlisle, who continued to check that all of his objects, all of his runes and protections, were where they should be. Satisfied, Carlisle took in his surroundings. He had been taken to a simple dwelling, the walls roughly fashioned from straw and mud, dark wooden beams laced through and stretching across the ceiling. An open fire crackled, casting flickering shadows around the dark room.

'Bit dingy,' said Carlisle.

'This is the City of the Dead, Mr. Carlisle, not the City of Jolly and Alive. Here,' said the Monk, offering a glass of brown, fizzing liquid.

'What is that?' asked Carlisle.

'It is cola. People usually drink it.'

Carlisle took the glass and sniffed at it suspiciously. 'If this is poisoned, I will be very annoyed.' After one last suspicious sniff, Carlisle sipped the cola

'We have so few willing visitors,' said the Monk, 'what brings you here?'

'Murder.'

'Oh?'

'I intend to commit one.'

'How exciting. Biscuit?' The Monk offered a plate loaded with a bounty of assorted treats.

'No. Thank you.'

'Are you sure? They're still warm from the oven.'

'I am sure,' said Carlisle.

The Monk shrugged. 'Suit yourself, I'm having one.' He put the plate down and took a biscuit, munching it with pleasure. 'Who do you intend to murder, if I might ask?'

'An angel.'

The Monk's eyebrows raised and he nodded, 'I see.'

'One of the first order.'

'It cannot be done.'

'I believe that to be a lie.'

'Suit yourself,' said the Monk. 'It's your neck on the line.'

'I have it from a very reliable source that the key to completing my murderous task is within this very city. Somewhere. A man. Or something that looks like a man. I do not suppose you could furnish me with his location?'

The Monk swallowed the last of his biscuit and went in for seconds. 'Never heard of such a person. Not here. Someone has been pulling your leg.'

'No. I do not believe so, not his style.'

'Even if such a man did reside within this City, you would not be able to leave with him.'

'Is that so?'

'You cannot take anything from this place. *You* may leave, as this place is not for you, but the rest of the things in the City of the Dead belong to it. They will remain. They cannot leave. They will not.'

'What if I go ahead and take him anyway?' asked Carlisle.

'You will not leave.'

'I am not accustomed to being told no, Monk.'

'You will become so here.'

Carlisle smiled. 'I think not.'

Carlisle took out the whip that hung beneath his coat and wrapped it around the Monk's neck, pulling tight until the Monk's face turned blue and his limbs ceased their twitching. Carlisle released the Monk and allowed the body to crumple to the floor. As it hit down, the corpse erupted in a cloud of black dust, leaving only robes behind.

Carlisle nudged at the empty robes with the toe of his boot. From within the garment, the key attached to its thin leather strap tumbled into view.

'Aha.' Carlisle bent down and retrieved the exit key, placing the strap over his neck.

He finished the last of his cola and stepped towards the door to leave the Monk's home. He paused, turned back, took a large chocolate chip cookie from the plate, and then left.

As Carlisle left behind the Monk's home, he found that the City of the Dead was more forest than city. The trees were giants, both in length and width, and looked as though they had been in a fire. The bark was black and grey and flaked under his touch, yet somehow the blackened branches were covered in fresh, green leaves still. Carlisle sniffed the air; smoke. He scuffed at the ground with the toe of his boot. It too was scorched.

Scattered around the forest were outcrops of small, simple buildings, much like the Monk's. Hovels, cottages, buildings that would not have looked out of place a few hundred years ago.

Carlisle walked on.

He had a knack for finding where he needed to be, so decided to trust his feet to lead him there. The magic in the air was bitter. His body naturally drew some of the background energy into himself, but the magic here made his body ache, his stomach churn. He turned his head and spat on the flaky ground as he walked, trying to get the bad taste out of the back of his throat.

He stopped outside a large stone building; a pub. Smoke billowed from the inn's chimney, and a wooden sign stuck out from the wall, creaking back and forth in the wind. *Dead Man's Folly* was scrawled on the sign in big red letters. Carlisle pushed the door open and entered. Much like a bar in a western film, the conversation within hushed and all eyes turned to the newcomer.

'Hello,' said Carlisle, grinning wolfishly. He made his way over to the bar, the patrons' eyes following him as he moved. 'Pint of ale, if you would be so kind,' he said to the barman, a sorry looking specimen with green, rotting flesh that looked like it might peel away from his bones at any moment.

'You're not dead,' said the rotting barman, his voice a wheeze.

'Not today, no, but who knows what the day might yet bring?'

The barman slid a full glass across the bar to Carlisle, who picked it up and turned to face the rest of the patrons. He tipped his head back, downed the drink in one, and tossed the empty glass over his shoulder.

'My name is Carlisle, the once and future King of the Uncanny Kingdom, and I am looking for the killer of angels,' he said. The bar's motley-looking customers looked at each other, then back to Carlisle. 'Well? Do any of you know where he can be found?'

One of the customers raised a hand.

'Yes, you with the eyeball dangling out of its socket.'

'You are not supposed to be here. This is the afterlife for those that do not die. You die.'

'Sometimes I do, yes, though I try not to make a habit of it. So, angel killer, I'm sure there's a grapevine in this wretched place, so feel free to pass it on and on as I weave my way through and through.'

Carlisle strode out of the bar and made his way further into the forest. Each building he came to, he entered and asked the same question, made the same request. It was laborious, tedious work, but often the best way to get what you want is to make yourself conspicuous.

'The killer of angels,' Carlisle cried to a group of children tormenting a bear, 'tell everyone, Carlisle is looking for him.'

'Piss off,' said one of the children, and the group returned to poking the bear with pointed sticks.

After walking for hours, and leaving threads everywhere he stopped, Carlisle took a seat upon a fallen tree and pulled an apple from one pocket and a paperback copy of *Wuthering Heights* from the other. He was three chapters and half an apple along when he was approached.

'You Carlisle, then?'

Carlisle looked up from his book to see a young woman stood before him. She had a mountain of yellow curls on her head and a very pleasant face… apart from the hole at its centre where a nose would once have sat. Carlisle slipped the book back into his pocket and swallowed a bite of his apple.

'I am delighted to say that yes, I am indeed Carlisle. Lucky old me.' He stood and walked towards the woman. 'Whom do I have the pleasure of addressing?'

'Lola. I'm Lola. Bastard lovechild of an eternal and a mortal.'

Carlisle had heard tell of the eternals. They walked forever between worlds and stars, realities and make believes, forever attempting to experience true emotions, but cursed to know only the cold empty nothing.

'Have you heard tell of why I am in your delightful, foul-tasting city, Lola?'

Lola looked over her shoulder, then back to Carlisle. 'Angel killer.'

Carlisle grinned. 'Ten points to you. And you have news?'

She nodded. 'You can find him where the river runs black.'

'Lola, why are you telling me this?'

'Huh?'

'What is in it for you? No one does something for nothing, but nothing is all I have to offer you. Take it or leave it.'

'I tell you 'cos he scares me. Comes to me when I'm in bed, sleeping, and gives me cause to shiver. I don't like him.'

Lola walked away, leaving Carlisle more than a little perturbed. He took a last bite of his apple, then tossed what was left and went in search of a river. That was not a difficult chore; he could sense the flow of water. When you are so connected to the Uncanny, it comes naturally. It was a narrow, fast-flowing river, but it was a clear blue, not black. Carlisle looked left and looked right, and then sighed. He took a coin from his pocket, flipped it into the air, and caught it. He looked to see which side was face up. 'Very well,' said Carlisle, and turned to follow the river down to his left.

The river wound its way through the forest, twisting and turning. Carlisle walked until his feet hurt, and he began to suspect that he had taken the wrong direction, but then, all at once, the clear blue water began fading to black. With each forward step it darkened and darkened.

There was a man sat on the bank of the river. He was small and wiry, with a hook nose and short, coarse brown hair that looked more like little porcupine spines than hair. He held a fishing rod and the line dangled into the black water.

'What kind of fish are there to be caught in water as black as that?' asked Carlisle.

'No fish, plenty of eels, though. Big fat ones, like from some sort of dreadful nightmare. They're as wide as your thigh, teeth like butcher's knives, smell like a busy prostitute's never-you-mind.'

'Delightful,' said Carlisle. He took a seat next to the fisherman. 'Lola told me I would find you here.'

'Did she? She still got no nose?'

'She was minus a nose when we spoke, yes.'

'Eels, you see. Took them to show her as she slept. Bit it clean off.'

'Would you rather I had not found you?' asked Carlisle.

'Makes no difference to me. My name is Horse, by the way.'

'What a stupid name.'

Horse nodded in agreement. 'My mother was not a wise woman, but she did like horses. Had a stable full of the finest, most handsome horses you've ever laid eyes upon. Champions. Could leap over houses, let alone fences. She'd have me ride them, my mother. Horse on a horse, she'd say.'

'Are you quite finished,' asked Carlisle, 'only you are stupefyingly boring.'

'Sorry, I do rabbit on, I've been told as much. You always rabbit on, Horse, that's what they say. Rabbit on horse. Ha. Like Horse on horse. That's funny, isn't it?'

Carlisle sighed and pinched the bridge of his nose, resisting the urge to push the man into the black water so that the eels would feast upon him. 'I am told you would be the person capable of terminating the existence of a first order angel. Would that be true?'

'Yup. I can do that.'

'How?'

'Just can.'

'That is a little vague.'

'Yeah.'

'Would you care to shed a little more light upon things?' asked Carlisle.

Horse shook his head. 'I can do it. Done it once before. Got nothing to prove to you or no one else.'

Carlisle was not the most trusting of people, but it mattered where information came from. In this case, it came from Giles L'Merrier. If he said that this was where the answer to his angel problem was, then it gave the information weight. What L'Merrier said could be counted upon.

Carlisle pushed down his natural inclination to doubt, and thought instead about the weight of his artefact in his right hand. How good that would feel once more. How complete he would feel. How right and powerful. How far from the sewer. 'Horse, I would like you to leave this place with me and slay an angel.'

Horse looked up at him with eyes that were far too close together. 'What's this angel ever done to you?'

'Enough.'

'Well, I do like killing things. Like killing eels. Like killing most anything. Especially, though, I like killing angels.'

'So you will do it?'

'Can't.'

Again, it took all of Carlisle's self-control not to kick the man into the river. 'You said that you could.'

'Can. But I can't leave here, can I? I'm the dead that does not die, and this is where I'm stuck forever.'

Carlisle smiled and pulled out the key that he had taken from the Monk. 'You cannot leave, but I can. I am still very much alive, so I am able to come and go, and I have the exit key right here.'

'So?' replied Horse. 'Won't do me any good. I'm not you, I'm me.'

'Oh, my ugly friend, the answer is simple.'

'Is it? Oh good. I prefer simple answers.'

'You will just have to share my body. Temporarily.'

'Right. Doesn't sound that simple, to be truthful.'

'The answer is simple, the process is not. It is also quite, quite painful.' Carlisle did not know, to be truthful, that what he was proposing would actually work. Trojan horsing the man out of the City of the Dead. But it was worth a try. 'So, Horse, what say you and I get a little closer?'

Horse nodded and pushed himself up on to his feet. 'Might as well. Eels aren't biting anyway. Must be sleeping at the bottom. Hope they're having bad dreams for keeping me waiting.'

Carlisle smiled and began to prepare himself for a houseguest.

26

A race against time.

It's always exciting in a film, that. A ticking clock, a bomb to defuse, a woman in a chamber rapidly filling with water screaming to be found, a hero coming through just as the final seconds ticked away.

Rita really, really hoped this race against time would not be such a close-run thing.

'So when you say an exorcist, what exactly do you mean?' Rita asked.

'I means an exorcist,' Formby replied. 'An exorcist-exorcist.'

'So, a bloke in a dog collar, "The power of Christ compels you", all of that stuff?'

'Yes. But different, too. Very special sort of Uncanny exorcist named Bob.'

'Bob?'

'That's him.'

'Right. Then take me to Bob.'

They left Ben back at Big Pins, despite his protestations. They didn't know how long this would take, or if it would prove successful. The last thing they needed was for both of them to be out and about as a full moon rose. No, damage limitation, Ben would stay behind and hole up in the basement before night came around. If he was going to change, he'd do it somewhere he wouldn't hurt anyone.

Rita checked her watch as she drove at speed through Blackpool towards Bob's house.

'Look at the road, look at the road!' Formby screeched as Rita almost drove them up on to the pavement.

'Shit, sorry,' said Rita. 'So, Bob. Who is Bob exactly?'

'Told you. Exorcist. Uncanny exorcist. Can talk the bad stuff out of you. Demons, ghosts, magic, whatever.'

'Hexes?'

Formby grinned. 'No.'

'Typical.'

'Trained at the Vatican under the Uncanny Order.'

'Wait, so there's a secret magic department in the Catholic Church?'

'Yes, secret. All kinds of things deep under Vatican City. Carlisle knows, he has stolen more than one thing from under there.'

Bob the exorcist lived at 23a Parker Avenue, a basement flat. Rita's car screeched to a halt outside and she and Formby hopped out. Rita checked her watch, then squinted up at the sky. It seemed like the day was already starting to bruise.

They scurried past the gate and down the grimy set of steps to the front door of Bob's flat, Rita bashing furiously at the door.

'Hello? Hello? Bob, open up!'

There was no answer.

'You did tell him we were on our way, right?'

Formby held up his phone to show the message he'd sent. 'Yes. He replied, look.'

Rita peered at the phone's screen to see Bob the exorcist had indeed replied with a little thumbs-up emoji, followed by a smiley face emoji.

Rita turned to the door and continued the bashing. No response came.

'Balls.' Rita took out the axe and smashed it against the door's lock until it sprang open.

'Bit rude,' said Formby, following Rita inside.

Bob's home was a mess. Actually, saying it was a mess was

insulting to the good name of mess. This place looked and smelled as though two crack dens had bumped uglies and birthed a super crack den. Rubbish was strewn everywhere; newspapers, food cartons with mould spilling out, dirty laundry. The curtains were pulled tight as if embarrassed that the world outside might see the horror within.

'This is the person that's going to save me from becoming a monster?' asked Rita, as they made their way into the living room. The only furniture there was a depressed-looking comfy chair with a tiny TV set perched on a crate in front of it. The walls were daubed in graffiti: arcane symbols, crosses, strange-looking creatures, and—if Rita was not mistaken—a shopping list.

'Bob is good,' said Formby, looking around the room. 'Bit messy, but good.'

'A *bit* messy?' said Rita, pulling her foot away from something sticky.

'Let yourself in then, did you?'

Rita turned to see a shambles of a man stood in the living room doorway. He was overweight, had a week's worth of beard growth, and the hair on his head was unwashed and unbrushed. In his hand was a plastic shopping bag.

'This is Bob,' said Formby, clapping his hands together.

Bob walked over to his chair, dropped the plastic bag on the floor, and dropped into it.

'You owe me for a broken door,' he said.

'Yes, sorry,' replied Rita, 'because now this place looks a right state.'

'Exactly.' Bob leaned down and pulled a can of lemonade out of the bag, opened it, and took a sip. 'Ah. Lovely sugar fizz. This her then, is it?'

'Yes,' replied Formby. 'Lycanthropy. Bitten by a master werewolf.'

'She's hexed, too, by the stink of her.'

'Hey,' said Rita, 'I do not smell.'

'Do a bit,' said Formby. 'Hex stink.'

Rita frowned and sniffed at herself.

'Can't force a hex out, you know that,' said Bob.

'Yes. Just the wolf,' replied Formby.

Rita waggled her watch at Bob and Formby. 'Not to rush you, but it's almost time for the sun to disappear, so…'

Bob the exorcist sighed, then stood and approached Rita, peering into her eyes. 'Let's have a look at you then.' He grabbed her by the jaw and looked down her throat.

'Is that strictly necessary?' asked Rita, though as her mouth wasn't able to close, it came out a little more garbled than that.

'Yup. Wolf in her all right. I can see it growling down there,' said Bob, then he let go of Rita's face and walked out of the room.

'Where are you going?' Rita asked. 'I did mention the urgency, right?'

'Getting me tools.'

Rita checked her watch again, then teased the curtains aside to see how it was looking outside. It wasn't looking good. Already the sun was dipping and she could see the moon starting to rise. It didn't look full, not yet, but she knew Magda could change that at any moment.

'Shit,' said Rita.

'Agree,' said Formby, who was now poking around in Bob's shopping bag. 'Ooh!' He reached in and pulled out a bag of crisps. 'Cheese & Onion, my favourite.'

'Got them for you, friend,' said Bob, walking back into the office with a small leather bag, the kind you might see a doctor carrying around on home visits fifty years ago.

'Okay, so what is it we're doing to get rid of this then?' asked Rita. 'Something simple and not painful sounds good to me.'

Bob chuckled as he opened the bag. He reached inside and pulled out a large, rusted tool of terror. A hand drill. Rita's face may have gone a little pale then. Bob chuckled again and dropped the nightmare thing back into the bag. 'Just a joke.' Formby broke out in a snigger.

'Yeah, laugh it up. Hilarious.'

Bob reached back into the bag and pulled out a water bottle filled with bright orange liquid.

'What is that?' asked Rita.

'A start,' said Bob. 'I can get this out of you.'

'Good.'

'Probably.'

'I'm sorry? Probably?'

'These things are not an exact science,' said Bob. 'Sometimes it just doesn't work and you ask, "Why didn't that work?" And the answer is "I dunno". So. Fingers crossed, eh?'

'Great. Feeling very worried now.'

'Either way, work or not, it's going to hurt. It's going to hurt a lot.'

Rita nodded.

'And I actually will have to use this,' said Bob, pulling the drill back out of the bag.

Rita felt the blood drain from her face again.

Magda stretched. She'd been sleeping, dreaming of running in the forest by her family home as a child. Night was almost here, and she had work to do.

She pulled out a piece of chalk and drew a pentagram on the sewer chamber's dirty stone floor. She knelt down and touched a hand to the chalk on the ground. 'Power. I grant it to you,' she said, and the pentagram glowed bright yellow as it accepted the Uncanny magic she was gifting it. Magda had given the pentagram life and purpose. Made it a tool, ready to use.

She stepped into the pentagram and sat down, crossing her legs. The spell was ready to cast.

Rita finished drinking the orange liquid and tried not to throw up. It tasted like death.

'What was that?' she spat, gasping.

'My own special mix. I can get you the recipe if you like,' replied Bob, as he put on his dog collar.

'Is that needed?' asked Rita. 'This isn't a demon. I mean, is it?'

'It's symbolic,' said Bob. 'There is a process, a routine. Each person has a different way to go about it. It's not the actions themselves that matter—they can be almost anything—it's the repetition. Like a mantra for meditation. These are the things we choose to do, choose to wear, choose to say, and they open the lines of power because we have decided they will.'

Rita nodded slowly. 'Right. Not really following that, but whatever you need to do to get this dog out of me.'

'Can I have this?' said Formby, waving a Kit Kat in the air.

'Right now?' said Rita.

'Sorry. Carry on.'

Magda always thought about the Creeping Oak before she cast a spell. Thinking about the tree, the winding iron staircase, the demon in its old woman guise at the top, helped her to bring calm to her mind before trying something so big. So dangerous.

She could feel the magic in the air around her starting to notice her. To become attracted to her more and more.

'I need you,' she begged, and ribbons of colour began to form, to sharpen, and dance around her seated form.

'I command you. I control you. I transform you.'

Bob chained Rita to the wall by her ankle, just in case.

'Any number of things could go wrong. You could try to escape before the ceremony is done. Or I could unleash the beast in you, you could turn and try to eat us.'

'Okay, let's get this over with.'

Bob the exorcist breathed in through his nose and clapped his hands together. Colourful sparks flew when his palms struck together. 'Oh Lord, I am your servant. I am unworthy. I ask of you your help. Your hand. Your guidance.'

The room darkened and Formby made his excuses and scuttled out of the door.

'This woman has the beast in her. The wolf.' Bob stepped forward and punched Rita full in the face. She staggered back and fell to the floor, clutching her nose that was now throbbing and dripping blood.

'What the hell, Bob?'

'Her blood runs. Her blood taints my hands.' Bob raised his hand up, her blood smeared upon it. He licked it.

'Oh, what the crap? Formby? This guy is mental!'

Bob began muttering words that Rita didn't understand, words that felt old. Older than old.

There were things in the corner of the room. In the dark. Rita could feel them. Could hear them chitter. She felt a deep-down horror begin to creep over her.

'Bob. I'm scared, Bob.'

Bob didn't respond. The ceremony had begun.

Magda pictured the moon in her mind's eye.

She pictured it large and full and so brilliantly white.

Beautiful.

Powerful.

The moon was God to her kind, and she worshipped it as she should. Revered it. But now she wanted to control it.

'In this place, in this dark, you will be full. Perfect. Powerful.'

The ribbons of magic began to whirl faster and faster, twisting into new shapes, becoming one. One spell, one magic, with one purpose.

'T'hum, latek, f'hum, latek,' Bob the exorcist chanted, over and over.

Ancient words of power.

Rita was starting to sweat. Her body shaking. Skin itching. Bones aching.

'It hurts,' she said.

Bob did not answer.

'Now, do as I ask. I am yours. I give you power.'

Magda was shaking too. This spell, this kind of magic, it was almost beyond her, even now. Almost beyond any magician. But she would be strong enough. She had it in her. Her will would not be denied.

The magic whispered back to her.

Told her it understood what she wanted.

Magda threw her head back and howled as the magic burst up from her, through the ceiling of the chamber, through the air above, up and up towards the moon.

Rita was curled on the floor, shaking so hard she thought she might give herself whiplash.

'I command you,' said Bob. 'You know me. You know my power. You know my purpose, foul thing.'

The unseen chittering things in the darkened corners of the room laughed and stomped their cloven feet upon the wooden floorboards; a tattoo of terror that made Rita's flesh crawl.

'Show me. Show me. Show me.'

Magda stepped up out of the sewers and on to the streets of Blackpool.

She looked at the sky, looked at the moon shining bright, and saw her magic, her will, begin to take effect. She thought of those she had turned so far. So many, ready to run through the streets and sit by her side. Ready to feast.

Rita screamed.

She could feel it.

Feel the beast within her.

The dark magic manifesting, pushing aside her sense of self, her memories, her everything. Pushing it under the black water and drowning it. Silencing it.

'Please!' she yelled. 'It's coming, it's coming!'

'Beast, hear me!' screamed Bob. 'I am your master, now. Not the moon, not the one who gave you life, just me!'

Rita felt her skin ripple. At any moment it would tear open and the wolf would start to push its way out.

Too late.

Too late.

It was over.

The exorcism had failed.

Rita wanted to cry, but was in too much pain.

So she whimpered.

But the whimper began to turn into a feral growl. The wolf was almost out. And the things in the shadows crowed and clapped and cheered.

Rita could not see the moon from inside the flat, but she could feel it. She could hear it. It called to her, to what was inside her.

It was too late.

'Dog, you are mine!'

She heard Bob say the words, just barely, and wondered why he was still fighting.

But Bob had not failed. Had not lost. Not yet.

He picked up the drill, kissed it, touched it to his forehead, spoke a single word that she could not hear, and then thrust the sharp end directly into her chest.

Rita howled. It didn't sound like her. It was the monster.

Bob began to turn the drill, Rita's flesh ripping beneath it, her rib cage cracking.

'Out! I cast you out!'

The drill glowed, tendrils of red washing around it as he drilled deeper and deeper. Finally—his face dripping with sweat—he yanked the drill free and threw it aside. The tool skittered away across the floor boards, leaving a bloody trail behind it. 'You no longer belong. You are of the dark and I send you back there.'

It was too late. Rita knew it. Could feel her teeth starting to itch, to change. Why was he still trying?

Bob stuck his fingers into the gaping wound he'd created and pulled something out of Rita's chest. It was alive. It writhed and shook, it was bone and teeth and dark fur, and it screamed, tried to cling to her insides, but it was no use. Bob pulled it free and threw it into one black corner of the room, where the unseen things caught it, tore at it, feasted upon it.

Rita could no longer hear the moon. Could no longer feel the wolf trying to suffocate her. Trying to rip its way out of her.

'It's done,' said Bob, and he clapped his hands together. The unnatural dark lifted and the unseen things were gone.

The curse was lifted.

Rita tried to open her mouth to thank him, but instead she saw static and fell unconscious.

27

Tina was the first to feel it.

She'd felt off ever since the party the previous night. The spiked drinks. That's what everyone thought. Some sort of group hallucination. It could happen, Brian said he'd read about it. The other option was absurd; some strange woman with big teeth biting them all, because firstly, that was make-believe. That was something that happened in a film, not in Blackpool. Secondly, none of them had any bite marks. Not even a bruise where they remembered being bitten. No, all they had was a rotten hangover.

John reckoned some member of staff with a grudge had done it. Maybe getting back at their boss, a little *fuck you* before leaving. Had to be something like that. Had to be.

Tina touched the place she remembered the woman with the piercing blue eyes sinking her teeth into. No mark, no wound. A little tender to the touch, perhaps, but what did that prove?

Tina's friend Marion was scared. It was getting dark and she couldn't stop trembling. Couldn't relax, couldn't stop the fist in her stomach from tightening with each passing minute. Marion remembered the woman with the blue eyes. The one they all agreed they'd imagined. But Marion had spoken to her. Had sat down and shared words. That didn't feel like she'd just imagined it. She'd been there. The woman with blue eyes had been there, surely. But just like Tina, and Brian, and all the rest. Yet there was no bite mark on her skin. She looked in the mirror again, touching the wound that wasn't there, remembering how it felt as the blue-eyed woman's teeth had torn into her flesh.

Brian could hear the moon. He tried to ignore it. The aftereffects of whatever had spiked their drinks, that was all. Must be. Just like the hangover that seemed to be getting worse as the day went on. A hundred times worse, the darker it got. Brian could hear the moon. Tina was upstairs. She'd crawled off to bed early, and Brian didn't want to disturb her. Anyway, he wanted to hear what the moon had to say.

His muscles aching, Brian got up off the floor. He'd been curled in a ball, trembling, sweating, for the past hour, but he couldn't ignore the moon any more. So he ignored his complaining body instead, ignored the fearful voice in his head, and he made his way stiffly over to the window. 'I can hear you,' he said, his voice hushed.

The moon was full. Brian opened the window a little. He wanted to hear more clearly what the moon had to say.

What it had to say was this: *Now. Now. You are born. Run. Feed. Be glorious.*

There had been twenty people at Tina's party, plus four members of staff.

They were scattered in homes all across Blackpool, and all of them could hear the moon, now. They hadn't realised it could speak before, but now they did.

Magda could feel them all. All of her children. She stood in the street, looking up at the full moon she had demanded, and basked in its glow. It warmed her, caressed her, made her strong.

One by one, a new voice, a new vision, was available to Magda. Each of the turned were falling to the floor, were screaming. It was such beautiful music. She could see what they saw, now they had become for the first time. They were part of her now, they were family. And they were just the first.

She went from wolf to wolf in her mind, speaking to them, soothing them, making sure they weren't scared, that they knew how special they were and that she loved them very much. Would care for them, lead them, feed them, protect them.

One was missing.

Magda frowned. Could it be that she was resisting her somehow? Magda searched again, washing around all of her wolves, but no. Rita wasn't there. A tear formed in the corner of Magda's eye and raced down her cheek. She had lost her. A death in the family.

Not to worry.

She would be remembered. Even as she had somehow thrown off Magda's gift to her, she would be remembered. Magda carried all of her turned ones in her heart.

She pushed the sadness aside, wiped the damp trail from her cheek, and smiled.

The pack was on its way to her.

Tonight they would run free.

Tonight they would be alive.

Tonight they would not hide, fear, or be ashamed of what they were.

For a short while, it wasn't alone. It could hear something weak called Ben Turner screaming, thinking, shaking, but it was strong and it pushed Ben Turner away until it could no longer hear him.

The moon.

The moon.

The moon.

It called to it.

I hear you, it thought, and it howled, throwing its big head back and opening its mouth wide to inhale air into its powerful lungs before unleashing its freedom call.

It paced the room it was in. No windows, no way to see outside, no way to see the moon.

Stone floor, walls, roof, a couch, a locked door.

It threw itself in a blind fury against the door, desperate to leave, to go outside, to feel the moon warming its fur, to run with the others. But the door held strong.

It whimpered and tried again, again, again, until it could taste its own blood on its big, sharp teeth.

Why was it being kept like this? Wanted to, needed to, had to run free and wild and eat, eat, eat.

Its ears pricked up as it caught its breath, readying itself for another attack on the door, as new sounds could be heard beyond.

Crashing.

Screams.

Cries.

Howls!

Its tail wagged and it paced in excited circles.

'It's okay,' said the voice of its master in its head, *'Calm down, free soon.'*

More noise, chaos beyond, and then a click and a clunk and the door opened to reveal a woman. A woman it knew, loved, would do anything for.

'Hello,' she said, then threw back her head and howled. It howled in reply, then ran to her, nuzzling its head against her, enjoying the feel of her hands stroking its fur.

'They kept you locked in here like you were worthless,' said its master. 'You are beautiful.'

Others like it surged into the room and there was blood upon their fur. Not their blood, the blood of others.

'Come on,' said its master, 'night is here. Our time. Let us go and greet the moon.'

It had taken Rita almost two hours before she'd recovered enough to leave Bob the exorcist's hovel of a home. Formby had been so concerned by her weakened, shaky state that he'd shared some of the food he'd liberated from Bob's shopping.

'You sure you're okay?' asked Formby, as Rita pulled the car to a stop next to the blind alley that lead to Big Pins.

'Yeah,' she said, but the truth was she was badly shaken. She put a hand to the place Bob had used the drill upon. It was tender and had left a cold, deep ache in her chest, but the hole had knitted back together thanks to some more potion and secret words. She'd rarely been more terrified in her life. She thought she was done, for sure. That it was all too late, that the wolf was upon her and every full moon from then on she was going to have to go through the terrifying, agonising process of changing. Of being submerged, pushed aside so a monster could take over.

It didn't take long to realise something bad had gone down in their absence. The front door of Big Pins had been turned to splinters. Formby slid back behind Rita as she removed the axe from her belt and slowly stepped inside, the magic-dampening bubble parting around her as she stepped inside.

Big Pins was a mess. Tables and chairs broken, windows shattered, glass shards littering the place, blood splatters everywhere. The place seemed empty of the living, but there were a few ripped-up corpses scattered around, one of which belonged to Tusk, the green-skinned monster she'd tangled with a while back.

'Holy shit,' said Rita, slowly taking it all in. Then a terrible thought struck home, 'Ben...'

Rita raced across Big Pins and past the bar, taking the door that lead down to the basement. The door to the room Ben had been locked in for the night lay wide open.

'Ben? Are you down there?' Rita wondered why she'd even asked. It was a full moon – if Ben was down there then he wasn't Ben anymore and she was in deep trouble.

She stepped into the basement, but the only person she found was Linton, sat on the couch, stitching up a wound on his stomach.

'Linton, are you okay?'

Linton looked up at her and frowned, then nodded, 'Mostly. I'm a tough bastard.'

'What happened? Was it Ben?'

'No. Others came. The woman you've been looking for, and a pack of werewolves at her side. They came here, ripped through the place and set your man free.'

Rita remembered Magda saying she was connected to those she'd turned. She knew where Ben was because Ben knew where he was, so she came to collect him.

'Shit. Shit, shit, shit!'

'Mm,' replied Linton.

'Wait, why didn't the magic dampening bubble thingy help?'

'Help what?' said Linton. 'Different kind of magic. Not controllable by anything. But you already felt that, yes?'

Yes, Rita had felt the wildness of the lycanthropy magic. It could not be tamed, even with the axe she wielded. An artefact of Heaven.

Rita checked her watch; it was a little after midnight.

'Okay. So Magda and her doggies of death have hours to run riot through Blackpool. That's a cheery thought.' She tried not to think about how many more deaths Ben might have on his conscience by the time the sun rose again.

'What to do?' asked Formby.

'Well,' replied Linton, standing, his wound now stitched up, 'I don't know about you two, but I'm going to clean up my bowling alley.'

'Right, thanks for the help,' said Rita as Linton left them. 'I don't suppose you have any ideas, Moley Molerson?'

Formby frowned. 'Perhaps a bite to eat, then consider all options.'

'Great. Brilliant idea.'

Formby grinned.

'I was being sarcastic.'

'Hm. So, do we eat or not eat?'

Rita sighed and slumped on the couch, head in her hands. 'I don't know what to do, Formby. They're out there and I can't stop them. I can't use this stupid axe because it can't control the magic, it'll just infect me again. We're screwed.'

Just as Rita was feeling sorry for herself—sorry for Ben and those he would encounter through the night—the last thing she expected to happen, happened.

'Rita.'

Rita's heart skipped. She knew that voice. She looked up to see a third figure was now sharing Big Pins basement with herself and Formby. A figure she knew all too well. A figure who had been murdered a few days previously.

'Hey, Waters,' she said.

'I'm sorry,' replied Dan Waterson, and then he ran at her and stepped into her body.

28

The wizards were worried.

Actually, that was a severe understatement. They were terrified.

The moon was full again. Had been forced to rise full. Just there, just in Blackpool. Such powerful magic, magic beyond the capabilities of any in the area.

'Something must be done!' said one.

'What? What can be done?' asked another.

The previous time, the spell had faltered—a test run, they assumed—but this time, this night, they could all feel it. Could feel the magnitude of the spell. Of the Uncanny disruption to the natural order. This night, the moon would stay full and the wolves would run amok.

Bullets of panicked conversation ricocheted about the Wizards' Chamber.

'Has he answered?'

'You know L'Merrier, he answers in his own time.'

'Push him!'

'He must see the pattern. Must see how she is building.'

'He'll have to face her eventually if she is not stopped here.'

The cave echoed with fears, with fury, with questions but no real answers. The Chamber had rarely been so full. Two dead wizards, the master werewolf with magic in their home, they were all at risk. They needed a wizard of L'Merrier's magnitude to deal with a situation this dire. A master werewolf without magic, as they should be? Any one of them could have dealt with such vermin, but this? This woman? This woman engendered only fear and doubt.

'We should form a union.'

'A union?'

'All of us should connect, become one, we could best her then.'

'A union has not been attempted in five hundred years. It is far too dangerous. Far too difficult to control.'

'It almost punched a hole in reality the last time it was tried. It cannot be risked again.'

'Then what do you suggest?'

They all felt it, a sudden cold that caused the skin to prickle. They turned to see they had unwelcome guests.

'So this is where you hide,' said Magda, her wolf pack at her side.

But no! This could not be. The cave was impenetrable. It had no entrance, had no exit. Chaos erupted as the wizards attempted to flee. Magda and her family did not try to stop them. The wolves remained still as Magda slowly circled the chamber, taking the place in.

'He showed me, the one who is sometimes Ben. He visited here and began to change, and I saw you all. Saw this place.'

The wizards were in a panic; they could not leave. Again and again they said the words, their own exit pass, but when they stepped forward they were rebuffed. Try as they might, the chamber would not allow them to leave.

'What have you done?' begged Ulner, the wizard in the blue, snug suit who had brought Ben into their sacred meeting place, unaware of what lurked within him.

'What have I done?' Magda replied. 'I have done the impossible. I have become a master werewolf with a greater grasp upon magic than any of you, and I have told this place not to let you leave.'

'Outrageous!' screamed the tiny wizard in the high-collared robe. He lifted the golden staff he held in one hand and pointed it at her. The end of the staff swarmed with orange light, orange light that blasted towards Magda.

Magda did not leap out of the way. Did not cower behind her arms and whimper. Did not even blink. The orange light, the burning spell summoned to reduce her to ash, paused a foot from her face, then turned back, back towards the tiny wizard, who then became an even tinier pile of grey ash.

The other wizards stepped back, reconsidering any rush to attack.

'You defile this place,' said Ulner.

'Yes. I do.'

The wolves began to growl, baring their jagged teeth, drool dripping on to the ground beneath their huge paws.

'You and your kind, you have called us vermin for centuries. People like me. My family. You have hunted and killed and thought it good.' Magda turned her back on the gathered wizards, showing how little she feared them, how contemptuous she was of them, and nuzzled with her hand the chin of the wolf that was once Ben Turner.

'What is it you want?' asked Ulner. 'No wizard in this place has hunted your kind, I can promise you that.'

Magda did not turn back to them. 'I don't care.'

'What do you want?'

Magda thought about her dead mother, laid out in their bathroom. Murdered. Slaughtered like a rat. She wondered just where her father's body had been left.

'I want only one thing,' replied Magda, 'one simple, small thing. An end to all wizards; for you to run in fear like my kind have done for centuries. To feast on your magic as my wolves feast on your bones.'

As one, the wolves, Magda's family, surged towards the wizards, and the cave became awash with screams and blood.

Magda thought that a very fine thing.

In time, the only wizards would be dead wizards.

29

It was fair to say that Rita Hobbes had not expected to see her ex-partner and best friend Dan Waterson again. At the very least, she hadn't expected to see him walking and talking. The last time she'd seen him he was being placed in a body bag and placed into the back of an ambulance, dead. Dead at the hands—and sword—of their boss, DCI Jenner.

'Waters?' Rita cried. 'What's happening?'

Rita could see where she was, what she was doing, but she was not in control of herself. She could see through the windscreen of her car as she drove it through Blackpool towards who knew where. It felt like she was very much a passenger inside of her own body. Waterson was in there with her. He was the one with his hands on the wheel.

'Waters, talk to me.'

'You know I hate being called Waters, Rita.'

'There he is! How's it going, pal?'

'Not great. I'm dead.'

'Yeah. Sorry. Partly my fault.'

'Partly?'

'Hey, I didn't know what was going to happen. I haven't exactly been in control of any of this shit, you know. Did I mention the whole wizards, monsters and hex thing?'

'You always did drop me in the shit, Rita.'

She laughed. 'So you're a ghost? What's that like?'

'So far, so terrible. Dying for a smoke, too. Well, not dying, what with the fact that I'm already dead.'

'But you were doing so well with the vaping...'

'I'm dead,' said Waterson. 'I think I can go back to the hard stuff.'

'Did you see Heaven?' asked Rita.

'No. Saw the inside of a morgue. Bit grim. Oh, I did meet an angel though.'

That made Rita's ears prick up, or at least it would have done if she'd have had any control over her body.

'The most beautiful person ever, ever, sat in a glass cube under the sea, right?'

'That's the one.'

The car pulled to a stop on a residential street. Two facing rows of terraced houses. Rita recognised the street. Gemma Wheeler, the woman she'd rescued from being sacrificed by Jenner, lived on this street. It suddenly became quite clear what was happening.

'Don't do it, Dan,' she said.

'Do you think I have any choice in the matter? It's that bloody angel, who has nothing but bad things to say about you, by the way. Not all of them entirely inaccurate.'

'Hey!'

'Sorry, did you or did you not say you were partly to blame for my murder?'

'Yeah, okay. You've got me there.'

'Tell me you can stop this, Rita. Please.'

Rita strained to regain control of herself, but not only could she not find a ledge to cling on to, she couldn't even find her fingers to cling on to it.

'You have to fight it, Waters. Fight Its control over you.'

'Oh, great, hadn't thought of that.'

'You know I've missed these little back and forths of ours.'

'Rita, focus, we're about to go and murder a woman with an axe.'

So the Angel was using Dan to finish off the sacrifices. Made sense. Easier to just shove Dan into her to pilot her around, to complete the sacrifices with the axe, than to try and free Jenner.

'Are you in control of yourself at all,' asked Rita. 'Even a little?'

'I can speak, I can say what I want, but that's it. The rest is just sort of happening. I've no idea how I was even able to step inside you and move you around like this. It was just natural. Like muscle memory.'

They got out of the car, Gemma's house was on the opposite side.

'Try and get me back in the car and drive away,' said Rita.

'Okay.' They walked away from the car and crossed the road. 'Didn't work. So the Guv was the bad guy,' said Waterson. 'I didn't see that one coming.'

'No, I don't think anyone did.'

'Where is he?' Waterson asked.

'Locked up, sort of. Alive. Off his rocker.'

There was a car parked up outside Gemma Wheeler's house. Two very bored uniformed officers were sat inside, listening to Capital FM. It was still only days since Gemma had been found, and the local police had no idea that the person responsible for taking her—for taking the other women too—was safely locked up in a dreamscape prison. So the officers were there to keep an eye on her, make sure whoever was behind her abduction didn't turn up to try again. Unfortunately for these two officers, Dan Waterson, a ghost who they wouldn't have been able to see, was inside Rita Hobbes, a hexed detective who they also couldn't see. They don't teach that in basic training.

Rita and Waterson were about to go inside Gemma Wheeler's house and finish what DCI Alexander Jenner had started. They made their way down a side alley and began climbing back fences until they found themselves in the back garden of Gemma Wheeler's house.

'I wonder what it's like back at the station,' said Waterson.

'Must be insane.'

'I'm dead, the Guv gone, they've no idea what happened to him, or that he was really a crazy piece of shit.'

They shoved the blade of the axe into the crack between the

back door and the doorframe and levered it open, wood splintering.

'Okay, no more messing around, Waters, we have to stop this.'

'I'm trying, but I've no idea how to even go about it. I'm in automatic.'

Gemma Wheeler was in her bedroom. They found her sitting up, reaching for her mobile phone. They swung the axe and Gemma screamed, leaping back, the phone tumbling to the floor.

'Rita?' screamed Gemma, her face a mask of shock. 'What…? What's happening?'

'It's okay, don't worry, I'm going to stop this,' was Rita's reply, but the words didn't come out. Only she and Waterson heard them.

'I don't think you are going to stop it,' said Waterson.

'Just try!'

'What do you think I'm doing?'

It was going to happen. They were going to murder Gemma Wheeler. Just back from the hospital and they were going to strike her down with the axe, which would then absorb her soul, trapping it with the others already inside. With Jane Bowan and Ellie Mason.

They stepped forward, the axe raised, as Gemma Wheeler opened her mouth to scream, but the sound never came out. Instead she looked past Rita-Dan to the man standing behind them.

'My, my, what a fortuitous moment for my return.'

They turned to see a tall, narrow, pale-skinned man in a long purple coat.

'Carlisle!' said Rita, not that he heard her.

'What the hell is going on?' demanded Gemma Wheeler.

'This does not concern you,' said Carlisle, who clapped his hands together, whispered a word under his breath, and thrust his hand into Rita's chest.

'What-what-what-are you doing to—?' said Rita Hobbes and Dan Waterson as ice blade fingers dug and probed and latched on to what was inside.

'There you are,' said Carlisle, yanking his arm back and pulling the deceased Dan Waterson with him.

Rita staggered back, the axe slipping from her fingers.

'Shit… how… I'm back!'

'So, did you miss me?' said Carlisle, grinning.

Magda perched atop a pile of dead bodies inside the wizards' meeting place as her wolves gnawed at the remains.

She looked down at them, their fur matted with the blood of the dead, and she laughed. She could feel the magic she had feasted upon surging through her. More and more she ate and the power, the connection to the Uncanny that her kind had been barred from for so long, strengthened. It was true that the price she paid for such magic was her soul, but she didn't care. All that mattered was this: stopping the wizards. Freeing her kind from fear. Avenging her slaughtered family.

The moon was full, the wizards were dead, and Magda was ready to step out of the shadows.

30

Carlisle was not a fan of hugging. In fact, as Rita hugged him, Carlisle tried very hard not to shove his fist through her chest again, this time to rip out her heart.

'You came back!' cried Rita.

'No, this is all a dream,' he replied with disdain before untangling himself from her.

'Sorry, bit overexcited. That was good timing on your part, otherwise I was totally going to twat Gemma with the axe.'

Gemma Wheeler was cowering, aghast, against the far wall, not entirely sure what was going on or if she was or wasn't in any immediate danger.

'You may unclench, Gemma Wheeler,' said Carlisle, 'you are out of the woods.'

'Oh. Good.'

'For now.'

'Not as good.' Gemma shuffled forward timidly to look at the ghost of Dan Waterson, who was currently curled up on the floor within a chalk circle Carlisle had swiftly sketched there to contain him. Gemma had seen the strange pasty man shove his fist into Rita, who for some reason had been about to murder her, and pull out this second person. This second person who she suddenly realised she recognised.

'Wait, that's… that's the other copper, the detective who came to the hospital to see me.'

'Yeah,' said Rita, 'that there is Dan Waterson, my ex-partner. Professional, obviously, I wouldn't touch him with yours.'

'Right. Didn't I read about him getting murdered on the beach a few days back?'

'Yeah, partly my fault, that.'

'Okay. So he's a… ghost?'

'A ghost that was being controlled to use me and finish off what the Magician had going on with you and the other kidnapped women.'

Gemma slowly sat down to catch her breath, and to try and stop herself from either breaking out into hysterical laughter or hysterical tears.

'Here,' said Carlisle, reaching into his pocket and pulling out a small, bull-shaped charm.

'What's this for?' asked Gemma, taking the charm.

'Keep that on you, always. If you are ever in similar peril, it will alert me.'

'Aw,' said Rita, 'you're a secret softie, aren't you, Carlisle?'

'Call me that again and I will remove your jaw.'

Rita grinned at him in a way that made Carlisle clench his teeth, only not to smile back.

'So,' said Rita, turning to look at Waterson in his chalk circle holding pen, 'ghosts can be unconscious?'

'Ah, how I have missed those razor-sharp deductive powers, Detective.'

Rita tapped her head, 'Not just a hat stand, mate.'

'Oh, good grief.' Carlisle crouched by Waterson's prone body, sniffing. 'Hexed.'

'I know,' replied Rita, 'by you know who, too.'

'What just happened?' asked Waterson, his eyes flickering open.

'Waters! Welcome back to the land of the living. Sorry, that was probably offensive considering the fact you're… hello!'

Waterson stood groggily and attempted to step forward, only to find he was unable to move past the boundary of the chalk circle.

'You will remain in there, ghost, until I either find a way to break the Angel's control over you, or, preferably, and quicker, I just destroy you utterly.'

'I'm leaning towards the first option, if I'm honest,' replied Waterson.

'Option one sounds good to me, too,' said Rita.

Carlisle opened his hand and tendrils of colour, ribbons of magic, began to swirl around it. 'I have no idea how the hex was rendered, it really would be easier just to destroy him.'

'Sword!' said Waterson.

'What about it?' replied Carlisle.

'The Angel thing, It said that was how it was done. The sword the Guv stuck me with had magic words carved into it or something, and that did it. That hexed me up.'

'There you go,' said Rita, 'no need for rough stuff.'

Carlisle snorted and closed his hand, the magic fading from view. 'We know how, but we do not know where the sword is. More than likely the Angel has it.'

'Actually I saw it almost buried on the beach earlier,' said Waterson.

Carlisle sagged. All of this helping was really very tiresome. He thought back to when he squeezed the life out of the Monk, and that cheered him up some. 'Okay, to the beach.' He clicked his fingers as he walked out of the room, and the chalk circle began to slide across the floor, buffeting Waterson forward.

'Oi, easy, not so fast!'

Rita turned to the wide-eyed Gemma Wheeler. 'You okay?'

'No. Obviously. Not at all.'

'Yeah, me neither.'

'Is all this ever going to stop? Am I ever going to be safe?'

Rita wanted to say something reassuring, but that would have been a lie. 'Keep hold of that charm Pasty gave you. We're doing our best.'

Not sure what to do next, Rita patted Gemma on the head, instantly regretted it, then left.

Carlisle refused to be a pig snuffling for truffles, and so it was left to Rita to search up and down the beach with a child's abandoned plastic shovel, trying to locate the sword that Jenner had used to murder Waterson.

'So,' said Rita, 'are you going to tell me what you've been up to while I've been battling werewolves?'

Carlisle lowered his copy of *Wuthering Heights,* both eyebrows raised. 'Werewolves?'

'Oh, something you didn't know, eh?' replied Rita on her knees, scraping at the sand.

'Actually,' said Waterson, pointing up the beach, 'I think it might have been a little further along.'

Rita sighed, stood, and began scraping a few metres up. 'Didn't you notice the full moon that shouldn't be a full moon?'

Carlisle looked up at the moon and tutted. 'So it is.'

'No big deal. Just a master werewolf who's able to do magic, which apparently they shouldn't be able to do.'

'Correct.'

'She's here offing wizards and turning non-wizards left right and centre. It's been a bit hectic.'

'Hm. Werewolves can be tricky,' replied Carlisle, his attention drifting back to his book.

'Ooh, is that it?' Asked Waterson, pointing.

Rita pulled out a stick from the sand. 'Pretty sure it's not,' she replied, tossing the piece of driftwood aside.

'If you must know,' said Carlisle, 'I went in search of an angel killer, as I said I would.'

Rita paused in her search. 'Did you find one? Please tell me you found one.'

Carlisle smiled. 'I do believe I have.'

'Well that's… that's amazing!'

'Yes. I am amazing.'

'I never said *you* were.'

'The implication was clear.'

The plastic spade struck something solid. Rita dug and scraped until shiny metal was revealed. 'Got it!' She grabbed hold of the sword and yanked it free of the damp, compacted sand.

'That's it!' said Waterson.

Carlisle closed his book and stood, waving Rita forward. She scuttled over and handed him the sword. Carlisle stroked the blade, running his fingers across the words and shapes that had been carved into it. 'Exquisite work,' he said.

'So, what now?' asked Waterson.

'Now this,' replied Carlisle, as his hands erupted with a white hot glow and the sword turned to a puddle at his feet.

'That's it?' asked Rita. 'Is Waters okay now? Is he free of the Angel?'

Carlisle scuffed at the chalk circle, breaking it, and Waterson stepped warily out.

'So?' said Rita. 'How do you feel? Any urge to get inside me again?'

Waterson raised an eyebrow. 'Get inside you? I wouldn't touch you with his, mate.'

'Is this really the time for innuendo?' asked Rita.

'Ach, you're no fun.' He considered Rita's question properly. 'No, the urge is gone. I feel like myself again. Well, except dead, of course.'

'Yeah.'

'You are welcome, by the way,' said Carlisle.

'Sorry,' replied Waterson, 'just, you know, still being dead, it's hard to get too jolly. So what happens now? Do I go to Heaven or something?'

Carlisle shrugged. 'You missed your initial window due to the hex. Perhaps you will be called at some point, perhaps you will be cursed to remain here, in this dreadful place.' He shuddered. 'In Blackpool.'

Rita saw Waterson crumple a little. 'Hey, it's okay. So maybe you'll be staying for a bit, we can be partners again! Rita and Waterson, best buddies, right?' Rita went to pat Waterson on the shoulder, but her hand passed right through him. 'Well, you get the idea.'

'If you would excuse me,' said Carlisle, 'I have an Angel to murder.'

'Okay, let's go and bash that twat up,' said Rita.

'No, you can stay here.'

'I appreciate the concern, but this is my life It's messing with.'

'Concern? You have my artefact. The artefact the Angel desires. The artefact I intend to possess again very soon. I would prefer you and it stay as far from the Angel as possible.'

'It's okay if you're worried about me, Pasty.'

Carlisle sighed and wondered if it would be so very bad if things went wrong and he was finally killed for good.

'Oh, by the way, can I maybe leech a bit of your magic?' said Rita, waggling the axe.

'You most certainly may not.'

'Oh come on, you heard me mention all the werewolves, right? Well, this thing is useless against them. I even touch one of them and it starts trying to turn me into a big murder dog.'

'You are not a quick learner, are you?'

'Agreed,' said Waterson, 'I almost went mad trying to show her how the new coffee machine at the station worked.'

'There is magic all around you,' said Carlisle. 'Each day you walk through a soup of the Uncanny. Look for it, use it.'

'Right. Okay, got it. I think.'

'She never did work out how to get the thing to make a latte,' said Waterson.

'You know, I'm starting to miss you being completely dead and gone, Waters.'

Waterson stuck his tongue out at her.

'So how are you gonna get there?' said Rita. 'To the Angel's prison?'

'I am Carlisle. Once I have been somewhere, I can always find my way back.' He flapped his long coat with a flourish, the sparkling lining briefly visible, and then he was gone.

'Well, that was fancy,' said Rita.

'So, who is he exactly?' asked Waterson.

'Bit of a bastard, I think. But mostly good.'

'Right.'

'Well, not mostly. Probably hardly at all, but I need him.' Rita looked out across the ocean and wondered just what it was that Carlisle intended to do. She flexed her fingers around the handle of the axe and hoped that she'd see him safe and sound again soon. He'd gone to kill an unkillable Angel on her behalf. Well, mostly on his own behalf, to get the axe, but still. Brave.

A sudden thunderclap of noise and air blasted Rita out of her thoughts and she turned to see a man she recognised stumbling towards her. He wore a snug, dark blue suit and had a pinched face.

'Ulner?' said Rita as he staggered forward, his suit torn, his face battered and dripping blood. It was the wizard who had taken her and Ben to their secret meeting place. She darted forward to catch him as his legs failed him and he dropped to the sand.

'Ulner, what's happened?'

'All of them. Killed… she killed all of…'

A chorus of low growls began to swell around them.

'Um, Rita,' said Waterson, as one by one, a large group of beasts, bigger than any man, with mouths full of sharp teeth, began to pad towards them.

'Shit,' said Rita, standing and brandishing the axe.

'Those are the werewolves then, I take it?'

'Pretty much. Ulner? Ulner, mate, you've gotta get up, we need to move.'

But Ulner did not get up, because Ulner was dead.

'Hello again, Rita,' said Magda. 'I see you have met my latest snack.'

'So what's the plan?' asked Waterson.

'Running,' replied Rita. 'I think mostly running.'

And off they ran as Magda knelt by the dead wizard and feasted upon his magic.

31

It was cold in the Angel's prison, and the thousands of candles that never burned out cast dancing shadows across the marble walls and pillars.

Carlisle stepped stealthily forward, leaning his back against one of the cool pillars and peering around it to see the Angel of Blackpool. It was sat cross-legged on the floor within Its glass box. Its eyes were closed and It looked perfectly serene. Patient. Beautiful. Carlisle was not fooled by Its pose though, by Its closed-eyed stillness. There was no way anyone stepped into this chamber and the Angel was not aware of it.

He stood up straight, brushed down his coat, and stepped from behind the pillar, striding towards the glass box. 'Good evening, I hope you are not annoyed by my late and unannounced drop-in. I know I hate visitors at such a dark hour.'

A smile spread across the Angel's face. 'Not at all. You amuse me, Carlisle.'

'I am glad.'

'How you walk this world with such confidence. With such wicked intentions.'

'Selfish, perhaps, but not all so very wicked.'

The Angel opened Its eyes and Carlisle shuddered as they fell upon him. It was as though he could feel icicles boring into him.

'So I got rid of the hex you placed on the late Dan Waterson.'

'Yes. Unfortunate.'

'Two plans in such a short space of time thwarted,' said Carlisle, circling around the glass box, the Angel not moving at all to follow him. 'All you want is to get out and stretch your legs and that hexed detective and I keep insisting on being the stick in your spokes. Insufferable of us, I know.'

'There are always more plans, Carlisle, do not worry. Do you think I would have just one game in play?'

Carlisle paused at that, then dismissed it. The thing was trying to slide doubt into his mind, but at a time like this, doubt could be deadly.

'I am glad to hear it. You have proven yourself to be a worthy opponent, and Lord knows there are so few of those.'

The Angel laughed Its birdsong laugh and the flames upon the candles swelled in brilliance.

'Such wonderful arrogance, Carlisle. It is delicious.'

Carlisle reached inside himself, to the places he had hidden Horse. He was in there, waiting.

'You are certain?'

'Of course,' Horse replied.

'Well,' said the Angel, 'shall we proceed?'

Carlisle reached inside of himself and took Horse's hand. Horse stepped out of Carlisle and looked around the marble chamber.

'We're here then,' he said.

Carlisle began to step back, ready to take his leave. He had no reason to wait around and get caught up in any fallout. He trusted the word of L'Merrier, but things often went wrong, it was the way of the world.

And something was, in fact, about to go very wrong.

Or very right, depending upon which side you were on.

'Well, I shall leave you to your murder, Horse,' said Carlisle.

Horse sniggered.

'And what, may I ask, is so funny?' asked Carlisle.

'This,' replied the Angel, slowly rising until It was stood upright, pointing at Horse.

Horse stepped to the right, but at the same time he stepped to the left. He was no longer one, but two, and, in truth, neither was

Horse. They were, instead, two animal mask-wearing fiends that Carlisle knew well. Carlisle had acted as a trojan horse to spring Horse from the City of the Dead, but it seemed that Horse himself had been playing a similar trick.

'I did say that I had been accused of rabitting on, did I not?' said Mr. Cotton, and the ears upon the ancient rabbit mask he wore twitched, though of course they did not, as it was just a mask.

Carlisle did not pause to reply. He reached into his coat, ready to flee, only for a pair of arms to clamp themselves around him, anchoring him to the Angel's prison. Carlisle could hear the grating, rasping breath of Mr. Spike against the inside of his hedgehog mask.

'Careful, do not break any bones just yet,' said Mr. Cotton, holding up a white-gloved hand.

'L'Merrier lied to me,' said Carlisle.

'Oh no,' said the Angel. 'I found Mr. Cotton and Mr. Spike once they had been rendered deceased and slipped out of their nightmare realm into the City of the Dead. So I stretched out and out and whispered to those that could hear me. Told a tale of a thing that could destroy a first order Angel. L'Merrier, he is such a very good listener. You can always rely on those that like to snoop to pick up any tasty titbits.'

Carlisle struggled against Mr. Spike's vice-like grip as it tightened incrementally, cutting off his lung capacity, bit by bit.

Mr. Cotton, hands behind his back, began to sway, to dance, his shoes tapping out a rhythm against the marble floor, as he moved closer to Carlisle.

'Brother of mine has spoken of you often, whilst we waited in that place; I do recall he murdered you once, did he not? I believe he craves seconds.'

Mr. Spike laughed, a gravel wheeze that smelled of decay.

32

DS Rita Hobbes and partner DS Dan Waterson, now deceased, had been running for some time, and their lungs were starting to burn. At least, Rita's were, Waterson found that he no longer had any breath to run out of.

Rita paused, leaning on her thighs, gulping down air. 'Bit like old times this, eh?'

'Yeah,' replied Waterson, 'except I'm a ghost, you have a magic axe, and werewolves are chasing us.'

'Yeah, other than that, pretty similar.'

A howl let them know they'd been spotted, and that it was time to run once more.

'So, do you have a plan at all?' asked Waterson.

'Mostly this,' said Rita.

'Right, it's just they seem very keen on killing you. I'm already dead, so I'm assuming I'm okay, but it doesn't seem like a gentle way for you to go.'

Christ, she could really do with Carlisle here to help. Instead, he was off selfishly risking his life trying to kill the unkillable.

Rita stopped. Blackpool Tower loomed over her. One-hundred and fifty-eight metres tall, it had stood by the sea since it was opened in 1894, and as werewolves ran at them from the front and from the back, it seemed like the only option to continue their escape attempt.

'Up,' said Rita. 'We go up.' Rita ran to the entrance, but it was the middle of the night, so of course it was secured. 'Shit!'

'Quick as you like, Rita,' said Waterson.

'Right.' Rita swung the axe at the door's lock and smashed the thing open. 'Oh, well that was easy. Come on!'

She ran inside, followed by Waterson. In front of them was the elevator. Without thinking, Rita darted inside and jabbed at the buttons, the door sliding closed just as a giant, furry head poked its way into the Tower's entrance.

'So what's the plan now?' asked Waterson.

'You know, you're just as annoying as when you were alive.'

'We're heading to the top of a tower, probably trapping ourselves. Not great, tactically speaking, that's all I'm saying.'

The elevator rattled as something bashed against the bottom.

'What was that?' said Waterson.

'A wild stab in the dark, but I think it's probably a werewolf.'

Another crash and the elevator rattled and scraped as it continued its ascent.

'The fuckers must be climbing up,' said Rita. 'Well, good. That's great.'

Rita hugged the axe to herself, more like a comfort blanket than a weapon, but then remembered what Carlisle had said on the beach. That magic, the Uncanny, was all around them. The axe should be able to tap into it, use it, if she could just find a way to do that.

'Okay, Waters, shut your gob for a minute.'

'I wasn't saying anything.'

'Is that shutting your gob?'

Waterson frowned and folded his arms.

Rita gripped the wooden handle of the axe in both hands and lifted it in front of her, closing her eyes. She tried to ignore the lift's movement, tried to ignore the howls of the monsters rushing up to meet them when the elevator reached its destination, tried to ignore the fact that she didn't really know what she was doing or if it would work. Instead, she focused on the axe. The axe was a lightning rod. A magnet. A sponge. She imagined all the magic in the air around her. She pictured the colours that she had seen. The colours of magic.

'Hey!' she thought, *'you will do my bidding. I wield the artefact, and you will do as I say.'*

Rita opened her eyes and saw the world around her anew. Ribbons of colour—reds, greens, blues, purples—whirled around her, around Waterson, around the axe.

'Now,' she said, and the magic rushed into the head of the weapon.

The elevator jerked to a stop, and the doors slid open to reveal five werewolves stood waiting patiently for them.

'Hi there, doggos, have this.' Rita swung the axe forward and colour blasted from the blade, smashing into the werewolves and scattering them like pins in a bowling alley.

'Holy crap!' said Waterson.

'I definitely agree with that,' she replied.

Like when she'd struck the dreamscapes of Mr. Cotton and Mr. Spike, like when she'd taken and used the magic thrown by the now deceased low level wizard Derek Nolan, Rita could read the magic. She was fluent in it. She could see it, feel it. She understood the sheet music perfectly and knew how to handle it, to mould it, to twist it into doing what she wanted. What she currently wanted was to knock anything that might come near them out of the way. She didn't want any of them dead, the werewolves were still innocent people under it all, doing something against their will.

The elevator's floor tore open and more of the werewolves rushed out of the lift shaft towards them.

'Eat this,' said Rita, and swung the axe. White light rushed out to knock the creatures back, but still they kept coming. Slowly backing away as the two groups joined forces and stalked towards them, Rita and Waterson found themselves at the edge of the room, an open air balcony beyond. Rita turned and smashed open the door and stepped through, the wind whipping her red hair sideways.

'Rita, I really think you might need to start, you know, putting a dog or two down. Unless you plan on having batting practice for the next few hours while we wait for the sun to come up.'

'They're people, Waters. It's not them doing this.'

Iron railings enclosed the balcony, put there to stop anyone from accidentally falling from the tower. In that moment, it also doubled as a cage to keep Rita and the monsters in one place.

Rita knelt down, placing the butt of the axe on the ground before her, and concentrated. 'More,' she said. The magic swarmed her and rushed into the axe. It was exhilarating. Despite the danger she was in, the proximity to hundreds of teeth hungry to tear into her flesh, Rita felt electric. Felt strong. Felt *sure*.

Flames rushed from the axe and along the balcony before them, beating back the werewolves that had begun to make their way out into the open air. Flames that somehow continued to burn whilst not harming the Tower itself.

'You know, you're actually pretty handy with that thing,' noted Waterson.

'Oh, it's easy when you get the knack,' replied Rita, blowing the axe's blade like the barrel of a smoking gun.

A sudden, blinding light erupted behind them and Rita and Waterson stumbled back as a ball of bright white rose into view beyond the railings. At the centre, raven hair billowing, was Magda, her blue eyes piercing through the glare.

'Get behind me,' said Rita.

'Already there,' replied Waterson.

'Rita, you rejected my gift,' said Magda. 'You could have been something so beautiful. So alive. I cried for your loss.'

'Thanks. Bit weird, but thanks. To be honest, I just don't think I could take all the fur. I can't even sleep fully under a duvet at night. I'm like my own personal hot water bottle.'

The railings screeched as they were torn aside, Magda floating through the gap before settling down on to the balcony.

'Magda, it's not too late to stop this,' said Rita.

'Why would I stop? This is what I want. What they *made me* want.'

'But those people back there, those people you turned, they're innocent. They didn't ask for this. They don't have a grudge to settle with any wizard.'

'Did I ask to be persecuted? Did I ask for my family to be murdered? Did any of my people ask to live a life of fear? Of hiding in the shadows?'

'Good point, but still, this isn't the way.'

'I am the wronged one,' Magda snarled, 'all of my kind are. Who cries over the body of a wizard?'

Rita lifted the axe, 'Look, I don't currently see a way out of this that doesn't involve me killing you to save all those people you cursed, all those people you've dragged into your vendetta, and I really don't want to do that.'

'I have no choice,' replied Magda, almost sorrowful. 'Look at what they made of me.' Flames erupted around her, her hands throbbing with magic, ready to be unleashed. 'I allowed myself to be tainted, allowed my soul to be someone else's property, just so that we would no longer live a life of constant fear.'

'I'm a detective, I'm not a killer, please don't make me do this.'

'I have no choice,' replied Magda. 'There is no going back—not after all I've done—and even if I could, what would that mean? Back to hiding? Back to being hunted like vermin? Put down under a wizard's boot like we are nothing? I will not be ashamed and I will not hide. No more. No more!'

Not waiting to be attacked first, Rita swept the axe in an arc and blue flames rushed towards Magda. The magic was meant to concuss, but unfortunately, Magda was not as easy pickings as her kin, and the flames around her reduced the spell to nothing before it struck home.

'Well, shit.' said Rita.

'A thought occurs,' said Waterson, holding up a finger.

'A thought is good.'

'What I did to you, jumping in, controlling you, maybe I should try that with her?'

'Do you remember how?'

'Yeah, sort of. Mostly.'

'Well then, what are you waiting for? Go get some, stud.'

'You are disgusting,' said Waterson, then turned and ran at Magda, leaping into her body.

The flames around Magda faltered and she staggered back.

'What are...?' she said, as the ghost of Waterson struggled inside of her, attempting to wrangle control.

'Take her down, Waters,' shouted Rita, turning to the burning balcony behind her to see the werewolves milling on the other side. Sooner or later one of them was going to try and rush through the fire to get at her. 'How's it going, Waters? Now would be a good time to call off the dogs.'

'I-and-what-will,' babbled Magda.

'Okay, that was gibberish, Waters.'

Magda screamed and Waterson was ejected, arms windmilling from her body.

'How dare you,' cried Magda.

'She's too strong for me, I barely know what I'm doing in there as it is.'

'Yeah, you always were terrible with women.'

'Hilarious.'

Rita leapt to the side as fire blasted from Magda – fire that would have reduced her to ash in a second.

Rita willed as much magic as she could into the axe, but looking at Magda, she knew she was outgunned. She was going to have to try and fight her way back down the Tower to try and escape, otherwise she was a corpse.

'Rita,' said Magda, 'don't fight us anymore. We are beautiful. To be so in touch with nature, with your own glorious, animal nature. We can change the world. All will be like me.'

'Okay, you're going full insane baddie now, so no thanks.' Rita dodged another volley, the spell scorching her heels.

'Another thought occurs,' said Waterson.

'Is it as foolproof as the last one?'

'The werewolves, they're not like her, right? Not as mentally strong?'

'They're pretty simple, instinctive, yeah. Why?'

'Well, then this horrible thing I'm about to do might work then.'

'What horrible thing?'

Waterson turned to the flames and sprinted through them.

'Waters, what are you doing?'

What he was doing was leaping into the body of one of the werewolves. He didn't have a fantastic grasp on the particulars of possession, not enough to control and subdue Magda, but these were just simple beasts. These he could probably do. The werewolf thrashed and bucked only for a moment, then paused, a look of surprise on its face.

It then leapt through the dying flames to stand at Rita's side.

'Waters, you could use a breath mint.'

'Get out of him,' roared Magda. 'Get out of him!'

'So what exactly was the end-point of this thought, Waters?' asked Rita.

The werewolf Waterson was inside of grunted in reply, then bolted forward, galloping towards Magda. She threw up her hands in defence, magic bursting forward, but the werewolf was big and heavy and hurtling forward at pace. It met Magda, wrapped its arms around her, and over the side of Blackpool Tower they tumbled, through the broken railings, and down, down, down to the ground below.

Rita darted forward and looked down to find Magda and the werewolf a dot on the ground. She turned, the flames she had created now dead, to see the other werewolves staggering from side to side in a state of confusion. Was Magda dead? Dying? Was the curse lifting?

She ran, dodging past the werewolves as they stumbled and lashed out wildly, and jumped into the elevator, making sure not to fall straight through the hole in the floor. She hit the button to go down.

Waterson met her at the bottom.

'Holy shit, was that a big boy move,' said Rita.

'Yeah, it was a bit heroic, wasn't it?'

'I mean, you are already dead, so you were basically safe as houses, but still.'

'Okay. Don't lessen it. I'm very brave, let's leave it there.'

Rita walked over to the two bodies stretched out on the ground. A werewolf and a master werewolf. Normal people would have died instantly upon impact, but lycanthropy magic was powerful, it fought to save, to cure, to fix. Already, the werewolves' legs were moving and Magda groaned, rubbing at her face.

Rita stood over her, axe raised, as Magda's eyes flickered open.

'Please,' said Rita, 'just stop. Cure these people and just...

just go.'

Magda smiled, but there was no mirth there, only sadness. 'You cannot understand. None of you can. They murdered my family.'

'So you kill them all?'

'They... they are all... guilty. Will not hide. Not again. Never...'

Every second that passed, Magda was growing in strength again. At any moment it was going to be too late. Rita looked to the werewolf on the ground; the person made monstrous by Magda. Cursed to turn every full moon, agonised and terrified. Cursed to murder and to feast upon the flesh of the living. She couldn't let it go on. She'd tasted what they had to go through and she couldn't allow it to continue and live with herself.

She had no choice.

'Damn you for making me do this,' said Rita. 'Really. Just fuck you.'

Magda reached up, magic starting to flicker around her hand. Rita raised the axe high. This time, she did not will magic into it. Did not talk to it and command it create the spell she needed. This time the axe was just an axe, and with a cry, she brought the blade down with all the strength she had, and buried it in Magda's skull.

Magda's limbs twitched for a second or two, and then the life left her body.

Rita pulled the axe free and turned away. Her hands were shaking, her stomach sick.

'Hey,' said Waterson, putting a phantom arm around her, 'you didn't have a choice.'

Rita knew that. It didn't make her feel any better. She'd been made a killer.

Then something that Rita did not expect happened.

A tree began to sprout from the ground next to Magda's body.

Not a young sapling, but a giant oak tree thrust from the earth and stretched up and up, its roots arching from the soil like spiders' legs. Once it had settled, an opening appeared in the trunk, and a plump old lady in an apron stepped out.

'Is there any point in asking what the hell is going on?' said

Waterson.

'Probably not,' replied Rita, stepping back, the axe in her hands.

The old woman did not pay them any attention, she made her way towards Magda, chuckling happily to herself.

'Out you come then,' she said, and Magda's soul sat up out of her body.

'Please,' she said, 'another chance, put me back. Put me back and let me try again.'

The old woman laughed good-naturedly as she pulled an empty jam jar out of her apron and unscrewed the lid. 'Now then, dear, a deal is a deal.'

Magda screamed and struggled, but it didn't phase the old woman. She took hold of Magda's soul and folded it down and down until it fit into the empty jar. She then screwed on the lid, and made her way back into the giant oak tree, which shrank back down and disappeared under the ground.

'Well,' said Rita.

'Pretty much,' replied Waterson. 'Hey, look,' he said, pointing to the werewolf he'd jumped inside of. Only now it wasn't a werewolf, now it was a naked man, sitting up, hair wild, wondering just what in the hell was going on.

'Hey, Ben,' said Rita.

'Hi,' said Ben. 'I feel like I missed something. He turned to see Magda's corpse beside him. 'Shit.' Ben scrambled to his feet, hiding his man-bits behind his hands. 'Is she...? She's dead, isn't she?'

'It's over,' said Rita. 'This is Dan Waterson, he's a ghost and he was inside of you a little earlier.'

'Right. Hello. Sorry, did you say "inside of", there?'

As Rita handed Ben her coat, more of the people who Magda had bitten began to emerge, confused and shaky, from Blackpool Tower.

'You do realise that no one else will be able to see that coat,' said Waterson, 'meaning your man there is still, basically, stark bollock naked.'

'Nope,' said Rita.

'Thought not.'

33

A week had passed since Magda fell from the top of Blackpool Tower, and Rita was still waiting for Carlisle to show up again.

Every day she tried getting people to notice her, or to step past the town's boundary, only to find that the hex still had its grip of her.

She'd asked Formby to search for any news of what might have happened, of where Carlisle might be, but every time she saw him, he frowned and shook his head. No news.

Well, no news was good news, isn't that what they say?

Yeah, no news was bloody awful news when your friend went to try and kill a monster. Carlisle had the biggest head, the largest seam of aggrandising self-regard, that Rita had ever come across. If he was able to come back, to lord some victory over her, he would.

All sorts of stories trying to explain the previous week's events had been thrown up in the news, from someone dosing the local water supply with a mystery hallucinogenic, to a strange case of mass hysteria. No one believed that the moon had actually been full for days longer than it should have been, or that werewolves had stalked the streets of Blackpool, because that was insane, impossible.

Rita touched a hand to the axe that hung from her belt. Every night, as she tried to drift off to sleep, she'd pictured the blade splitting Magda's skull. She felt the shockwave of the impact travelling up her arms. She saw Magda's limbs twitching their last. She hadn't had any other choice—Waterson kept telling her as much—and she knew it was true. She'd saved all those people, Ben Turner included, from a living hell.

She'd done the right thing. Sometimes the only choices available were bad ones, but you still had to make a choice.

She leaned back on the bench, smelling the salt air, looking out to sea as the sun dipped into the water like a molten coin. Soon the moon would be up. A natural moon. A natural moon in a world that was anything but.

'Hey,' said a voice behind her. She turned to see Ben Turner. He'd started to grow a beard and was wearing glasses with non-prescription lenses in, a baseball cap clamped on his head.

'Hey.'

'Thought I'd wear clothes today,' he said, gesturing at his not-naked body.

'Pity. I'd grown accustomed to looking at that tight little arse.'

Ben smiled. 'Waterson said you'd probably be down here.'

'Yup. Just me and my guilty conscience. How are you getting used to living in hiding, then?'

'It's not great. Though there are some perks.'

'Like?'

'Like, I don't suppose you fancy grabbing a drink at all? With me?'

Rita looked out at the ocean. Somewhere out there an angel was imprisoned.

'Okay, but only if you're paying,' she said, then turned her back on the ocean and walked towards the road, Ben falling in step beside her.

The End.

NIGHT TERRORS

1

Tap-Tap-Tap.

Liam squeezed his eyes tight, turning everything black and pink. He pulled his covers close.

Tap-Tap-Tap.

It was just a tree branch tapping against the window pane.

That's all it was.

That's all it always was.

Tap-Tap-Tap.

The wind whipping against the big tree in the back garden. That one, long, gnarled branch that reached out from the trunk like a witch's finger, flicking forward and hitting the glass. At least, that's all it was in the day. In the day, it was just a tree in the wind with a branch that needed to be cut, but at night, when he should be asleep, it was anything but.

Tap-Tap-Tap.

Liam was eight years old, and like all eight-year-olds, knew that monsters and ghosts and bogeymen of every stripe were very real and knew where he lived.

Where he slept.

Most grown-ups didn't seem to believe in the things that hid in the inky black, which was really stupid as far as Liam was concerned. If he, a child, knew monsters were real, then an ancient grown-up should know for sure.

'Just go back to your own bed, Liam,' Mum would say when he appeared at his parents' bedroom door, wide-eyed and knees trembling.

'You're too old to be such a scaredy cat,' Dad would chime. 'The dark can't hurt you.'

Liam knew Dad was wrong about that. For as long as he could remember, Liam had been aware of the things in the dark that others couldn't see. There was no question in his mind; he'd known for sure that there were strange things lurking in the shadows. One evening, back when he was six, he'd pointed out of the top deck of a bus at a man with horns walking down the street, but his mum had acted like she wasn't able to see him. Told him to stop playing up or he'd get no chocolate. And Liam had shut up, because he really wanted that chocolate.

Tap-Tap-Tap.

Liam believed in all sorts of stuff, but especially ghosts. He'd seen them his whole life, not that he was aware of it at first. He'd be yammering away to someone as a toddler, only for Dad to ask him who he was talking to. Wasn't it obvious there was a girl in weird-looking old clothes sat cross-legged with him on the carpet, telling him to do bad things? Liam would point at her but Dad would just frown and sigh and chuckle and shake his head.

Yes, Liam saw things. These days he'd learned to keep most of it to himself for fear of being called a liar, of being punished.

Tap-Tap-Tap.

It was no good, he was going to have to get out of bed and check, otherwise he'd never be able to sleep. Yes, it was just a tree branch, but also maybe not, and what then?

He slowly sat up and pushed his covers aside, toes wriggling as they met the carpet.

'I know you're just a stupid branch,' he said, the words sounding hollow in the darkness.

Liam edged across the room until the heavy, blue curtains were within reach. He took a breath or two, his heart fluttering like a butterfly's wings, then grabbed hold of the curtain and pulled it open.

He could see the tree outside, the branch reaching towards

the window. The wind wound a ribbon around the branch once again and it *Tap-Tap-Tap*-ed at the glass.

'See, told you,' said Liam.

He let the curtain fall back down. He was thirsty. Liam walked over to his bedside cabinet but the glass perched there was empty of water. He didn't remember drinking any of it, but he supposed he must have done. He picked up the glass and headed for the door. It was always strange walking through the house at night, when the whole place seemed like it was holding its breath, eyes closed. It felt wrong, like he was a burglar sneaking around, looking for the best bits and bobs to steal.

Or perhaps he was a murderer. A killer with a knife ready to cut. Liam waggled his eyebrows and bared his teeth.

Stupid tree, waking him up.

He walked past his parents' bedroom; the door was closed but he could hear both of them inside, asleep. Dad's low snore-drone, Mum's higher pitched. He wondered how either of them could sleep next to the other when they were making such a racket.

Liam yawned and scratched at the mass of dark blonde curls that reached almost to his shoulders. Mum had begged him to agree to a haircut, but Liam liked having so much fat, wild hair. It was like he had a lion's mane.

He reached the bottom of the stairs and began to tiptoe in an exaggerated manner towards the kitchen, glass in hand. He was a robber, and if he made too much noise the house would open its eyes and see him.

Liam shivered a little in his Batman pyjamas as his bare feet met the cold tiles of the kitchen floor. He could see the tree dimly through the window, its wide trunk like an elephant's leg. Sometimes demons lived in trees, Liam had read that somewhere. Or heard it. Or watched it on TV, or something. He wasn't exactly sure where he'd learned that fact now that he came to think about it, but it was true. Demons could live in trees. If you found the way in you'd see a winding staircase, and up and up you'd go, until you found the demon squatting all evil and damp-skinned at the top, smelling like bad breath and old socks. You could sell your soul for stuff then, if you wanted. Liam wasn't sure why you'd ever sell your soul. Even if he wanted something really, really, super badly, he would never let no stupid demon have his soul. Not for all the chocolate in the world.

He carefully turned the cold tap so the water wouldn't burst out all noisy, and filled his glass.

There was someone sitting at the kitchen table.

Liam turned round sharply, almost spilling his water.

He hadn't noticed anyone there when he walked in, but then, as he'd been filling his glass with water, he'd just sort of known that someone was sat there, watching.

'Who are you?' asked Liam, voice a whisper, toes clenching.

At first, the shape sat at the table was too shrouded in dark to make out.

'Don't you recognise your old dad, son?' replied the shape.

Liam could feel the sink pressing against his shoulders.

'Dad?'

'That's right. Do you want to sit on my knee? I'll tell you a story. A really good story.'

It did sort of sound like Liam's Dad, but the words were empty, like they weren't even real. Like they were pretend. Like he could swat them away with the back of his hand and see that no one had said anything at all.

'I heard you snoring in bed,' replied Liam.

'Oh. I must be sleepwalking then,' he replied, and then the dark seemed to melt away a little and Liam could see it was his dad after all. 'See? Here I am. Your loving dad. Your mother and I love you very much, despite everything.'

Something didn't seem right. 'Are you okay?' asked Liam, wishing the door wasn't quite so far away.

'Of course,' replied Dad, 'everything is fine, fine, fine.'

The silence crushed down for a long time, and Liam wondered how long it had been since he'd taken a breath. Finally he gasped and gulped and then began to walk towards the door.

'Don't you want to hear my story?' asked Dad.

'I'm tired,' replied Liam, stopping and turning and wishing he'd just kept on going.

'Are you sure? It's a good story.'

Liam noticed for the first time that his dad's eyes seemed to be too close together. It wasn't his dad at all. He wondered what it was and what it wanted.

'Maybe another night, Dad,' said Liam. 'I've got school.'

'Oh,' replied Not Dad. 'I was going to tell you about all the birds in my head.' He reached out a hand, upon the palm of which was a wet clod of mud, fat worms wiggling. 'Don't you want to feed my birds, Liam?'

'Sorry,' said Liam, wondering how he was even managing to talk with his throat being so tight and his heart now not a butterfly but a pot full of exploding popcorn. 'Good night.'

'Okay,' said Not Dad, 'that's fine. Everything is fine, fine, fine.'

Liam walked quickly from the kitchen and headed up the stairs, gripping his glass still, the water inside spilling down his pyjamas and splashing his bare feet. He heard his dad's snore as he passed his parents' bedroom.

He closed his own bedroom door and pushed a chair under the handle so no one could get in.

2

It was only midday, but the sky was black as tar.

DCI Alexander Jenner, his robes caked with mud and grime, was sat on the ground, eyes glassy, slowly eating a stick of bright pink candy floss.

'How's your week been, Guv?' Rita Hobbes asked her old boss as she strolled towards him, her long, red hair flowing in the breeze.

They were in the Night Fair, only not the real one. The real Night Fair was a place for Uncanny folk to visit: to play games, to have their palms read, to wander through a hall of mirrors, and more besides. This Night Fair—the pretend, dream one—was a prison built to keep Rita's old boss trapped; to isolate him from the Angel of Blackpool's power. It was a dreamscape of Rita's making, created using the axe that hung from her belt and patted against her thigh as she walked. As the name suggested, it was always night at the Night Fair. The sun never rose. The sky was a blanket of black covered by a light dusting of stars; a brush dipped in white paint and given a flick.

Jenner carried on chewing at his candy floss, staring through Rita.

'I'm not going to lie,' she said, hopping up on a stall's counter, legs swinging, 'you're starting to smell a bit ripe. What happened to the new clothes I bought you?'

'I like my robes,' Jenner replied around a mouth of fluffy pink sugar.

Rita noticed that the box of supplies she'd delivered to Jenner a week previously was in the same place she'd set it down, unopened, clothes, food, and drink left untouched.

'There's actual fruit in there, you know, Guv. A man can't live on sugar alone.'

'What do you care?'

'Oh, we've reached the self pity stage have we? That's not going to wash with me, Guv. And by the way, if I didn't care, you'd be dead already, so think about that you… you big, murdering freak.'

Jenner sighed and carried on munching.

DCI Jenner had been Rita's superior back when she was on the force – her partner, Dan Waterson's, too. Of course, at the time, neither of them had known that he was a crazed murderer, sacrificing women so an evil Angel trapped in a prison beneath the sea off the coast of Blackpool could break out and take Its revenge on God. If she'd known that, she'd have brought it up in one of their daily debriefs for sure. At the very least, she'd have raised the issue with H.R.

Rita smirked, then felt bad. People had died. Waterson had died.

'How much longer do I have to stay in here?' asked Jenner.

'Dunno to be honest. Most likely forever. What part of, "You murdered a bunch of people, you nutty dickhead," isn't getting through to you?'

'I only did what I did for—'

'Yeah, yeah – you only did it for the greater good, or whatever bullshit it was you were planning to babble. Save it. People died. I've got two of them trapped in here.' She patted the axe that contained the souls of the two women Jenner had sacrificed before she'd been able to stop him: Jane Bowan and Ellie Mason.

Jenner turned his attention to the axe, and Rita saw a spark of life in his eyes for the first time since she'd arrived. 'Give it to me,' he said, his voice hoarse.

'Yeah, not happening that, weirdly.' The spark in Jenner's eyes reminded her of the way Carlisle would sometimes look when he saw the axe. She wondered if and when the time came for her to give it up, whether the need to wield it again would gnaw at her the same way.

Carlisle.

Rita frowned. It had been over a week since she'd seen him. Since he'd said he had something that might be able to kill the Angel. To stop It doing any more harm and free her of the hex that had made her invisible to anyone not touched by the Uncanny. The hex that had erased her life completely and trapped her within the boundry of Blackpool.

Over a week, and no word. Not a single sighting or message from him. Rita tended to try and look on the positive side of things, to hope for the best until she had evidence of the worst, but she was finding it tricky to believe Carlisle was anything other than a pile of ash on the marble floor of the Angel's prison.

'So, Guv, you ready to tell me how I get Jane and Ellie out of this axe?'

Jenner said nothing.

'It's just that they keep bothering me when I'm trying to get some sleep in. Asking how much longer they're going to be stuck in limbo. It's annoying if nothing else.'

'They are trapped. I am trapped. You are trapped. Trapped, trapped, trapped.'

He was babbling, but at least he was talking. The way Rita saw it, Jenner had seemed a little more reachable each time she'd visited. Less desperate, less foaming-at-the-mouth loony. Perhaps, like a junkie, the longer he was away from his drug—from the Angel feeding him power, whispering in his ear, controlling him—the cleaner he would get. The healthier and more open to reason.

Rita hoped so.

Despite everything, she still hoped her old boss could be made to understand what he'd done. Would come to regret it, and perhaps be able to help the women he'd killed, and Rita herself, in some way. One day, he'd change. One day he'd come to terms with reality, as weird as that reality was.

'One day I'm going to step out of this prison and stab you in the throat,' said Jenner.

Okay, so rehabilitation was a *little* way off yet. Rita shook her head, hopped off the stall counter and headed for the exit.

'See you soon, Guv. There's some nice cheese in the box. Go on and live a little.'

As Rita stepped through the Night Fair's ornate, wrought iron gates, the flaming torches on top of each gate post flickered. The world around her shimmered, and the next thing she knew she was walking through the gates of the real Night Fair, the one on Blackpool Pleasure Beach.

A grumpy looking ghost was waiting for her, arms crossed.

'Hello, Waters. Looking pretty fly for a dead guy.'

'Enjoy your little chat with my murderer, did you?' asked Dan Waterson. His hair was short and neat, and he was dressed like a Geography teacher on the first day of term.

'He was a riot, as always. He's starting to smell a bit, though.'

'Like what?'

'You ever sniff between your toes in the summer after wearing trainers all day?'

'Rita, even though I'm dead, you still find new ways to disgust me.'

Rita grinned, happy that she still had her best friend at her side. Even if he was dead.

'So, why are you waiting for me?' asked Rita.

'I knew it. I bloody knew it.'

'What?' Rita wracked her brain, trying to remember what she had clearly forgotten.

'You said you'd put a reminder in your phone!'

'I did! For, uh, what… exactly?'

Waterson kicked at a discarded Coke can in exasperation, but his foot passed through the thing, and the follow-through almost sent him sprawling. His eyes darted to Rita as she tried, and failed, to strangle a smirk.

'Just come on,' he said, 'we're going to be late.'

Rita followed, remembering how Waterson had always complained about her timekeeping.

'You'll be late to your own funeral,' he'd say.

'Oh…' Rita stopped as she remembered the forgotten thing. 'Balls.'

3

The sky was bright blue with barely a wisp of cloud to break it up. This, to dead detective Dan Waterson, felt disrespectful. Funerals were meant to be sombre affairs. Grey skies, heavy rain, black umbrellas. Not this. This was holiday weather. Sunbathing weather.

Dan had mentioned his funeral to Rita about eighty times, and forced her to add it to her phone so she wouldn't forget. And yet still—somehow—she had failed to do so, and now the pair had arrived as the service was already underway.

'Made it,' said Rita, gasping for breath outside the entrance to the church, its large wooden double doors open, a picture of Waterson propped up on an easel in the foyer.

'*Made it?*' replied Waterson. 'We're ten minutes late.'

'Po-*tay*-to, pa-*tah*-to,' she replied, brushing his annoyance aside.

Leaving the bright day behind, they stepped inside the church. Rita felt the temperature inside, cool and crisp upon her skin.

'You look like a right twat in that picture,' she said.

Waterson frowned. It was a blown-up picture of the one his mum kept in a frame on her mantelpiece. It had been taken years back, when he'd first been accepted into the force. Back then he'd thought a moustache suited him. He had been mistaken.

They joined the other mourners, who were sat before a vicar with desperate hair fastidiously teased over his bald head. Waterson's coffin sat off to one side.

His coffin.

That was weird.

Yes, he'd seen his dead body after his murder—in fact he'd spent several miserable hours with it at the morgue—but since he'd last seen it, he'd come to think of his ghostly form as *him*. Whatever that was—that length of flesh and bones and hair and teeth—that wasn't him. How could it be? That thing was dead.

'...a respected officer, who always put others before himself,' droned the vicar, as though he had known Waterson in life.

Okay, so he was dead. Sure. No getting around that. He was dead and his rotting body was packed into a box that was about to be trundled through a sheet of flames and burned to a handful of ash. And yet here he was, still talking and thinking. It was all a bit weird, and he wasn't sure he'd ever quite get used to it.

'Your mum looks good,' said Rita, pointing out the woman with tight, white hair, dressed in a form-fitting black dress and red high heels.

'She always did like a funeral,' replied Waterson, trying not to let his mind slip into thoughts of how she must be feeling. How she must have felt when she got the news of his death. Things were bad enough without picturing that.

'You know, I never thought your mum liked me much,' said Rita.

'That's because she didn't.'

'Right.'

'She once referred to you as, *"That flame-haired, mouthy trollop who bounces from man to man like a shameless hussy"*. So.'

Rita laughed. 'She says that like it's a bad thing.'

The two spoke at normal speaking volume as, of course, no one else at the funeral could see or hear them.

'Pretty decent turnout,' said Rita, nodding appreciatively.

It was true, there were more people there than Waterson had expected. Family, friends, work colleagues. Waterson almost found himself welling up a little. Almost.

Waterson didn't like being a ghost.

He couldn't touch, couldn't taste, and worst of all, he couldn't sleep. He had no idea how slowly time moved until he was unable to miss large chunks of it by sleeping. Whilst Rita, and Ben Turner, and his mum, and everyone else snoozed away for hours on end, Waterson wandered and paced and grew increasingly agitated at the relentlessness of consciousness.

At first he thought he'd give anything to taste a cold pint of beer again. Now all he wanted to do was sleep. Just for a few minutes. Just close his eyes and not be there. Not be anywhere.

He wondered if souls got to sleep when they found heaven. Somehow, he'd missed his opportunity to ascend after dying. Formby, the mole-man looking eaves who Rita was now friends with, said it was because he'd been murdered, but eventually his time would come.

Waterson was already tired of waiting.

'You're thinking about leaving me again, aren't you?' said Rita, reading his expression.

'Oh, always.'

'You bastard.'

Waterson smiled despite himself. 'It's not easy, you know. Being this.' He passed his hand through the wooden pew in front of them. 'Being nothing. Just fog with a memory.'

'Oh, very poetic.'

'Shut your face.'

Waterson noticed a little girl with hair so blonde it was almost white, sat a few rows in front of them. She was wearing a hairband with bunny ears attached to the top. He couldn't for the life of him think who she was, nor why someone would take a child to a funeral wearing bunny ears. Who did that?

'Okay, so you're dead,' said Rita, 'but would you really rather be dead-dead? Just nothing and gone?'

'No, of course not, but… you wouldn't understand. You don't know how this feels. I just... I want to know my options, that's all.'

'What do you mean?'

'How long is this going to last? Me wandering around and not going to Heaven? Is there a way for me to speed things up so I can get there quicker?' He wiped a hand down his face. 'Christ,

I don't even believe in God, let alone an afterlife. This is completely ridiculous.'

Rita reached out a hand to place over Waterson's, which did not go well, what with it passed right through him.

'Thanks,' said Waterson, sarcastically.

'Waters, there's something I really want you to know,' said Rita, her eyes wide.

'What? What is it?'

'You looked really, really shit with that child-molester moustache.'

Waterson blinked, frowned, went to say something mean back, then burst into giggles. Rita joined him, and after almost a full minute, they just about managed to regain control of themselves. That was the moment Rita realised someone was watching them.

'Uh, who is that?' she asked, pointing to a small boy on the front row with a mass of curly blonde hair. The boy was looking back over his shoulder in their direction.

'That's Liam, my cousin Carol's kid.'

'Right. Am I crazy or is he looking right at us?'

'Don't be daft, he can't be.'

Rita waved a hand at Liam, and he waved back.

'Holy shit,' said Waterson. 'Well, that's... weird.'

But that was not the weirdest thing that was going to happen at Dan Waterson's funeral.

The sound of someone knocking on wood caught everyone's attention. The knocking was loud, insistent. The vicar stopped talking and turned to look.

'Is that...?' started Waterson.

'...coming from your coffin,' finished Rita.

Knock-knock-knock.

The sound was indeed coming from the coffin. Someone inside was rapping their knuckles against the wood, and as the only person in there was the late Dan Waterson, it was more than a little disconcerting for all present.

Knock-knock-knock.

'Maybe I'm not dead,' said Waterson.

'Or you're a zombie, that can happen.'

'Can it?'

'I dunno, you're a ghost and I've got a magic axe, so I reckon it's open season for weird shit.'

The knocking stopped.

The vicar turned from the coffin and back to the mourners, eyes darting wildly. 'Well, I… well…'

The coffin lurched forward and toppled to the stone floor with an almighty crash of splintering wood. As the church echoed with cries of surprise, the coffin lid flipped open and Waterson's corpse was vomited from within, dressed in a suit that Rita recognised. It had once been his date suit.

'Fuck me,' said Waterson.

Rita darted forward as everyone else instinctively backed away.

'Uh, Rita,' said Waterson, pointing at his dead body.

The body was twitching and writhing as though something was alive inside.

'What the Hell is goi—' started Rita, but she hadn't finished her sentence before the corpse sat up as though jerked into the air on invisible strings.

There were screams as mourners shot from their pews and charged for the exit. Rita pulled the axe from her belt, fingers flexing around its wooden haft. It tingled against her skin, connecting to the magic that surrounded them, ready to do as she asked.

'Dead, uh, Waterson?' she said, trying to get the corpse's attention.

The corpse—its skin bubbling now—turned its head to her and smiled. 'Ms. Winters says hello,' he said, in a voice that scuttled out of his mouth like a spider across a basement floor.

Rita blinked, lowering the axe. 'What did you say?'

Dead Waterson laughed.

And then exploded.

Millions of maggots erupted from inside the corpse, smothering Rita.

'Fuck!'

'Jesus!' said Waterson, as Rita fell back, thrashing wildly at the maggots that seemed to be increasing in size with each heartbeat. Seemed to be growing vicious teeth that bit and bit as they attempted to burrow their way inside of her. They wanted to bite and wiggle their way in. To lay their eggs that would hatch and make Rita explode, too.

The desire to descend into panic was almost overwhelming, but Rita pushed past it. Pushed past the maggots and their insistent teeth. She levered her way up into a kneeling position and gripped the axe in both hands. The axe, when it made contact with someone's magic, allowed her to use it as her own. But Carlisle had told her that it could do more than that, because magic was all around her. All around everyone, every second of every day, just waiting to be called upon. If she concentrated, she wouldn't need to steal someone else's magic, she could make the axe aware of the magic in the air and draw upon that instead.

She closed her eyes.

She could feel it.

Not the maggots nipping at her flesh.

No.

She could feel the magic, old magic, ancient magic, that rolled around the church in great waves.

'You see it too?' she asked, and the axe twitched in her grip.

She told the axe to feast, to open wide. It throbbed in her hands as the magic swarmed towards it. The axe was a black hole swallowing all the light in the room.

The magic asked her what she wanted of it.

'Burn them. Utterly. Completely. Now.'

The magic wagged its tail.

Rita opened her eyes, grunted, and slammed the handle of the axe against the stone flagstone in front of her. Magic—great washes of purple and red and yellow—burst from the axe blade. A tsunami that raged around the church, turning every maggot it came in contact with to ash.

It lasted all of two seconds before the church was maggot-free.

'Well,' said Waterson, 'that was… well.....'

Rita stood, blowing the blade of the axe like she was Dirty Harry and she'd just plugged some guy good.

'All in a day's work, partner.'

'My body, the maggots… that wasn't normal.'

'Definitely not normal.'

Rita nudged at the tattered remains of Dan Waterson's corpse.

'A coincidence that something like this would happen at my funeral? To my corpse?'

'Unlikely.'

'Yeah. Thought so. What now?'

Rita spotted something on one of the pews. She walked over and picked it up. It was a hair band with a pair of tatty old rabbit ears attached to it.

'Now we put on our detective trousers.'

Rita wished Carlisle was around to help.

4

Carlisle was and wasn't sat at a table outside a charming little Parisian cafe, enjoying a cup of black coffee and a croissant. He teased at the flaking pastry as a young couple on a bicycle—the woman in the saddle, the man on the crossbar—rolled past, giggling. Carlisle considered tossing the pastry in their direction with some velocity. But he didn't. Instead, he sipped the coffee, delighting in its bitterness, then placed the cup down and stretched out in his chair until his long purple coat reached down to the pavement. He closed his eyes and let the sun warm his chalk-white skin,

Carlisle was in a bad situation.

He had been in bad situations before. In fact, a high percentage of his long existence had been spent sandwiched between a bad situation and a probable, painful death. A couple of times he'd even toppled right over into death, but he'd always had an ace up his sleeve. A get-out for when the Reaper came a-calling and laid a cold hand upon his shoulder.

This time he'd been all out of aces.

This time, unless he thought of something fast, his number was up.

'Is this seat taken?' asked the Angel of Blackpool.

Carlisle frowned and opened one eye to see the Angel stood

before him, tall, delicate, beautiful, wearing brilliant white robes that seemed to hum they were so bright.

'This is my fantasy,' Carlisle told the Angel. 'I do not believe I handed out invites.'

The Angel pulled out a chair and gracefully lowered Itself on to it. Carlisle grimaced and sat up, tearing off a chunk of croissant and gnawing upon it.

'They shall kill you,' said the Angel.

Carlisle sipped his coffee as the young couple on the bicycle looped through the imaginary scene again.

'You know, I've never actually been to Paris. But I did stab a man to death somewhere in the south of France one brisk winter's afternoon a hundred years back. Jacques, I think was his name. Terrible lisp. Missing half an ear on the right side from a bar room brawl. Stank of stale sweat. Funny, the things you remember, wouldn't you say? When I think of him I could swear I can still smell that rank odour, and yet for the life of me I cannot recall why I sunk my blade into his belly, nor why I cut out his heart and fed it to a sow.'

'Perhaps we might assist each other.'

Carlisle raised an incredulous eyebrow. 'Asking for help? From little old me? My, my, you must really be hitting rock bottom.'

Carlisle had gone looking for a way to kill the Angel of Blackpool, and had been tricked into thinking the answer lay in the City of the Dead, beneath the streets of Manchester. A man named Horse had been that trick.

'What is it like to be the one being used for once, hm?' asked Carlisle.

The Angel did not answer, but Its eyes grew darker, just for a moment.

There had been no man named Horse, it had been Mr. Cotton and his brother, Mr. Spike, in disguise, and Carlisle had smuggled them out of the City of the Dead and back to the Angel of Blackpool's prison chamber. The plan had been for them to then carry on assisting the Angel, but it seemed as though Mr. Cotton and Mr. Spike had had other ideas.

'Help me and I can help you,' said the Angel.

'And how would you do that?'

'Escape. Life. Your artefact.'

Carlisle felt his stomach tighten and his heart jump at the mention of his artefact. The axe that Detective Rita Hobbes currently had in her possession. The craving to hold it, to use it once again, itched at him.

'And I suppose, after I assist in some unspecified manner, I will be permitted to dance off into the sunset? How gullible do you think I am?'

A hint of a smile teased at the corners of the Angel's mouth. 'Gullible enough to be fooled into smuggling Cotton and Spike from the City of the Dead.'

'Well, if you're going to bring that up, it is rather the pot calling the kettle black, wouldn't you say?' Carlisle finished off the pastry and gestured to the waiter to bring him another.

The Angel opened Its mouth to speak once more, but before It could utter another word, It turned to smoke and was wafted away by the arriving waiter, who placed a plate with a fresh pastry before Carlisle.

'Ah, thank you on two counts,' said Carlisle, glad the Angel had gone.

'What did It want?' asked the waiter.

Carlisle looked up, irritated at the imaginary waiter's question, only to find himself looking into the fraying, ancient rabbit mask of Mr. Cotton.

'Oh,' said Carlisle.

'Found you,' replied Mr. Cotton. 'Very rude to hide from pain, Carlisle, you know how much my brother enjoys inflicting it.'

Carlisle sighed and looked around at Paris one last time. 'My apologies to you and yours, you third-rate cretin.'

Mr. Cotton's rabbit mask frowned, though of course it did not, as it was just a mask.

'Get on with it, then.'

The table in front of Carlisle was tossed aside as Mr. Spike, sporting his dank hedgehog mask, burst from beneath, white-gloved hands reaching for his face.

And in the time it took to blink, Paris was gone.

Carlisle was in the Angel of Blackpool's prison chamber, the ice-cold of the marble floor pressed against his cheek.

Everything hurt.

Carlisle wanted to say something smart and condescending—he *always* wanted to say something smart and condescending—but if he were to open his mouth, he knew the only sound to emerge would be a ragged, blood-flecked scream.

His eyes fluttered open, the giant, vaulted chamber coming into focus, its huge columns reaching up and up, flickering candles stretching out all around like a wax forest set ablaze.

Carlisle had been made a pin cushion, only instead of pins, jagged shards of glass punctured his flesh. His stomach, his arms, his legs, his neck; every part of him stung sharply, every nerve end shrieking. He wanted to run, to get up and race away from this chamber, but he had been pinned in place. Mr. Cotton was using some of his newfound power to stop him from creating an exit. He was stuck.

'Back in the room, Carlisle?' asked Mr. Cotton, stepping into view, hands behind his back.

Carlisle glanced over to the glass box containing the Angel of Blackpool. It was on Its knees in the centre of the prison, hands resting on Its thighs, head bowed, hair hanging down. Its brilliant white robes pooled around It like a puddle of milk.

Carlisle could see black fingers of smoke weaving through weaknesses in the glass, reaching across the chamber, winding around Mr. Cotton. Cotton reached up a white-gloved hand and toyed with the Angel's power. Power that he and his brother-in-anguish were now feasting upon. Using. Unleashing.

Both the Angel and Carlisle had been taken for fools. He had to applaud Cotton and Spike for that. At least, he would have applauded if it didn't hurt quite so much to move, and if his right hand wasn't pinned to the ground by a shard of glass.

'Can you feel the fear?' asked Mr. Cotton.

'I fear nothing,' growled Carlisle.

'Not your own fear, dear one, you keep that locked in tight, but fret not, my brother and I shall unlock it in time. No, no, I refer to the fear of the town beyond. Of Blackpool. How wonderful a tool this Angel has proven. We plug in and are amplified. Day or night, the people of Blackpool are now our buffet.'

Mr. Cotton began to tap dance, causing the sound to rattle in Carlisle's ear, which was still pressed to the ground. He let out a weary groan as he rolled on to his back and looked up to the ceiling, half-hidden in the gloom.

The nightmare brothers had not returned to assist the Angel of Blackpool. They had decided they were done waiting for It to give them what was promised. Carlisle had gone to the City of the Dead looking for a weapon to use against the Angel, only it was Cotton and Spike that had found one. A set of words. A sentence that allowed them to leech the Angel's celestial magic and amplify their own particular set of skills.

Now they would not need to focus on just one person at a time. One dream turned nightmarish. Now they could keep a whole town in their thrall. No doubt if the Angel was not trapped within Its glass box It would put a stop to this, to being used and ignored and double-crossed, but trapped It was. Carlisle was unsure—despite the rather dicey situation he found himself in—whether doing as the Angel asked and helping It was altogether the best idea. Even if he could have done such a thing.

The damp rasp of Mr. Spike's breath against the inside of his hedgehog mask let Carlisle know that the torture was about to begin again.

'You… you know… that breath of yours is… is torture enough…'

Mr. Spike giggled as he oh so slowly slid a new piece of glass into Carlisle's side. His screams echoed around the marble chamber, and Mr. Cotton danced in time to the music of pain.

5

Ben Turner scratched at the beard he'd started growing since becoming a fugitive. He wasn't sure that it suited him; the beard or being on the lam. But then it wasn't as though he'd had much of a choice in the matter, and being a fugitive was certainly more appealing than the alternative. Ben was pretty sure he wouldn't flourish in a prison environment.

A cheer went up from the second bowling lane in Big Pins—the main hangout for Uncanny folk in Blackpool—momentarily nudging Ben out of his self pity. A woman who Ben had it on good authority was a six-hundred year-old vampire was high fiving a three-foot goblin. Perhaps low fiving would be more accurate.

Vampires and goblins, and more besides. Ghosts! Ben had seen them all in the last week, ever since he'd been taken under Rita Hobbes' wing. Each new addition to the Uncanny roster should have been cause for alarm, but since he himself had been turned into a werewolf, it was easier to just accept the monsters and move on.

At times like this, when Ben was sat alone, three or four drinks deep, his mind would start to wonder how many people he'd murdered. How many had died between his teeth since Magda had turned him into one of her pets? Since she'd afflicted him with this curse. He knew of one for sure, Alan Crowther, the front desk security guard at Ben's old office. He didn't remember the actual murder, he had little to no memories of being in his wolf form, but he knew that he had been the one to end Alan's life.

So how many more?

He'd turned more than once, and other bodies had been discovered in the wake of Magda's reign of terror. Other people had been turned by Magda, so perhaps the additional deaths had been at their claws, but Ben didn't know that for sure. Perhaps his tally of the dead lay north of one.

It was very strange, knowing you were a murderer, whilst also knowing that it was completely out of your hands. Knowing that the you who had done the biting, the ripping, the gouging, wasn't really *you* at all.

Rita had told him more than once that he shouldn't feel any responsibility for what he had done when he was under the control of the lycanthropy magic, and he knew that she was right. She was right, and beautiful, with really great hair. She was right. And yet Ben couldn't shake the guilt that rested its rotten hands upon his sagging shoulders.

He wondered where Rita was right now. He pulled out the new phone she'd given him and started writing out a text, then deleted it and pocketed the thing. He was being needy. He had to start pulling himself out of this rolling funk. Still, it would've been nice to have seen Rita's face right about then. To see her smile, and the way she would tease at the ends of her thick red hair as she spoke to him.

A giant hand placed a fresh pint of beer on the table in front of Ben. Linton stood there, a hulking tree of a man with almost grey skin and a face that wasn't prone to anything so everyday as expressions.

'Thank you, Linton,' Ben told the owner of Big Pins.

'Welcome,' Linton replied.

'Just thinking about how many people I might have murdered again,' said Ben, in as cheery a manner as possible.

'Hm. More that you didn't kill than you did.'

'Well, true. I definitely didn't kill more than I did. Never looked at it like that before.'

Linton nodded, then turned and made his way back to the bar, where the vampire lady was impatiently waiting to be served.

Rita had already been using Big Pins as her home, and had now persuaded Linton to let Ben use the basement as a place to sleep. The same basement he'd previously been locked inside of so when the full moon rose and he changed, he'd be safely stashed away.

He didn't have any memories from the times he'd turned, apart from one. A memory of being in that basement, a raging beast, looking up to see the door open and finding Magda framed there, a maternal smile on her face, brilliant blue eyes sparkling, reaching a hand towards him.

Just that one memory.

Ben shook his head and finished off his previous drink, pushing the empty glass aside and reaching for the new pint.

Okay, thought Ben, *got to think of something else. Something other than guilt and murder and Magda.*

He wasn't entirely certain why Linton had been so open to him staying under his roof. He certainly didn't have any money to pay him. Rita had waggled her eyebrows and said she could be persuasive. Ben had asked if that meant she was sleeping with Linton. The dead arm she gave him convinced Ben that he was mistaken.

'He's open to my whims, Benny. There's a magic dampening bubble protecting this place,' Rita had said. 'But still, you get a lot of bad sorts wanting to cause trouble. It doesn't hurt to have a bad-ass like me waving an axe about. Also, beneath that gruff exterior, Linton is a big old soft touch.'

Ben smiled, began to drink his fresh pint, and thought about texting Rita a funny cat video he'd seen online.

Rita was about to knock on the door of a basement flat when her phone chimed.

'Who is it?' asked Waterson.

Rita sniggered, then put the phone away. 'Ben. Ha, how is that whole kitty fitting in a jam jar?'

'Aw, isn't that sweet?' said Waterson, batting his eyelashes.

'Shut up.'

'You *lurve* him.'

'He does look hot with that beard.'

'Roughs him up a bit.'

'Keep your ghostly fingers to yourself, Waters.'

Waterson rolled his eyes as Rita began knocking at the weathered door. He eyed the mounds of rotting rubbish piled high in the narrow gap between the flat and the wall that reached up to street level. He was sure if he had a solid foot to nudge it with, a hundred fat, greasy rats would explode from within.

'This place is disgusting,' he said.

'Wait until you see inside. Bob is not exactly the house proud sort.'

'Seeing as you've been knocking for almost a minute, I think he's also not the in-at-the-moment sort.'

'Have a look.'

'Excuse me?'

'You're a ghost. You can, you know, walk through shit. Walls and stuff. Just walk in and have a nosey.'

Waterson made to complain, then wondered what it was he was complaining about and stopped. He certainly felt offended in some way that made no sense. He frowned and stepped through the door.

'Is he in?' Rita asked through the letter box.

'Give me a bloody second, will you, you annoying woman.'

'All right. Sexist.'

Waterson sighed and looked around at the crack den he had wandered into. The wallpaper of the corridor was missing in great, torn patches. The carpet was a disaster. Waterson was, for the first time, glad he was a ghost and lacking the necessary nose to smell the place.

He took the first door and found himself in the front room of Bob's flat, which was even more foul than the corridor. Mounds of takeaway cartons and wrappers were everywhere, many with maggots squirming around in the leftovers. Numerous plastic bottles lay strewn about, full of what looked suspiciously like piss. It wouldn't be how he would decorate a living area himself, but then to each their own.

A man, who Waterson assumed was Bob, the rancid inhabitant of this armpit of a flat, was asleep on an old armchair, the room's only item of furniture. Bob was overweight, with greasy hair plastered to his fat egg of a head. He wore a pair of trousers that may once, many moons ago, have belonged to a smart suit, and a t-shirt with a picture of Hellboy on it.

There was a crash in the corridor and Rita joined him.

She looked at Waterson's raised eyebrow and shrugged. 'Got tired of waiting. You found him then?'

'Well, I found the king of all the tramps here, who I'm really hoping isn't the man you brought me to see. The man you said might be able to help me.'

'Yup, that's Bob the Uncanny Exorcist.'

Waterson sighed and pinched the bridge of his nose. 'Fuck my afterlife.'

Rita liked to think she was a good friend. Well, sometimes. It depended on the situation. She knew Waterson was having trouble with his situation. She knew, because he never stopped harping on about it. She'd promised to try and help him, to at least get him the best information she could about what might be in store for him. When he might be finally called to Heaven, or how he could, perhaps, speed the process up. Bob the slobby Exorcist here had been trained at the Vatican. It seemed to Rita that he might be as good a person as any to ask about such things.

She wasn't happy about it though.

Since being hexed, Rita's whole life had been taken from her, her existence wiped away like words on a blackboard. It was all gone, and no one, friend, lover, or vague acquaintance, had any memory of Rita Hobbes having ever existed.

And then Dan Waterson had appeared, her best friend and partner on the force, and he'd *remembered*. Yes, he'd been murdered and was now a ghost trapped in this earthly realm—bummer—but she'd got her friend back. A piece of her old life.

No wonder she wasn't exactly filled with giddy joy at the prospect of losing him.

But still.

He was her best friend, and Rita was, mostly, a good friend. So here they were. She would help him and try and bite her tongue.

'What's he doing?' asked Waterson, breaking Rita's train of thought.

'Hm?'

'Is he drawing in his sleep?'

Rita looked down at Bob, whose left arm was twitching. A small pad was sat on his lap, a pencil clenched in his hand, jerkily moving across the page.

'Well, that's weird,' said Rita.

'What isn't weird these days?'

Rita looked at the pages. Bob wasn't just thrashing out random squiggles, there were clear, legible words there. Pictures too.

Fear. Fear. Fear.

Hungry. Will eat. Eat and. Will. Feast. The dark dark dark.

Bob's hand dropped and Rita could see now what he had been sketching. She stepped back and shivered.

Rabbit ears.

The tension was broken as Bob spluttered awake, coughing and wheezing and reaching into his trouser pocket to pull out a crumpled packet of cigarettes. As he lit one and drew deeply on it, his cough slowly abated. He waved at Rita and Waterson, apparently not at all perturbed to wake up and find two people had let themselves into his home.

'Did you break my door again?' Bob asked around the cigarette clamped between his thin lips.

'Yeah. Sorry about that. But if you don't answer, what do you expect me to do?'

'I can't see any holes in that logic,' he replied, causing Waterson to snort out of his nose. 'I see you brought a ghost with you this time, then.'

'Hello,' said Waterson. 'Yes, I am her dead friend. You keep a lovely home.'

'What do you want?'

'I died and didn't, you know... ascend. To Heaven.'

'Right.'

'You're connected to all this God stuff,' said Rita, 'do you have any idea how long it might take for Waters to be called up?'

'Or if there's any way to jump the line,' added Waterson.

Bob scratched absent-mindedly at the worn crotch of his trousers. It was not pleasant.

'Murdered, were you?'

'Yes.'

'Killer been caught?'

'Yup,' replied Rita.

'That should be that then.'

'Well, it clearly isn't, because,' Waterson waved at Bob.

'Ever heard the phrase, "God moves in mysterious ways"? Well, it's true. Another, less known phrase is, "God is a forgetful son of a bitch". You'll get the go-ahead at some point – trying to force it will only slow things down. Probably.'

Waterson sighed and turned away. Rita was glad he did as she was, briefly, unable to keep the smile from her face. Okay. So. He would leave her at some point, but not yet. For now, she had her friend.

'How long can "at some point" take?' asked Waterson.

'A week.'

'Oh, okay. Not too bad.'

'A month.'

'A month?'

'A decade, a century; can't really put a timeframe on it.'

'Awesome.'

Bob stubbed his cigarette out on the tatty arm of his chair and flicked it into a darkened corner of the room before reaching into his pocket to fish out a new one. As he did so, the pad of paper on his lap was dislodged and slipped to the floor. Rita bent down to retrieve it.

'What were you doing? When you were asleep?' she asked.

'Sleeping, mostly,' replied Bob, sparking up his fresh smoke.

'You were writing while you were conked out. In this pad. Drawing too.'

'Oh, that's just some automatic writing. It's a thing. Sometimes it's good to know what your unconscious mind is preoccupied by.'

Rita turned the pad to him. 'Fear.'

Bob frowned, 'Huh. Not that surprising. Been having a lot of bad dreams the past week. Shit your bed sort of dreams.'

'Nice,' said Waterson.

Rita pointed at the rabbit ears sketch. 'What about this?'

Bob squinted at the drawing and shrugged. 'Maybe a mutant rabbit was chasing me. I don't remember the details of my dreams that well, as a rule.'

'Are we done here?' asked Waterson. 'I like to spend as little time in places that horrify me as possible.'

Rita nodded but didn't take her eyes off the rabbit ears sketch.

6

Liam wasn't the least bit surprised to see the ghost of his Uncle Waterson at the funeral. He'd seen plenty of ghosts before, and he thought if he were ever to turn into one, he too would visit his own funeral. He felt as though he had recognised the woman with him, too—the one with the red hair—though he wasn't sure why, as he knew for a fact he'd never seen her before.

He hadn't seen too much of what had happened to Uncle Waterson's body. Not after the coffin had fallen and the body had rolled out. They'd rushed him out of the church and hadn't been that keen on discussing it further with him. All they'd said was that the coffin had obviously not been set down correctly. Somehow.

Liam had felt weird looking at the dead body as it had spilled out of the coffin. It sort of looked like his Uncle, and also didn't. Like it was missing some of him. Maybe that's what the ghost was. The missing bit that made the body look weird without it.

It was almost half-twelve, and Liam was sat in class, third row back, his table right next to the window looking out on to the playing field. It was maths, which meant Liam would usually be bored.

Today he wasn't bored.

School had been weird.

He'd felt it as soon as he'd stepped through the gates two

days previously, and the feeling had only got heavier with each passing day.

Nervous. Tired. That's how everything felt. Each day more peoples' eyes—kids and teachers—started to get a distant look to them.

Today Miss Hethers, his maths teacher, had it.

She was trying to talk to them about something boring, most probably fractions, but she kept stumbling over her words, forgetting what she was saying, her hands twitching on top of her desk like she was playing an invisible piano.

Liam looked at the girl who was sat at the desk next to his. Her name was Molly. She had dark skin and an explosion of hair upon her head. She was scribbling something in her workbook over and over. Liam couldn't quite make out her doodles as she was bent over her book, her left arm shielding it from curious eyes.

'Sorry,' said Miss Hethers, as she lost her way again, 'I'm afraid I didn't have a good night's sleep.' She reached into her handbag and pulled out a thermos of coffee.

Billy Martin, head shaved, skin awash with a riot of freckles, was fast asleep, resting his head on his arms. He looked like he was shaking.

Liam rose slightly from his seat and leaned over in Molly's direction. From that angle he could see what it was she was working on. She wasn't writing down what Miss Hethers was saying, wasn't noting down numbers or equations or anything like that.

She was drawing rabbit ears.

Formby shuffled into Big Pins, nose twitching. Rita waved him over from a table in the back, and he hustled over, weaving a scenic route that took him past anyone sat with company. As he went, he snaffled up pieces of conversation, ears restlessly taking in anything that might be of value to others. It wasn't purposeful behaviour, it was second nature. Formby was unaware that he was doing it, though some of Big Pins' patrons were, and clammed up as he neared them. Smart people knew to keep their lips sealed when an eaves was close by.

'Got you one in,' said Rita, as Formby finally finished his walking tour and joined her, Waterson, and Ben Turner at the table.

He let out a little cheer and clapped his fingerless glove-wearing hands together, his exposed fingertips dark with dirt. He saw the full pint of beer and unopened packet of cheese and onion crisps sat waiting for him and lowered himself on to a stool, opening the crisps with one hand whilst raising the pint glass to his mouth with the other.

'Multi-tasking,' said Rita. 'Impressive.'

Formby grinned, exposing a mouthful of sharp, little, yellow and brown piranha teeth. His chin and cheeks were covered by bristles turned white with age.

'Have you ever heard of toothpaste, Formby?' asked Waterson.

'Yes. Heard of everything, me.'

'Anything for me yet?' asked Rita.

'Listening. Listening, listening, always listening.'

'And what have you heard?' asked Waterson.

Formby frowned and scratched at his head, raising a little cloud of dandruff. 'Dreams.'

'Bad dreams?' said Rita, leaning forward.

'Very bad. Lots and lots of very bad dreams.'

Rita reached into her coat and pulled out Bob's pad of paper that she'd kept after leaving his squalid flat. She flicked through the pages, found the one she was after, and slapped it down on the table, pushing it towards Formby. 'Well?'

Formby leaned forward, squinting. He reached out and traced the rabbit ears drawing with a grimy finger tip.

'Not dead and gone?' he asked.

'That's what I'm starting to wonder,' she replied.

'Wait,' said Ben, 'is this about those two mask-wearing, uh, things, you told me about?'

'Mr. Cotton and Mr. Spike,' Rita replied.

'Right. I thought you said you, sort of, killed them. Or something.'

'I did something to them. I've no idea how it affected them. Maybe it killed them, maybe it just slowed them down. I don't know. It got them out of the way for a while, at the very least. Maybe this is just a coincidence.'

'Bad dreams, rabbit ears there, the little girl wearing them at my funeral,' said Waterson. 'It seems like the evidence is starting to stack up.'

'*Circumstantial* evidence. That's all it is for now. We need more so we know for sure.' Rita grabbed the pad of paper, rolled it up, and slipped it back into her coat pocket. 'If we know it's them for certain, we can find them and we can stop them. Somehow.'

Formby finished his pint and let rip a deep, bassy belch.

'Good God,' said Waterson. 'I'm dead and even I feel like I can taste that burp.'

Formby sniggered and began licking the now empty bag of crisps.

'You good to keep on snooping?' asked Rita.

'Yes, yes, I will listen. Sooner or later, someone says something. Someone who knows.'

'How can I help?' asked Ben.

'Oh. Ah…'

'Rita, I'm going mad here. I haven't stepped outside in over a week.'

'I know, I know, but you're still too hot.'

Ben grinned and raised an eyebrow. 'Why, thank you.'

'Hilarious. You know what I mean. You murdered someone a matter of days ago and the police are still on red alert looking for you.'

'I grew a beard, and I have this hat, look,' Ben pulled out a blue baseball cap and put it on.

'Eat your heart out, Scarlet Pimpernel,' said Rita. 'I still think, maybe, one or two of the more observant officers might see through your cunning disguise.'

Ben sagged and nodded.

'If it's any consolation, I really liked the funny cat vid. Keep that shit up.'

Ben laughed, then sighed and took off his hat. 'Fine. Okay. But I can't stay in here forever.'

'I know. We'll work it out, I promise, okay?'

Ben nodded, then headed off to the bathroom.

Rita turned to see Waterson grinning. 'What's that shit-eating grin about?'

'So, when are you two tying the knot?'

Rita attempted to punch Waterson on the arm, but tumbled to the floor with a startled yelp as her fist passed harmlessly through him.

Formby bent down to look at the fallen Rita. 'More drinks now, please, yes?'

Ben washed his hands and splashed some water on his face. After he grabbed a paper towel and dried himself, he balled the wet paper in his fist and threw it across the bathroom in frustration. He sighed and leaned against the sink. He knew Rita was right to keep him indoors and out of harm's way. People might recognise him. The police definitely would. And he trusted her. More than trusted her.

But it didn't make his circumstances any less frustrating. He'd dodged one prison for another, and it couldn't go on forever. There would have to be some sort of solution eventually.

He thought about Sally, his ex. The girl who had dumped him. She'd have heard about what he'd done, of course. About how he'd torn a man to pieces. He wondered how she'd taken the news. If she thought that dumping him had been a lucky escape, or if she didn't believe a word of it. She knew him better than just about anyone, surely she would never believe he would do such a thing? She might have thought him capable of boring a man to death, but not eviscerating.

He thought about his little desk at Briers & Travers, the office he'd worked at as an accountant for more years than he cared to remember. He was surprised to feel a little pang of nostalgia for the place. That routine, that normality. The office banter, office drudgery, the people you looked forward to chatting to, the ones you looked forward to avoiding and chatting about. No doubt he would be the one they spoke about these days. The single topic of conversation. Steve would definitely be heading that up, Ben's colleague, the man who'd bully him into going for an after-work pint or six. Steve would have a bunch of Google alerts set up so he caught any scrap of news on his friend the fugitive. Ben could picture him strutting about the office, doing the rounds, doling out every fresh morsel.

Ben smiled. Turned out he missed that tosser, too.

He sighed and pushed himself away from the sink, ready to rejoin Rita and the others. It was no good feeling sad about what was lost, it didn't help, it was pointless. Time to accept, to move on, to embrace the crazy world he'd found himself in. The crazy people he now called friends. The crazy redhead who he might, maybe, call more than a friend soon. He took out his phone and started looking for new cute cat vids to send Rita.

'They keep you as an indoor pet now?'

Ben's heart lurched. He recognised that voice. It was like that voice was part of him.

He looked up to find Magda standing in front of the door, her long, black hair tied back, her brilliantly blue eyes boring holes through him.

'No,' Ben whimpered, back pressing up against the sink again, 'this isn't… you're dead. I saw your body, you died.'

Magda was a master werewolf, and the sole reason he was a fugitive. Ben was quite correct, Magda was dead. She'd fallen from the top of Blackpool Tower and had Rita's axe buried in her for good measure. Magda's soul had then—Ben had been told—been claimed by a demon. Yes, Magda the werewolf, who had infected Ben with her curse, was indeed deader than dead. And yet she was stood before him, a cool smile teasing at her lips.

'Do you not miss my gift?' she asked, and bared her teeth, large and sharp.

'It wasn't a gift.'

'To be so free, so untamed. The smell of the hunt on the air, the excitement. I will give you that gift again, Ben.'

'No, I don't want it. I don't want it!'

He didn't see her move, but Magda was pressed against him, teeth grazing his neck, ready to sink into his flesh and turn him into the beast.

Ben's heart beat so fast he thought he might have a heart attack. His stomach was a knot, his thoughts a cavalcade of wild terror.

'Let the wolf out, Ben. Let it out.'

'No!'

Ben shoved Magda back.

'I won't be that thing again! I won't kill again!'

The top of Magda's head began to bulge, and the sound of her skull cracking echoed around the tiled bathroom. Rabbit ears began to emerge from the top of Magda's head, white fur slick with gore, blood pouring down her face.

'Alan Crowther is waiting for you, Ben Turner, he is very, very cross with you.'

Her rabbit ears twitched.

And then Magda was gone.

In the weeks since she had been freed from the nefarious clutches of the Magician, Alexander Jenner, Gemma Wheeler had seen quite a lot of Rita Hobbes, so she was not at all surprised to answer her front door and find the grinning Detective and her frowning partner stood before her.

'Come in then,' said Gemma, 'I'll get the kettle on.'

'Cheers, ears,' said Rita, and followed her inside, Waterson at her heels.

Something about her experience at the hands of Jenner, Mr. Cotton and Mr. Spike too, meant that unlike most normal people in Blackpool, Gemma was aware of both Rita and Waterson.

Minutes later, Rita reached up from the couch to accept the mug of tea Gemma offered. 'Nice one.'

Waterson looked at the mug pointed in his direction. 'I'm dead.'

'Oh,' said Gemma. 'Do you not like tea when you're dead, then?'

Waterson thought about correcting her, then nodded instead. 'That's right. Gone right off the stuff.'

'Fair enough.' Gemma placed the unwanted mug on the coffee table. 'Extra cup for whoever wants it.'

'How have you been?' asked Rita.

Gemma frowned and wobbled her head. 'Pretty good, you know. All in all. All things considered. Alive and not murdered, so that's good.' Gemma looked at the mug of tea she'd placed on the coffee table, then over to Waterson on the couch. 'Oh. No offence. Sorry.'

'None taken.'

'Was that offensive?'

'A bit.'

'Right.' Gemma sipped at her hot tea. 'I hope you haven't come with bad news.'

'Why would you think that?' asked Rita. 'Can't a girl drop in on a friend for a bit of tea and banter?'

'Yeah. But when you bring the frowning ghost it makes me suspicious.' Gemma's eyes went wide. 'Oh! He's not got out, has he? The Magician bloke, Jenner, has he escaped? Am I in danger?'

'No, no, nothing like that, promise,' replied Rita.

'Okay. Good. I'm still not keen on the idea of being sacrificed.'

Rita laughed and drank her tea. She had once dated Gemma's cousin, a uniformed officer. She'd liked him a lot, he was fun, and cute. Well, "dated" was a bit strong for what the status of their relationship had actually been. They drank together. They occasionally saw films together. They quite often had loud, energetic sex together. He'd been keen to make things more official and "normal", as he'd put it, but Rita had never been eager to turn it from a good shag into a boyfriend/girlfriend thing. She'd had every intention of leaving Blackpool for one thing, so falling in love with someone there would have been a disaster. Of course, now she wasn't able to leave Blackpool anyway due to the hex. Funny how things turn out. She found herself sad that, whatever their relationship had actually been, he no longer remembered anything about it. The way he'd look at her with those big puppy dog eyes after they'd had sex, hoping against hope that she'd let him stay overnight.

'We just dropped by to ask you a question,' said Waterson, shaking Rita from her reverie.

'Okay then,' said Gemma, 'fire away.'

'I was just wondering if you'd been experiencing any bad dreams recently,' said Rita.

'Well, I was traumatised by a man in robes wanting to chop me up with an axe, not sure if you remember, so yeah, I've had the odd bad dream here and there.'

'Right. Sorry. But I mean something more specific.'

'You mean the rabbit mask dream?'

They'd all had dreams about the rabbit mask, the one Mr. Cotton wore. All of the women who Jenner had intended to sacrifice had seen the mask in their nightmares for as long as they could remember.

'Have you?' asked Waterson.

'No. Not that I remember anyway.'

'You're sure?' said Rita.

'Why would I lie?'

'No, right, of course.'

'From what I can remember, the only mask I've dreamed about recently was the goat one the Magician was wearing. Doesn't mean I haven't seen the rabbit mask in my dreams too, of course, but I don't remember it if I have.'

Rita finished her mug of tea and placed it down beside Waterson's unwanted one.

'Thanks, Gemma. For the drink and for putting up with more questions.'

'That's all right. Most people pussyfoot around what happened to me. Worry I'll break down and get all embarrassing on them.'

Gemma walked them to the door.

'Phone me,' said Rita, 'if you see anyone in a rabbit mask, in your dreams or otherwise, let me know. It's important.'

'Promise.'

They said their goodbyes and Gemma closed the front door behind them.

'So what now, then?' asked Waterson.

Rita rested her hand on the handle of the axe. 'Time for another home visit.'

Rita had visited Mr. Cotton and Mr. Spike's house once before. The hidden house nestled within their dream realm. She'd saved Carlisle and put an end to the nightmare of Cotton and Spike. Now she was not so sure that the end had been as permanent as she had assumed.

Waterson watched as Rita held the axe tightly in both hands, eyes closed, lips moving silently. The axe head strobed with colour, ribbons of magic whirling around it.

'Right then,' said Rita, opening her eyes and swinging the axe so that the blade stuck into, well, nothing. Into reality. The colours burst from the axe and an opening appeared.

'We couldn't just take the bus, then?' asked Waterson.

'Not on any route, Waters.'

'Okay, magic portal it is then.'

Rita had been to the house before, and the axe remembered the way.

Detective Hobbes and Waterson stepped into the portal, into the wound in reality, and found themselves in a darkened room.

'Oh, Jesus,' said Rita.

'What? What is it?' replied Waterson, on high alert.

'It bloody stinks in here.'

Waterson gave Rita an evil glare as she pinched her nose and the magic portal closed behind them.

Rita flicked the light switch and the candelabras affixed to the walls sparked and sputtered into life.

'Okay, how does that work?'

'Buggered if I know,' said Rita, 'but then this isn't an ordinary house. This is all the stuff of dreams.'

They were in a nursery. Sat in the corner of the room, a large wooden rocking horse eyed them balefully. Vines reached up through the floor, through the thick shag carpet, wrapping themselves around the horse. The vines had also claimed a chest of drawers, a wardrobe, and an empty crib.

Rita pressed her foot down on the carpet. It squelched and brown liquid oozed to the surface. The whole nursery was in a state of decay. Rotting. Overtaken by vegetation that thrived in the putrefying room.

'Come on, we're on a wabbit hunt,' said Rita, wiggling her nose.

Waterson rolled his eyes and followed behind.

Cotton and Spike's home was large and old and in a state of advanced decomposition. It was as though the house itself had been a living thing, and Cotton and Spike had been its beating heart. Its soul. Without them, it was a husk.

They moved as quietly as they could down the corridor, past the eyes of the oil paintings that lined the walls. Old, cracked paintings of men in powdered wigs and frilly ruffs. Rita wondered if the people in the portraits could see her, whether their eyes were following her as she walked. That's the sort of thing you'd expect in a nightmare, and this was where nightmares lived. Where nightmares were born.

She and Waterson made their way down the grand staircase, each step loudly announcing their presence. If anyone was home, they would definitely know they had unexpected guests by now. Yet Rita was pretty certain that she and Waterson were the only people present. No one else had walked the halls and rooms here for some time.

'I take it you can deal with this pair if they do appear unexpectedly?' asked Waterson.

'I twatted them last time, I can do it again.'

Rita opened the door to the large dining room that she had found Carlisle's corpse in the last time she had been there. Part of her hoped she might find him there again, though alive this time. At the far end was a large table laden high with rotting piles of food. The smell was overpowering, and brought tears to Rita's eyes.

'Another win for team dead and can't smell,' said Waterson, eyeing the terrible, putrid mountain.

Rita rushed from the room, slamming the door behind her, and tried not to empty her stomach on the floor. The whole house stank, but that room was just a little too much. She composed herself, wiping the spittle from her lips using the sleeve of her coat.

'They're not here,' she said. 'No one's here.'

They checked the rest of the house just to be thorough, ducking and stepping over the vines that crept along every floor, every ceiling. If Cotton and Spike were behind the strange events of late—and Rita knew in her gut that they absolutely were—they were holed up elsewhere. Well, they could skulk where they wished, but she'd find them.

She only hoped she might find Carlisle, too.

Carlisle's eyes flickered open.

He'd been unconscious for a while, passed out from the pain. That was probably the only thing that had kept him from being dead already. Mr. Spike didn't like playing with things that couldn't feel fear, couldn't acknowledge pain, so when Carlisle had passed out, he'd left him to go and find tastier treats.

If Carlisle had passed out even a few seconds later, he would have died. Too much damage, too much pain; his body would have finally given in. Mr. Spike was unrivalled in his ability to keep his victims alive. To slowly tease out his tortures so that the poor person at his mercy would live as long as possible, and in acute agony. But even someone as hardy as Carlisle could only take so much. Sooner or later—likely very much sooner—Carlisle would perish.

He glanced around, ears straining for any sound, for any evidence that either Cotton or Spike were present, that they would carry on the abuse once they saw him conscious again, but neither were there. It was just him, his body a battered, slashed, purple mess, and the Angel, still kneeling with Its head bowed in the centre of Its glass box.

Carlisle grunted and pushed himself up, wincing as the glass shards that pinned him dug into the flesh. Slowly, agonisingly, he removed any glass and, his body complaining viciously, propped himself into a sitting position against a column and tried to catch his breath.

He had one chance, and it wasn't a favourable one. It would most likely lead to his death in another way, but at least it would not be directly at the hand of Mr. Spike or his rabbit mask-sporting, tap-dancing brother.

He had to relinquish his physical body.

Hopefully temporarily.

He had to step into the astral plane to be able to bypass the lock they had placed upon him, and reach out for help.

There were three problems with this last resort he now found himself embracing. Well, four.

Firstly: he might not find anyone prepared to help him. Or capable even. Which would be annoying. Annoying and lethal.

Secondly: a body left behind in this way would start to deteriorate. It would rot, physically and mentally, the longer it was abandoned. Even if he found help, Carlisle might return to his body to find it degraded beyond repair. He had no idea how long his body would allow him to step outside of it before it passed the point of no return.

Thirdly: he had little experience of this sort of excursion. He had, briefly, stepped out of his body once before, but that had been a mistake. A spell gone wrong. He'd rather swiftly clambered back inside himself when he realised what had happened. The astral plane was not easy to traverse, so his lack of experience meant he might well be tossing himself into a blender. A leaf in a hurricane. No control, no sense of where he was, or where anything else was. His consciousness could drown in it.

So far, so terrible; but those first three thumbs down weren't even the thing he was most concerned about.

There were... things that hunted for vacant bodies. For physical forms that had been left unprotected. Almost things that ached for true existence, for actual substance. Anyone travelling to the astral plane would first place themselves within a powerful spell of protection: shapes and words sketched on the ground that they would use to fortify their Earthly form. The almost things, the desperate creatures without form that searched for a body to call home, would be kept at bay by these protective spells. Without them, Carlisle would be erecting a giant neon AVAILABLE FOR OCCUPATION sign next to his battered and bruised body. The things were like sharks, they could smell an empty body from miles away. Would his otherworldly whereabouts help hide him? Carlisle hoped so, but he doubted it. Death was one thing, but the idea of something else using his body as their own *offended* him. Turned his stomach on a primal level.

But he had no choice.

He had been backed into a corner and he was going to have to take a leap of faith.

'What's life without a little risk?' he muttered quietly to himself.

He brushed down his coat, squared his shoulders, closed his eyes…

...and then he was gone.

7

Marie Dwyer had butterflies in her stomach.

She clenched and unclenched her hands, her grey-painted nails digging into her palms, and hoped to God she wasn't smiling too insanely.

Marie was sat in The Grapes, a cosy pub a few streets away from Blackpool's seafront, snuggled down a dead end street. An absurdly handsome man named Carl Cooper, with gorgeous green eyes and a jawline that made her knees weak, was sat opposite, telling Marie about his dream of setting up a chain of coffee shops. If she hadn't been so madly hot for him she might have pointed out that the likes of Costa and Starbucks seemed to have the monopoly on coffee shop chains, but right now her heart and, well, her crotch, were doing the thinking, and both of those things were prepared to agree with anything the man had to say. Especially anything dirty.

'I think, within five years, I could have a shop in Manchester, Birmingham, Carlisle, maybe even Newcastle.'

Marie tucked her mousy brown hair behind her ears and carried on nodding.

Carl Cooper ran a cute little coffee shop called Blaffee, which—Carl had excitedly explained—was a combination of the words 'Blackpool' and 'Coffee'. It had come to him in a dream ten years previously. Marie had been visiting Blaffee on a twice-daily basis during the working week for the past six months. Every day, on her way into work, she would swing by for her morning Cappuccino, served with a smile that made Marie's heart jump into her throat. In a good way.

'Have I told you you're my favourite customer?' Carl Cooper would say each and every time. And, each and every time, Marie's cheeks would flush red and she'd laugh, handing over her money and walking out of the shop, both elated at the interaction and crushed that he hadn't asked her out.

And so she would go back at lunch. Another coffee, this time with a slice of cake, perhaps, or one of the sandwiches Carl made with his own large, manly hands.

So that was her routine, ever since she'd stumbled to work hungover one day and passed a shop she'd never noticed before. Ever since she'd shuffled inside to guzzle something that would fool her brain into thinking her body wasn't collapsing like a failed soufflé.

This twice-daily visit, angling for a date she was too nervous to initiate, had already cost Marie a fortune. Blaffee was ludicrously overpriced to the point that Marie had been forced to go to the cheap supermarket for her weekly shop, just so she could protect her Blaffee fund.

And then it happened.

Marie had gone to the counter with her empty coffee cup and placed it down.

'Thanks. Thank you!' she'd said, wearing a grin wider than her face.

'Marie, I don't suppose you'd like to—'

'Yes I would, thank you! I mean… what were you going to ask?'

And suddenly everything was roses and puppy dogs. Now here they were, sharing drinks and jokes and flirty smiles, and Marie was pretty sure they'd end up having at least two kids and a cottage somewhere green with a lake within walking distance. All she needed was to lock in a second date and perhaps a goodnight kiss.

'Wow, I didn't realise how late it was,' said Carl.

'I know, it's gone quick, hasn't it?' Marie replied.

Carl Cooper handed Marie her coat, and they walked towards the exit, stepping out of the warm fug of the pub and into the crisp night air. The sky was clear above, and Marie pulled her coat tight as she looked up at the stars.

'What a lovely night,' she said, and Carl Cooper agreed.

He turned to her. He was really close, and Marie could feel his breath on her skin. Could feel his heat.

'So, I've really enjoyed tonight,' he said.

'Me too. A lot.'

'Will I see you in the morning for your coffee?'

Marie smiled and nodded and smiled some more.

There was a held-breath pause and the stars shone brighter. Eyes darted to mouths, and then Carl Cooper leaned in and pressed his lips against Marie's. The kiss lasted all of three seconds, but Marie was pretty sure she was now fully pregnant.

'Can I take you out again?' asked Carl Cooper.

Marie nodded and said yes and reminded him that he had her number and he should very definitely call.

As they parted, walking in opposite directions, Marie could still feel Carl Cooper's lips on hers. A phantom kiss. She squealed, punched the air, and did a brief funky chicken dance. Maybe this was *it*. Maybe this was *love*.

She turned to a shop window to see how happy her face looked. She saw two faces looking back. One her own, framed by its long, straight, brown hair, the other a stranger. At least, she assumed it was a stranger, as the face was hidden by a tatty old rabbit mask.

She turned to see who the person was, but found herself alone in the street. Confused, she looked back at her reflection, but this time only saw her own face.

Unease began to chase the butterflies from Marie's stomach.

She shoved her hands into the pockets of her coat and resumed walking.

She only made it another few steps.

There was a girl standing half in and half out of an alleyway. The girl was young, around six years old, and, like Marie, had long, straight, mousy brown hair. Her eyes were small but her smile was big.

Marie recognised the girl. She looked just like she had the last time she'd seen her, twenty years ago.

'Laura?' said Marie, in a voice that sounded like someone speaking from behind a locked door.

The girl giggled and stepped into the alley, disappearing from view.

Marie looked up and down the empty street, the stars silently looking down from above, and knew she should turn around and walk the long way home.

She walked towards the alley.

Laura was stood waiting for her, a couple of metres into the alleyway, partially shrouded in gloom, her face invisible.

'Laura?' Marie asked once again.

Laura giggled.

'You're dead,' said Marie.

Laura had been Marie's sister, younger than her by a year. They'd been on a family holiday to Devon and the two of them had been splashing around in the sea while their parents lay stretched out on towels, eyes closed, slowly crisping under the summer sun.

It all went wrong so fast. As though death had only needed a split-second, a single moment of distraction, to reach out and sink its bony fingers into life. The waves had been surging towards them, and Marie and her sister had been screaming and laughing and jumping over them. Only, one time, Laura didn't come up from beneath the salty water, ready to jump the next wave. Marie had ducked under trying to see where Laura was hiding, but couldn't see her. She'd ducked under again and again, confused, scared.

Mum had screamed and Dad had sprinted into the water, sunglasses flying off his head as he ran splashing past Marie, diving and swimming towards the face-down body floating on the surface.

Marie hadn't stepped into the sea since her little sister had died. Hadn't even gone to a beach. And now here she was. Her dead little sister, looking just as she had before she drowned, stood in an alleyway, waving Marie forward.

Marie didn't believe in ghosts, but maybe ghosts didn't care if you believed in them or not.

'Help me, Muzzy,' said Laura, using Marie's pet name.

'Laura, you're dead.'

'Oh,' said Laura, as though this was the first she'd heard about it. 'Step in the alleyway, Muzzy, and give me a hug.'

Marie shivered as the shock began to recede, replaced by fear, by the certainty that she should start running. Unfortunately, the realisation came too late.

Laura laughed as limbs shot from her body and wrapped around Marie, pulling her off her feet and into the alleyway.

The street was empty, but the stars saw it all.

Tap-Tap-Tap.

Liam sighed.

Tap-Tap-Tap.

He was going to try and ignore it this time. Ignore the stupid tree branch slapping his window and ignore the image of his dead uncle's empty corpse that had decided night time was the right time to pay Liam a house call.

Tap-Tap-Tap-Tap-Tap-Tap-Tap-Tap-Tap.

Liam got out of bed and made his way to the curtains.

He'd asked his dad about cutting the branch off, but his dad looked tired, his eyes dark, cheeks unshaven. Mum had been looking frazzled recently, too. They weren't alone, of course. Everyone seemed on edge these days. Tired and ready to jump at the slightest noise.

Tap-Tap-Tap-Tap-Tap-Tap-Tap-Tap-Tap-Tap-Tap-Tap.

Liam lifted the curtain. The corpse of his dead Uncle Waterson leered at him through the window. Liam yelped and stumbled backwards, the curtain dropping down to hide the ghastly sight.

'Are you afraid?' asked a voice.

Liam turned to see who was talking, but couldn't find the source. 'Where are you?' he asked. It had not been his dead uncle's voice. Was this another ghost come to haunt him?

His blankets began to pull back, then a white-gloved hand reached up from behind the bed and waved at him.

Liam ran to his bedroom door and flung it open, only to find his dad stood waiting outside.

'Do you want to feed my birds now?' asked Not Dad, holding out a clump of mud squirming with fat worms. Not Dad no longer had eyes, and snapping bird beaks thrust out of the empty sockets.

Liam moved back as Not Dad stepped into his bedroom.

'I'm not scared,' said Liam.

'Oh?' said the voice from behind. 'That will not do at all.'

Liam's heart beat-beat-beat as two large rabbit ears rose into view from behind his bed.

'Oh, it's Mr. Cotton,' said Not Dad. 'He told me I'd see much better without my eyes, so he tore them from my head with a corkscrew. Now I see the dark much more clearly.'

Not Dad lifted a worm to one of the vicious beaks, and it ripped it hungrily from his hand and pulled it back inside Not Dad's skull.

Marie sat up.

She was not in the alleyway, she was on a sandy, golden beach, the sun beating down on her sweating brow.

She struggled to her feet, brushing the sand from her clothes, trying to work out what in the hell was going on. She was asleep, that must be it. She didn't actually remember getting home from her date with Carl Cooper. Getting into bed and closing her eyes, any of that. But she must have done, because all of this, and seeing her dead little sister in the street, that wasn't normal. None of this was possible, it all seemed like a nightmare, so that's what it must be.

Marie felt almost happy for a moment as she convinced herself that she'd cracked it. If she just ignored the fact that she was sure she never got home and never went to bed, then she didn't have to be scared anymore, and everything made sense.

There were bodies in the sea. Hundreds of them. Thousands.

Little corpses of little girls, face-down, bobbing on the tide as the lazy waves rolled towards shore.

'It's okay, I'm just having a nightmare, that's all. I'm fast asleep and in the morning I'll think about that kiss and I'll see Carl Cooper on my way to work when I go into Blaffee for my morning pick-me-up.'

As each dead Laura was washed on to the sand it slowly rose to its feet. It looked at Marie and giggled. Giggled and walked towards her.

'I know this is a nightmare, and I'd like to wake up now.'

'Your fault,' said the dead Lauras. 'Let me die, your fault your fault your fault your fault your—'

Marie turned away. Her dad was stood before her. She was grown up but her dad towered over her like he had when she was little. He grabbed her arm painfully.

'How could you let that happen to your little sister?' he yelled through rabid dog teeth. 'Your fault! Your fault!'

Marie screamed and pulled her arm free. She ran from the beach, through the scrub of grass, and the dead Lauras ran at her heels, laughing and screaming and accusing and begging.

'Wake up!' said Marie, eyes almost blind with tears. 'Wake up, wake up, wake up!'

She ran into something solid and landed hard on the ground. She looked around wildly, wiping tears from her eyes. She was no longer on that beach in Devon, and the many dead Lauras were nowhere to be seen. She was back on the street in Blackpool she had been on before she stepped into the alley. She looked behind her, at the alleyway's black maw, and shivered.

'Are you quite all right?' asked the person Marie had run into.

'I'm not sleeping, am I?' Marie asked as she looked up.

The blank glass eyes of a rabbit mask looked down at her. Marie stood up, trembling.

'My name is Mr. Cotton, and that is my fine brother, Mr. Spike.' He pointed a white-gloved hand behind her, and Marie turned to see a second figure dressed in an old-fashioned suit, its material dusty, faded, frayed. Marie could hear Mr. Spike's breath rasping against the inside of his hedgehog mask.

'Who are you?' she asked.

'Connoisseurs of terror,' replied Mr. Cotton, and the rabbit mask smiled, though of course it did not as it was just a mask.

'This is a nightmare, please tell me that's true.'

'Oh, that is very true. But you don't need to sleep to experience our gift. Soon, every waking moment shall be a nightmare, and we shall have very full bellies indeed. Is that not so, brother of mine?'

Mr. Spike nodded and made a horrid gurgling sound.

'As a special treat,' said Mr. Cotton, 'how about my brother takes off his mask and shows you the true face of terror? Would you like that?'

Marie ran.

'I do not believe she desires said treat, Mr. Spike. But not to worry, they will all see your face, given time.'

Marie spent the rest of the night wide awake, TV blaring to fill the silence, checking and re-checking that all the doors and windows were locked.

All across Blackpool, people were having bad dreams, whether they were asleep or not.

Rita Hobbes was no different. She was in the void again. In whatever formless, empty space inside the artefact—the axe—that the sacrificed souls of Jane Bowan and Ellie Mason were trapped within.

'Hello? You two playing hide-and-seek?' asked Rita, now used to her regular sleep trips. She couldn't say she enjoyed them, as each time she spoke to the souls of the trapped women it just reminded her that the axe she wielded was essentially their prison. No, it wasn't her fault they were trapped inside, but she was a police detective—or had been—and failing to provide help where help was needed was the kind of thing that gnawed at her.

'Come out, come out wherever you are, girls,' she said, kicking at a stone that wasn't there.

A shape began to emerge from the grey fog.

'Ellie, is that you?'

It was not Ellie.

'Hello, Rita Hobbes,' said the Angel of Blackpool.

Rita made to grab her axe, then remembered she was inside the axe. Or her unconscious, sleeping mind was inside it at least. Somehow.

'Where's Carlisle?' she demanded, trying not to look nervous.

'Why so nervous?' asked the Angel.

Damn.

'I said, where is Carlisle?'

'In a Parisian cafe within his mind, at least he was the last we spoke.'

'Right.' Rita rolled that one around in her head for a few seconds. 'I'm sorry, what? Are you saying he's alive or not alive?'

'I have not harmed him.'

'Well, that's good.'

'Others have.'

'Not so good.'

'I… request your help.'

Rita attempted to reply in at least three different ways, before simply giving in and laughing. Loudly.

The Angel waited for her to finish. 'Release Alexander Jenner from the dreamscape you fashioned to imprison him.'

'Yeah, unlikely.'

'Release him and the power shall be his again.'

'Sort of why I won't be doing that.'

The Angel began to flicker and fade, Its mouth moving but the words missing.

'What? What is it?' asked Rita. 'Why in the name of my arse would I ever help you, or release the guv? You're off your angelic rocker.'

'...power… his… will flow… away from… to him…' Its voice came through like a detuned radio, slipping in and out.

'Sounds like we're about to lose our connection, so let me make this clear before you get cut off. I've only got one thing I'm going to offer you, you big twat.' Rita held up her middle finger. 'That's all yours. Now go with God.'

The Angel of Blackpool's face creased in silent fury, and then It was gone.

'What a total arsehole,' said Rita. But she found herself smiling. Carlisle was alive.

Probably.

The wind roared in Carlisle's ears, only it wasn't actually the wind as he didn't actually have ears.

He was not exactly sure how much time had passed since his astral form had vacated his body. It could have been seconds. Or hours. Or years. Time was a nebulous concept when one was traversing the astral plane.

Reality shook and rushed and warped around him, a kaleidoscope of images, sounds, times, realms, realities, all jammed together and behind and on top of each other. Noisy, disorienting chaos. No up, no down, no here, no there, no clear sense of anything to get a grip on.

Carlisle was in big trouble.

He opened his mouth to say "Shit" but had no idea whether he had a mouth or how to use it, forcing him to think the word "Shit" instead. It was a rather understated way of expressing how deeply in trouble he was.

He tried to ignore the madness surrounding him, and reached out to get hold of one true thing. One real, alive, solid thing that might anchor him as he tried to get to grips with reality as it bucked and raged and tried to shake him off.

Patience.

That's all it would take.

Don't get overwhelmed. Don't let that seed of panic take hold and bloom.

The sound of everything assaulting him at once began to fade as he willed himself into a state of calm.

He was Carlisle. He could find his way through anything, and do it with style.

He was Carlisle.

...so scared, is he following...?

There! An Uncanny voice in the madness.

He wasn't sure if he had hands, but he reached out as the beacon wafted in and out.

'...ears and the birds in Not Dad's...'

Almost there. Reality scratched at him, tried to shred him, but the beacon was shining bright and clear. A lighthouse beaming into the fog to lead his ship to safety.

'...so dark, I shouldn't be out here so late at...'

Carlisle screamed, though of course he didn't scream at all, and the whirl of chaos shuddered to a stop.

A small boy on Blackpool beach. He was in his pyjamas, his feet were bare, his cheeks red, eyes too. He was shaking and crying in the cold, and he was worried about going home because of the terrors, the terrors, the terrors, even though he was brave, really, and knew that the dark hid secrets that others couldn't see. Knew about the Uncanny without really knowing about it at all. *Was* the Uncanny.

'Who's there?' asked the boy, asked Liam, aware of something holding on to him. 'Are you going to try and hurt me, too?'

Liam felt as though he could almost see a person. Tall and pale, with a long, dark coat and a wicked grin spreading across his face.

'Many thanks,' said the almost-there person with a slight bow, and then he was gone.

Liam rubbed the last of the tears from his eyes, his toes curling in the damp sand. He'd run from home, scared by the rabbit mask and Not Dad with his head full of birds, but he'd have to go back.

They were only nightmares, probably. Nightmares in the awake world. He thought that lots of people were seeing these thing now, too.

He looked out to sea and saw things reaching out from the horizon. Things he had not been able to see just moments before. They looked like smoke trails, the kind a plane left as it passed overhead, only these were black. They reached out from the sea and arced high across the water, over Liam's head and then down into Blackpool. Thousands of them, writhing like snakes.

Yes, Liam thought a lot of people in Blackpool were having bad dreams that night. Perhaps even worse than bad dreams. Liam thought the nightmares meant them all harm.

He wrapped his arms around himself and tried not to shiver.

8

Joan looked down at the dead bird that had been deposited on her kitchen floor. Its neck had been torn open and a wing was missing. She clucked her tongue with annoyance and retrieved a plastic bag from the cupboard, dropping the poor creature inside and placing it into one of the outside bins. She wasn't squeamish about it, she'd had more than one grisly present left for her over the years.

'Birds, rabbits, even had a bat, once. Lord alone knows how they caught that bloody thing,' Joan had told her young neighbour just a few days earlier. 'It's not down to *my* cats, you understand, Mandy. No, no, no. Jackson, Mr. Tabby and Ginger would never dream of killing anything. They're very cultured cats, you see. I've brought them up from newborns to act in a respectable manner. Plus they're very well-fed; they've no need to go trawling the garden like common animals.'

Well-fed was certainly one way of putting it. All three of Joan's cats were more than a little on the chunky side. She couldn't help but lavish attention and treats upon the trio. There came a point when they struggled to squeeze in and out of the cat flap into the back garden, but instead of putting the chubby threesome on a diet, Joan had had a larger cat flap installed.

'No, no, no, not *my* cats. They would never leave such things in my kitchen. That's the thing with cat flaps, you see. It helps my cats get out and about, but it lets other things get inside.'

Joan's neighbour, Mandy, was a single mum who had left the father of her child to bring up little Ashton alone. Not that Joan held that against her, it was a modern world after all. You have to move with the times. Would've been a scandal if Joan had done the same in her time of course. Just imagine the horror if she'd bundled up baby Celia and done a midnight flit from Frank! Her mum would have disowned her, and that was just for starters!

But no, that wasn't what happened nowadays, and who was she to look down upon it? Truth was, she admired Mandy in a way. Being strong enough to go it alone with a little kiddie. They'd had a cake and pop party for his second birthday only the other week. Cute as a button, he was.

Joan's daughter, Celia, had never had kids of course, and it was too late for that now. Celia wasn't a young woman anymore. She could maybe adopt, though. Joan had mentioned that once or twice, read up about it down at the library even, but Celia wasn't interested. *'I'm not the nurturing sort, Mum,'* she'd said, over and over again.

Joan knew it, and she wanted her own daughter to live the life that felt right for her, but a part of her, in the pit of her stomach, hadn't stopped longing for grandchildren. She supposed a head-shrink type might say that's why she doted on her cats the way she did, and had taken such an active interest in little Ashton.

Well, maybe it was, but then who else was she going to dote on? Celia was all the way down in London, Frank dead for almost twenty years, no grandchildren; should she just sit there alone and let the cold creep in? A loving heart was a healthy heart. That's what Joan always said, when people stopped to listen.

'You know, one time, after getting that bigger flap fitted, I actually came home to find a fox asleep in my kitchen. Not a small one either; a big ol' boy! Chased it round the place with my broom before I managed to shepherd it back through the flap. Cheeky thing! So regal though, foxes, don't you think? Make a riot of your rubbish bins, of course. That's the thing you see, that's the thing with these cat flaps: other things can get inside. Things that aren't supposed to. That's why I know it isn't my cats leaving these presents. It's that big, black moggy from across the road, oh, I've no doubt about that. I see him skulking across my back fence when I'm washing the dishes. I've been over there to tell Mr. Wright about it more than once, but you know that grumpy old codger. Not interested. Ah, well. What's the harm though? Probably wants a little extra love and food, that's why he comes round my kitchen. Can't see Mr. Wright offering much in that department.'

Joan had taken to calling the black mog Charlie Boy. She'd wave to it as it passed and call out its new name. Poor thing wouldn't come near when she was around though. A nervous mite. Clearly, Mr. Wright had not treated him well.

'Lord alone knows what I'll find coming though that cat flap next, Mandy.'

Joan sank to her knees on the kitchen floor with difficulty. She dunked a sponge into the bucket of soapy water and scrubbed at the tiled floor. She liked to keep a good household, always had done. Point of pride. Now that Celia was coming back in the morning to stay for a few days, she was making sure every inch glittered.

'You'll be able to eat your dinner off the toilet seat by the time I'm through!' Joan had said to Mandy, hooting with laughter.

It had been so long since Celia had been up for a visit. Going on a year now. Had to cancel her trip earlier in the year, work needed her, so she said. Celia was always so busy, and so very far away. Joan had made the trip a few times over the years, down on the train, but the older she got, the more of a drain it was. So now she sat at home and waited for Celia to find the time. Or a "window", as Celia liked to call it.

She didn't blame her daughter—of course not—she had a busy life. She was a success! Built that interior design business up from the ground, now she had a whole host of people who worked under her. Joan bragged to anyone who would listen about her clever daughter down in London with her own business. Joan liked to think that it was something to do with her own flare for keeping a tidy home that had rubbed off on her daughter. Helped cultivate the spark that had flared up into such a wonderful skill. Well, it certainly wasn't down to Frank. Football, beer, and naps, that's all he'd been interested in.

Joan grunted as she pushed her way up and on to her feet. She made her way to the counter and put a pot on the stove, then poured some milk into it. She'd always liked a cup of hot milk, ever since she was a little one and her own mum had made it for her. She smiled as she watched the milk begin to bubble.

She glanced out the window. It was pitch black. Mad old woman, staying up all hours cleaning a house she'd already been over twice that day.

Joan went to lift the pan of milk off the stove when a streak of movement caught her attention.

'Ginger? Jackson? Mr. Tabby? That you, there?'

She turned to look, and as she did, something shot between her legs. Joan shrieked as the creature hit her ankle at speed, causing her to lose balance. She threw out her arms to steady herself, but it was no use. In what seemed to her like slow motion, Joan fell, twisted, to the floor.

She knew as soon as she hit down that something had broken. She felt it go. Heard it, like a rifle shot. She would have screamed out, but the pain was so sharp and sudden that it robbed her of the power to vocalise, and instead her mouth stretched wide in an anguished mute cry.

'Okay… okay…' She took a few calming breaths, then tried to move, crying out in pain. She was broken good, she wasn't going anywhere.

She wasn't going to be able to make it to the phone. Even if she wasn't as busted up as she was, she didn't have the strength to drag herself to the other side of the house for the land line, and she knew her mobile phone was all the way upstairs. No, she was going to have to stay right where she was until her daughter arrived. Maybe… maybe, when Celia found her this way, she'd decide to stay for longer. Look after her. Maybe she'd even want to keep a closer eye on her. Visit more often, or split her time between here and London to take care of her poor old mum who could no longer be trusted on her own.

Perhaps this wasn't such a terrible thing to have happened. Maybe it would even be a good thing.

Something moved at the other end of the kitchen. Joan lifted her head and squinted. A small, dark shape was sat on the floor a few feet away.

'Who is that? Ginger?' Joan knew that it wasn't. 'Oh… Charlie Boy? Charlie Boy, that you over there?' The dark shape shuffled into view, then sat looking directly at Joan.

'It is… it is you, isn't it?' The cat just looked at her, quite still and unconcerned. 'Not your fault, that's okay, you weren't to know.' Joan was surprised to see her neighbour's cat actually inside her house, sitting there, calm as you like. He was always so wary and liked to keep his distance usually, but now there he was, fearless.

'Decided to come inside at last, Charlie Boy? After a little attention, I'll bet.'

Charlie Boy stood, eyes unblinking, and padded across the floor towards her, stopping by Joan's head.

'Hey there, Charlie.' Joan didn't like the cat's eyes. Something was wrong with them. Something that made her heart flutter. 'Okay… okay… now you just go over there, Charlie. You just—'

Charlie Boy bit Joan's face.

She screamed and flapped at the hissing cat, causing it to back off, but not to run away entirely. Instead, it took back its position at the other end of the kitchen and sat staring at her with its amber eyes.

Joan touched the wound on her face, her breath quick, and felt the blood smear between her fingertips and cheek.

'Scat…! You scat, you hear me? You get out of my house!' Charlie Boy ignored her. 'This is my house, you get out of here!'

Squeak.

Three more cats entered through the cat flap. 'Ginger, Jackson, Mr. Tabby, you be careful of that bad cat! Be careful now!'

Joan's three cats sat beside Charlie Boy. Their eyes didn't look real. It looked as though someone had removed them and sewn on glass ones. Joan began to feel very frightened. She used what little strength she had to push herself as far back from the cats as she could, until she was pressed up against the larder door.

The cats stood.

'Please don't.'

As one, the cats made their unhurried approach, their glass eyes never leaving her.

'Please.'

The cats hissed as they swarmed her, needle teeth and claws flashing as they attacked again and again. Joan lifted her arms to try and protect her face from the worst of it, but they were too many.

Not my cats, not my cats, oh no! I've brought them up from newborns to act in a respectable manner.

As quickly as it had started, the attack stopped.

Joan lowered her lacerated arms, a sharp pain in her chest. The cats had their backs to her. They were looking towards the cat flap.

'Well... oh my...oh dear...'

Joan gulped down air and tried to ignore all the blood.

Squeak.

The cat flap was pushed open by a tiny hand.

'Please,' Joan begged. 'Please, I need help.'

The hand was joined by a second, then two arms slid inside, followed by a head. It was a small child, no more than two years old. Joan recognized the child; it was Ashton, her neighbour's little boy.

'Oh, Ashton! Be careful! Go get your mummy! Ashton, don't come in here! Don't!'

But the boy didn't listen. He wriggled and squirmed and breathed in hard as he struggled to make it in through the cat flap. Finally, he twisted just right, something in his body cracked, and he slithered in like a snake.

'No, Ashton! Run! Can't you see the...'

Joan stopped. Something was wrong with Ashton. She could see it in the way he held himself. Like something else was wearing an Ashton disguise. Something frightening. There was a cracking sound and two rabbit ears forced their way up and out of the child's skull.

The boy wandered over to Joan, his gait strange, disjointed.

As he reached her, he crouched low on his haunches and looked into her eyes.

'Please don't, Ashton.'

The boy stood and made his way over to the cutlery drawer. He pulled it open and retrieved a large carving knife. It looked so large in his tiny hand that it was almost comical.

The cats shuffled closer to watch.

'Please don't.'

Ashton placed a small, cold hand on Joan's right arm, holding it tight.

That's the thing with cat flaps, you see. It helps my cats get out and about, but it lets other things get inside.

Joan tried to go elsewhere as Ashton and his knife went about their business. She was dancing with Frank the night he asked her to marry him. She was holding Celia for the first time, her eyes so large and full of trusting wonder. She was in that hotel room with her old boss, just that one time, just that one mistake.

'It's okay, Ashton. It's okay. Don't you worry none. It's okay. It's okay. It's okay.'

As her head fell to one side, she saw two men in old-fashioned suits and animal masks watching. They raised their white-gloved hands and began to applaud.

9

Formby liked to think he heard all of Blackpool's stories. All of its secrets. One way or another, anything worth knowing, and a whole lot not worth knowing, found its way into his ears. Sometimes, amongst all the endless babble, one clear story rang out. This was one of those times.

The story was fear.

He was waiting in the car park behind the offices that contained, among other things, the psychiatry practice of Alison Parks. Formby knew a lot about Alison Parks. He knew she was forty-five years old and carried more weight than she was happy about. That she had grown up in Burnley, but moved to Blackpool when she was fifteen, when her parents relocated for work. He knew that she had never been married, and had no desire ever to be, although she did wish someone would actually ask her, just so she could turn them down. That way everyone else would know it was her own choice, rather than through a lack of opportunity. He knew she liked eating apples, and hated the taste of butter.

He knew all of these things and more, as he'd spent quite a bit of time over the years in her company.

He knew she was a good psychiatrist, and also a very, very bad psychiatrist.

She was a good psychiatrist because she was excellent at her job. She knew how to listen, how to make people feel heard, how to help them unburden, accept, challenge, move on. Patients would recommend Doctor Parks to their friends.

She was a very bad psychiatrist because she broke her clients' trust once a week in return for a taste of magic.

Formby looked up as the fire escape door slammed closed, and Alison Parks, in a grey pencil skirt and pink blouse, her dark blonde hair back and pinned into a bun, scurried across the car park and joined him on the wall he was sat upon.

'Morning,' said the eaves.

'Morning. Absolutely dying for a fag,' replied Alison, pulling out a pack of cigarettes, lighting one, and placing it between her red-painted lips. 'Christ, that's better,' she said, head tilted back, eyes closed, as smoke seeped lazily from her mouth and nose.

She was in the grip of more than one vice, Alison. She went through at least one pack of cigarettes a day, often more, depending on how stressed she was. She liked a drink too, usually starting with two large glasses of wine with lunch, and she kept a hip flask in her purse for the occasional pick-me-up nip between clients. More nights than she'd care to admit she would find herself falling asleep in front of the TV, having slipped into an alcohol-assisted stupor.

Then there were the painkillers. And the gambling, mostly on football. Yeah, Alison Parks had a taste for a lot of things that were bad for her, and magic was just another on the list. One that she happily ignored her hippocratic oath for.

Formby, as an eaves, liked to gather all the secrets he could, and who hears more secrets than a psychiatrist? It hadn't taken him long to sniff out Alison Parks and her compulsive bad habits. A free taste or two and she was on the hook. No, it wasn't entirely ethical on Formby's part, but since when had an eaves ever worried about ethics?

Alison Parks had her addictions and he had his: information.

'Have you stories for me?' he asked.

Alison opened her eyes and nodded her head eagerly. 'And have you got a little something-something for me?'

Eaves used magic for nourishment, and to build impossible mazes to conceal their dens, to keep themselves and their clan safe from reprisals. They do not, as a rule, hand over their hard-earned magic to others, but this was a special case. Alison was so juicy with secrets that it was worth giving away a weekly taste for all that she provided.

'I do,' replied Formby. 'Secrets for main course, magic for pudding,'

Alison licked her lips and began telling him anything and everything she remembered from the sessions since last she'd met Formby.

She told him of the man who would fish his own poo out of the toilet, seal it into little plastic bags, and then store it in a giant chest freezer in his basement.

She told him of the woman who was abused by a relative when she was young, and how, now that the relative was dead, she wished she'd been the one to send him to his early grave.

She told him of the six-year-old girl whose parents had found her more than once holding a pillow over their newborn child.

Most of all, she told him about the nightmares.

Over the last week, more and more of her patients had been enduring terrible nightmares, and some of them claimed they had not been asleep when they were experiencing them. That they had been suffering a sort of waking nightmare, their unconscious mind bleeding into their waking hours.

There was the woman who claimed, after a date, to have seen her dead little sister. Actually, to have seen numerous copies of her dead sister, floating out at sea.

There was the little boy who believed that a ghost pretending to be his dad, only with a headful of birds, was visiting him at night.

More and more patients pushing aside their normal litany of worries and fears to talk about nightmares—daymares—and, more often than not, about a pair of men in old dusty suits and tatty animal masks.

There was a lot to take in, and Formby took it all.

Rita grabbed a packet of crisps from behind the bar at Big Pins then poured herself an orange juice. Yawning, she shambled her way across the room to the table where Waterson was sat.

'Morning, Waters, still dead?'

'Afternoon, Rita, still an annoying old tart?'

'You know it, brother.'

Waterson smiled and watched as Rita began her cheese and onion crisp breakfast-slash-lunch. He really, really wanted to taste food again. Taste anything, really. He'd contemplated trying the trick the Angel had made him do. Jumping into living people's bodies and trying to control them, just so he could pop down to a cafe and gorge on a giant, greasy full English Breakfast, washed down with numerous cups of tea. His sense of right and wrong wouldn't let him do it though. It didn't matter that, if it worked, he wouldn't be hurting the person he briefly inhabited, he was still making them do something against their will. Taking ownership of their body, their life.

Maybe if he found someone willing to let him hop inside for a while, though…

He wondered if he could find someone who might agree to that. Then that would be all fine, right?

'What's with the face?' asked Rita, noticing the ruminative expression weighing heavy upon Waterson.

'Just, you know, thinking.'

'Right. It'll give you wrinkles, that.'

'I think I might be a little past wrinkles, but thanks for the concern.'

'Good point, one of the perks of being dead.'

'Oh, one of many.'

'So what did you get up to last night?' Rita asked.

'Just a little bit of slowly going insane, wandering the streets on my own for hours, wishing I could go to sleep for even a quick half hour to numb the relentless horror of constant awareness.'

'Oh, nice. As long as you're keeping yourself busy.'

Waterson sighed, then laughed, and shook his head.

'The Angel of Blackpool paid me a visit last night,' said Rita, matter-of-factly.

'What?' replied Waterson. 'Is It out? How did It get out of the prison?'

'It didn't, I don't think. Not properly. It just came to speak to me in a dream.'

'...Okay.'

Rita gave Waterson the same middle finger she'd offered up to the Angel.

'Classy,' said Waterson.

'Look, I dunno how It did it, or how, or, you know, whatever. But It did.'

'Fine. Why then?'

'It wanted me to release Jenner.'

'Well, sure.' Waterson frowned and sat back, shaking his head. 'So it just came to you and asked?'

'Yup,' replied Rita, taking a sip from her orange juice.

'So this bastard, evil Angel just popped into your dream to politely request that you release the crazy person who is in Its control, murdering women, and who, by the way, also murdered me?'

'That's the long and short of it, yeah. Weird, right?'

'Very weird, yes. Did It think you were just going to say, *"Oh, all right then, if you like,"* and that would be that?'

'They do say God moves in mysterious ways. Maybe Angels do, too.'

'Most of what you do has always mystified me, and you claim to be part angel, so that sounds about right.'

Rita laughed and waved at Ben Turner, emerging bleary eyed from the steps that lead down to the basement where he slept. He ignored her.

'What's up with wolf boy?' asked Waterson.

'Hey! Don't call him that.'

'All right, you touchy bitch.'

The entrance to Big Pins opened and Formby shuffled in.

'It's like that man has a radar for when people are eating,' said Rita.

Formby hustled over and sat at the table, hands fretting, not once attempting to grab any of Rita's crisps.

'Spill it, Formby,' said Rita. 'What have you got?'

'Death. Bad dreams and death.'

Rita and Waterson looked down at the kitchen floor where Joan Barnett had been found dead. There was blood where the body had been removed, and forensics officers were slowly going about their hunt for clues, unaware of the ghostly man and the hexed woman who had joined them.

Rita crouched down to get a closer look at a drawing of a pair of rabbit ears that had been finger-painted on a cupboard door in blood.

'It was definitely them,' she said. 'Has to be. Can't be any doubt now.'

Formby had told them all the things Alison Parks had told him, about her clients bad dreams. The bad dreams that were happening even while they were awake. Of the many sightings of scary men in animal masks. And then he'd told them about this. An elderly woman found dead by her visiting daughter.

'We already knew it was them,' said Waterson as Rita stood back up.

'We assumed so, but now we know for sure. And this is a step up in their activity. They've been scaring people, but now it looks like they've moved on to killing, too.'

She knew Cotton and Spike fed on fear, and when would the fear be sweeter than when a person knew for sure they were dying?

'A lot more people are going to end up dead if we don't get our arses in gear,' she said.

'So what do we do now exactly? We're on the back foot as far as I can see.'

Rita walked out of Joan's kitchen, out of her house, wishing she didn't feel quite so powerless.

Alison could still feel the magic in her system. The soothing warmth that made her brain gently crackle with pleasure.

She wished Formby would visit her more than once a week, but he said he didn't want to give up more than one taste every seven days; that it would be irresponsible. He just wanted to keep all the good shit for himself, that's what Alison thought. Well maybe she'd find another of the, well, whatever it was he was. There must be more of them. Little, ugly, pointy-eared people with sharp teeth and bad breath. She knew he had a family nearby, or a "clan" as he called it. Just as he'd snaffled up information from her, she'd made sure to coax the odd thing out of him. If he wouldn't supply the amount of magic she wanted, then she'd find someone in his clan who would.

'You've been telling tales on us,' said a man Alison had not realised had entered her office.

She sat up, shaking herself out of her thoughts, out of her beautiful, numbing stupor. It was work time. Who was it she was supposed to be seeing next?

'Uh, sorry, away with the fairies there,' she said, then looked for the first time at the man stretched out on the couch in front of her. He wore an old-fashioned brown suit with a waistcoat and pocket watch, his hands in dirty white gloves resting upon his chest. On his head he wore a decaying rabbit mask.

'My brother and I do not mind, you understand. We are not trying to hide ourselves away from the detective, are we, brother mine?'

A grunt from behind caused Alison to turn and find a man in an identical outfit, only wearing a hedgehog mask.

'Who are you? What's going on?' she said, worry starting to worm its way past the soothing effects of the magic.

'We're much too strong for her to do anything about, thanks to the effect of our Angel friend, but still. Nobody likes a tattle-tale, Doctor.'

The man in the rabbit mask swung his legs around and slowly rose to his feet.

'I said, who are you?' She reached for the phone on her desk but a gloved hand slammed down against hers and pinned it to the desk.

'I believe you know who we are, Doctor. I am Mr. Cotton, and the man causing your wrist some amount of discomfort is my fine, fearsome brother, Mr. Spike.'

Alison was shaking. 'No, that's not… those were just…'

'Your clients' nightmares? Yes, that is us.'

It was impossible. Some sort of shared psychosis. It was rare, but it happened; whole communities experiencing the same delusion.

'I'm afraid we must punish you now,' said Mr. Cotton. 'Loose lips sink ships, after all.'

'I didn't say anything!'

'Oh, I'm afraid you said everything, you little piggy. And now, I do believe my brother would like to show you his face.'

Mr. Cotton gestured to Mr. Spike and bowed. Alison could hear Mr. Spike's excited breathing as he began to tease off his mask.

Alison Parks' next client was a young boy. His name was Liam, and he sat in the waiting room alongside his mum and dad. His parents were worried about their boy's increasingly strange behaviour, not least of which was a recent incident that involved him going missing in the middle of the night, only for Dad to find him walking home in his pyjamas, barefoot.

When Alison's receptionist tried and failed to raise her on the phone, she knocked on the door instead. 'Hello? Doctor Parks? Your two o'clock is here. Doctor Parks?'

The receptionist opened the door, Liam and his parents stood just behind her. Inside the office they found Alison Parks, her body splayed out on the floor, eyes wide and terrified, a hair band with rabbit ears atop her head.

Liam stared at the dead body as the receptionist screamed.

10

Reality was a spooked cat trying to wriggle free of Carlisle's desperate grip and dart off into the bushes.

'Stop squirming,' said Carlisle, as though the universe would nod its head and settle into his arms for a nap.

The boy on the beach had been an anchor point, something that Carlisle had been able to latch onto to prevent his form drifting apart, but that did not mean what happened next would be easy.

He needed an ally. Someone he could trust who could help him escape from Cotton and Spike's clutches. This presented some issues. Carlisle was not the sort of person who had nurtured warm relationships over his long life. There was, to be blunt, no one with the ability to help him who would do so out of the kindness of their own heart. Why help a fiend like Carlisle twist free of his trap only to put their own ankle in its rusty jaws?

This forced Carlisle to do something he preferred to avoid wherever possible; to make a promise. A promise to help whoever helped him in whatever manner they pleased. It put him in a weak position, and Carlisle hated to be in a weak position. To be in someone's debt. Then again, Carlisle also hated being in an about-to-be-very-deceased position, so a promise would be made.

First things first though. Although the boy had anchored

Carlisle to some extent, had stopped his violent spiral towards the mountainside, he was still not practiced in the art of astral travel. He could not walk, or fly, or catch a bus to his desired location. There was a knack to it, to moving from one place to another, and it was a knack that seemed to change with each new attempt.

Carlisle's first thought had been Giles L'Merrier, the mighty wizard and master of the dark arts, who currently lurked within his antiques shop in Soho, London. But chances were that L'Merrier would not lift a finger to help him, even if he offered up a thousand promises. L'Merrier was the very definition of mercurial, and was as likely to delight in Carlisle's comeuppance as he was to assist his release. Carlisle was glad that his actual stomach was elsewhere, otherwise it would be clenching painfully as he pictured the smug look spreading across L'Merrier's face as he told him of his situation.

Perhaps it was lucky then that, not having mastered the knack, Carlisle found himself not within L'Merrier's shop of Uncanny antiquities, and instead sat in a booth at London's Beehive Pub, a bar for Uncanny types, sat opposite a ghost that he did not recognise.

'You are not Giles L'Merrier,' said Carlisle. His words sounded muffled, like they were coming from behind a closed door.

The ghost, handsome, dressed in a slightly dishevelled black suit, blinked and rubbed his eyes. 'Where did you come from, mate?' he asked, squinting at the vague approximation of a man that had appeared at his table.

'Who are you?' asked Carlisle.

The ghost scratched the bristles on his chin. 'Name's Jake Fletcher, what's it to you?'

'You are dead,' said Carlisle.

'Oh, is that what happened? I wondered why I didn't get any Happy Birthday messages this year.'

Carlisle didn't smile at the ghost's witticism. Instead, he concentrated on remaining where he was as the material plane did its best to reject his astral form.

'How did you come a cropper then?' the ghost asked.

'I'm not dead,' replied Carlisle. 'Not yet anyway.'

'You sure? You look proper ghosty to me. And pale. You're paler than an Irish shut-in's rear end, mate.'

Carlisle wished very much that his physical form were with him so he could reach over and squeeze this person's soul until his eyes bulged.

'I need help,' said Carlisle. Perhaps the astral realm had somehow read his needs and delivered him to a person able to assist him.

'That right?' said the ghost. 'Well, you're in luck, pal, you've found the Spectral Detective. So what do you need doing?'

'I require—'

'How do you like Spectral Detective, by the way?'

'What?'

'Spectral Detective. Trying to brand myself. It's all about branding these days.'

'Please stop.'

'I thought *Ghost Detective* at first, straight to the point, no messing around, but Spectral Detective has a little extra oomph to it, am I right? A little more poetry, maybe. Less on the nose.'

'Please.'

'*Dead Detective*, that was the next one. My mate Jazz Hands offered that up. I liked the alliteration, but it sounded a bit morbid to me. A bit defeatist.'

'Forget it,' said Carlisle. 'I don't care how dire my situation is, nothing is worth this torment.'

Spectral Detective Jake Fletcher blinked, and the pale stranger was gone. 'Rude,' he muttered, then licked his lips and gestured to the landlord for a fresh pint.

Carlisle's world was shifting colour and sounds again: disparate places, smashed together, piled high, overlapping impossibly. He hadn't intended to leave the ghost quite so swiftly —perhaps he could have helped in some small way—but Carlisle's astral form refused to linger any longer, and he found the phantom too aggravating to fight the irresistible pull.

Carlisle reached out again. Concentrated on a person and imagined arriving wherever they might be. He knew of an angel named Vizael who might be able to lend a hand. Carlisle had never had any direct dealings with the angel—and by all accounts he was not just ancient but beginning to lose his marbles—but an angel was an angel.

He pictured the old man and reached out, the astral winds shoving him this way and that. He opened his eyes. He was sat on the slope of a hill covered in blood red grass. He had arrived in the wrong place once again. Carlisle sighed and looked up at the sky, which swam with rolling waves of fire. He had passed into a new realm, attached to but not part of the everyday.

'The Dark Lakes,' he sighed.

Carlisle had never been to the Dark Lakes, but he recognised the place from the Uncanny texts he had read over the centuries. It was a realm that housed an army of the dead awaiting a beast known as the Magic Eater to lead them into battle. Or so the story went. Carlisle was not sure how much of that he believed himself. People were prone to exaggeration in the name of a good yarn.

'All true,' said a small voice at Carlisle's side. He looked down to see a short figure had joined him on the red hill's slope. It was a fox, stood upon its hind legs like a person. A Roman helmet was perched on its head, and in one paw it gripped a small axe.

'I do not appreciate my thoughts being read, fox,' said Carlisle.

'Oh, weren't you speaking out loud? Or in my little head?' said the fox, tapping his helmet with the hilt of his axe. 'I cannot read minds, not me. I am just a humble fox. But I know the Dark Lakes and I know the Magic Eater, too. The Red Woman rules this land and desires his hand.'

'Well, that is fascinating, but I am not here to learn the local history.'

'Why then?'

'I require help.'

'I help. I help a lot, ask Joseph.'

'I do not know who that is.'

'I do. I know what his face looks like and everything.'

Carlisle longed to lift the fox and kick it so hard it would sail up and into the sky of fire.

'I am trapped,' he said, 'beyond the reach of most, at the mercy of things born from the nightmare realm.'

'Oh,' replied the fox. 'Not nice.'

'No. I seem to have found myself here, which means, I hope, that perhaps you might be of some assistance. In return I will give you a promise, to use when and as you please.'

'Ooh, that is a pretty price indeed,' replied the fox, grinning, its little sharp teeth gleaming.

'So, can you assist me or not?'

'Maybe. Might be able to. I know people and things and hidden stuff, too.'

'Then take me to someone who can help and the promise is yours.'

'No need to offer a promise, I'm a good fox.' He grinned again and then began making his way down the hill towards the black lake that sat at the bottom. Carlisle followed.

'Where are we going and who shall we meet there, fox?'

The fox waved Carlisle forward with his axe, his white-tipped, red bushy tail bobbing along behind him. 'Follow me, see-through person, I know where the Yellow Man rests.'

Carlisle stopped for a moment. 'The demon?'

'Big demon. Very big and bad. I know lots of people, you see, some are bad but they can still help if the price is fair.'

'I understood the Yellow Man had fallen.'

The fox snorted. 'Nothing so old can be wiped away for long. Specially not a high demon like him.'

They reached the edge of the lake and the fox pointed at the water.

'There is no boat,' said Carlisle.

'Need to walk in. Get wet. *Get wet and count to five, and the Yellow Man shall arrive.*'

'Thank you, fox.'

The fox grinned and walked away, whistling.

Carlisle looked out at the lake, then began to drift into the water. He could not feel the cool of the water, and it did not cling to him, making him damp, as there was nothing to make wet. He moved forward, eyes closed, and counted out loud, '1-2-3-4-5.'

He opened his eyes.

He was no longer stood in the water, and he was sure he was also no longer in the Dark Lakes. He was in another realm altogether. At first it was dark, so Carlisle was patient, allowed his eyes to adjust. Gradually, his surroundings began to fade into view. He was in a cave. Thick tree roots snaked their way down from above, clinging to the damp walls. The ground was wet. He crouched to look closer and found that the cave had an inch-thick carpet of blood. He wondered if that was what the tree was feeding upon.

He moved forward, his astral form passing above the blood, drifting deeper into the dark.

The Yellow Man was waiting for him.

'Here at last? The cave told me you'd turn up one of these days, Carlisle.'

He was, as his name suggested, yellow-skinned. From toe to hair, he looked as though he had been fashioned from gold. Two entirely black eyes watched Carlisle, an easy smile upon his face. From the top of his head, two large antlers twisted. He was naked and draped over a throne that appeared to be alive. Pieces of flesh, of bone, sewn together. It twitched beneath him, emitting dull cries of pain.

'That does not look very comfortable.'

The Yellow Man laughed. 'The pain of others is always comforting,' he replied with a voice as smooth as velvet. Carlisle was already wondering if this visit had been the best of ideas. That was the last time he'd take advice from a fox.

'Oh, he's a good fox,' said the Yellow Man, 'and he has brought you to somebody who can indeed help you squirm free of your situation.'

'You can?'

'I am the Yellow Man. A high demon. I have met the Beast and tamed it.'

'For a while,' replied Carlisle.

The cave grew darker, just for a moment, as the Yellow Man's face twisted into a snarl. As quickly as it appeared, it was gone, and the easy smile was back. 'You know, I'm quite the fan of Mr. Cotton and Mr. Spike's work. They do fashion such delightful nightmares.'

'Yes, a great couple of lads,' replied Carlisle. 'Why would you help me?'

'I have heard your offer. It is very attractive.'

'What would a high demon need of a promise from me?'

The Yellow Man clicked his fingers, his throne of pain thrashing in fear beneath him. Hands began to reach out of the cave walls, each of them clutching a jar with a screw-top lid. Inside each jar—and there were hundreds of them—was a swirl of light.

'You want me to promise you my soul?' asked Carlisle.

'By jove, I think he's got it! It really would be a treat to add you to my collection. Oh, the other demons would be green with envy. Apart from those that are already green, of course. I wonder what colour *they* would turn?'

'So you help me and I spend eternity in a jar? A tempting offer.'

'I would let you out from time to time. You are special, I would have other uses for you. You are not like these ordinary souls. You are a thing of the dark, like me.'

'I am not evil. Well, as such.'

'You are on our side.'

'I prefer not to join teams.'

The Yellow Man inspected his cuticles. 'Make your choice, Carlisle. You can accept my help or you can die.'

Carlisle began to back away. 'I believe I shall explore alternatives.'

'Oh, there are none. I'll be seeing you very soon.'

The Yellow Man clapped his hands together and the cave was torn from view, sending Carlisle spinning into a whirl of nothing.

11

Alison Parks' corpse lay naked on an autopsy table in Blackpool Hospital's morgue.

Rita frowned. It had only been a few hours since Formby passed on information from Alison about the web of nightmares Cotton and Spike were weaving across Blackpool, and now here she was, dead. The idea that it could be a coincidence was difficult to swallow. Now, as she and Waterson looked down on her dead body, it was clear it was not.

Alison's eyes were wide and terrified. Red tracks trailed down from them and across her cheeks; tears of blood. Rita had tried to close Alison's eyes, but they sprang back open each time. Her jaw hung wide, unhinged in a silent scream. A piece of glass had been used to carve a rabbit into her chest.

Whenever Rita found herself stood beside a dead body—which, due to her chosen profession, was often—she would flash back to her first. His name was Gavin Dylan. There had been many since him, some murder victims, some suicides, some accidents. As the deaths piled up the names and faces had drifted further and further from reach, but not Gavin Dylan's. He had been found abandoned in an alleyway.

He'd been rake thin, mid-length, dark brown hair that stuck slick to his head and face. He wore a pair of faded jeans that were too big for him, a Metallica hoodie swamping his top half. His eyes had been half-open, and he'd almost bitten his own tongue in half. His neck had been slashed three times.

He was the first murder victim Rita had been assigned to, and she had never found the person responsible. Ever since that day, she made sure she remembered Gavin Dylan and how she'd failed him. It kept the fire in her alive, pushed her on to make sure she would never let any other victim down. Never again.

'How do we find them?' asked Waterson, a hard edge to his voice. 'Cotton and Spike.'

Joan Barnett and now Alison Parks; two deaths in quick succession. Rita knew in her gut that it was just the start. Every day that passed with Cotton and Spike out in the wild would lead to more bodies. They weren't content with giving people sleepless nights anymore, they wanted to push people until their bodies gave out in fright.

'I don't know,' replied Rita, trying to push Gavin Dylan aside.

'Perhaps they shall find you,' said Alison Parks.

Rita and Waterson lurched back as Alison sat up and turned her head to look at them, her hands toying with the bunny-shaped wound in her chest.

Rita pulled the axe from her belt and gripped it in both hands. 'Get out of her!'

'She wanted to scream, you know,' said Alison. 'We would not let her. As my brother showed her his true face, she opened her mouth wide and wide and wide, and yet nothing came out. I took each scream when it was still deep in her throat and I claimed them as my own. I placed them between my teeth and chewed and swallowed, and now her screams live in my stomach. Yummy.'

'Use your bloody axe and burn that thing up!' cried Waterson.

Rita wanted to, her body was willing her to. She could feel the magic surging into the axe-head, begging to be used, but if she did what she had done at Waterson's funeral they'd still be no closer to trapping Cotton and Spike. They'd slip away again and she'd have learned nothing.

'Why don't you stop hiding and face me properly?' said Rita. 'Or are you too chicken shit after I kicked your dusty arses last time?'

The body of Alison Parks stepped off of the autopsy table. She plucked a scalpel from a nearby trolley and slashed at the flesh of her belly. Then again.

'Jesus,' said Waterson, as blood began to flood from each fresh wound. Each new cut brought a new waterfall of red, an unnatural amount of blood, washing down her body, flooding the tiled floor as she shuffled forwards.

'Are you afraid?' asked Alison Parks.

'Fuck you,' replied Rita.

Waterson wasn't quite sure what happened next. He certainly did not remember them concluding their business at the morgue. One moment he had been backing away as the possessed, self-harming corpse of a psychiatrist walked towards them, and then...

...well...

...then what?

He looked around.

He was in his mother's house.

The one she'd lived in for the last fifteen years, ever since his dad had passed away. They'd had a large, four-bedroom detached place when he was growing up. Two whole spare bedrooms. One his dad used as a study, the other he had been allowed to use as he pleased. He'd been sad when she sold the house.

'It's just me rattling around in there on my own. It's too big for me.'

And there was the unspoken truth. The house was haunted. Not by spirits, but by memories. Every room, every corridor, every nook and cranny held a thousand different memories. A step creaking on the stairs could throw her back to a different time. Some find that sort of thing comforting at that stage of life, he knew it caused his mum nothing put pain. It was just a brick box reminding her of what she had lost and what could never be again.

So she sold it, downsized, enjoyed the extra money she made

in the sale. Even started going on little holidays by herself, something he never thought she'd have the nerve to do.

Wait, wasn't he just in the morgue? He'd got lost in memories there for a moment, forgotten that something was up. Something was wrong.

'Hello, Daniel.'

He turned to see his mother. She was dressed like she had been at his funeral: black dress, red heels.

'Mum, you can see me?' Waterson's heart beat hard in his chest, but he was dead and had no heart to beat. What was going on?

'Thought I'd seen the last of you,' she said, dismissively.

'I'm sorry. I'm so sorry.'

'All I ever wanted was to be alone. I was glad of it, when your dad finally popped his clogs. I'd been fattening him up for years, praying for that pig's heart to finally give up the ghost.'

'You loved Dad.'

'Puh. Then there was you. You were his idea, you know. Never forgave the pig for that. I never wanted no brat.'

'Stop it.'

'Every moment you were inside me, growing. A tumour I couldn't get ripped out. Every time you moved in my womb I thought I was going to be sick.'

Had his mum always had rabbit ears?

'Shut up. Just shut up, that's not true!'

'Listen to you, wailing and stamping your feet. Just like when you were little. Needy little waste of skin. Well, you're dead now, too, thank the Lord. Look, I bought new shoes specially, do you like them? Red, like the blood that magician made you spill when he stuck you like a pig. You're a pig, your dad a pig; a pair of piggy bastards.'

Waterson couldn't take it anymore. He ran from his mum, from the house.

Rita wasn't sure what had happened.

She was in a corridor and it was dark, too dark to make out much in the way of detail, but detail wasn't needed. She knew where she was. She felt it on her skin, she smelled it in the air.

Moorsgate Children's Home.

The building she'd called home as a kid.

'But that's..'

Impossible.

It was impossible.

Moorsgate burned to the ground when she was just fourteen years old. She'd seen it happen. No, no, she'd *made* it happen. It was being fumigated and all the kids and the staff were being housed in local bed and breakfasts, and that's when she'd taken her chance. A box of matches, a couple of cans of paint thinner. She knew which window had the latch and could easily be forced. They never fixed stuff like that at Moorsgate. It wasn't a place where things got fixed, it was a place things were allowed to break down and degrade.

In she'd wriggled, falling the metre to the hard, wooden floor below.

She'd been listening to her Walkman, to a tape she stole from Woolworth's a week before. A Madonna best of. As she bopped to *Borderline,* to *Vogue,* to *Holiday,* she splashed the thinner around, singing and laughing and *alive.*

You needed a key to get in the front door, but not out. She'd opened the door and stood, looking into the guts of the building she hated, one last time. Then she lit the match and the building went up, the flames as eager as Rita to scrub the place from the face of the Earth. She watched for a few seconds while Madonna implored her to express herself, and then she turned and ran—ran faster than she'd ever thought possible—as though she'd cast off a rucksack full of rocks.

It was gone.

Demolished after the firemen had finally put out the flames.

And now she was stood in its corridors again.

'Nice try, boys, but you have to get up early in the morning to pull the wool over this bitch's eyes.'

Rita passed the axe from hand to hand, strolling down the corridor, taking in each bit of the dreamscape recreation.

'I know your dirty tricks, remember? You think I'm gonna what? Fall to my knees and cry or something? Fat chance, big ears.'

She turned the corridor to find Alison Parks' dead, naked body stood waiting for her. Alison raised a hand and waved. 'Hello Rita. Remember when you wet your bed with tears and piss and you felt so alone and wretched and unwanted? It was just in that room there, wasn't it?'

Rita did remember. It had happened on more than one occasion. Ms. Winters had heard her muffled sobs as she passed by. She'd poked her head into the room and told her to keep it down. *'Don't be such a big baby,'* she'd said. The first few times she'd wet the bed, Ms. Winters had smacked her legs with the back of her hand. After that, it was the belt. She hadn't let on after that. She would just get up early, strip the bed, and wash it in the sink.

'I had a giant turd of a childhood,' said Rita, feigning a yawn. 'You've got me. I feel terrible. Can we move on?'

The door to what had been her bedroom opened and Ms. Winters stepped out. She wore a thick-knitted jumper, a pair of black jeans, her dark hair severely short.

'Hobbes, who said you could go wandering the corridors after lights out?'

Despite herself, Rita felt her heart rate quicken, her hands shake.

'There it is,' said Alison Parks, stroking her long, rabbit ears.

'Answer me!' demanded Ms. Winters. 'Well, did someone steal your tongue, you wretched little monster?' Rita saw she was holding a belt. It was doubled over and Ms. Winters' hands squeezed it, knuckles white.

'Mm,' said Alison Parks, 'that really is very moreish.'

'Oh, fuck you to the moon and back,' replied Rita, then stepped forward and swung the axe, embedding its blade in Ms. Winters' skull.

'No television for you for a month,' slurred Ms. Winters, one half of her face hanging slack.

Rita could feel what Ms. Winters was made of. She wasn't real, of course. She was a toy, fashioned by a master.

'Piss off,' said Rita. 'And by the way, everyone talks about how rank your breath is behind your back.'

The simulation of Ms. Winters existed just long enough for surprise to register on her face before Rita told the dream magic to turn her into something more pleasing. Ms. Winters broke apart, became a cloud of butterflies, and fluttered off into the dark.

'That all you got, Bugs Bunny?'

Alison Parks lifted the scalpel and dragged it down her forehead, face, neck, chest, stomach, crotch. She peeled herself open and Mr. Cotton, his old suit and tatty rabbit mask coated with gore, stepped out of her. The remains of Alison Parks crumpled to the floor behind him, a boneless sack of skin.

The rabbit mask grinned at Rita, though of course it did not as it was just a mask.

Waterson had not experienced the nightmare magic of Cotton and Spike first-hand before, but after running from his mum's house and pulling himself a little more together, he put two and two together and grew very cross indeed.

How dare they do that to him? To make his mum say those things, even if it had just been an empty, pretend version of her.

'Okay, you tricked me, congratulations. You spooked a ghost.'

Rasping breath. Waterson whirled round, but he was alone on the street. Houses with their lights outs, curtains closed, pressed in at him. Were they getting closer? The road narrower?

Rasping, damp, rancid breath in his ear.

He turned again, but he was still alone.

'Okay, who is that? I know this is just a waking dream thing, so you might as well come out.'

One of the doors opened and a man in an old suit and a hedgehog mask stepped out. Waterson had seen neither of the men, of the *things*, he and Rita were after, but he'd heard enough to recognise who had joined him.

'You must be Mr. Spike. The one who doesn't talk.'

Another door on another house opened, and a second Mr. Spike stepped out.

'Okay. Nice trick. You should play Vegas.'

A third door, a third Mr. Spike.

'I might just be off then,' said Waterson. 'Places to be.' He began to hustle his way down the street as more and more doors opened, and Mr. Spike after Mr. Spike stepped out to stare at him with the empty, glass eyes of his mask. It was, to put it mildly, really putting the willies up Detective Dan Waterson.

He realised he was no longer just walking fast but sprinting. He was desperate to get off that street, but the damn thing seemed to be never-ending. An infinite stretch of opening doors and Mr. Spikes.

He was dead, what did he have to be afraid of? He couldn't die again. Or could he? Could the dead die? He didn't really want to find out.

He was dead! Why on earth was he running? He could just think of a place he knew and he'd zap right over there and away.

'Big Pins!' He closed his eyes.

'Yes, the dead can die,' said Waterson's mum.

'Shit it!' replied Waterson as he ran from his mum's house to find a street full of Mr. Spikes waiting to greet him from an endless expanse of doorways. He turned back and made his way through the house, past Not Mum.

'Such an ugly baby. It was all I could do not to drown you every bath time.'

Waterson ran through the kitchen and to the back door. He threw it open, raced through the backyard and over the wall to the alleyway that ran on that side of the street.

As his feet hit down on the cobbles he straightened up to find himself stood not behind, but in front of his mum's house again, the endless Mr. Spikes looking back at him, waving their white-gloved hands.

'Oh, come on!' said Dan Waterson, wondering if things could possibly get any worse.

The endless Mr. Spikes began screaming and sprinting towards him.

Things could always get worse.

Rita was sat in the orphanage canteen at one of the long, wooden tables that all the kids had sat at, breakfast, dinner, and tea. She was spooning a bowl of rice pudding into her mouth.

'I always hated rice pudding,' she said.

'This is a nightmare,' replied Mr. Cotton, who was sat opposite her, his mask and clothing still dark with Alison Parks' blood, his stained white-gloved fingers fanned out on the table top before him.

'So, I didn't finish you and your brother off, then?' she asked, adding a spoonful of strawberry jam to the pudding and swirling it around.

'Finish us off? That is not possible. You can stomp on us, cut us, burn us, and we shall return, given time. Wherever a child quivers beneath their bed covers, we shall be reborn.'

'Well, bully for you. Where is your brother, by the way? Is that mute little prick going to jump out at me at any moment? Sneak up behind me with a balloon and a pin?'

'Brother mine is currently occupied elsewhere, terrorising a ghost.'

Rita frowned. So Waters was in a nightmare of his own.

'You can't have thought this would really fool me,' she said. 'I've tasted your magic, I've used it, made it my own.'

Mr. Cotton opened his mouth and a spider with legs as thick as pipe cleaners scuttled out.

'Gross, stop that,' said Rita.

Mr. Cotton picked the spider from his mask and crushed it in one hand before swiping the small, squished thing aside. 'Please, continue,' he said.

'What's your game then? What do you and the Angel have in mind?'

'Angel? We are not Its worker bees. We do as we please, and fear is what we please.'

Okay, so the Angel wasn't involved. Cotton and Spike were

flying solo. Was that true? Should she trust the word of a nightmare monster?

'Do you know where Carlisle is?'

Mr. Cotton nodded once.

'Is he dead?'

'Hard to say. Perhaps, perhaps not, you things of bone and meat do die so easily. So deliciously.'

'Are you going to try and kill me?'

Mr. Cotton's mask smiled. 'All good things come to those who wait.'

Rita finished the rice pudding and dropped the spoon into the bowl as she stood. 'Okay, I'm bored now. Time to kick seven shades of shit out of you.'

She raised the axe and swung it at Mr. Cotton's head. He did not attempt to get out of the way. Instead, he let the axe pass through him, his head drifting apart like smoke before reforming into that same masked face.

'Strike one,' he said, and the rabbit mask wriggled its nose.

'This one is going to sting,' she replied, kneeling and slamming the butt of the axe against the floorboards. She could feel the dream magic, the nightmare magic, all around her. She willed it into the axe and it obeyed. The colours, dark, corrosive, washed around her mind, scraping their nails across her thoughts as she reshaped it, unleashed it with a war cry.

Flames erupted out of her at all angles, swamping the orphanage, devouring Mr. Cotton. He sat calmly and waved as the dream construct surrounding him was reduced to ash. 'You cannot harm us anymore, Rita Hobbes. But the damage we shall do to you…'

When the spell was finished, Rita stood and looked around at what she had done. 'That's the second time I've burned this shit hole down. I'm not going to lie, it felt just as good as the first.'

Waterson was running in circles. Through his mum's house, through the backyard, over the wall and then emerging impossibly at the front of the house again. Round and round again, the endless, screaming Mr. Spikes so close at his heels that he could feel their noisy, damp breath caressing the hairs on the back of his neck.

He tried again and again to jump anywhere but the street he found himself running loops through, but it seemed as though the parameters of the nightmare he'd been shoved into wouldn't let him free of it.

'You got your ugly dad's fat face, too.'

'Fuck off, Mum!' he cried as he rushed by once again.

As he burst into the backyard for what must have been the fiftieth time, he became aware that he no longer heard the pack of Mr. Spikes in pursuit. He stopped at the yard's wall and turned. A single Mr. Spike peered at him through the kitchen window.

'What's the matter?' asked Waterson. 'Tired out from all the running? I ran three different marathons when I wasn't dead, you were always on to a loser, mate.'

Mr. Spike reached up and began to remove his hedgehog mask. Waterson was pretty certain that the last thing he should do was see what lurked beneath that rotting mask.

He turned back to the wall, only now the wall was a hundred Mr. Spikes', all slowly removing their masks.

'Shit. Shit!'

Everything was that same mask. The world was the sound of Mr. Spike's rasping breath. Wherever he turned, the mask's glass eyes looked back, his own horrified face reflected back at him. A pair of white gloves inched it up and up and—

An axe erupted out of one of Mr. Spike's masks, cleaving it in two.

'What?' said Waterson, more or less reaching the end of his tether. He crouched and looked through the gap that had been created, to see a familiar face looking back.

'Come on then, idiot,' said Rita, waving Waterson forward from beyond the split in Mr. Spike.

'You know that looks really, really weird.'

'Shift it!'

Waterson ran forward and jumped through the gap in reality as Mr. Spike's teeth chattered in frustration.

12

Ben Turner sat on his bed in Big Pin's basement and tried not to think about what he'd seen in the toilets.

Tried not to think about Magda, the woman who'd bitten him, turned him monstrous, appearing there and speaking to him.

He clenched his hands together to try and stop them shaking.

He knew she hadn't really been there. Of course he knew that, she was dead. Very, very dead. Thanks to meeting Dan Waterson, he'd been made aware that ghosts were a thing, but that hadn't been Magda's ghost. For one thing, her soul had been claimed by a demon (and it was vaguely worrying how readily he accepted that. Souls, demons, no big deal. His entire world had expanded in an instant).

So Magda was gone. Properly gone, soul and all. He knew it hadn't really been her, back to turn him once again. Back to make him her hungry, faithful hound. No, this was nothing but a waking nightmare. Part of Rita's investigation, something to do with those masked dream monsters. A nasty trick meant to terrify him.

Well, it had bloody well worked. A-Plus results to the mask-wearing bastards.

Okay, it was nothing but a trick. Cool. He understood that. The thing was, Ben really needed to go to the toilet, and was now afraid to go by himself. Which was crazy. He'd been alternatively sat on his bed and pacing his room for the last hour, trying to work up the courage to just walk upstairs, cross the bar, and head into the toilets.

He eyed the empty plastic bottle on the floor again.

No, he wasn't going to pee in a bottle, that was daft.

Before he could talk himself out of it, he stood and left the basement, feet heavy and unwilling. Upstairs, Linton was giving a man with horns a pair of bowling shoes.

Ben's heart was beating way too fast.

'Get it together, you tit,' he mumbled to himself.

He placed his hand against the door to the Gents, took a breath or two, then pushed his way inside.

The toilets were empty: a urinal, a couple of sit-down stalls, the sinks. He didn't like the way he looked in the mirror, wide-eyed and pale-faced. Ben hustled over to the urinal, unzipped, pulled out, and sighed in relief as he had one of the longest pees of his life.

Satisfaction washed over him, the fear that the nightmare might repeat itself fading now as the pain in his bladder abated.

So of course, after washing his hands, he passed the stalls on his way to the exit to see Magda standing inside one, waving.

Carlisle was struggling to find his way home. To find his way back to his body.

Who knew how much damage had been suffered, to his muscles, to his mind. Not to mention the things that hunted for empty bodies. Had the almost things sniffed him out yet? He hadn't meant to be apart from himself for so long, but it was difficult to judge the passing of time when in an astral form. All he knew was, he felt deeply that he'd been away for longer than he should have.

It had been a waste of time. He'd found no one who could help. His only option now was to get back into his body, to try and regain a little strength, then jump out and have another go. That was if Cotton and Spike didn't murder him before he was able to try for a second time.

'Find me,' he said. A mantra. A rope to hold on to as the raging waves and winds of sights and sounds battered against him. Tried to send him tumbling into the jaws of nothingness.

'Find me.'

The rope tugged him forward ever so slightly. He was a horse sinking into quicksand, his rider vainly attempting to pull him to safety.

'Find me.'

The only place he'd found potential help was with the Yellow Man, but the price was too high. He also did not like the idea of the dark claiming him as one of its own. He thought of himself as a rogue, a bastard, a swindler, a killer, but since when did all that make a person evil? Very presumptuous.

'Find me.'

Was that salt water? The sea? Waves crashed overhead; real waves this time.

'Find me, find me, find me.'

The water was gone. An Angel was on Its knees inside a glass box.

'Haha!' said Carlisle, relief coursing through his astral form. Now to slip back into his body, catch his breath, restart any of his organs that might have failed in his absence, and then he'd try again. Then he really would find his way to L'Merrier and offer him a fistful of promises if that's what it took. This would not be the end of Carlisle. A couple of mask-wearing freaks weren't going to put a full stop upon his existence. He was Carlisle, and he would hear their masks crack beneath the heel of his boot.

He soon found one small problem standing in the way of his continued existence and thirst for revenge.

His body was gone.

'Well, fuck,' said Carlisle, and his muffled words echoed around the marble walls of the Angel of Blackpool's prison.

Ben Turner was breaking the number one rule Rita Hobbes had given him.

He was outside. Outside, in public, and on his own.

After running like a scared rabbit from the latest Not Magda to appear, he'd found himself several streets away from the sanctuary of Big Pins without even realising he'd left the place. His mind was a spinning top of fear, and all he knew was that he had to go, go, go.

And now here he was, approaching the seafront. He should turn around and get back quick-sharpish before things turned from bad to worse and he was recognised. He wasn't even wearing his baseball cap, and his shades were sat on the bedside cabinet.

Yes, he should absolutely turn around and speed-walk back to Big Pins, head down, not making eye-contact with anyone as he rushed back.

But he didn't.

Fresh air.

He'd been trapped inside for so long. And yes, he knew it was for his own good, but he was going stir crazy. His reaction to the pretend Magda was proof enough of that. He knew it was a waking dream, but it had twisted him up inside. Maybe if he'd had something else to focus on as he drifted around Big Pins like a ghost, but he hadn't, and so the dream had wormed its way under his skin.

It would be okay. *He* would be okay. He'd just sit on that bench over there and watch the sea for a few minutes. Shake off the inside air, clear out his head, and then he'd go back. Rita wouldn't even know he'd left.

He made his way over to the bench and sat, glancing around to see if anyone was looking at him, but there was hardly anyone around. He was okay. He was fine.

Ben Turner closed his eyes and stretched out his legs, leaning his head back and enjoying the sound of the waves crashing, of the seagulls crying, of the traffic passing by behind. After a few joyful minutes he opened his eyes and pulled out his phone. He searched for an appropriately adorable cat video, then sent it to Rita. He wondered what she was doing at that moment.

'Okay,' he said, putting his phone away. He leaned forward, ready to stand and make his way to Big Pins, when he realised he'd been joined on the bench. A young boy with a mass of dark blonde curls was sat at the other end.

'Why do I hear a wolf when I look at you?' asked the boy.

'I… I'm sorry?'

'My name is Liam. I can see stuff. See even more stuff now since the ghost thingy.'

'Right. I should probably be off,' replied Ben, standing.

'It's coming from the sea,' said Liam.

'What is?'

'The bad stuff. Everyone's having nightmares, even when they're not asleep, and it's all coming from the sea.'

Nightmares? Ben pushed away the image of Magda waving at him. This was the case that Rita, Dan, and Formby were investigating. Could this boy actually know something helpful? Perhaps Ben could help out after all.

'I've had the waking nightmares,' said Ben, sitting back down on the bench.

'I think we all will pretty soon. I think all day every day will be nightmares.'

'You said something about the sea. What did you mean?'

Liam turned and looked at Ben for the first time. 'Can't you see them?'

'See what?'

Liam pointed out to sea. 'The black fingers.'

Ben squinted, but all he saw was the tide, the sky, the seagulls circling.

'I couldn't see them at first, but then a ghost came to me. Well, I think he was a ghost, he was all see-through anyway. I was stood on this beach and scared and the ghost whispered to me and passed through my head, I think, and then I could see more than before. Then I could see the black smoke fingers and I think I got what they meant.'

'Can you show me?' Ben asked.

Liam shrugged. 'Dunno. Maybe.'

Liam reached out with one hand and Ben took it.

'Can you see them? The smoky black fingers?'

Ben could see them.

There were hundreds of them, thousands. Thin trails of dark

smoke starting way out on the horizon and arching over them both before dipping back down all across Blackpool.

'That's what's causing the nightmares?' asked Ben, staring up in wonder at the writhing, snake-like trails.

'Think so. Part of it, at least.'

Liam pulled his hand away, Ben blinked, and the smoke trails disappeared.

'Okay, my friend, she's going to want to know about this. Do you think you can show her?'

Liam shrugged and nodded and Ben pulled out his phone, ready to call Rita. He did not manage to make the call.

'Stay right where you are, sir.'

Ben's heart sunk as he turned to see two uniformed police officers, batons drawn.

'Benjamin Turner, I am arresting you on suspicion of murder.'

Ben turned to see Liam, hands in pockets, wandering away up the beach.

13

Mr. Cotton and his brother in terror, Mr. Spike, were stood in the cool of the Angel's marble prison.

'I wonder what you dream about,' Mr. Cotton said to the Angel of Blackpool, which was still on Its knees in the glass box, hands resting on Its thighs, head bowed, pure white robes pooling around It.

'What say you, brother of mine?' asked Cotton of Spike, but Spike did not answer as he was sulking. His favourite plaything had gone missing.

'Never fear,' said Mr. Cotton, and the mask he wore smiled and wiggled its nose in mirth at the very idea that they should know fear (though of course it did not smile or twitch its nose as it was just a mask). 'Person by person, town by town, country by country, we shall spread across this world and infect all with our beautiful terror. None shall escape. Sooner or later, Carlisle shall fall under your boot again.

Mr. Spike made a wet sound that might have been joy, and clapped his hands, the dirty white gloves he wore creating a cloud of grey dust as they were struck together.

Mr. Cotton raised a hand and toyed with one of the thousands of smoky tendrils that wormed their way from the Angel and through imperfections in the glass box. Imperfections the Angel had spent close to an eternity creating so that It could eventually escape Its bonds. Now Cotton and Spike were using them for their own ends, amplifying their natural gifts many times over.

'Have I ever told you of the first person whose heart I caused to stop with blind terror, brother mine?' asked Mr. Cotton. He had, but he enjoyed the telling, and Mr. Spike was always such a good listener.

'There was a child, a miracle, born to a mother and a father who had long since accepted that they would not be gifted with such a thing. I watched the birth, watched the new parents weep tears of pure joy. At night, as they slept, I sang to the child and it wiggled its fat little legs in pleasure, her tiny heart, no larger than a plum, beating strong and firm.'

Mr. Cotton clasped his hands behind his back and began to sway in time to his words, as though they were the dreamiest music imaginable.

'Every night I watched the baby as it became aware of itself. Of the world around it. Of the two big things like itself that cared for it. Such pure, reciprocated love, brother of mine, oh, it did warm my innards. One night, I took a knife from the kitchen drawer and I introduced myself to the mother, her hair long and golden, her eyes a bright, bright blue. She did not want me in the house, but I explained to her that it was all fine, fine, fine. I used the knife upon her and then wore her face as my very first mask. I went to the child's crib and lifted it by the neck. It weighed not much more than a bag of sugar. With the child in one hand, the knife in the other, and peering through the eyeholes of a face that was not my own, I waited for the father to arrive home from work. When he finally arrived, his eyes did open wider than any I had witnessed before or since.'

Mr. Cotton's feet tapped out a rhythm against the marble floor, and Mr. Spike clapped along, his breath eager against the inside of his hedgehog mask.

'The father made sounds the likes of which I had never heard. He could only make sounds and not words. As he took in what greeted him that evening, words had been stolen from him. As I began to whittle away at the child, the father clutched his chest and crumpled to the floor like a marionette whose strings have been sliced.'

Mr. Cotton stopped his dance and turned to his brother, bowing. 'Now, is that not a story to be cherished, oh brother? There have been so many since, and soon there will be many, many more. But you must never forget where you came from.'

Mr. Cotton held out a hand and Mr. Spike took it. 'Come, there is no rest for the wicked.'

And in less than a moment, the Angel was alone.

14

Despite Waterson's insistence, Rita refused to share her experience of the dreamscape she'd been subjected to.

'Hey, I told you what mine was about,' complained Waterson.

'Your mother being a bitch is hardly fresh information.'

'Oi! She wasn't being a bitch, they were making her. She never thought the things she was saying.'

They walked to Big Pins in a heavy silence for almost another minute before Rita mumbled an apology.

'As always, you are forgiven,' replied Waterson.

'Look, it was just something from my childhood. Something I dealt with at the time.'

'Moorsgate?'

Rita didn't reply, which was all the confirmation Waterson needed.

They entered the blind alley, Big Pins' spluttering neon sign lighting the way home.

'They really are sneaky little bastards, eh?' said Waterson as they stepped into the warmth of the bowling alley and headed for the bar.

'Oh, the most bastardy of bastards, but don't worry, we'll be giving them a good boot to the bollocks soon enough.'

'Right. How, exactly?'

Rita frowned as she took a stool and waved Linton over. 'Not sure on the specifics just yet, but it'll come to me.'

Waterson smiled and took the seat next to her.

'Linton my man,' said Rita, 'a pint of something wet, if you please.'

'He's gone,' Linton replied with a grunt.

'Who's gone?' replied Waterson.

'The other one. The one who isn't you and isn't her.'

'Ben?' said Rita.

'If you say so,' Linton replied, pulling her a pint.

'Shit,' said Rita slamming her fist on the bar top. 'Shit! I told him to stay put, I told him he wasn't safe!'

'Maybe your doggy needs more obedience training,' replied Waterson, swallowing back a smirk as Rita glared at him.

'This isn't funny, he's a wanted man. Wanted for murder, remember?'

'I'm sure he's fine. He's not stupid, I don't think. He's probably just gone for a quick, well-disguised walk around the block. No doubt he'll be walking back through that door safe and un-incarcerated at any moment.'

Rita leaned past Waterson to look at the entrance, willing it to open. Her phone ringing made her jump and almost fall from the stool.

'Ah, that's probably him now. Maybe he has a new cat video for you.'

Rita scowled at him as she answered, 'Hello? .... Okay.' She hung up.

'Was it him?'

'It was him.'

'See, he's fine.'

'Yeah, he's in jail.'

Waterson nodded. 'Fine-ish?'

Rita swigged half of her pint in one, then headed for the door. 'Ghost Boy, with me.'

Waterson followed. 'I told you I don't like Ghost Boy.'

Liam felt his phone vibrate for the tenth time in the past hour. He pulled it out of his pocket and turned it off. It was just his mum again, wanting him to go home.

He sat down on the beach and watched the fingers of smoke dancing in the sky.

The man he'd been talking to had been arrested, but the police hadn't been interested in Liam. They seemed far more excited about the person they were bundling into the back of their police car.

'Are you still there, ghost?' Liam asked.

He didn't like being at home at the moment. The bad things came even when it wasn't past his bedtime, and his mum and dad didn't want to listen to him. He knew they must be seeing things too. They looked tired and were snapping at each other.

He wondered what the nightmare tendrils made them see. Did the man in the rabbit mask come to them, too? Maybe his dad would see a Not Liam with a fistful of soil and a headful of hungry birds.

'Ghost, it felt like you needed help, and I like to help, so if you're around, you can come back and talk to me.'

He picked up a stone and threw it into the waves.

Rita and Waterson crossed the forecourt of the police station they used to work at, en route to their old workspace on the second floor. Rita wondered how her ex-colleagues were dealing with the loss of three of their number in quick succession.

When it came to Rita, they'd simply forgotten she ever existed, but they'd have felt the absence when her workload—inexplicably to them—began to land on their desks instead.

And then Waterson was murdered.

And not long after that, Alexander Jenner, the guv, disappeared.

It must be drama central up there, Rita thought.

'Christ, something awful just crossed my mind,' she said, as they approached the station's automatic doors.

'What? What is it?'

'With Jenner gone, you would have been the most likely candidate to take his place.'

'And that's awful why?'

'That's not the awful part. You're dead. Which is awful but also not the awful part. With you not around, and me not around, who do you think they'll have shoved in Jenner's old office?'

Waterson stopped in his tracks. 'Oh, Christ.'

'Exactly.'

'Not Collins, surely?'

DI Collins, a sack of spoiled meat with a stuck-on moustache. A man whose favourite hobby was blocking the Men's toilet on a bi-weekly basis.

'On paper, he's the one they'd have turned to,' said Rita.

Waterson crossed himself as they stepped into the station. 'God help those poor bastards.'

Liz Peters was behind the booking in desk. Apart from her, the reception area was empty. They walked over to her, unseen and unheard, as she scrolled through her phone.

'I like what you've done to your hair, Liz,' said Rita, 'that copper tint you've had done really suits you.'

'Do you think so?' said Waterson. 'She looks like Carrot Top to me.'

'You're overly critical, you know that, Waters?'

'You should hear the things I don't say about you.'

Rita shot him a look, shook her head, then gestured towards Liz Peters. 'Okay, in you pop then,' she told Waterson.

The plan to spring Ben Turner from his cell was simple: they would open its door and walk out with him. The Angel had shown Waterson how to hop into people and work them like a person-suit. Waterson wasn't exactly an expert at it, but he reckoned he'd be able to work whoever was holding down the booking desk for as long as it took to slip in the back with the key, let Ben out, and escort him to Rita's car.

'Okay, here I go.' Waterson rubbed his hands together and closed his eyes.

'You're not moving,' said Rita, after several seconds of silence.

'I'm preparing myself,' hissed Waterson. 'Takes a bit of focus. Skill. Artistry.'

'Sorry, didn't mean to upset you, you diva.'

Waterson ignored her and got back to focussing. 'Okay. Brace yourself, Liz, I'm coming in.'

Waterson stepped forward, through the booking desk and into Liz Peters.

Liz looked up from her phone briefly in surprise, her eyebrows disappearing beneath her copper-coloured fringe, hands grasping at nothing. After a moment, she seemed to relax and lifted her hands, turning them back and forth as though seeing them for the first time.

'Waters? You in there?'

'See? *Artistry*,' replied Waterson, with the voice of Liz Peters.

'Okay, smart arse, let's go.'

Waterson opened the door, allowing Rita to join him.

'Do you have the keys we need?'

'Right here,' said Waterson, patting the big ring attached to Liz Peters' belt.

'Okay, jail break time.'

The pair first made their way to the security office, the one containing the equipment that recorded footage from the many cameras dotted around the station.

'Your go,' said Waterson.

Rita pulled the axe from her belt, gripping it in both hands, and closed her eyes. Without looking, she could see the magic and she willed it into the axe, telling it what she wanted of it. And the magic obeyed. It surged from the axe-head and swamped the recording equipment.

'Oh,' said Waterson, 'I sort of expected it all to catch light. Or at least a bit of fireworks.'

'Sorry to disappoint.'

Waterson shrugged. 'Is it done anyway?'

'Yup,' replied Rita, sliding the axe back into her belt as they vacated the room. 'All footage has been wiped and the cameras fried. No one will see poor Liz Peters setting a prisoner free.'

'All right, Liz?'

Waterson and Rita turned to see a uniformed officer swaggering towards them, his eyes roaming up and down the body Waterson was currently inhabiting.

'Uh, hello there…' Waterson tailed off.

'Jenkins!' said Rita.

'...Jenkins,' Waterson continued.

'Karl Jenkins!' Rita prompted.

'Karl Jenkins.'

'Correct,' said Karl Jenkins.

'Hello, Karl Jenkins. Bit busy, so...' Waterson pointed down the corridor, ready to leave Karl Jenkins behind.

'Did you mean what you said last night?' asked Karl.

'Did I…? Pff. I mean…'

'Just say yes!' Rita implored.

'Absolutely,' said Waterson.

'Even the bit about wanting to stick your tongue so far down my throat you'd be able to taste what I had for dinner?'

'Oh, disgusting,' said Waterson. Rita elbowed him. 'Disgustingly hot, I mean.'

Karl smiled. 'I'll be at the Dog from eight. Wear something nice.'

'Right. Sounds great. Wait, didn't you get married last year?' said Waterson, remembering how he'd dodged the work drinks celebrating the nuptials.

'Yeah. Karen. Cracking lass.'

'So…?'

'So there's a pint and a bag of crisps with your name on it,' said Karl, swaggering past. He paused and leaned close to Liz Peters, so close that Waterson could feel the man's spittle in his/her ear. 'And maybe, if you're lucky, there'll be more than that on offer.'

Karl Jenkins slapped Liz Peters on the arse, then strode away without looking back, a jaunty whistle on his lips.

'You're well in there, mate,' said Rita.

'Shut up,' replied Waterson, wiping his damp ear with his sleeve (her ear/her sleeve).

They hustled through to the cells and found the one holding Ben Turner. Rita opened the little hatch and peered through, Ben was sat on the small cot.

'Did someone request a rescue?'

'Rita!' Ben stood and ran to the door.

'What's up, handsome?'

'Oh, you know, one of those days.'

'What happened to not being stupid?' asked Rita.

'Did you get the latest cat video?'

'Yes, it was adorable.'

'Get out the bloody way,' said Waterson, placing the correct key into the cell's lock.

'Why is she helping exactly?' asked Ben.

'Oh, that's Waters in someone else's body.'

'Right. Have you done something different with your hair, Dan?'

'Hilarious,' replied Waterson as he opened the door. 'Now let's get a wiggle on, I think this body is going to vomit me out any minute now.'

'Aw, but you'll miss your big date with Karl!'

'Shut it,' replied Waterson, not giving Rita the satisfaction of seeing the shit-eating grin she was sporting.

Liam turned his phone back on and looked at the screen. Three more missed calls. He wondered if his mum had phoned the police yet. He stood, ready to run back home before he was in any more trouble.

'Got to go, ghost,' he said, turning from the sea.

There was a shape rippling before him. Liam stopped and took a step back.

'Ghost. You came back.'

Carlisle reached out a hand towards him.

15

Ben Turner had never been so grateful to find himself in Big Pins. Sure, he'd basically swapped one cage for another, but at least the bowling alley wasn't an *actual* prison.

'Big man,' said Rita, signalling with her axe to grab Linton's attention, 'the heroes have returned from their quest. We shall celebrate with much booze and bar snacks.'

Linton grunted and set about providing the requested. Meanwhile, Rita lead Ben and Waterson to the table Formby was sat at, cradling a half-pint between his small, filthy hands.

'Heard he was in prison,' said Formby, touching his ears.

'You heard right,' Ben replied, pulling up a chair.

'Ben here was a big, big idiot,' replied Rita.

'Thanks.'

'But he's learned his lesson, right?'

Ben nodded and accepted a drink from the tray Linton set down. 'Lesson learned. From now on, I'm going to stay in my kennel like a good dog.'

'So,' said Waterson, trying not to lick his lips with jealousy as he watched the other three tucking into their drinks and snacks, 'what exactly made you break the really very simple and, I believe, only rule Rita gave you?'

'I was going mad cooped up in here, okay? A lot has changed

all at the same time, and it's just been sitting on me, crushing me. I just needed to breathe for a minute.'

'A lot has changed?' replied Waterson, raising a hand. 'Recently deceased bloke over here, hexed out of her life over there. Join the club, mate.'

'All right, zip your lip for a second, Waters,' said Rita, butting in. 'It's not a competition.'

'But being murdered and turned into a ghost means I win though, right? At least you got a magic axe. What do I get? Bugger all, that's what.'

'Ben,' said Rita, reaching out and placing a hand over his. 'I understand, okay? This whole thing is mad as a box of frogs, and there's no right or wrong way to cope with it.'

'Though me running out and getting arrested was the wrong way, right?'

'You are correct,' replied Rita, grinning.

'You know, the whole time I was sat in that cell, I wasn't worried. I knew you'd come for me.'

Rita met Ben's eyes and held them. She felt her cheeks start to flush, her heart flutter. Suddenly, it seemed very, very hot in there.

'Uh, I did most of the heavy lifting, thank you,' said Waterson finally breaking the spell. Rita busied herself with coughing and fiddling with her bag of nuts.

'Thanks, Dan,' said Ben.

'Waterson. Only my mum calls me Dan.'

'She calls you Daniel,' said Rita.

Waterson gave her some serious side-eye, then left the table to stretch his legs, which was something he found he needed to do even though he didn't strictly speaking have muscles that required stretching.

'I'm not sure Waterson likes me all that much,' said Ben.

'Oh, that's just him. He's a pissy little bitch to most people, you get used to it. Even enjoy it. Plus he was murdered recently, as he keeps pointing out. That'll bring out the grump in anyone.'

'He doesn't like me much, either,' said Formby.

'That's because you smell,' replied Rita.

'He's dead, he can't smell nothing,' said Formby, checking his breath against a grimy hand and recoiling at his own stench.

'He might not be able to smell it, but intellectually he knows it. Always liked things very clean, that boy. I think his first word was "bleach".'

Formby sniggered, then his eyes went wide and his pointed little ears twitched as he looked at Ben. 'Oh!'

'What?' replied Ben. 'What is it? Do I have food in my beard?'

'You have information. New, tasty information.'

'How on earth do you know that?' asked Ben.

'Can see it in your eyes, the way you sit, you have news.'

'What news?' asked Rita, turning to Ben.

'I met a young boy, before I was arrested.'

'Okay,' Rita replied warily. 'You were arrested on suspicion of murder and not suspicion of… anything else, right?'

'Har-de-har. He was a weird little bloke. Kept talking funny, and I think he knew I used to go, you know, a bit wolfy. He showed me something. He took my hand and pointed out to sea and suddenly I could just see them.'

'See what? Tell!' said Formby, desperate to taste some fresh information.

'They were like smoke trails. Thousands of them.'

Rita leaned forward, 'Sorry, did you say smoke trails?'

'Yeah, they reached out from the sea and over into Blackpool. The boy said that's what's causing all the nightmares.'

Rita sat back. 'The Angel.'

Carlisle was drifting apart.

Having made it back to the marble chamber that the Angel of Blackpool was trapped within, Carlisle found it increasingly difficult to keep himself together.

Astral projection was a tricky thing to keep a grip on, even for those trained in the art, and Carlisle was very much not trained in the art. After so long roaming free, and with his body now M.I.A, Carlisle was increasingly at the mercy of the astral plane's raging, vicious winds. He could feel himself being pulled apart. His form drifting. Smoke in the wind.

He frowned, or thought about how a frown would look if he were still able to frown. If the astral approximation of his face wasn't now spread across several metres.

There wasn't enough time. To keep himself together he needed to get to his body, now, or at the very least find an anchor point he could cling to. A shell to crawl inside of like a Hermit Crab.

But he didn't have one.

He di…

...gone for a moment. The gaps between thoughts, between sentience and nothingness were growing longer.

So this was…

...end.

Fog and…

'Got to go, ghost.'

A flare!

That voice. He'd heard it before.

With his last ounce of effort, Carlisle found himself stood before a small boy. The same small boy who'd anchored him the first time.

'Ghost, you came back,' said Liam.

Carlisle, unable to even remember what words were, rushed forward into the boy. The sound of the raging winds cut out, all Carlisle could hear now was the boy's heartbeat. That had been far too close. Another few seconds and his essence would have been stretched too thin. He would have drifted into oblivion. It seemed as though he'd pulled himself out of the fire at the last moment once again. He laughed.

'What's so funny?' asked Liam, far less perturbed at being possessed by a phantom than one might have expected.

'Everything, depending on your point of view,' Carlisle explained, delighted to find that he could speak again, if only inside the boy's head. Now his form was settled inside of a receptive, Uncanny form, he was safe, he was strong.

'What do you want with me, ghost?'

'I am not a ghost. Ghosts are of the dead.'

'Are you not dead, then?'

'I've been dead a few times,' replied Carlisle, 'but not currently, no. I am in my astral form.'

'Astral?'

'Astral.'

'I don't know what that is.'

'I am overcome with shock.'

Carlisle was secure inside Liam, but he wasn't able to control the boy's body. His astral form did not afford such luxuries, he was just a passenger.

'There is something of the Uncanny to you, boy,' said Carlisle.

'The what?'

'The strange. The out of the ordinary. When I first left my body, you shone like a lighthouse. We connected.'

'I could see the smoke fingers after that, and what they meant.'

'You anchored me, and in return gained extra insight through me. But you could only have provided me such a service if you were of the Uncanny world already. No ordinary human could do such a thing.'

'I have always seen weird stuff. My mum and dad say it's just me remembering bad dreams, or making stuff up.'

'No. Either they do not know or are choosing not to see. Magic is connected to you in some small way.'

'So I'm special?'

Carlisle laughed. 'Oh no. Magic has touched you, but that is all, you are just one of thousands. About as special as a ten pound win on a scratch card.'

Carlisle felt Liam's body sag a little.

'Buck up, boy, you're still part of something most will never even be aware of.'

'Yeah. And that actually is pretty special, isn't it?'

Carlisle held in a long sigh so as not to dispirit the donkey he was riding. Finally, he said, 'Now I have a very important mission for you.'

'What?'

'We need to locate a piece of chalk.'

Rita was confused.

'You're sure?' she said. 'Dark, smoky trails reaching from the sea and into Blackpool?'

Ben nodded. 'That's what I saw.'

'The Angel of Blackpool's magic,' said Formby.

'But Mr. Cotton said him and his brother weren't working with the Angel. That this was just the two of them.'

'Maybe they were lying,' said Ben. 'I don't think they're exactly trustworthy.'

'Yeah, but why bother? It doesn't get them anything to pretend the Angel isn't helping them. It's not as though, if I found out, I could stop the Angel anyway. It's way too powerful.'

'Perhaps,' said Formby, his long, yellow fingernails scratching at his stubble, 'Mr. Cotton and Mr. Spike have found a way to use the Angel's power for themselves.'

'You think they might have, what? Tapped into the Angel somehow?'

'Maybe. Could be.'

'Wait…' Rita sagged back.

'What is it?' asked Ben.

'The Angel, It sort of came to me. When I was asleep. I *think* it was the Angel anyway, and not a trick, but either way I did think It was trying to trick me.'

'Trick you into what?' asked Formby.

'Into helping It. Perhaps this is why. It's being used.'

'So you think Cotton and Spike really are using Its power for themselves?' said Ben.

'If they are,' replied Formby, 'then the whole of Blackpool is in very bad doo-doo.'

'Oh, you absolutely are,' chimed a new voice.

They looked up to see who it was that had joined them. Only Rita recognised him. 'No…'

His name was Gavin Dylan, the victim of the first murder

case Rita had ever investigated. The one she hadn't been able to solve. The one whose memory had been a sliver of ice in her heart ever since.

'Why did you fail me, Rita?'

Gavin Dylan, his neck slashed three times, blood oozing from the wounds, reached out a hand towards her.

16

Liam's mum was not at all impressed with him.

'You little monster!' she yelled, teary-eyed, gripping him so tightly that Liam thought she might crush him to death.

'Mum…' he said, just about audibly.

His mother pushed him back, keeping a tight grip on his arms. 'Your dad is out there right now, driving around looking for you! Why do you do these things, Liam, and why can't you answer your bloody phone?'

'Chalk,' said Carlisle, from inside his head.

'Just a minute,' replied Liam.

'You were not gone for just a minute,' said his mum, 'it's been hours! You're too young to be galivanting around the place on your own. Ten more minutes and I was calling the police.'

'I climbed inside you for help, not to bear witness to a tiresome domestic,' said Carlisle, wishing he had access to his magic so he could push the ranting, blubbering woman into another realm and get on with the task at hand. Namely obtaining chalk and locating his body.

'Maybe I should go and wait in my room?' said Liam.

'Yes! That's where you can sit until your dad gets back so he can…' she broke down again and gave Liam another desperate, relieved hug.

'Sorry, Mum. It was the bad dreams.'

'Okay. Okay. Go on up, then.'

Liam felt bad, of course he did. No child wants to see their mum cry, and the fact that he was going to make her worried again very soon only made him feel even more guilty as he trudged heavy-footed up the staircase and closed his bedroom door behind him.

'She's going to be really angry.'

'She already appears to be at the very apex of angry,' replied Carlisle.

'Do we have to leave again straight away?'

'Yes, unless you want us to lure my monster-infested body to your home?'

Liam did not want that.

'That is what I thought. Now hurry, chalk, let us get on with this so I can get out of your extremely cramped body.'

Liam dropped to his knees and dragged a box out from under his bed. He tossed away the lid and dug around inside until he found a box of coloured chalks.

'There! Knew I had some. Mum bought me them ages back, barely used them, though I'm actually pretty good at art so I don't know why.'

'What a thrilling anecdote. Let us away.'

Liam opened his bedroom door. He could hear his mum in the hall downstairs. 'I'm telling you, he just walked back in, he's okay, he's safe.'

She was on the phone to his dad, and also blocking any escape. Liam closed the door again, quietly, then scampered over to his window. He opened the curtains and pushed up the sash window. The tree stood waiting, that one, long branch reaching out towards him.

'The branch might snap,' he said, warily eyeing the alarmingly thin limb.

'Indeed.'

'I'd fall and hurt myself.'

'Yes.'

'I could break my leg, or worse.'

'You should meet Detective Rita Hobbes, you both have a gift for stating the blindingly obvious. Now get on with it.'

Liam scrambled up to the window ledge and reached out for the branch. He looked down at the ground below. If he fell it would be on to grass, not concrete or paving stones, but it still seemed an awful long way down. Long enough to hurt *a lot*.

He grabbed the branch in both hands and swung out. The world seemed to go head over heels as the branch bent, his grip slipped, his stomach leapt into his mouth, and then his descent abruptly stopped as his arms wrapped around another branch, jarring them almost out of their sockets.

Body shaking, Liam descended, dropping down the final few feet to the grass, his heart a thrash metal kick drum.

'Well, you made rather a meal of that,' said Carlisle.

'I did it!' Liam cried, exhilarated.

'Hurry along, we have a trap to set.'

Liam ran for the garden fence, tumbled over, and sprinted away.

At some point between witnessing the dead Gavin Dylan and standing up, Rita had realised she was no longer inside Big Pins, and was instead in a dirty alleyway.

'Really?' said Rita, axe in her hand, ready. 'Didn't we just do this?'

Gavin Dylan stepped into view at the other end of the alley, a pair of rabbit ears sprouting from the top of his skull. 'Rita Hobbes, the defective detective.'

'I'm starting to think you have a personal issue with me, cottontail.'

'You did attempt to murder my brother and I.'

'Wow, you really hold a grudge.'

Rita gripped the axe and closed her eyes, the dreamscape magic around her rushing into it. She crouched and slammed the butt of the axe against the rain-slicked ground at her feet and unleashed the magic. She'd told it what she wanted, re-shaped it to do one thing: burn away the dreamscape. Destroy the pretence. Return her to the real.

But when Rita opened her eyes she was still in the alley.

'Oh. Well, that's not fair.'

'Nothing is fair, Rita Hobbes. Take poor Gavin Dylan here. Throat cut and tossed away in a dank alleyway. Worthless.'

'He wasn't worthless,' Rita replied through gritted teeth.

She attempted to destroy the dreamscape again, to bust out of it, but the dreamscape refused. She tried to talk to the magic and felt her throat tighten. She struggled to catch her breath. This was much more powerful than any magic she'd felt from Mr. Cotton before. It was overwhelming, heavy, and he controlled it entirely.

'He was a junkie, Rita. Just another drug-addled nothing taking up space. Is that why you didn't do him the good turn of bringing his murderer to justice?'

Rita swallowed. Her throat was dry, her arms trembling. She had to try again. She had the axe, she could tell the magic what to do. Had to. She pulled the magic into the axe again and slammed the handle down on the ground. She watched as the spell raged from the axe and burned the alley away like it was made of dry paper, only to reveal an exact copy beneath.

It was the Angel's power, it must be. The extra strength it afforded Cotton. The lies it created, the terrors, couldn't be pushed aside. She was nothing, the power of the axe was nothing. Over and over she tried to burn the dream, to scrub it clean, and time and time again it remained.

'His mother committed suicide, do you remember?'

'Shut it.'

'A few months after you arrived at her front door to tell her the bad news. Your words planted the seed, and away she went. Sucking on exhaust, dear, dear, dear.'

'Show me,' Rita asked the magic around her. 'Show me, show me, show me.'

The picture flickered and settled. Rita could see it, the Angel's power, a smoky tendril coiling around Gavin Dylan, around Mr. Cotton, just as Ben had said it would be.

'I know you're leeching from the Angel,' said Rita.

'Oh? Did Ben Turner see and go running to teacher, just like the headshrinker?'

Alison Parks.

'Perhaps he should get the same treatment as her? What say you?'

'You go anywhere near him…'

Gavin Dylan melted away and Mr. Cotton stepped forward, a large smile stretching across his rabbit mask. He gestured to the ground, a pair of feet were visible, poking out from the dark; was it Gavin Dylan?

'Shall we take a look?' said Mr. Cotton.

Something wasn't right about the feet. Rita remembered every detail about Gavin Dylan. When he'd been found he was wearing a beaten up pair of blue Converse trainers, but the feet she saw were wearing dark brown leather shoes.

'Ben?'

She darted forward to find the dead body of Ben Turner.

Rita staggered back, hand to her mouth.

'Poor little doggy,' said Mr. Cotton sadly, as he looked down at the corpse in the dirt. 'He trusted you would protect him, too. Another failure, Detective? How do you even live with yourself?'

Rita gripped the handle of her axe so tightly that she thought she might turn it to dust, but she had to hold on to something, it was the only thing stopping her from losing her grip on sanity. From taking what she saw at face value. This was a dreamscape, that's all it was. Those feet, that body, hadn't been there when she first arrived.

'Ben Turner, whose greatest hope in life was to find a woman who would love him, and that he could love in return. Such a simple, ordinary wish. A wish unfulfilled.'

The dreamscape pressed in on her. Too strong, too much to push back. It was endless, endless power and she was nothing.

'That's not Ben,' said Rita.

Mr. Cotton giggled and clapped his white-gloved hands. 'Oh, you have me, Detective. It's a fair cop, as I believe the saying goes.'

He clicked his fingers and Ben was replaced by Gavin Dylan, just as she remembered.

'I wonder where the real Ben Turner is?' he said. 'My, my, and my again, I do hope nothing tragic becomes of him. Would that not be awful, Rita Hobbes?'

'Get out of here, go!' Rita yelled at Ben Turner.

He ran to the basement door, half relieved to be getting out of the firing line, half ashamed to be doing so.

But what, exactly, could he have done? He was just Ben Turner, ex-accountant, ex-werewolf. He didn't have any power to deal with this sort of thing. No magic axe, no magic anything. The best thing he could do was whatever Rita told him to do.

So he bolted across Big Pins and into the basement, locking the door behind him. The door that had kept him in when he'd still been affected by the lycanthropy curse. The one that had prevented the beast he turned into from getting out and causing bloody havoc.

Breathing heavily, Ben slowly backed down the stairs, straining to hear what was going on beyond the door, but he couldn't hear anything. There should have been a giant fight going on, magic exploding, people screaming, that sort of thing, but there was only silence.

Confused, he made his way back up the basement stairs and pressed his ear to the door.

What was going on out there? Were Rita and the walking corpse having a polite chat? A gentle whisper in a far corner over a pint and a packet of crisps?

Ben frowned and moved his head from the door. Maybe it was over already? Rita had smacked the corpse with her axe, and that was that.

He placed his hand on the door's lock, ready to open it, when he realised he could actually hear something. It wasn't coming from the other side of the door though, it was coming from inside the basement.

It was someone's breath, rasping.

Ben turned around to see.

Dan Waterson was in a park.

'Okay…'

This time he was not surprised to find himself transported somewhere. This is what they did, Cotton and Spike, picked you up and dropped you in some nightmare construct.

'Right then, what is it this time?'

At first he didn't recognise the park at all, then he turned to see a set of swings. The metal frame was rusted and the two swings had metal chains and a simple wooden slat to sit upon. That's when he realised where he was.

'Grafton Park.'

He'd been six and angry and ran out of his mum's car in an area he didn't live in. He'd been full of fury and had found himself in a park. In this park. He'd sat on the swings, hoping his mum would be frantic with worry. With terror. That'd teach her for shouting at him just because he'd spilled his can of pop across the back seat.

'Oh,' said Waterson, 'right.'

A man had approached him that day as he sat on the swing, his skinny legs dangling, bottom lip pouting. A man with matted hair and missing teeth. He'd run his dirty fingers across Waterson's face and laughed like a lunatic. Little Waterson had tried to run, only for the man to grab hold of the scruff of his jumper. Waterson had struggled and screamed and kicked and the man had laughed and laughed. Eventually, he'd wriggled out of his jumper and sprinted blindly across the park and out on to the road, only to bump into his mum, who was halfway between fury and relief. For a moment it looked like anger would win out, but it only to took one look at her boy's face for that to melt away. Waterson had experienced nightmares of the laughing man for years after that.

And there he was, that same man, shuffling towards him now.

'You know, you're smaller than I remember,' said Waterson.

The man opened his toothless mouth and began to laugh, only for his form to ripple and warp.

'Um. Okay,' said Waterson.

The Laughing Man rippled once more and was replaced by the flickering, not quite there form of a new person. Only it wasn't a person, not really.

It was an Angel.

'...leas... enn...' said the Angel of Blackpool, Its voice broken into pieces.

'What? You want me to lease something?'

'..se... ner.'

Waterson wondered what the purpose of this was. He'd been terrified on a deep, awful level by the Laughing Man as a child, but he'd never been scared of the Angel. Not like that. Why were Cotton and Spike swapping out that old, primal feeling fear with *this*?

'...if... stop them... release... have to release Jenner...'

And then the Angel was gone.

Liam was on his hands and knees sketching with a piece of chalk on a paving stone.

'What are these?' he asked.

'They are shapes that hold power,' replied Carlisle.

First Liam had drawn a large, unbroken circle. Within that circle he had then been asked to draw tiny symbol after tiny symbol in an exact pattern. A pattern that began skirting the inside radius of the chalk circle, then spiralled closer and closer to the circle's centre.

Liam could see the shapes he had to draw in his mind's eye. He would close his actual eyes and there they were, one after the other, and he could recreate them easy as pie.

'What sort of power?' he asked.

'There are creatures. Almost things. Creatures without physical form who hunger for one. One of these bodiless bastards stole my body while I was in my astral form, and is no doubt taking it for a joyride, hell bent on causing chaos and murder with the thing.'

The magic that had been used to bind Carlisle to the prison

didn't work with the almost thing inside of him. Magic was a contract, and with a different person inside, the contract was broken. The binding spell useless. And so his hijacked body ran free.

'Why does it want to murder?'

'Why? You might as well ask why a spider catches a fly. Because they do. Because they must. And now that one of these things has my body, it can do so with reckless abandon.'

'Unless you get your body back and stop it.'

'Precisely.'

Liam closed his eyes and saw the final shape that he was required to draw.

'What will this circle do to it?' he asked as he drew a triangle with all sorts of weird squiggles within it that looked like they might be letters of some sort, but Liam had never seen letters like them before.

'Two things. Firstly, if the thing in my body is within reach, it will attract it.'

'How?'

'We will place bait into the circle. The words and symbols will make the bait the tastiest thing for miles around. It will radiate, like an angler fish's lure in the dark depths of the ocean. Irresistible.'

'What's the bait?' replied Liam, sitting back on his knees to take in his completed handiwork.

'*You* are the bait.'

'Oh.'

'Do not worry, it is quite safe.'

Liam was not absolutely sure that he believed Carlisle. 'What if your body is too far away for the bait to work?'

'Then I shall do my best to push you out and take over your body.'

'Oh. Can you do that?'

'Let's hope we do not need to find out, I would not wish to be so small a second time.'

'What's the other thing it can do? You said two things.'

'It will trap the thing. My body. The circle is meant for it and it alone. Once it steps within it, it will not be able to step out again unless the circle is broken. Now come along, get into the circle and wriggle around like the tasty bait you are.'

Liam looked at the circle, unsure that this was the best course of action. 'What if I don't?'

'I did mention pushing you out and taking over your body, did I not? You would be dead, which most people are not altogether keen on.'

Liam stepped into the circle. He looked down at his feet to see the chalk words and symbols he had sketched had begun to glow a pure, brilliant white.

'The trap is activated,' said Carlisle. 'Now we wait.'

'You know you said you left your body to go looking for help because you couldn't leave where you were?'

'Yes.'

'Maybe you should have just stepped out of your body, waited for one of these things to come get you, then followed it out and grabbed your body back. Been easier, probably.

Silence.

'Carlisle?'

'Shut up.'

Rita whirled around, axe at the ready. The alleyway and Mr. Cotton were gone. She was back in Big Pins.

She shuddered, her chest untightening. Cotton and Spike had been terrible before, but with the Angel's power too, she wasn't sure how she was supposed to stop them. She could still feel the power of them. Mr. Cotton had been showing off, flooding the dreamscape with this fresh power and showing her just how puny she was. How useless and scared she should be. She'd swatted away at it with her axe and hadn't even left a scratch.

'Rita.'

She turned to see Formby and Waterson.

'Are you two okay?'

'Fine,' said Waterson. 'Still dead, but otherwise in top condition.'

Rita slumped down on a bar stool. 'We're in such deep, deep

shit here.'

'What is it?' asked Waterson.

'Their power. The Angel's power. It's just… it's too much.'

'Hedgehog!' said Formby.

'What?' replied Rita, looking to the wide-eyed Formby who was pointing past her.

'Oh crap,' said Waterson.

Rita turned to see a figure stood in the open doorway to the basement. He wore a hedgehog mask and was holding up a white-gloved fist stained red with blood.

Rita jumped up, wielding her axe.

'Get out of here, you spiky prick!'

Mr. Spike opened his fist and what he had been holding clattered to the floor.

'Are those… I think those are teeth,' said Waterson.

Rita remembered Ben Turner, dead behind the bins.

'My, my, and my again, I do hope nothing tragic becomes of him. Would that not be awful, Rita Hobbes?'

'No…'

Mr. Spike was giggling.

'What is it?' asked Waterson, but Rita wasn't listening.

She ran at the giggling Spike, who was busy smearing the blood over his mask. She screamed and swung her axe, but it didn't stick into Spike, into his body. Instead, it tore through him, causing his 2D image to rip in two and disappear.

'Ben!' She ran down the basement steps, almost tripping over her own feet in the process, and burst into the basement.

Ben Turner was curled up on the floor.

'It's not real. That's not him.'

She took a step towards him. A pair of bunny ears on a hairband had been slipped on his head.

Waterson stepped past her and went to Ben, kneeling down next to his body, Formby following.

'It's a trick. It's just a trick, right?' said Rita, but she knew the truth.

Formby looked up to Rita. 'He's gone.'

Rita sat down on the basement steps, wrapping her arms around herself. It was cold down there.

17

Bob the exorcist woke in his ratty chair, the only stick of furniture in his rundown excuse for a front room.

'Still alive,' he said, not quite certain if he said it with surprise, sadness, or relief.

Bob had been chosen by the Vatican to serve as an exorcist when he was just six years old. Bob was originally from London, so it might come as a surprise that he was pulled in by the Vatican, but their Uncanny arm had people everywhere, searching for new soldiers in their fight against the dark.

Bob's parents, devout, fearful, had been delighted. He had shown a natural affinity with the dark and the things that dwelled there. It came as easily to him as breathing.

'That's the power of our Lord and Saviour, Robert,' his handler, his trainer, had told him.

He had developed into one of their frontline people. The first to be sent to the worst places imaginable, saving innocent people from the machinations of demons, and worse.

But there is always a price to pay for playing with the dark arts.

Most in his line of work did not live very long. Toiling with dark magic took a toll on a man's body. Ate it up. Turned it against itself. The mind, too. There were many ways an exorcist for the Vatican could go. Perhaps something they fought would fight back. Or the dark magic would infect a body with cancers, or push a person to suicide.

And the things in the black, the creatures from the pit, they were always waiting. As soon as you stepped into battle against them, announced yourself as their opposition, you were added to a list. It was not a good list to be on. Sooner or later, if the dark magic didn't eat you up, something would slither out of a corner to scratch you off that list. That was the price paid for doing the Lord's good work, and Bob had accepted that.

Eventually, sickened by the hypocrisy he saw in his own world—a world he had always believed to be on the side of the light—he had walked away. That's how he found himself sat in a basement flat in Blackpool of all places, waiting for the end to come.

He meant to go down fighting. To bloody a few noses. But the waiting was torture. He'd been there for years now, and he could feel the eyes upon him. All day, all night, they were watching.

Drink and junk food and pretending he didn't give a fuck helped. He lived that way for long enough that it fooled his own mind into not caring, into shrugging off any fear, any anticipation.

Apart from when he woke up. He'd remember then.

He struggled up out of his chair, a half-empty can of lager clattering from his lap and on to the floor, the remains of the drink gurgling out.

'Shit.' He bent down and grabbed the can, saving about an inch of liquid. 'Waste not want not.' He drank the warm remains before tossing the empty can into a darkened corner.

He thought he saw something flinch out of the way. A patch of dark in the darkness. Bob ignored it, reached into a plastic bag on the floor by his chair, and pulled out a fresh can of beer, foam exploding as he opened it.

'Breakfast of champions.'

He wondered what time of day it was. There was no real light bleeding through from the tiny window high on the wall, so it must be late. He hoped a bakery close-by would still be open, he wanted to chase his lager with a nice pie. And then another lager or six at the pub. 'Don't wait up, dear,' he said to the dark corners of the room and headed for the front door.

He opened it to find two people stood outside waiting. One was a young boy with thick, blonde, curly locks. The other was a tall, absurdly pale man in an almost floor-length, purple coat. The man appeared to be trapped within a chalk circle, and was not at all happy about it, though his teeth-gnashing and foam-mouthed raving had been silenced by the spells he saw drawn within the circle.

'My name's Liam,' said the boy.

'Hello Liam.'

'The ghost inside me that isn't a ghost wants you to kick a monster out of his body.'

Bob the exorcist looked from the boy to the silent lunatic with murder in his eyes, then back again. 'You'd better come in then,' he said and walked back inside.

The pie would have to wait.

Mr. Spike had done terrible things to Ben.

Rita hadn't seen them, but she could tell from the expressions on Waterson and Formby's faces that his killer had taken pleasure in the killing. They hadn't needed to kill her to get their kicks. Instead, Cotton and Spike had prodded at her and found a way to get a response they could feast on. And now they had it.

As she'd stepped into that basement and seen Ben Turner's body—so strangely small looking, like he'd shrunk in death—her mind had recoiled with anger, with fear, with horror.

Oh, they must have liked that.

They must be having a good laugh about it right now. A little revenge on her for how she had dispatched them.

Waterson sat down next to her in a booth upstairs. She was watching the last cat video Ben had sent her, replaying it over and over again.

'Hey.'

'What happened to his ghost, Waters? Is he okay somewhere, do you think?'

Waterson opened his mouth to speak, paused, then started again, 'I… I don't know. I'm sorry.'

Big Pins became blurry and Rita angrily brushed her sleeve across her eyes. Any tears she shed would only be giving Cotton and Spike more of what they wanted. She would grieve once she had beaten the shit out of them.

'I'm really not the hugging type,' said Waterson.

'I know.'

'Plus I'm a ghost, so couldn't hug you even if I wanted to.'

'I know.'

'But just know that I am. In my head, I'm hugging you.'

Rita smiled. 'Thanks, Dan.'

Waterson blinked in surprise. 'I think that might be the first time you've ever called me Dan.'

'It was weird, wasn't it?'

'Very weird. Stop it.'

'Understood, Waters.'

Waterson laughed, then stopped, feeling guilty. 'You'll stop them, you know,' he said.

'I hope so.'

'They'll rue the day they picked on Rita Hobbes.'

'Everyone does.'

'And wherever Ben is, whatever's happened to him, to his soul, it'll be resting easy, because he knows you're going to twat those fuckers.'

Oh, she would. Somehow she had to. She was going to be their worst nightmare.

The chalk circle slid across the floor, nudging the man within it forward, until it was stood against one wall.

'My mum tells me off if I draw on the walls,' said Liam, looking around at all the pictures, shapes, and words daubed all over Bob the exorcist's living room.

'My mum's dead,' said Bob, 'so she doesn't tell me fuck all.'

Bob peered closer at the eyes of the man trapped in the circle. 'Who is he, then?'

'His name's Carlisle.'

Bob turned to Liam, eyebrows raised. 'That so? A bloody celebrity, in my humble flat. What an honour.'

Carlisle scowled inside of Liam, he knew when he was being taken the piss of.

'I don't think he liked that,' said Liam, shuffling on the spot.

'Do I look like I give two tits what he thinks?' replied Bob. He'd heard of Carlisle, of course. Most with any connection to the Uncanny had heard of Carlisle. Most of what they heard was not good. 'So you went and slipped into the astral, did you? Without safeguarding your body? I thought you were supposed to be smart.'

Liam listened. 'He says there was no other option at the time. He was trapped with an Angel and Mr. Cotton and Mr. Spike.'

'Shit does like to mix with shit,' said Bob.

Liam peered into a darkened corner of the room. 'How is it so dark over there? Light's on, but I can't see the corner. Or that corner over there.'

'Can't always shine a light on evil,' replied Bob, taking a mouthful from his can and unleashing a bone-rattling burp. He scrunched up his nose and wafted a hand in front of his face. 'Talking of evil... Christ, what have I been eating?'

'Carlisle is saying lots of loud, rude words now.'

'Simmer down in there, all right?' replied Bob. 'I'm not in the habit of helping out bastards, at least not in the past, but you're catching me on a good day, so I'll help you get your body back.'

'He says thank you. It sounded like he was saying it through clenched teeth. (...) What? Well, it did!'

'I have something I want in return though, no freebies today.'

'What is it?' asked Liam.

'I know the sort of thing Carlisle offers, and I want the same.'

Liam frowned as he listened to Carlisle. 'He says okay.'

'So I get a promise?'

Liam nodded.

'It better be a big promise.'

'He says it is.'

'Okay then,' said Bob the exorcist. 'Better get me tools, then.'

Bob walked from the room and through to a kitchen. The sink looked like it was giving birth to a creature made of mould and turds. It was not the most hygienic of kitchens.

Bob grabbed an old-fashioned leather bag; the kind doctors on call had used a hundred years previous. He'd been given the bag and its contents after graduating the training the Vatican had given him. It contained the tools of an exorcist's trade: the complete apparatus for dealing with a demonic entity and deporting them from a human host.

Most in Bob's business preferred to clean their tools regularly as they became rusted, bloodied, gore-coated. Bob did not clean his. Not ever. For one thing, he hated cleaning. For another, he believed the remnants of past jobs only amplified a tool's potency, like a cooking pot that was never scrubbed completely clean, the chef believing it enhanced the flavour of the next dish.

'He wants to know if this will damage his body much,' asked Liam, keeping his distance from the thrashing, grasping arms of Carlisle's body, despite the fact he knew it could not reach beyond the circle to grab him.

'Hard to say, really,' replied Bob, re-entering the room. 'He's got an almost thing lodged in his body, and prising those dicks out can be tricky. Sometimes they slide right out with a little levering, sometimes you've got to hack and hack and hack, and by the time you've wiped the blood off your face to take a look at things, the almost creature is gone, and you're left not so much with a body as a pile of meat confetti.'

Bob dropped his bag on the chair and opened it, pulling out a hammer.

'Let's get to work then.'

Linton had closed Big Pins—something that was almost unheard of—to help Formby take Ben Turner's body to the police. Formby knew an officer they could hand it off to who would make sure the right things happened. Make sure his friends and family knew he'd passed on.

'I know this isn't the best of times,' said Waterson, as Rita poured herself a gin and tonic.

'What is it?' she asked, frowning at her drink and splashing in another hefty slug of gin.

'There was this weird thing in my dreamscape.'

'Okay. Like what?' Rita slumped back on to a stool and drank.

'Well, at first, it was like you'd expect, something from my life that I was scared of, but then it changed into something else. *Someone* else.'

'Who?'

'The Angel. Your big bad, so to speak.'

Rita sat up and frowned, more focussed now on Waterson than her drink.

'It wanted me to release the guv.'

Rita recalled her own interaction with the Angel of Blackpool. How it had come to her in a dream and asked the same.

'Do you know what?' she said.

'What?'

'I think we should give It what It wants.'

'Right. That feels like a really, really—and I'm going to add a third really here—bad idea.'

Rita stepped back behind the bar and poured herself another drink.

'Oh, it's the worst idea ever.'

Carlisle did not like the thought of a thing being inside his body. He didn't even like when other people wore his clothes. He once tore a man's throat out for trying on his coat. This was, of course, much worse. He felt it on a primal level, the revulsion at someone—or to be more accurate, some*thing*—using his body as their own.

'Jesus,' said Bob. 'I should leave the thing inside you, Carlisle, just to teach you a lesson. And it's not as though you don't deserve it, things you've done.'

'Tell him to keep his weasel words to himself,' said Carlisle.

He glanced to the corners of the room, the too-black places

that had unnerved Liam so. There were things there, he could sense them. Almost see them. The price of Bob's chosen profession, no doubt. Heinous bailiffs waiting to emerge from the shadows and claim their debt. Carlisle wondered why people like Bob willingly did what they did when the cost was so very high and so very unavoidable. Was doing the right thing really worth all that?

Bob stood in front of Carlisle's possessed body, just an inch from the chalk circle. He pulled a rather nasty looking knife from his leather bag and raised it above his head, mumbling words that Carlisle did not understand. As Bob continued with his invocation, the knife blade began to glow, white hot.

Carlisle heard whispers. Many voices, overlapping, all seeping from the darkened corners of the room.

'Stay where you are,' Carlisle ordered Liam. 'Do not get close to the dark corners.'

As Bob continued to chant his strange words, white tendrils began to weave from the corners towards Bob. Should he warn him, Carlisle wondered, or was this all part of it? Was he leeching dark magic to use as his own? Was that how this was going to play out? Carlisle had seen a lot of things in his long life, but had never witnessed a Vatican-trained exorcist at work.

The tendrils of light wrapped around Bob as the almost thing in Carlisle's body thrashed and raged. It seemed to Carlisle that it knew exactly what was going on, and did not care for it one bit.

And then the whispers stopped, the tendrils of light disappeared, and Bob ceased his chant. All was quiet.

'What now?' said Carlisle. 'Ask him.'

'I hear you,' said Bob, raising a hand. 'What happens now, is this...'

Bob the exorcist stepped into the chalk circle and thrust the knife into Carlisle's heart.

18

Nightmares can happen whatever time of day a person sleeps, but at night, when the moon is high, that is when nightmares are at their most potent. When even the sublimely crafted horrors conjured by Mr. Cotton and Mr. Spike are given extra depth.

Mr. Cotton walked the streets of Blackpool, his white-gloved hands clasped behind his back as the dark fingers of the Angel's power writhed around him. Each house he passed he could feel discomfort within. Dreamers shifting in their sleep, moaning half-formed sentences as their covers grew damp with sweat.

'Do you hear their cries, brother of mine?' asked Mr. Cotton as Mr. Spike stepped from nowhere and joined him. 'Fear. Ah yes, they are playing our song.'

Mr. Cotton licked his lips, he could still taste Ben Turner's terror upon them. Could still hear Rita Hobbes' anguish as she discovered the man's dead body. Yes, that certainly wiped the smug grin off the hexed detective's face.

'Was that not something to savour, brother?'

Mr. Spike giggled behind his mask.

'And yet, that is such a small morsel. What we have done to the ex-wolf. What we have created so far in this tired town. Tentative steps only. Is it not now time to throw off these self-made shackles to see what we can really do? I do believe that it is time to turn up the screams.'

Mr. Cotton began to dance.

Elaine Travers turned over in her bed, unsure if she was awake or asleep. The room around her was a warm fuzz. A perfect cocoon.

A cough.

Elaine's muscles turned into piano wires as she realised she was not alone.

On the chair in the corner sat a man, face shrouded by the dark, his chest heaving up and down.

'Who is it?' asked Elaine Travers, reaching for her glasses on the bedside table. Maybe it was her brother, Simon, who had come up to stay for a few days and was sleeping in her spare room. What was he doing sat there, though?

She slid on her glasses and turned on the bedside lamp, but still the man remained in the dark.

'Simon?' said Elaine her heart speeding. No, that wasn't Simon, too big for Simon. Her brother was a short man, five-foot-six on a good day; this person was much larger, much wider.

Elaine realised who it was. All of a sudden she knew. It was the trousers. She could see the trousers, poking out from the dark that hid the rest of him. The trousers were mustard-coloured cords. She remembered being six years old, covers gripped tight in her hands, stealing a look through scrunched up eyes and seeing those trousers walking towards her bed.

Remembered his hand reaching towards her.

'Uncle Alan?' whispered Elaine.

Uncle Alan leaned forward.

'Hello, little one,' he replied, a smile on his face and a hungry look in his eyes. Eyes that twitched this way and that across the covers hiding Elaine's body.

Uncle Alan had been dead for thirty years.

'I'll tell mum,' cried Elaine, as Uncle Alan stood. He had a knife in his hand.

'Don't worry, little one,' he said, 'everything is going to be fine, fine, fine.'

Elaine cowered and closed her eyes.

Mike Lewis always went to pee at least twice before he settled down to sleep. Sometimes it drove him to distraction, curled up in bed, wide awake, waiting for that familiar urge to occur so he could throw back his covers, pad down to the toilet, relieve himself for a second time, and finally get some rest.

It had been a habit of his since he was five, when his dad died. At first he'd just wet the bed, but it made his mum so cross with him that he'd taken it upon himself to make double sure he didn't do it again. It was a comfort thing; he didn't want to be causing his mum any more distress, and as the months and years passed, it had become a trigger that flipped the switch on his brain and let sleep take him.

Mike shook off, flushed the toilet, and went to the sink to wash his hands. As the warm water rushed out the tap and he rubbed his hands under it, he could already feel his pillow calling him.

It was as he turned off the tap that he saw that someone stood behind him in the bathroom.

'Please, no,' said Mike Lewis as he turned to see his mad Auntie Alice.

He'd been ten and alone in the house when Auntie Alice had turned up and let herself in. He didn't like to think about what happened next, but the look on her face, the awful sounds she was making, that was always there.

He'd heard a family friend commenting how Auntie Alice wasn't the first in the family to, "Lose her bloody mind", and from that point on, Mike had worried that one day that's how he would end up. How he would look.

He turned away from Auntie Alice, her teeth grinding, feet shuffling, and saw his own face in the mirror, a leer of sheer insanity across his face.

He screamed and fell backwards, hitting his head against the edge of the bath as he went down. As he lay on his back, blood spreading across the tiles, he looked up to see a man in a mask, crouched in the bath.

Empty glass eyes were the last things Mike Lewis saw.

Will Devon had always had this thing about bats.

He had no idea where it came from. Did not recall any incident in his past, in his childhood, that might have brought about the deep, frantic revulsion he felt for them. He'd once asked his mum if she remembered any reason for his hatred of the things (and he always used the word "hatred" when discussing it with others, as "fear" felt so silly). His mum said she had no idea why he disliked them so much, and that they were a daft thing to get in a tizz about anyway. How often do you come across a bat?

Will couldn't even enjoy a Batman film, his aversion to the flying rats was so all-consuming. A friend once told him he should go and see a hypnotist. One had helped her quit smoking, maybe she could do something for him too. She'd given Will the hypnotist's details, but Will had never got around to doing anything with them. He didn't really believe in that sort of thing. As far as he was concerned, for hypnotism to have any effect you had to actually believe that it would. It was a placebo, and without that faith he'd just be handing a wad of cash to a charlatan.

Will stopped to pull up the zip on his coat while his dog Pepper pissed against a tree. He was strolling through London Square, giving Pepper his final walk of the day before the two of them called it a night. Will enjoyed taking these late night walks with Pepper. The streets were mostly empty, just the two of them roaming around, tiring each other out.

Pepper had finished and was walking over to Will when he froze and cocked his head to one side.

'Come on, boy,' said Will.

Pepper made a strange noise in the back of his throat, and began to back away.

'Pepper, come on, time for sleepy-byes.'

Pepper barked once and ran into a bush.

'Jesus,' said Will, annoyed. He turned to look at what might have spooked Pepper so much. Was there another person out there taking their dog for a moonlit walk? Pepper always was antsy around other dogs, ever since he'd gone up to one a few years back and it had given him a deep bite on the leg for his trouble.

Will squinted, but he couldn't see any other dog, nor any other people.

A flash of movement in the corner of his eye. Will turned and looked up to the sky, trying to make out what it was he was seeing.

At first it looked like a little black cloud growing larger with each second. Then Will realised it wasn't growing larger, it was that it was moving closer, which was very, very strange. And what was that sound? A whooshing sound, over and over. Wings beating?

Will's eyes widened.

That wasn't a cloud.

He hoped it was just birds, but his gut knew the truth.

'Pepper!' he yelled as he turned, a sharp pain in his chest, as the bats descended and Will was swallowed up.

Pepper poked his face out of the bush and whimpered as Will Devon thrashed, screaming, desperate. Soon he was on the ground, in the dirt. It would not be long until he stopped screaming. Until he stopped moving.

A white-gloved hand reached out and stroked Pepper's silky, chocolate fur.

'There's a good boy,' said Mr. Cotton.

19

Rita Hobbes had never believed in a life for a life. Through all her years on the force, she'd believed in bringing the guilty to justice, and justice did not include death. Could not include it.

This new life of hers, post-hex, was making that an impossible ideal.

She wanted Cotton and Spike dead. She wanted them to feel fear, to know their end was coming, and then to die. She wanted the Angel of Blackpool dead too, if such a thing was even possible.

Her stomach churned as an afterimage flashed in the dark each time she blinked.

Ben Turner's corpse.

Cold.

Still.

Dead.

'Are you sure this is the best idea?' Formby asked again.

'I don't see what other choice we have,' replied Rita, walking towards Big Pins' exit. She paused and turned to Formby. 'Stay here.'

'I can help. Maybe.' Formby knew that wasn't true.

'Me and Waters have got this,' she replied.

'You're sure I shouldn't stay here and keep the mole man company?' asked Waterson.

Rita gave him a look that could have stripped paint from a door.

'I was only asking!' said Waterson, following her out.

'Who is the mole man?' Formby asked Linton, a confused look on his face.

It was obvious as soon as they stepped from the blind alley that hid Big Pins from the ordinary people of Blackpool, that something wasn't right.

'It takes a lot to put the shits up a ghost,' said Waterson, 'but consider this spook spooked.'

Rita felt it itching at her skin, like she was covered in bugs. A heavy, thick spell lay over the entire city.

She took out her axe, tightened her fingers around the wooden haft, and closed her eyes. 'Show me.'

She looked up and saw them. Hundreds of dark lines weaving through the night sky. Thousands of them. It was just as Ben had said: the Angel's power, Its magic, spreading far and wide across Blackpool. On this night, Cotton and Spike were spreading fear, spreading death, on an epic scale.

She wondered how many people had died already. Wondered how many more would end up that way before the night was through.

She realised her hands were shaking as she strode towards Blackpool Pleasure beach, the huge fun fair that also, unbeknownst to most, housed the Uncanny Night Fair, and inside of that, the dreamscape prison where Alexander Jenner was incarcerated.

Sweat prickled her brow and her eyes darted from one shadow to the next. The spell Cotton and Spike were weaving was intoxicating. Heavy. Undeniable. They weren't even attacking her directly, but it was like suffering fallout from a nuclear blast. The side effects were eating into her anyway.

'This is really, really, bad, Waters.'

'I am getting that impression, yeah.'

A man ran past, screaming.

'They certainly know how to create an atmosphere, your mask-wearing friends.'

Rita was already running.

She found the screaming man on the ground, desperately scuttling backwards.

'What? What is it?' she whirled round, axe at the ready, but couldn't see what it was he was running from.

'Maybe he's having a panic attack,' said Waterson.

Rita crouched by the man, 'Hey, it's okay, you're safe now.'

The man looked at her, sweat pouring down his face.

'What is it?' Rita asked. 'What's wrong?'

'Nothing is wrong,' replied the man. 'Everything is fine, fine, fine.'

His torso ripped open and two bloody hands thrust out, grabbing Rita by the neck.

'Holy buggering shit!' yelled Waterson, jumping back.

The axe fell from Rita's hand as she tried to wrench free of the choking hands closed around her windpipe. This wasn't a man running from a nightmare thing created by Cotton and Spike, he *was* a nightmare thing. The man laughed hysterically as more arms reached out from his torso and grasped Rita.

'Everything is fine, fine, fine!' His left eye bulged alarmingly, then popped out of the socket, a crow's head poking out, screeching furiously, beak snapping, eager to chew on Rita's face as she was pulled forward.

'Axe!' Rita managed to force out, as she beat ineffectually at the arms wrestling her inside the nightmare man.

'Right! Shit,' said Waterson. He fell to his knees and grabbed at the axe, but his phantom hand passed right through.

'Axe!' Rita garbled again, as she strained to turn her head to the side, the crow's wicked beak scraping her cheek, drawing blood.

'Okay, okay,' Waterson told himself. 'Solid. I am a solid.' He did his best to make his hand corporeal, and slowly reached out for the weapon.

It moved.

He didn't pick it up, but it had reacted to him. For the briefest of moments, he'd willed himself solid enough to nudge it. Waterson was so exhilarated that he actually laughed. Rita's strangled screams soon put an end to that.

She was pressed right up against the nightmare man's open torso now, one shoulder leaning into him, his rib cage opening and closing like the jaws of a steel trap as the crow in his head pecked angrily at her face.

'You'll like it inside me,' said the nightmare man. 'No, not like it, those are the wrong words. You'll sit inside all broken and pained and screaming those good, tasty screams and we'll be best of friends forever and ever.'

Waterson tried to concentrate, tried to block out Rita's anguish, the nightmare man's gloating, the crow's angry squawks, and reached out again and again for the axe. Each time it would move, just a little, but he couldn't grab it, couldn't lift it. If he had a few hours to practice, he was sure he could actually do it. But he didn't have hours. He barely had seconds left.

'Come on!' he yelled in frustration, but the axe merely nudged forward again.

Rita felt herself starting to go limp, the fight draining from her as the lack of oxygen began to take its toll and the world turned dark and fuzzy around the edges. She thought she could hear Waterson saying something. Shouting something. But the nightmare man's laughter drowned out everything, even the crow's screeches.

Rita was pissed off.

Even as the black hole of unconsciousness promised to make everything okay, she felt the fury in her stomach burning. They were going to win. That pair of mask-wearing freaks were going to win and Ben's death would go unpunished. All the deaths in Blackpool.

She'd failed.

Then the laughter stopped and she felt herself crumple to the ground.

'Rita,' said Waterson, rushing to her side.

'Wh… what the…?' she managed, gasping for air, eyes streaming, as she struggled up on to her elbows. She looked to where the nightmare man had been and saw only a little pile of ash on the ground.

'How did you…?'

'It wasn't me,' Waterson replied.

'You must never rely on the help of a ghost, Detective,' said a new voice.

Rita turned to see a tall, narrow man with the whitest of white complexions and the most wonderful, dark purple coat stood before her.

'Well,' said Carlisle, the devil of all grins across his face, 'what did I miss?'

Carlisle sat on the bench facing the sea, looking up at the thousands of smoke fingers stretching out of the water, from the Angel's prison, and arcing high above them into Blackpool.

'So, do you want to tell me where you've been?' said Rita. 'I thought you were dead.'

'Do I detect worry? How sweet of you.'

'You'll detect a pissed off woman with a sharp axe if you don't spill, Pasty Pete.'

'I'd tell her,' said Waterson. 'She once threw a full cup of coffee at my balls because I forgot to tell her there were free doughnuts in the staff canteen.'

'Very well,' said Carlisle. 'I was inside a small boy.'

There were a few moments of silence after that.

'Okay,' replied Rita, finally.

'You have a depraved mind, Detective.'

'So that whole time you were.. .whatever it was you were doing... inside a small boy?'

Carlisle shifted, uncomfortable. 'I was… trapped. At the hands of Mr. Cotton and Mr. Spike. Trapped within the Angel's prison.'

'What happened?'

'I am no longer trapped.'

'Wow, and you say I have a talent for stating the obvious.'

Carlisle smiled and breathed in the night air. It felt good to be back inside his own body. No, it felt better than that, though he also felt as though he needed a scalding hot shower, or eight, to get rid of the stink of the almost thing that Bob the exorcist had forced out.

His smile faltered as he recalled the price he'd paid. A promise. A *big* promise. To be called in at any time. Carlisle was not bound by many things, he had spoken more lies and half-truths in his life than most, and thought nothing of letting people down. But if he offered a promise, he did not welch. He did not like the feeling of being in another's debt, of knowing he could be made to do something helpful at any given moment.

He wondered just what it would be that the doomed exorcist would ask of him.

'So,' he said, 'it would appear that Cotton and Spike are having a grand old time with this wretched resort of yours.'

'They've expanded their operations, so to speak,' Rita replied.

'Indeed. Normally they go person by person. Their scope, their power, limited. Now,' he gestured to the smoke tendrils spreading far and wide, 'they are playing with everybody.'

'It's the Angel's power, boosting them, isn't it?' said Rita.

'It is. Partly my fault. I may have, inadvertently, brought Cotton and Spike back from where they were held, after which they were able to leech the Angel's magic.'

'You *what*?' said Waterson.

'Yeah, that doesn't seem like a smart move on your part,' said Rita.

'I was… tricked.'

'Oof, that's gotta sting that mountain-sized ego of yours, hey?' said Rita. Carlisle did not respond. 'Ben Turner is dead,' she continued. 'They killed him.'

Carlisle nodded slowly. 'One question.'

'What?'

'Who is Ben Turner?'

'Who is he?' Rita began, blood boiling, rising up off the bench.

'Easy there,' said Waterson. 'He was one of the people turned into a werewolf.'

'Ah yes, the wolf business, it had quite slipped my mind.'

'He was a friend,' said Rita. 'He was one of us, and Cotton and Spike murdered him.'

'I feel your fury, Detective,' said Carlisle, 'and I share in it. The indignities I suffered at their hands. Well, I would very much enjoy hearing what it sounds like when *they* scream.'

'Can you stop them?' asked Rita.

Carlisle shook his head. 'I do not believe so. Not with the Angel's power at their disposal.'

Rita flopped back on the bench and sighed. 'Yeah, I was afraid you were going to say that. I was able to knock them back on my own the first time we faced off, but now... I mean, you can feel it in the air. Feel it all around us.'

'Power upon power,' replied Carlisle as the nightmare magic caressed his skin.

'In that case,' said Rita, 'I think I have a plan.'

'Detective,' said Carlisle, looking at how shifty her eyes had become, 'I have a sneaking suspicion that you are about to do something extremely stupid. I wish I could say this surprised me.'

'Okay, I'm just going to come out with it, so get ready to mock me, you lanky twat.'

'Consider me cocked and ready to fire.'

'I'm going to release Jenner from the dreamscape prison.'

Carlisle nodded, 'As usual, I am correct. That is a plan of pure insanity that will almost certainly spiral towards disaster—'

'—yes, but—'

'—and I absolutely agree that it is what we must do.'

Waterson, while surprised that Carlisle was on board for suicide, did enjoy the look of astonishment on Rita's face.

'You... I'm sorry, what?'

'I take it the Angel reached out to you, too?' asked Carlisle.

'Yeah.'

'And me,' said Waterson raising a hand.

'Hm. It seems as though It will mix with anyone.'

That was definitely a dig, so Waterson did his best not to react.

'I believed the Angel was trying to trick me,' said Carlisle.

'Me too,' said Rita.

'And in truth, It is.'

'It is?'

'Oh, absolutely, Detective, but it is also the only next step if we wish to bring an end to Cotton and Spike's reign of terror.'

'With the awesome side-effect of the Angel taking control of Jenner again,' added Waterson. 'The reason I'm dead, in case anyone's counting.'

'People die every second of every day,' said Carlisle.

'If Jenner is released,' said Rita, 'then, according to the Angel, the magic Cotton and Spike are controlling—the magic we can see above us—will automatically move over to Jenner, leaving those masked turds with only their own magic to throw at us.'

'Yes,' agreed Carlisle.

'And we know that, do we?' asked Waterson. 'I mean, we know for a fact that with Jenner out, all the magic will go to him and we can get rid of the other two. It won't just split between them and we have three super-powered arseholes to deal with?'

'There's no knowing for a fact,' said Carlisle, grimly.

'Well, super,' said Waterson. 'All I can say, and this is definitely a first, I'm glad I'm already dead.'

Rita had all of the same doubts as Waterson. There was no knowing how things would play out. And even if they did go like they hoped, and Cotton and Spike were pushed aside, they still had Jenner to deal with.

'A Jenner who will be much more powerful than when you last faced him,' said Carlisle, reading her expression. 'There are many more fissures in the Angel's prison than there were. The compromised structure has been deteriorating at an increased rate. Forcing Jenner back into the Night Fair you fashioned may prove difficult.'

'I imagine "difficult" is a big, fat understatement, yes?' said Waterson.

'Oh, the biggest,' replied Carlisle.

'Tell me you see another way, Casper,' said Rita. 'Really, anything you've got, I'm open to it.'

Carlisle stood and spun so that his coat fanned out like a

cloak, the sparkling lining, like a galaxy of shining stars. 'I do not. The choice is yours, Detective.'

Rita took a look out at the sea as the waves lapped against the shore. She thought about Ben Turner's body, curled up on the basement floor.

'Let's end those fuckers.'

20

The twisted iron gates of the Night Fair appeared before them, and Rita, Carlisle, and Waterson paused, watching the flames that burned atop each gate post flicker in the cool night breeze.

'We're totally, totally all in on this suicide mission, then?' said Waterson.

'Feel free to run and hide, ghost,' said Carlisle.

'I'm not a coward,' he replied.

'You're also dead, so have a little less skin in the game,' said Carlisle. 'And I mean that both figuratively and literally.'

'Okay ladies, enough bickering, time to put on our shit-proof trousers.'

'I do believe you missed your calling as a poet, Detective.'

Rita grinned and flexed her fingers around the handle of the axe. What they were stood before was not one gate, but two. One lead to the Night Fair itself. The *actual* Night Fair. The other, the one only Rita could see, lead to the dreamscape Night Fair. The one she had fashioned using Cotton and Spike's magic and tricked Jenner into stepping inside of, severing his connection to the Angel.

'So here's the plan,' said Rita.

'Oh, do tell,' said Carlisle.

'Let's say all goes as smoothly as Waters' chin...'

'A crack about my inability to grow a beard. Nice,' he replied.

'...Jenner emerges, takes on the Angel's power again and no doubt twats the living shit out of Cotton and Spike for fucking It around, leaving us with the extra-extra-extra-powered Jenner to deal with.'

'Not good,' said Carlisle.

'He might be strong, but we have the prison I built all ready and waiting, we just need to push him back inside.'

'What if he doesn't want to be pushed?' said Waterson. 'What if he legs it away from the entrance?'

'It's not fixed. It doesn't exist in the same way the actual gate we're looking at now does. I can use the magic, with the axe, to position the door anywhere. All we need to do is place the gate to the dreamscape directly behind Jenner and throw everything we can at him so that he takes a single step back.'

'One step,' asked Waterson.

'One step. That's all we need to do. Easy, right?'

Carlisle raised an eyebrow. 'Delusion is a most comforting disorder, Detective.'

'Shut up, it'll work. It'll probably work. It has to work.'

Carlisle looked at the axe Rita was wielding. His artefact. A thing he had longed to possess again for so very long. He felt the urge to reach out and snatch it from her, as pointless as he knew that idea to be. It would not accept him, not unless she willingly gave it. This was something Carlisle was doubtful, at this point, would ever occur. Not without killing the Angel of Blackpool, and it seemed as thought that was impossible.

He wanted the artefact. Craved it.

'Oi, stretched-out Johnny Depp,' said Rita, clicking her fingers.

Carlisle grimaced and turned his attention back to the gate. 'Get on with it then, I am eager to toss myself with reckless abandon towards certain death.'

'That's the spirit,' replied Rita and lifted up the axe, ready.

'Well, look what we have here, brother,' said an all-too-familiar voice.

The group turned to find themselves flanked by Mr. Cotton and Mr. Spike.

'Hello, you two,' said Carlisle. 'Apologies for taking my leave without a goodbye, but I was desperate to stretch my legs.'

'Never fear, Carlisle, perhaps my brother will stretch them and stretch them until they are torn from your body altogether. What say you, Mr. Spike?'

Spike gurgled and grunted and nodded his hedgehog mask.

Rita swung at the air. 'Stay back unless you want an axe to the neck, you murderous pieces of shit.'

'Poor, poor doggy. I do believe he whimpered and begged as my brother showed him his true face. Such delicious fear, such ripe torment. Yummy.'

Rita nodded to Carlisle.

Carlisle nodded back.

They moved as one. Rita sprinted forward, axe raised, ready to strike a point in reality and open the dream realm wide, while Carlisle pulled charms from his coat and threw them in the direction of Cotton and Spike.

There was an explosion of light as each charm struck home, causing Cotton and Spike to warp like images in a funhouse mirror.

Rita swung the axe, only for a tree to burst from the ground and seize it in one of its limbs. Rita whirled around to find she was no longer in front of the Night Fair's gate, but in a forest. She could see movement between the trees in the distance. Wolves stalking.

'Fuck-shit,' cried Rita, yanking the axe from the tree. 'Carlisle?' she yelled as she warily looked at the wolves in the dreamscape she'd been swallowed by. No reply.

She gripped the axe and willed the dreamscape's magic into it, then swung again and created an exit. She stepped through the opening and found herself on top of a building this time. Another dreamscape.

She turned as something thudded down behind her. It was Ben Turner.

'Why?' he asked, blood streaming from his eyes. 'Why did you let me die, Rita?'

'Oh shut it,' she snarled, magic erupting from the axe-head and turning the pretend Ben to ash. She swung the weapon again and stepped through the opening into a third dreamscape.

'Carlisle! A little help here!'

She was in an abandoned factory, rats the size of dogs scampering across the grimy concrete floor.

Mr. Cotton sprouted up from the floor, the ears of his rabbit mask waggling. 'Why do you struggle so?' he asked. 'Fear is natural. Death inevitable. And both are so very, very delicious.

'You're going to lose, you know that?' said Rita, brandishing the axe. 'Fear never wins. Not ever. It might seem overwhelming for a time, but in the end it's beaten.'

Mr. Cotton clapped. 'Did you get that from a greeting card?'

A wheezing sound from behind. Rita turned to see Mr. Spike, his shoulders shaking from laughter. She began to back off, trying to keep both brothers in her eye-line as they watched her retreat.

'You know, Rita, I do believe it might be time for you to finally leave the game. What say you, brother?'

Mr. Spike clapped his hands together.

'We were holding something of a grudge. Childish, I know.'

'Well, I didn't want to be the first to say it,' replied Rita, heart hammering.

'You bested us once and we wished to draw out your pain. We did not want to shoot you in the head, we wanted you to bleed out, ever so slowly. We wanted the same for your wicked friend, Carlisle, but it is a fool who allows danger to remain while there is work to be done.'

Mr. Spike grunted and ran at Rita. She swung the axe but missed, slicing the air and tearing open a fresh hole. Meanwhile, Spike crashed into Rita and brought her to the ground.

'Carlisle!'

Mr. Spike sat on her chest and Rita swung her fists, trying to dislodge him, but her blows had no effect. He grabbed her face with one filthy glove, a centipede squirming from the sleeve of his jacket and skittering across her wild-eyed face.

'You called?' Rita looked up to see Carlisle poking his head through the door the axe had created. He peeled the hole open further, stepped through, and clapped his hands together, unleashing an explosion of light and a deafening boom. The dreamscape, and Cotton and Spike, melted away, and Rita found herself back before the gates of the Night Fair.

'Rita!' cried Waterson, rushing over to her as she grabbed the axe and climbed shakily to her feet. 'Is that it? Did you stop them?'

'No,' replied Carlisle. 'That is beyond either of us at this point.'

'Well,' said Waterson, 'hurry up and open the bloody prison thing!'

Rita didn't need telling twice. Axe in hand, she stood and turned to the gate.

Mr. Cotton stepped out of nothing to block her way. 'So that is your plan, is it? A calculated risk? I applaud you, really I do.'

Rita swung the axe, burying the head in Cotton's rabbit mask as Spike bundled into her side, knocking her from her feet and the axe from her grip.

'The power is ours,' said Cotton, pulling the axe from his mask and tossing it aside.

Carlisle darted towards it. Mr. Cotton swept a hand across the ground beneath Carlisle's feet, causing it to jut out and propel him through the air. Carlisle's journey was soon halted by a wall that sent fists of white static blooming into his vision.

Rita struggled as Mr. Spike planted himself atop her chest again and giggled.

'Get the fuck off me!'

'Such bad language. Have you ever heard the like, brother mine?'

The mouth of Mr. Spike's hedgehog mask opened wider and wider and wider still, though of course it did not as it was just a mask. Great strings of thick drool seeped from within, making Rita recoil with revulsion as they struck her face.

'This magic, the Angel's magic, belongs to us now,' said Mr. Cotton, hands clasped behind his back as he danced towards Carlisle. 'It will not be taken away. We will use it in Blackpool. When this small place is drained of fear, of terror, of life itself, we shall move on. We shall wander this Earth bringing the gift of anguish with us.'

Carlisle stumbled up, blood dripping down his face, into his eyes. He wiped the sleeve of his coat across his face and staggered towards the axe, only to find himself spinning wildly through the air again, the Night Fair's wrought iron gate stopping his journey this time.

Waterson edged his way towards the fallen axe, a forgotten man. It seemed Mr. Cotton and Mr. Spike were so concerned with Rita and Carlisle that they saw no threat from him. Which was fair, he wasn't sure there was anything he could do to threaten them. But his best friend needed him, so he was going to try.

He knelt before the axe and reached for the handle.

His hand passed through.

'Can you feel our power now, Carlisle?' said Mr. Cotton, as a groggy Carlisle used the bars of the gate to haul himself to his feet.

'You really do... enjoy the sound of your own voice,' replied Carlisle, spitting a glob of blood on the dirt.

Mr. Cotton laughed and clicked his fingers. Vines sprouted from the ground and wrapped around Carlisle's arms, his legs, his neck, strapping him to the metal gate.

'Come on, concentrate,' hissed Waterson, reached for the axe. The handle shifted, ever so slightly, before his hand passed through it once again.

Rita kicked out, bucked, fought, as Mr. Spike giggled, a tongue snaking out of the mask and licking her cheek.

'Oh, you dirty prick,' she yelled, twisting her head away.

Waterson tried again. The axe did not budge.

'Hm,' said Mr. Cotton, rubbing at the chin of his rabbit mask with one hand, 'I wonder how to make this worse.'

'You could just keep on talking, that's torture enough,' replied Carlisle, straining to push his right hand into his coat pocket.

Mr. Cotton clicked his fingers. 'Aha! Thorns! Of course.'

Carlisle grunted as vicious thorns grew from the vines that pinned him, sinking into his flesh and causing crimson to leak from his chalk-white skin. All the same, he carried on straining for his pocket, trying to ignore how moving his arm only caused the thorns to drag and tear at his flesh.

Cotton and Spike were beyond powerful now, their dreamscape magic a thought away, able to do as they pleased. Able to make the ground shake and vines sprout at a moment's notice, all built from the stuff of dreams, the substance of nightmares.

Waterson's hand passed through the axe handle again and he almost cried out in frustration.

'Do you know,' said Mr. Cotton, turning his attention to Rita, 'I do believe it is finally time for my brother to show you his true face.'

'That's okay,' replied Rita, 'let's do it another time.'

Mr. Spike raised his hands up to his hedgehog mask and Rita writhed and kicked and struggled, terror overwhelming her.

'There it is,' said Mr. Cotton, delighting in her fear, 'delicious anguish, fresh from the oven.'

Carlisle's hand reached the object he was after. A fire charm.

'Oh, this is going to hurt,' he said to himself.

Mr. Spike's mask edged up—slowly, slowly—he and his brother delighting in the anticipation. Rita tried to close her eyes but found that she couldn't. Tried to turn her head away, but Spike's hand locked it in place.

She didn't want to see.

Didn't want to see.

Rita realised she was screaming.

And she wasn't the only one. Waterson yelled in anger, in frustration, in hopelessness at how useless he was, and swiped with one, last, futile attempt at the axe. He almost fell back in surprise. He could feel the axe handle. He looked down, wide-eyed, as he lifted the weapon.

'I did it… I fucking did it!' he screamed.

Mr. Cotton turned to see Waterson standing, axe in hand. 'Oh, naughty, naughty ghost. Ours, I think.'

He stepped towards Waterson.

Rita could taste blood in her throat.

Carlisle put the right words together, ancient words, and the charm reacted. It was created to throw at an enemy, to engulf them in flames. Carlisle would not be throwing it. Fire rushed up around his coat, raced along the vines, eating away at them until Carlisle stumbled forward, free of their grip, and struggled out of the blazing coat.

He'd had that coat for over a hundred years. Now he was angry.

The magic rushed into him and he punched out a fist, sweeping Mr. Cotton from his feet, halting his advance towards Waterson. Carlisle spun on his heel and yelled out an oath, swinging his fist again and knocking Mr. Spike from his position on top of Rita.

'Detective!' he said.

Rita rolled and stumbled to her feet, body trembling. 'Waters!'

Waterson threw her the axe.

'No!' yelled Mr. Cotton, reaching out, vines bursting from the ground, following the path of the axe as it spun, head over handle, towards Rita's hand. Carlisle was ready and swept a hand across, unleashing a spell that turned the vines to ribbons.

The axe found Rita's hand.

No time for relief, no time for a snappy remark, with the sound of Mr. Spike's wet, furious grunts at her back, Rita swung the axe at the Night Fair's gate. It stuck in nothing, stuck in reality, and Rita shoved the handle, opening a bright, white gap.

A door.

An exit.

'It's okay, it's okay, everything is going to be fine, fine, fine,' said Mr. Cotton, as the smoky fingers of the Angel's magic that stretched from the Angel's prison and wound around Mr. Cotton and Mr. Spike broke away and rushed into the door Rita had created. It was like a black hole gobbling up all available light.

'I think it's fair to say,' said Rita, as Cotton and Spike stepped back, 'that you pair are royally fucked.'

A figure stepped out of the door Rita had created, his eyes blazing with a furious white light.

'I am very upset,' said Alexander Jenner with the voice of the Angel of Blackpool.

As Mr. Cotton and Mr. Spike attempted to get away, to escape into a maze of dreamscapes, Jenner reached out a hand. 'No, no. Stay.'

Cotton and Spike fell to their knees.

'We still have similar desires,' said Mr. Cotton. 'Errors of judgement have been made, but I believe we can come to a new understanding and put this sorry business behind us.'

Mr. Spike gurgled and grunted and nodded.

'Is that so?' said the Angel. Jenner's fingers clicked and the masks that Mr. Cotton and Mr. Spike wore burst into flames. They screamed and struggled, but the Angel would not let them fall or run or roll. Would not let them throw off their masks.

Rita thought about all the terror they'd been responsible for. She thought of the women's souls inside her axe, trapped still. She thought about Ben Turner, dead on the basement floor.

The flames edged down their bodies, and before long, they were nothing but twin piles of ash, blown by the wind.

Rita stepped back as Carlisle and Waterson joined her.

'Yay for teamwork?' she said as Jenner—as the Angel—turned Its gaze to her.

'Thank you, Rita Hobbes,' said the Angel.

'Did you see me?' Waterson asked Rita. 'I only bloody picked something up!'

'Still in a shitload of danger here, Waters, let's put a hold on any celebrations for a bit.'

'I do not suppose you would like to step back inside of your prison of your own free will?' asked Carlisle, as Jenner's body began to rise into the air in a ball of crackling, bright white magic.

'Okay,' said Rita, axe in her hands, 'the door to the nightscape is behind Jenner; all we have to do is make him fall back, just an inch or two.'

'Oh, is that all?' replied Carlisle.

'We can do this,' said Rita. 'Ready?'

Carlisle sighed and drew strength from the magic in the air around him. 'Ready.'

'Then let's do this.'

Rita and Carlisle ran at Jenner.

And then things went very, very bad.

21

Carlisle was not in a good way. For one thing, his coat was a smouldering heap, all the charms within it lost, all the bits of protection stitched into it, ash. He felt almost naked without it.

He ran his fingers gently along one of the tree roots that snaked down the walls of the cave to feast upon the thick layer of blood that coated the ground. It pulsed under his touch. Writhed.

Carlisle felt weak, which was not something he was used to. Both magically and physically, he was beaten down. He had not recovered from the torture Mr. Cotton and Mr. Spike had inflicted upon him, nor the damage done by his astral jaunt and exorcism.

Punishment on top of pain on top of punishment. And then there were the beatings he had just suffered in the battle against Cotton and Spike, and then in a fruitless attempt to move the Angel-possessed Jenner so much as an inch. They had been no more capable of moving it back than a bug was capable of winning a fight against an oncoming truck.

Carlisle stumbled, faltered, wrapping his hand around one of the roots to stop himself from collapsing to the bloody cave floor.

He wondered if the detective was dead already. Wondered what she had thought as he ran from the battlefield and she screamed after him. Had she felt betrayal? Thought him a coward? A part of the dark showing its true colours at last? It annoyed him that he cared.

'You called?' asked a figure, rising from his twitching throne of flesh and bone.

'Unfortunately so,' replied Carlisle with a smile, turning his attention from the hundreds of roots, to the nonchalant demon who claimed this place as his realm.

The Yellow Man.

The demon smiled, his golden skin glowing, his antlers scraping against the roof of the cave as he stepped forward.

'I see you have made friends with your body again. Good for you.'

Carlisle bowed a little, wincing in pain as he did so. 'Thank you, I find I am able to squirm out of even the most hopeless of situations.'

'That's one of the things I've always liked about you, Carlisle. You're a scrappy son of a gun.'

Carlisle was not sure he liked being referred to in such a cutesy way, but he was not so stupid as to argue with a demon. Or with *this* demon anyway.

'So you would now like to take me up on my kind offer, is that right?'

Carlisle frowned and nodded. 'Unfortunately, I appear to have temporarily taken leave of my senses, yes.'

'And all for no personal gain, by the looks of it? But, in fact, to help *others*. What has become of you, man?'

'It seems I may have grown a conscience,' replied Carlisle, spitting the last word out as if it was a piece of rancid meat.

'A conscience,' the Yellow Man frowned and placed a hand to his heart. 'Perhaps even a sliver of empathy sprouting up from the cracks in the concrete? I'm really sorry to hear that. It's the sort of thing that leads nowhere good.'

'It is most tiresome, I can assure you.'

The Yellow Man laughed and clicked his fingers. The hands, grasping their screw-top jars, each containing a soul, began to emerge from the cave walls.

'Would you look at that,' said the Yellow Man, pointing to one jar amongst hundreds. 'I've got a nice, empty jar all waiting for you.'

He stepped over and took the empty jar, tossing it up into the air and catching it again. 'Do you think I'll be able to squeeze you in there?'

Carlisle stepped back. 'Do not get too excited. I may offer you my soul, but I have no intention of actually dying. I intend to outlive the great Beast Itself.'

The Yellow Man laughed again and the mocking sound echoed throughout the cave. 'It's good to have a goal in life, Carlisle. But no, I'm afraid sooner or later, you'll be part of my collection.' He tossed the empty jar at the wall, and a fresh hand emerged to catch it before it struck the stone and shattered.

'Oh, I would be the pride of your collection, I'm sure.'

The Yellow Man lowered himself onto his throne again. It writhed and whimpered beneath him as it took his weight. 'I have to ask you if you're sure. Just a formality, you understand.'

Carlisle thought about Jenner, about the Angel, about Rita Hobbes. He thought about all the pain that had been inflicted upon him. The indignities. 'I am.'

'And that is what you want in return for your sacrifice?'

'Get on with it.'

The Yellow Man smiled, 'It's already done.'

Carlisle looked to the empty jar that he would one day be trapped within. Another tight spot to find a way out of. He smiled, he was sure he would think of something.

He turned, wishing he had a long coat to sweep as he did so, and strutted away from the demon.

'Carlisle?' said Rita. 'Carlisle!'

'He's legged it, the bastard!' replied Waterson, as the two cowered from the blazing magic that rippled around the floating body of Jenner.

'You think you can put me back in my box?' asked the Angel. 'I am not as I was, not as you last faced me. I am more with each heartbeat that passes. With every blink of an eye, more of me escapes my bonds and rushes out into the world.'

Rita swung the axe and magic erupted from it, bursting

towards Jenner. A flick of Jenner's hand and the spell melted away.

'You are an ant before me. A termite, nothing more. Abase yourself, you grovelling insect.'

'Up yours!' yelled Rita.

'I'm really starting to think that we should follow Carlisle's lead and make a run for it,' said Waterson.

'We can't,' replied Rita. 'We have to stop him, have to stop *It*.'

'How? What can we do? It's hopeless!'

'I believe I shall kill you very, very slowly,' said the Angel. 'I will tweak every nerve ending so you are in an endless rapture of pain. You will beg me for death. Beg me. And I shall answer, no.'

Rita knew Waterson was right. They should run. They should run away and hide. She gripped the axe, willed the magic that flooded into it to obey her. To do what she wanted, what she needed. Magic gushed forth, eager to do as she asked, but it was a water pistol against a tank.

They were going to have to turn their backs and escape, and that meant more deaths. A lot more deaths. She thought again about the two souls trapped within the axe. That had just been the start. She wondered how many more were going to die because she couldn't bring this thing to justice. Because she'd let the genie back out of the bottle.

'What on Earth?' said Waterson. Rita looked to see what had drawn his attention.

'Carlisle?' said Rita, shocked.

'Just had to pop out and pick something up,' he replied.

'Your eyes…' said Rita.

They were entirely black.

'Carlisle, what is that I see in you?' asked the Angel.

'A gift for you,' he replied.

A sneer bent Jenner's face and he thrust out a hand, magic rushing from him towards Carlisle, ready to strip the flesh from his bones.

Carlisle leapt to the side, rolled, and rose up on one knee. He could feel what the Yellow Man had given him. Could feel the dark power boiling inside of him. Time seemed to slow down.

'Are you ready?' he asked the darkness, and the darkness howled in anticipation.

Carlisle gritted his teeth and reached out.

The darkness flooded out of him. A writhing, screaming, demented thing. Carlisle trembled, opened his mouth to scream in agony as the dark scraped through him.

The Angel lifted both hands in surprise, in horror, as the convulsing flood of torment swarmed over the body it was using, over Alexander Jenner.

Rita watched in shock as layer by layer the thing Carlisle had unleashed stripped Jenner away. The clothes went, then hair, skin, organs, muscles. All the pieces were torn from him, turned to dust, and blown away until there was nothing left but the faint sound of his screams, and then even that was gone.

Alexander Jenner was dead. The body utterly destroyed. The soul erased. The Angel's puppet gone.

'Well… holy bloody buggering shit,' said Rita.

Carlisle smiled then toppled sideways to the ground. Rita and Waterson rushed to him.

'You are welcome,' said Carlisle, breathing heavily.

'What *was* that?' asked Waterson.

'Ghost, you do not believe I will tell you and the detective all of my secrets, do you? It would ruin my mystique.'

Rita smiled and hugged him, and Carlisle was too weary to recoil.

'Sorry about your coat.'

'It was a nice coat,' said Carlisle.

Trying not to make it obvious how much pain he was in, Carlisle rose slowly to his feet. Feeding that darkness through him had scratched his every nerve, shown him pain like he had never experienced. He put a fist to his chest; it was still in there, the connection. Perhaps he had enough in him for one more big effort.

'So… did we win?' asked Waterson.

'No,' said Rita. 'Well, a bit, but also no.'

'Okay. Not sure if I should be happy or worried.'

'You saw how much magic is escaping from the Angel's

prison,' replied Rita. 'We can't ignore It anymore. Too much of It is free.'

'The detective is correct. With Mr. Cotton and Mr. Spike out of the way, and so many weak spots in Its prison, it is only a matter of time before the Angel is entirely free of Its bonds.'

'So what do we do?' said Waterson.

'*You* do nothing, ghost,' replied Carlisle.

'Liking this plan so far,' said Waterson.

'I take it I'm not off the hook this time?' asked Rita.

Carlisle smiled, the dried blood on his lips cracking, 'No. You are very much in the hot water.'

Rita laughed and rested the axe against her shoulder, reaching out a hand. 'Let's dance.'

Carlisle took her hand in his, and then Waterson was alone.

Rita blinked and she was in the Angel's prison. The giant marble pillars, wider than ancient trees, stretched high above. The only sound was the whisper of the flames that burned endlessly upon the thousands of candles spread across the floor throughout the chamber.

'Can't say it's a thrill to be back here,' said Rita.

'Look on the bright side, this will hopefully be the last time.'

'Fingers crossed.'

'Of course, it may be the last time as we're about to die an agonising death.'

'You're a real ray of sunshine, Carlisle.'

They rounded a pillar to find the Angel stood waiting at the centre of Its glass box.

'Don't mind us dropping in for a home visit, do you?' asked Rita.

The Angel of Blackpool smiled. 'You surprised me, Carlisle. I did not expect you to go to such lengths. To give so much of yourself.'

'What does It mean?' asked Rita. 'What did you give?'

Carlisle ignored her.

'In the end, all you have done is destroy a man's body. A body

I would soon have no use for, anyway.' The Angel pressed a hand against the glass wall of Its prison. The wall glowed and hundreds of dark cracks appeared. 'Can you see? I tapped, and I tapped, and I tapped. Created imperfection upon imperfection; enough for some of me to emerge. Soon the damage will be too much and the structure will fail. This glass box shall shatter, and I will step out of this place. Where I tread, I will leave nothing but dust and pain and darkness. I find that good.'

Carlisle pressed a fist to his chest. The dark was waiting. He wondered if he had the strength to survive a final use of the gift the Yellow Man had bequeathed him.

He looked up to see the Angel smiling.

'Now.' Carlisle commanded, and the dark tore from him, surging towards the glass box. It wriggled its way inside, forcing itself through the cracks, whirling around the Angel, attacking it. The Angel did not move, did not fight. It closed Its eyes, Its smile never faltering.

Finally the dark was used up and Carlisle slumped to the marble floor.

'Carlisle,' said Rita crouching by him. 'Carlisle, don't go and bloody die on me again.'

Carlisle smiled and sat up, leaning back against a pillar.

'It did not work,' he said, and laughed. 'Not enough. Not enough.'

The Angel ran the back of one hand against Its nose and looked at the smear of blood upon it. 'Is it my turn now?'

The candle flames flickered violently, throwing shadows around the chamber. The glass box trembled, filling with the Angel's smoky tendrils, which began to snake out of the glass prison's imperfections and wind towards the prone Carlisle. The magic wrapped around his neck and tightened.

'Do not worry,' said the Angel, 'soon it shall all be over.'

'Leave him alone!' screamed Rita, and swung the axe at the magic tendril throttling Carlisle. The axe was wrenched from her hand and thrown across the chamber, the blade embedding in one of the pillars.

'You did well, Rita Hobbes,' said the Angel. 'Be happy. Be proud, yes? Be proud.'

'Eat my arse,' she replied and ran towards the axe. It was useless, she knew that, but she didn't care. If this was it—if failure was all she had to look forward to—then she was going to go out fighting. Was going to go out like the couldn't-give-a-shit, pain in the rear end that she'd been her whole life.

She wrapped her hands around the handle of the axe, ready to pull it free of the pillar.

And then she stopped.

'Oh…'

She could see it. Feel it.

She told the axe to take more.

To take more, and more, and more. To fill itself up and be ready to do as she asked.

The axe obeyed.

'Can you feel the end approach, Carlisle?' asked the Angel.

Rita pulled the axe from the pillar and turned back to the Angel.

'Oi, fuck face,' she said.

The Angel turned to her, and Its smile began to falter. 'Oh.'

'"Oh" is right,' said Rita. 'You're done, mate.'

She swung the axe and magic flew from it, surrounding the glass box, and in a matter of less than a second, it sealed every imperfection.

Carlisle coughed and gagged and fell to the side, gasping for air, as the magic that had been choking him died.

'No. No!' said the Angel.

'Oh yes, mate.'

'What… what did you do?' asked Carlisle.

'We've been a bit thick. Jesus, we've been stupid. Because you know what this place is made of? Do you know what they used to create this prison?' Rita turned back to the Angel and grinned. 'Magic. I mean, Celestial Magic, but magic all the same. And what does this axe let me do? Ooh, I'll answer that as well for those not following: it allows me to take another thing's magic and use it as my own. So I just fixed that wanker's glass box.'

The Angel snarled and beat Its fists against the glass walls. 'I will escape. Time is nothing to me! You will live and you will die and I will use the sharpened point of my will to destroy this prison once and for all!'

'Well, yeah, you will be able to do that, eventually. Give you another few thousand years and you might be free. Oh… unless…'

Rita swung the axe and another glass box formed around the first.

'Shit, double the work now, sorry mate.'

'Stop,' said the Angel, pressing Its back against the glass wall of the first box.

'But I'm just getting in the swing of things,' she swung the axe and a third glass box appeared around the other two. She turned to Carlisle and grinned. '"Swing of things", do you get it?'

Carlisle rose to his feet. 'My body is in agony, but I believe having to hear that pun is the thing paining me the most.'

'Have mercy,' said the Angel, falling to Its knees.

Rita's smile faltered. 'Mercy? Did you give Jane Bowan mercy?' She swung the axe and a fourth glass box was created. 'How about Ellie Mason? Either of them get any of this mercy thing?' A fifth glass box appeared. 'Then there's Dan Waterson; where was his mercy?' A sixth glass box. As each was created, the others within shrank, and the Angel shrank with them. Rita swung the axe again and again, over and over, swung it until her arms screamed in agony and she finally stumbled to her knees, the axe slipping from her grasp.

Carlisle rested a hand on her shoulder. 'Well done, Detective.'

She smiled and looked up at the nesting doll of prisons she had created. Boxes within boxes within boxes. So many, that the Angel of Blackpool was no longer visible, Its voice hidden.

'Consider…' said Rita, gasping for air. 'Consider that a life sentence with no chance of parole, you prick.'

'Shall we leave?' asked Carlisle, reaching out a hand.

22

Liam sat up in bed. His parents had been furious with him, of course they had, but their relief soon washed away any anger. Liam thought that was partly down to their own experiences since the nightmares had began to seep into Blackpool.

He had told them how terrified he had been, and that was why he was trying to escape. Trying to escape the monsters that came to him in the dark. His parents had looked at each other, and he could see in their eyes that they knew something of what he was talking about. He wondered what they had seen. What things had scared them.

Now, as he sat in bed with the lights out, he no longer felt afraid. Things felt different now. He believed that whatever it was that was behind the smoky fingers, that had been delighting in Blackpool's fear, was gone. He could sense it in the air, a calmness. A cleanness. A bad taste that had been washed away.

He also didn't feel afraid because he knew for sure that monsters existed. That the strange thrived. And he knew, absolutely, that he was part of it. That the weird lived in him and he could see it. Interact with it. Be a part of it. And if he was part of it, then what was there to be afraid of?

He thought about the man he'd helped. The not ghost whose body he'd helped retrieve.

Carlisle.

He wondered what part he'd had to play in burning away the nightmares that had swamped Blackpool. Felt good that he himself had played some small role in others sleeping soundly.

Liam settled down into bed, closed his eyes, and for the first time in a long time, had the most marvellous of dreams.

Rita and Carlisle approached the blind alley that hid Big Pins, exhausted and battered.

'Thank you,' said Rita.

'For what?' replied Carlisle.

'For coming back. For helping.'

Carlisle shifted uncomfortably. 'It was purely self-serving, I assure you.'

Rita smiled and shook her head. 'What was it you gave up for that power you unleashed?'

Carlisle didn't meet her eyes. 'Oh, nothing. Nothing at all. A promise, that's all. I do hate to make promises.'

Rita frowned, knew he was covering, but thought it best not to probe any further. 'So what now?'

'I imagine you will get very drunk and bitterly regret it tomorrow.'

'That's a given. But I meant what next for me and you? I'm still hexed. Seems to me that's not going to change. The Angel is beyond reach, and even if It wasn't, it seems like that twat's unkillable. So the hex is gonna stay.'

'Indeed.'

'Which means…'

'Which means you will not give up the artefact.'

Rita rested a hand on the handle of the axe that swung from her belt. 'If this is it for me, this is my life, then I need it.'

Carlisle nodded. 'I believe… I believe it is time… I let it go.'

'Can you?'

'I do not know, but it appears I have little choice. At least I know that it is in safe hands.'

Rita and Carlisle met eyes and she smiled, Carlisle smiled back.

'Okay then,' she said, and stepped into the blind alley. Carlisle did not follow.

'Are you not coming?' asked Rita. 'There's a gallon of beer with your name on it.'

'I think not. I believe I have spent enough time in this stain of a place. London calls me. If nothing else, I need a new coat, and they have the best tailors.'

Rita dithered, not quite sure what to do, what to say. 'Will you come back?'

Carlisle looked up at the night sky, 'Who can say? Impossible things happen all the time, Detective.'

Rita stepped forward and hugged him. 'Thanks. Thank you. For everything.'

'Please let this be the final time you hug me,' said Carlisle. Rita laughed and released him.

'Goodbye, Detective.'

'Until the next time. Be good, hey?'

Carlisle smiled. 'Good? Me? The very idea.'

Rita watched as Carlisle walked away. Watched until he turned a corner, out of sight.

'Where's he off to, then?' asked Waterson, stepping in beside her.

'Everywhere, I think,' she replied.

'Not dead then?'

'Not dead.'

'Pity. It's not all that bad. Well, actually, it's terrible. Just the bloody worst. But look at this.' Waterson lifted his hand to show he was holding a beer mat. 'Impressive, right?'

Rita laughed and wandered up the blind alley towards the spluttering neon sign of Big Pins. 'Right then, I'm going to get wankered.'

There is an Angel.

The Angel of Blackpool.

A wicked creature that wanted nothing but bad things. Selfish things. Revenge, murder, screams, pain.

It rages within a prison, within a prison, within a prison, within a prison, and on it goes, an endless chain. Each link stronger than the last.

Unbreakable. Impossible.

It rages. It screams. It cries. It beats Its fists against the glass and begs for mercy.

No mercy will come.

In Its endless prison, the Angel of Blackpool will remain.

Unseen.

Unheard.

Forever.

The End.

LEAVE A REVIEW

Reviews are gold to indie authors, so if you've enjoyed this book, please consider visiting the site you purchased it from and leaving a quick review.

BECOME AN INSIDER

Sign up and receive **FREE UNCANNY KINGDOM BOOKS**. Also, be the **FIRST** to hear about **NEW RELEASES** and **SPECIAL OFFERS** in the **UNCANNY KINGDOM** universe. Just visit:

WWW.UNCANNYKINGDOM.COM

MORE STORIES SET IN THE UNCANNY KINGDOM

The Branded Series

Sanctified

Turned

Bloodline

The London Coven Series

Familiar Magic

Nightmare Realm

Deadly Portent

The Spectral Detective Series

Spectral Detective

Corpse Reviver

Twice Damned

The Dark Lakes Series

Magic Eater

Blood Stones

Past Sins

Strange Stories

Apocalypse Hill

36798587R00336

Printed in Great Britain
by Amazon